MW01145710

RAINCOAST
GOLD

A NOVEL

G.A. PACKMAN

RAINCOAST GOLD

Copyright © 2020 by G.A. Packman.

All rights reserved. Printed in the United States of America. No part of this book may be used or reproduced in any manner whatsoever without written permission except in the case of brief quotations embodied in critical articles or reviews.

This book is a work of fiction. Names, characters, businesses, organizations, places, events and incidents either are the product of the author's imagination or are used fictitiously. Any resemblance to actual persons, living or dead, or events is entirely coincidental.

ISBN: 9781896794419

First Edition: December, 2020

10 9 8 7 6 5 4 3 2 1

"I didn't set out to join a movement or become part of a trend: I simply cut myself loose from the moorings of my life."
     Lou Allison - Gumboot Girls

ONE

THE PILOT CAREFULLY GUIDED HIS CESSNA EAST THROUGH THE islands, over churning whirlpools at the narrows and up the verdant old growth inlet, staying close to the deck to avoid the mist and low cloud. From the jump seat Wayne peered north out the side window at the scenery below, lost in thought, not sure if calling Ted to come all the way up from Vancouver was a good idea. He still didn't know why he'd taken this job for a fly by night gold mine north of Prince Rupert. Then he remembered. It was because he'd bet heavily on the last hot junior mining stock that then ended up declaring bankruptcy. Even though he'd been a high flying consultant in the fast lane for the past ten years and had made lots of money, he badly needed the cash now.

As they approached the New Discovery Gold Mine, Wayne leaned forward and tapped Ted on the shoulder. He pointed down at the mine site coming up on the northern side of the inlet and at the cabins on the shore nearby. Ted shrugged, raising his hands, to say, 'So?'

The pilot throttled back, adjusted the plane's attitude and dropped down for a landing. Aluminium floats hit the choppy water and the plane shook as hollow pontoons rattled over wave tops before settling to become paired watercraft. They taxied to the dock and floating camp.

Wayne greeted the man watching from the camp barge above as he climbed steel rungs welded onto its side. Once up on deck he motioned back and forth to Ted and addressed the man, saying, "You guys obviously know each other." The man's name was Jack.

Wayne's predecessor had hurriedly left the company six weeks ago and this was Ted's first time back. Wayne watched as the two men shook hands and exchanged familiar pleasantries. With few words and an expansive sweep of his thick arm the man indicated they were welcome to look around. He tossed Wayne keys to a leased pickup sitting beside a cluster of fuel drums above them on the timber crib landing.

The pilot pushed his plane out and fired up the single engine. He would be back in three hours.

Wayne hauled his lanky frame into the truck on the driver's side and pulled the consulting company ball cap down tight over his shaggy sandy coloured hair trimmed by the current live-in girlfriend back in Vancouver. Ted climbed in opposite. They drove up the slope, past large fuel storage tanks and the generator, and on up a road to a clearing that afforded a surround view of the mine and mill operations including the tailings pond below. The mine portal was higher up the mountain, just below the snow line. A treacherous switch back road connected the two.

"So what did you want to show me?" asked Ted turning away from the view to look straight at Wayne, in the direct and almost confrontational manner he would always employ to control situations, and people. "Everything looks fine to me."

Wayne Dumont had been with Ted Sullivan's firm, TDS Engineering, since grad school in marine biology. With his PhD he'd managed monitoring projects and environmental assessments over the past ten years for progressively larger companies to help them meet government requirements. Pipelines, mines, oil and gas, hydroelectric, his work had covered the field. The higher the profile and the bigger the challenge, the more he revelled in it, taking on the government officials and making them look silly. Wayne was a master at bending a story and a data set to fit the clients' needs.

He hesitated momentarily before regaining his cocky self-assurance, knowing he was bigger than this two bit mining operation, but resigned to his current financial circumstances. He needed the money and besides, this Prince Rupert job would only be for a couple of months. Wayne pointed and said, "If you look across there you can see where the tailings pond containing all that grey mine waste slurry and water has almost over-topped the dam."

It had been a rainy spring and a big storm had blown through just before Wayne arrived on the job. The erosion channels on the face of the dam were as obvious as the initial signs of slumping. "And the poly liner could be ripped," he said pointing to the seepage they could both see in the wetland below the dam. "I guess that would have happened during installation?" Wayne looked straight at Ted, gauging his reaction.

This mine was Ted's project and had been all the way from conception through construction of the tailings dam and now during operations. "What exactly are you saying?" Ted asked, in a tone clearly intended to shut down further discussion on the subject.

"I'm concerned about dam integrity and a tailings spill once water gets in and liquefies the dam core. It's a salmon stream below that wetland and there are a bunch of granola back to the lander types living down there along the shore. You know, the ones that have objected to this mine from the beginning. I haven't seen them mentioned in any of the reports you told me to use as a guide for my reporting."

"I wouldn't worry too much. Just do your rounds and complete the templates you've been given. Now, let's see what else you've got."

They drove further up the valley, steep slopes rising to partially cloud shrouded snow-capped peaks on both sides. Along the way, Wayne pointed out an area where waste rock from the mine adit was being dumped. Discolored runoff was clearly visible. "I think the rain and sulphides in the rock are combining to produce sulphuric acid. Look, that discolored runoff extends all the way down the gulch and into that stream."

"I know what acid runoff is. What do you mean there might be acid runoff? The tests came up negative."

"Well the tests must have been wrong, cause I've seen acid runoff before and this is it. Plus I checked the pH myself," said Wayne confidently. He'd done his work well and wasn't about to be contradicted on the facts and the data.

"Are you questioning the tests I had done by the lab in Vancouver?" asked Ted with an edge.

"I'm looking at the real world situation and there it is," Wayne replied self-assuredly.

"Alright, we'll look into it," said Ted without conviction, "But there's no need to include that in your reports until it's confirmed. Anything else?"

"Didn't Ron check the pH? It's in the monitoring protocol the company agreed to with the government. It's in the terms and conditions for this operation. It's required."

"We'll talk about that later," said Ted glaring at Wayne to clearly signal he didn't want to discuss the subject any further.

They both knew the government approved templates kept reporting so narrow the real story would never be captured.

"On those templates everything's in compliance right?"

"Yeah," said Wayne reluctantly, before adding, "except the pH."

4

"Well then there's no problem. Just keep doing your job."

"Okay boss," said Wayne, "let's just continue the tour."

Wayne turned the pickup around and headed back down the mine road toward the inlet. At a turn, he slowed and veered off to the right through some underbrush and onto an overgrown old logging road. When he finally stopped, Ted asked, "What the hell did you bring me here for?"

"I want you to see something."

Ted shrugged his shoulders, threw his hands in the air and looked at his watch, communicating frustration and impatience at being forced to waste his valuable time on such inconsequential matters.

Wayne got out of the truck and motioned for Ted to follow, which he did reluctantly. He led Ted through a thicket of aggressive devil's club stocks before he stopped and pointed down. At his feet, water flowed out of the ground into a pool created by a small hand-fashioned earthen dam someone had made. In the dam was a green garden hose.

"Those guys down there on the waterfront are hippies left over from the seventies, living in a bit of a time warp."

"I know they're there. Who cares?" said Ted impatiently.

"They get their water from here. It's going to be contaminated if the tailings dam leaks or even worse, fails."

"They're living there illegally. So, again, who cares?"

"Maybe illegal, but they're not moving. This is all they've got."

Ted shrugged again, signalling so what.

"If mine contamination spreads, the mine will be illegal too. At that point, who's got rights? Meanwhile, these people could be poisoned and the salmon they harvest in this stream could be gone."

Ted looked sternly at Wayne again, eyebrows raised. He rubbed thumb over forefinger right in Wayne's face, in the age old way of underlining money implications. If the mine shut down and the client couldn't pay, then they would both feel the pinch.

Wayne looked away, resigned. "Okay. I guess we can go then. I just wanted to talk these things through with you."

Back at the camp barge, the mine manager, Klaus, invited them into his office.

Wayne surveyed the room he was becoming familiar with: vinyl floor, vinyl covered drywall panels with vinyl strips at the joints, mud on the floor and a film of dirt on the cheap desk.

"How was your tour?" Klaus asked, indicating they should sit in the worn vinyl and steel office chairs opposite. "Pretty impressive operation eh? There's a lot of money being made here, and a lot was invested to get things up and running."

Ted smiled in agreement as he nodded to Wayne and sat down. "It's a small mine but rich and efficient." Returning his attention to Klaus, he expressed thanks for the opportunity to tour the site.

"Anything catch your eye?" asked Klaus making a good show of playing the game.

Ted looked over at Wayne sitting in the second chair and then back at Klaus again. "Everything looks good. Wayne will just keep coming in and doing his reports as usual."

Klaus answered with a big smile, his pale blue eyes boring directly into Wayne's. "That's why you're our favourite consultants. Everyone in the industry says so. Wayne here has been doing a good job. He's experienced and knows exactly how things work."

Wayne met Klaus' penetrating stare then glanced at Ted who nodded with a terse smile. He looked beyond Klaus out the window to the forest rising from the water on the far shore of the inlet. The sound of propeller blades reversing thrust came just before the plane crossed the field of view in a shroud of spray. Wayne stood and extended his hand to Klaus. "Plane is here. We'd better get down to the float."

Klaus shook hands and yelled out the door, "Hey Jack. Take these guys down to the float to get picked up. And make sure they give you back the keys." He paused before adding, "Can't have you guys running off with the keys to our trucks can we?"

With Wayne and Ted aboard, the plane taxied back to the middle of the inlet and the pilot revved his engine. As they clattered over wave tops and lifted off, Wayne could see the cabins on the inlet's north shore, basking in a shaft of afternoon sunlight that shone like a beacon through the cloud cover.

Back in Prince Rupert, Wayne dropped Ted off at the downtown terminal to catch the shuttle bus and ferry ride to the airport out on Digby Island. On departing, Ted said, "I know I can count on you Wayne. You've always been loyal to the company and our clients no matter what it takes. Remember, don't be like that loser Ron."

TWO

THAT NIGHT WAYNE COULDN'T SLEEP. SINCE ARRIVING A MONTH ago, things hadn't felt quite right. The trip with Ted out to New Discovery Gold had been weird and increased his discomfort. Ted had always been in it just for the money but this was beyond what he'd seen before.

In the grey light of early morning the apartment, built in the heyday back in the 70s, looked tired. The smell of coffee brewing perked him up so he called Kathy in Vancouver to talk things through. She was at work by now and busy. Right away he realised his mistake.

"Wayne, when are you going to leave there and come back down to Vancouver, if you're coming at all? You didn't have to volunteer for this stupid little job in Rupert. Sounds like the last guy didn't like it much either." Her impatience was impossible to miss. "What happened to him anyway?"

Wayne turned on his laptop while he waited for her to finish and then said, "I think he got fired. That's kind of why I'm calling. I need to talk things out with someone."

Completely overlooking Wayne's situation, Kathy carried on her rant. "And that old boat you bought. What's going on there? What were you thinking? You must be planning on staying or something."

"It wasn't much money and you know I've wanted to get a boat to fix up and do some of my own consulting and survey work, and maybe some commercial fishing. Back here on the north coast was the perfect opportunity to try and this is the perfect boat. And like I said, it didn't cost much either."

He listened for a response but Kathy just sighed heavily into the phone and then sharply hung up.

Wayne stared into his cup exasperated. He dressed and tried to work at the kitchen table. He had to get some kind of report done for Ted so the mining company could send it to the provincial environment guys up in Smithers. Unable to focus, he packed up everything and put on rain gear. The truck was wet inside again and he thought, 'Really need to deal with the leaky weather stripping on the old beast. Will the rainy season ever end?' He quickly corrected himself. 'A break from the rain is too ridiculous to contemplate.'

He drove the short distance downtown, parked and walked south, up the hill to Third Avenue, wondering if it wouldn't have been just as fast to walk all the way from the company apartment. The rain was coming down in sheets though and rebounding off the sidewalk. He turned east onto Third and then stepped through a weathered glass and steel door into the office building and climbed the old worn terrazzo stairs to the company's fourth floor office. He unlocked the door and could immediately see down the length of the office and out the window facing north to the harbour. In good weather the snow covered peaks of the Coast Mountains extended magnificently to the east, but not today. Today Wayne would miss that therapeutic view. As he sat down to work, he couldn't get the picture of that hose in the little dam collecting spring water out of his mind. He knew that water would sooner or later be contaminated, or even lethal if they ever spilled cyanide or mine tailings or diesel.

Wayne played with the digital photos from his mine visits and composed appropriate captions, trying to fit them into the report template he'd been directed to use. He had to ensure none of the photos were from angles that might hint at the problems he knew were there. There was no place to put in the pH data he'd been collecting. Until this job, the projects he'd worked on were always big and impersonal. You never saw the people, the project opponents, face to face in their homes. This closeness was new and it was getting uncomfortable.

Eventually he gave up and went out to grab a coffee at at the café down by the water. By now the rain had let up and maybe the walk would do him good. Maybe there'd be someone at the coffee shop he could talk to. Living in the apartment by himself, with all the gloom and rain, was starting to get to him, starting to make him question his own judgement. And that was a new experience too.

He walked into the coffee shop and saw Susan sitting in her usual corner by the window, monitoring the comings and goings, looking for stories for the local paper. He got a coffee and scone and sat opposite her, offering half the scone. She accepted.

"Well you don't look too good," she said inspecting him as she broke off a piece of the biscuit.

"Up all night. Couldn't sleep," said Wayne, eyes down to hide his fatigue.

"Still have to fly high in the morning though, eh?" said Susan, suggesting she did not really want to hear his personal problems, unless it was something she could use in the paper. They had met around town and in the coffee shop. She gave the impression she found him to be pretty arrogant but new and maybe intriguing. She flicked her shiny black hair over her shoulder and said, "Everything OK?"

"New Discovery Gold," said Wayne tersely, assuming that said it all for anyone living in Prince Rupert.

"Oh shit." She laughed and added a sarcastic, "Good luck with that. They're on our traditional lands you know."

"Yeah, no kidding," said Wayne sipping coffee and holding the scone with his other hand. "Should've stayed in Vancouver. Should've taken a break until the next big job, instead of getting mixed up in this mess."

Just as Wayne was about to expand on his problems, a group entered the shop looking like they'd just stepped out of a commune. The three of them, dressed head to toe in wet rain gear, lined up for coffee and looked around as they stood, essence of forest and patchouli wafting off them. Susan nodded pleasantly in their direction and they nodded back.

The youngest, who was pretty in a wholesome sort of way and looked to be in her mid-twenties, stared straight at Wayne.

"I know you. You were out at the mine yesterday," she said in a loud direct voice, "and lots of times before that. We had our scope on you."

Wayne's heart stopped as he tried to maintain his poker face and looked from her to Susan. He knew that squatters lived out by the mine but he didn't actually know them, had never talked to them. Susan rose from her chair and approached the group.

"Hi Dave, Starshine, Hello Cedar. Come on over, while they get your order. They'll be a while. I guess you've seen Wayne around. You might want to meet him." Susan waved her arm in Wayne's direction. "This is Wayne Dumont the new consultant. Wayne these are Dave, his wife Starshine and their daughter Cedar. They live near the New Discovery Gold Mine. Sounds like they've seen you up there."

Wayne rose and extended his hand, which each one of them rejected in turn. Wayne sat. They picked up their orders and he watched as they proceeded deliberately to the opposite side of the coffee shop, hanging up their wet rain gear and fleece on the rack there.

"They've been here a long time," said Susan in a low voice.

"Yeah, looks like it. Expect to see moss growing on them."

"Now be nice," Susan admonished gently with a smile. "They've always been on the fringe and like it that way. Dave used to do log salvage and they lived in an abandoned cabin across Prince Rupert harbour, at Salt Lake, for a while. That's where Cedar was born. With the mill closing and trucks taking over log transport, the log salvage gig kind of dried up. They moved to another cabin up the coast, at an abandoned log dump in Mirage Inlet. Everything was fine for them until New Discovery Gold showed up and invaded their little utopia. They've been fighting the mine ever since. They show up at all the meetings here in town and in lots of news clips."

Wayne broke off a piece of scone and put it in his mouth while he studied them. Eventually he asked, "What do they do for money?"

"As you can see from their clothes, except for Cedar they don't spend much. Get welfare of course. But Dave does some fishing, for food mainly, occasionally commercial but under the table. They have a garden, chickens, goats, a dog. The usual hippie ensemble. They do crafts and sell them in town. Probably grow and sell some weed too. Who knows?"

"The girl, Cedar is her name? She looks different."

"Cedar's more sensible. She was homeschooled by Starshine but went to high school in town, staying with family friends. Now she works as a Teaching Assistant and stays with friends over at Dodge Cove, commuting with them across the harbour to town each day."

Wayne sipped his coffee and tried not to stare.

Susan carried on. "The mining company wants them out. That's where you come in. The enemy."

"Now you can see why I didn't sleep last night."

"Wasn't too hard to guess, given the work you do." Susan paused before adding, "For a tough hotshot consultant, you were pretty easy to read on that one."

"I saw stuff nobody wants me to report," said Wayne, sipping his coffee, hiding behind the cup.

"I know. Don't tell me though. I might have to put it in the paper. That's what happened to the last guy up here from your company. Ron. He tried to get info out and they fired him on the spot. Had to find his own way out. I heard he's back in Newfoundland now."

Wayne leaned over the table on his elbows, running his hands through shaggy hair and over tired brown eyes. He looked dismally up at Susan. "You know, I've never really been comfortable with my life. Always have to measure up. You know."

Susan looked at him, exasperated. "You're not going to unload a bunch of personal shit on me now are you? It's too late my friend. Apparently you're already branded."

"Can anything be done?" asked Wayne, gazing across the room at Cedar and her family.

"You'll have to figure that out for yourself, I guess. It's like the people that go to AA, first you have to admit you have a problem."

*****

"Damn, I can't write this garbage," said Wayne to the yellowing bare walls. He swivelled his chair to stare out the office window, field notes lying on the desk, boring a hole into the back of his head. The images still staring out from the screen.

It was clear that Cedar and her crowd didn't like the fact he was associated with the mining company and they had probably been looking into his past. Everyone in the environmental justice scene had. It was all there in the news clips, the transcripts from multiple hearings in public registries across the country. He was the guy. The high flying spin artist for big project proponents – pipelines, oil sands, mines, hydroelectric; if it was big and controversial Wayne had been there one way or another. Gold mines were the smallest and he really hadn't cared much about them. For gold mines he'd just mailed in the standard lines and company commitments that would never be met. It was a formula, and he'd written it.

It was clear by now that most of the mining companies were concerned mainly with raising money in the capital markets to pay the big salary promoters, board members and corporate enablers, rather than actually digging holes in the ground. A public offering provided capital for the good life for a few years while some two bit exploration was done, releasing cherry picked results to fuel excitement and entice naïve people to throw in their hard earned money. Pumping up the stock, fleecing the suckers is what the promoters and brokers called it after market closing in the bars off Howe and Pender streets, and even he'd been one of the suckers himself more than once. He couldn't help getting swept up in the game.

The ravens were circling at New Discovery, squatters, activists, federal and provincial enviro cops, and the investors. Wayne didn't want to be the last one holding the dynamite on this one when the situation blew, which it surely would. Things had been bad enough out there at the mine site but now they were talking about enhanced onsite gold recovery with cyanide. That could spell trouble at a site like this. 'How far will I let myself go?' he wondered.

The last rays of the early spring sun lit the far side of Prince Rupert harbour in a golden hue, against a backdrop of thick dark cloud. The white superstructure of an anchored freighter, illuminated by the sun, stood out starkly against a charcoal grey sky. It was strung out on the tidal stream, waiting for another load of raw logs going to create jobs in

China, or somewhere else outside Canada. He'd worked a bit on that kind of bullshit too.

Wayne rose from his chair, put on his Floater jacket and headed for the door, taking all this with him in his head. He parked the laptop and files in his old truck and walked to the nearest bar.

Susan was there, sitting in a corner, watching for stories and pretending to drink. Her rumpled Gore-Tex jacket hung on the chair back. Dark hair hanging down past her shoulders partially screened her eyes. Wayne sat down opposite and ordered a draft. There were only a few other patrons, mainly retired fishermen who chatted quietly about the heydays of big money in halibut, salmon and herring. Hundred thousand dollars from trips only lasting a week. Those were the days. It was the wild-west back then. There were also a few construction types in the opposite corner, watching the Canucks and Flames on a flatscreen, no sound. A couple of them wore New Discovery Gold ball caps.

"So my friend, how goes the battle with the devil?" she said with a welcoming smile.

"About even odds for the moment. I really need the money but I can't sleep or work right now. I need someone to give me a boot in the ass and tell me what to do," said Wayne managing a smile and accepting a beer from the server.

"I guess you'd better call your mommy then, mister big shot consultant," said Susan with derision. She knew Wayne's mother was a society overachiever back in Toronto, who pushed him constantly. It had been an ongoing and off-putting topic of late night conversation.

Wayne threw up his hands. "Thanks," he said and took a long pull of whatever watered down brew they were selling as draft beer that night.

"Seriously," said Susan with more empathy. "What are you going to do?"

"I don't know. If I send in a real report I'll be fired on the spot for sure. Ted, my boss and the owner of the company, made that pretty clear and I really didn't need to be told. But I need the money right now, quite badly."

"Maybe you shouldn't have bought that boat."

"Now you sound like Kathy. That's what she said to me, right before she slammed down the phone."

"Damn. You really are in the shit," said Susan, smiling and pushing her chair away from the table with the back of her knees as she stood. "Let's play pool. Get your mind re-focussed."

Well into the game, two of the squatters came into the bar. It was Dave, and Susan leaned over to tell Wayne the other one was known as Jimi.

"Well if it isn't the great Wayne," said Jimi approaching aggressively. "I've heard about you. Actually I've been watching you, at the mine and elsewhere."

"Oh yeah, like where?" said Wayne, not sure how to take this guy.

Jimi adjusted his frayed homespun woollen toque, ran grimy fingers through his unkempt blond beard and said, "In the online public registries where your lies and manipulation are manifest for everyone to see. When New Discovery was making noises I went to hearings in the Yukon on Turning Point Gold. That was really some display you put on there. Even I was impressed by your arrogance and gall."

Susan looked at Wayne with questions in her deep brown eyes. Their game wasn't over but Wayne put down his cue and said to Susan, "Keep the money". He grabbed his coat and walked out the door, into the dark and the rain that now pelted down.

In his truck, he hung his head and sat with hands on the wheel. Drips came down through the weather stripping just missing his left hand. His pants were getting wet. He drove home via the government wharf where he sat for a moment in the dark looking down at his new boat. Well, it was new to him anyway, but actually had been built back in the 1930s. A real classic troller he was determined to restore.

When he flicked the lights on at the company apartment, it was after nine p.m. It was not a warm light. The place was spare and cold and damp.

On a whim, Wayne gathered up his laptop and report and sat down at the cheap Swedish dining table. He opened up the files and went to work, dropping digital photos into the template boxes, crafting captions, and inserting text. He added extra categories and boxes to the company template and filled those too. At about 2:00 a.m. he finished, sat back and hit the 'Send' button. He put his head down on arms splayed across the table. That was it. Now he was done.

At 2:30 he packed up his personal laptop, files and digital records and left the apartment. It was cold, with a northwest breeze blowing in from the Gulf of Alaska, and no moon. Maybe a long sought high pressure ridge was finally coming in to blow all the rain inland. He piled everything into the truck and drove to the office.

Third Avenue was bare except for the stragglers from the early morning bar closures. His feet made the familiar morning sidewalk sound of soles on broken glass as he walked up to the building. Wayne smiled to himself at the crunches. He used his company key to enter.

In the office he gathered up all the digital and paper copies he'd been making since his first visit out to the mine site. He'd had a premonition about how things might end from the outset. He struggled to carry the boxes of duplicate files down the stairs. Outside the street level door he looked all around the shadows as he pushed through and then turned back to lock it. He saw no one in the gloom as he shoved everything into the truck and climbed in the driver side.

The boat was his fail-safe. Wayne parked at the wharf and, carrying a box and the company laptop, he carefully edged down the slippery steep low-tide ramp to the floats below. His boat was moored along a finger float, away from the orange glow of piling mounted lights. He jumped aboard, unlocked and opened the fish hold. He climbed down the vertical rungs into the hold a couple of times to get everything stowed safely away. After he climbed out, he looked all around again and then re-locked the hatch cover. He'd get a better lock tomorrow.

*****

WAYNE WOKE AT 10:00 A.M. IT WAS SUNDAY AND THE SUN streamed through the half closed blind slats, turning the wall opposite from dingy to bright stripes against grey shadows. From the bed he watched cedars and fir trees swaying green in the breeze against a deep blue sky. Hays Mountain was visible to the top for once. The high pressure ridge had come in and it was going to be a beautiful early spring day. Everything was good until he remembered, like a lightning bolt cleaving his brain, that he'd sent in the report last night and now he had to wait.

At the waterfront café, the waitress brought bacon, eggs, home fries, toast and strong black coffee, essential to get going and last the day if needed. The place was busy. It had been overcast and raining for quite a while and everyone was coming out to enjoy the sun. The chatter was about boats, fishing, the old days, politics and whether New Discovery Gold was ever going to pay its bills in town. Lots of people worried about that. Wayne savoured breakfast, listened for a while, paid and went down to his boat.

"Hey Wayne, how you doin' with your new boat. She's a beaut," said Gus as Wayne shuffled along the float with his gear. "You were lucky to get her. Not many of those left."

Gus Gustafson was a weathered veteran of the north coast, of Norwegian descent like so many of them. He'd started fishing for the cannery with his father and then carried on his whole life.

"Well I bought her, so I guess I'm lucky," said Wayne setting his gear down, glad to have someone to chat with. "Before I paid I read the marine survey, but not too carefully cause the price was good and there aren't too many left of these old boats built by those Japanese-Canadian guys. They built a helluva boat. Superb craftsmanship with the best wood: oak; yellow cedar; and, Douglas fir. Guess I'll go over her with a fine tooth comb and see what I've got."

Wayne grabbed his things and swung aboard with one hand on the rigging, surveying his baby.

"Yup, *Molly B*'s a pretty little troller alright. You'll appreciate that double ended hull in a following sea," said Clarence climbing off his boat and coming over to join the conversation. He slurped coffee that looked and smelled like light crude, smacked his lips and smiled to show gums and missing teeth. "Thirty three feet of comfort. You set her up right and you'll be able to live aboard just like me. We'll be neighbours. What d'ye think about that?"

"Sounds perfect Clarence," said Wayne with a smile as he fished in his pockets for keys.

Wayne's cell phone rumbled. He held up a hand to Clarence and answered.

"Wayne. Is that you?" Kathy's voice had an immediate edge to it.

"Hi Kathy. I'm good. How about you?"

They briefly reviewed their respective mundane daily routines, warming up before Kathy really started in.

"So do you know when you're coming back down? I'm feeling trapped here. Just going to work and coming home. What am I supposed to do?"

"Well I'm here for a while. We need the money you know."

"We wouldn't if you hadn't sunk a bundle into that phony gold mine stock."

Wayne was frustrated that she'd manoeuvered him onto defense so quickly. "They had good reserves. Everything looked like a sure thing. How was I to know they were bleeding cash?"

"Should've been more careful," mumbled Kathy sounding frustrated and angry, maybe with herself.

"What? I couldn't hear you?"

"Never mind. Old subject. What are you doing today?"

"Right now I'm down on our boat, starting to really go through it. See what we've..."

At that point Kathy blew. "You mean your boat. I didn't want any part of that piece of junk."

"You haven't even seen her."

"I know, but it's still a piece of junk. We have no money."

"Don't worry. We'll get the money from this job. Ted's paying me a big bonus for being here."

"You ever ask yourself why?" asked Kathy, losing patience. "That son of a bitch never gives anything away without getting more back for himself."

"No. I assumed it's because I'm the best at what I do and right now I'll take what I can get it."

"You mean the best at twisting the truth, lying, deception. That's what you do. Are you doing it again on this job? You're doing it with me right now and I can see right through you."

Frustrated and fed up, Wayne said, "Look Kathy, I've got to go. There's a boat coming in to raft up and I need to fend him off and take his lines." He clicked the phone off and turned to face Clarence. Clarence had gone back aboard his own floating home, a beautiful troller built in the renowned Wahl yard in Prince Rupert, but badly in need of clean-up and repairs.

Wayne threw his arms in the air and shrugged, to no one. He used a key to open the lock on *Molly B*'s cabin door and stepped inside his new cocoon. The wheelhouse was cozy, just enough room for two if the second person stood in the companionway leading down two steps to the twin berths below, in the bow. An oil stove and sink made up the galley down there too, port side aft of the forepeak berth.

Wayne went down the companionway, sat on the starboard berth and leaned across to light the stove opposite. The boat needed warming up to drive off the damp. He looked around considering what needed to be checked out and what could be done that morning. He decided to work on the electrical system and check the wires and connections at the main terminal board. Exposing the opening under the cabin, he wriggled in with a headlamp on. The diesel engine was right there and on the side was the electric terminal board. He wormed his way further in to get a good look.

While his head was well into the bowels of the engine compartment he was startled by a knock on the hull. He hadn't heard anyone coming down the float and wondered who it might be.

"Hey Wayne. You in there?" It sounded like Susan.

He backed his way out, trying to avoid cramping up, and raised his head out the companionway enough to see her climbing aboard. She wore non-skid sea boots and a heavy water proof jacket.

"Oh hi Susan," said Wayne on his knees and looking up and aft to where she stood in the cabin door. "Nice to see you. What'cha ya doin' down here on a Sunday morning?"

"Well I was out for breakfast and then it's so nice I thought I'd walk around down here. You know, see if you were around. I had a hunch you'd be puttering around your new baby and it looks like I was right."

"Yeah you were. I'm just going through and checking things over more carefully. Hope I don't find anything bad, although I'm pretty sure this boat was well cared for."

"Need a hand?"

"Maybe you could confirm that the nav lights go on when I reconnect the wire."

"Right-ho. Just say when."

Wayne contorted himself back into the engine compartment and re-connected the wire to its proper terminal.

"How's that?" he yelled. Susan yelled back in the affirmative and Wayne secured the connection. Together they checked some other connections: cabin lights, radio, radar, GPS. Finally Wayne extricated himself and stood. "Thanks Susan. That was a big help. Saved me going in and out all the time."

"So what now?" she asked.

Her boots and jacket said she was ready for a boat trip. "How 'bout we go for a good run. I need to clear the injectors out on this old diesel. Maybe catch a spring salmon."

She enthusiastically agreed and Wayne hit the ignition. The diesel coughed and belched before rumbling to life. A puff of oily black smoke blew out the exhaust pipe above the cabin and the engine warmed up, settling into a steady rhythm as it reached operating temperature. Susan cast off the mooring lines and he manoeuvred the engine controls and rudder to work his way out of the tight mooring spot. They passed by the floating breakwater and out into Prince Rupert harbour.

Wayne perched on the lone stool set behind the wheel, next to the portside controls. Susan stood in the companionway leaning on the varnished mahogany of the dash. It was cozy but they both had a 180 degree view of the bright blue harbour through the surrounding cabin windows.

The boat sprang to life as they encountered a light chop on clearing the harbour entrance past the container terminal. At the coal terminal they turned west heading into the sun at a seven knot cruising speed. Looking seaward between coastal islands there was nothing between them and Haida Gwaii hidden beyond the horizon. The open Pacific lay beyond that archipelago. Behind them a gallery of snow-capped peaks crowned the skyline, lit to the brightest white by the sun.

Wayne increased the revs to push *Molly B* up to her eight and a half knot maximum hull speed and the engine ran fine. After a run around Digby Island they turned back into the harbour, past Metlakatla and Crippen Cove.

Susan pointed to the Tsimshian village of Metlakatla saying, "Look, there's my parents' house. The place where I grew up. And lots before me. The village has been there for thousands of years. Way before you traders and settlers came along."

On a whim Wayne suggested Susan toss in a line which she did and soon caught an average sized spring salmon. Back at the wharf, he manoeuvred *Molly B* to bring her in next to the float, and Susan dealt with the mooring lines competently. Wayne closed up the cabin and told her to keep the salmon, hoping sometime she might invite him for dinner.

As she was leaving, Susan asked, "So, I've been wondering, what did you end up doing with your report?"

Wayne looked at her nervously and asked, "Is this for sure off the record? Just between you and me, as friends. You know I need someone to talk to but you can't put this in the paper, right?"

"Yes. For sure. It's just between you and me."

Wayne shuffled his feet and looked all around them before hesitatingly telling her. "I closed my eyes and sent in the real report."

"Wow. Good for you. But I bet you're in a lot of shit now, aren't you?"

"I guess. We'll see what happens. Worst case I lose my job, get kicked out of the apartment and have to find a place to live. That's what they did with the last guy," said Wayne, hoping for a lifeline from her.

"That's terrible," said Susan.

*****

"MAY I HELP YOU?" ASKED THE LIBRARIAN AT THE LOCAL LIBRARY main desk.

"I'm fine I think," said Wayne gazing around, looking for the newspaper racks. "I just want to go through the old newspaper clippings for Prince Rupert. The current paper and the old Daily News."

"The Daily News is out of business," said the woman with shoulder length wavy brown hair wearing what appeared to be a hand knitted sweater.

"Yes I heard that. I just wanted to go further back, maybe into the 90's or the 80's. Do you have the papers themselves, or are they digital or on fiche?"

"Come on over here," she said, leading Wayne through the turnstile and the reading area to the periodicals.

"Some of the more recent papers are here," she said, pointing to the stacks. "The older papers can be found on this computer and the even older ones are on fiche. You can use this reader. We just haven't got the resources to digitize them. The digitized records go back to about the mid 90's and, for anything predating that, the fiches are in these file card drawers. The fiche index is here in the top drawer. Someday we'll get all of these records digitized if we ever get the money. You looking for anything in particular?"

"I'm interested in Mirage Inlet," said Wayne familiarizing himself with the layout, "and the New Discovery Gold Mine."

"That stuff is all through the papers. Lots of history. Lots of controversy. Lots of coverage. Help yourself." She started to walk back to her desk but turned to add, "You may be a while."

Wayne settled in, going through the most recent papers first. He found an article by Susan herself, last year, before

Wayne arrived. In it she detailed companies in town that had not been paid by New Discovery Gold. There was mention of the mining CEO she had tried to contact but his secretary in Vancouver said he was out of the country on vacation, apparently in the Cayman Islands. Susan had wrapped up the article by pointing out how people had looked forward to and supported the mine, because of the jobs and investment in the community.

Wayne continued to plough through the papers and records on the library's computer, gaining a better picture of the mining company and the way it conducted business. This was the first time he'd really focussed on pulling back the curtain on the business practices of one of his clients. It had always been better to just not know.

One common thread in the news articles was the presence of a group of objectors who were apparently squatters living in a few cabins up Mirage Inlet at a place they proclaimed as Blissful Cove, although there was really no cove to be found, just a gentle curvature of the shoreline. Going back into the records on fiche, Wayne came across a photo showing a back to the land family living up the inlet. A mother with long dark hair in long floral dress. A father in denim overalls and t-shirt with a black beard, long hair and an old punched out fedora. A boy and a little girl toddler, just able to walk. Wayne looked at the picture and decided to make a copy to ask Susan about.

When finished, or more accurately when he was dizzy from flipping through articles and photos, Wayne thanked the librarian and left. Avoiding the office and email, he walked across town to the newspaper office to visit Susan. Heavy clouds overhead made the streets dark and a steady rain had settled in, again. A few people walked along the streets but not many. The back street of the newspaper office was deserted.

He pulled open the glass front door and found himself at the main reception counter. A push button phone rested on the worn oak trimmed counter top and to the right was a message spike clogged with old messages, along with a bell to ring for service.

Behind the counter was an off white plaster wall, with glass windows. Through the window, Wayne could see Susan, busy with her head down working at her computer, perhaps on an article he thought. She was dressed in a red and black checked shirt and black sweater, jeans and boots. Her hair was pulled back but dark strands still dangled over her face. The computer screen gave her an ethereal glow.

When Wayne dinged the bell, Susan along with all the others in the news room looked up. Seeing who it was, she smiled and rose. As she came out through the door and approached the reception counter she said, "Wayne, what are you doing here. Not going in to work today?"

"Just in the neighbourhood," said Wayne smiling at her, making an outward show of a self-confidence he did not feel.

"Thanks for the ride yesterday. That was fun."

He opened his shell to let her peek inside his real state of mind. "Actually I'm mainly killing time if you really want to know. Don't want to go to the office. Don't want to find out what they're going to do to me."

"Yeah, that's a tough one. Like we discussed, they tossed the last guy, Ron, like it was nothing. Right out on the street with nothing. Poor guy had to get himself out of town, back to Newfoundland."

"Yeah, that's what everyone says alright," said Wayne, fingers thrumming the counter the only physical evidence of his agitation and uneasiness. "Nobody at work really talks about it though. Hazard of the business I guess."

"Nice company you work for. Why'd you take this assignment? Oh yeah, you needed the money."

Changing the subject, Wayne said, "I was over at the library just poking around, looking at old newspaper articles dealing with Mirage Inlet and New Discovery Gold."

"You should have come here. This is the newspaper after all. We have our own archives you know."

"Yeah, I guess you're right. I should have thought of that," said Wayne pleased that she had made the offer of help. "And I didn't want to take you away from your work because, remember, I'm just killing time and avoiding the office this morning."

"That's right. Thanks for that. But remember you can use the archives here any time. Just ask and I'll make the arrangements."

"Thanks Susan. There is one thing I want to ask you about. I got this copy of a picture." Wayne reached into the inside pocket of his Floater jacket and drew out a piece of photocopy paper. He unfolded it and pressed it flat on the counter for her to see. She turned the picture, looked at it and smiled.

"What's the smile for?" asked Wayne, intrigued and wondering what she saw.

"This is a family from Mirage Inlet."

"I can see that. It's in the caption."

Without raising her head, Susan glanced up into Wayne's eyes. "Well you know these people."

"I do?"

"Sure. They're the squatters that saw you out at the mine, the ones laying into you every time they see you here in town, at the coffee shop, at the bar. That cute little girl grew up to become Cedar."

"Wow. That's quite a change. You mean they've been fighting the mine for that long?"

"That's right. They built their cabins out there on Crown Land after the valley was logged out. The old log dump made a nice gravel base to build on, where the A-frame used to be.

And there's the indentation they call Blissful Cove that's sheltered a bit from Arctic outflow gales that rip down these inlets in the winter. Dave worked as a faller during the logging. He was injured and gets disability. Jimi does log salvage or he did until the pulpmill shut down. I guess he may still do a bit for the sawmill when he can find good timber logs. Starshine and Jimi's partner, Chelsea, help out with that. They're all quite settled there."

Wayne leaned over the counter to examine the picture more closely, considering the image and the information he'd just received. "Did New Discovery try to get them moved off the land?"

"Oh yeah, that's for sure. They tried. Dave led a big fight, on the water and on the land. They painted the mining company as the devil, with quite a bit of success too. Ultimately everyone reached a stand-off and that's where it still sits today." She paused, as if considering the situation. "Except the mining continues, unabated."

"Hmmm, makes you think," said Wayne, looking up at Susan and rubbing his forehead with his hand, his elbow propped on the counter.

"Yes it does," said Susan, turning the picture back to Wayne's view. "You came into this situation on the side of the company. Whose side are you on today? Have you checked with your mommy to see if you're still supposed to be the big bad consultant?"

"Come on Susan. I'm trying to do the right thing. I just sent the report in didn't I?"

"We'll see I guess," said Susan with a sceptical look.

"That was a nice salmon yesterday, wasn't it?" he added, trying to change the subject to something less confrontational and more engaging.

"Yes it was," said Susan, failing to offer the hoped for invitation to dinner. "Anyway, that's enough about the mine and the squatters. I'd better get back to work."

"Guess I'll go then," said Wayne looking straight into Susan's deep brown eyes, hoping for answers, knowing that that only he himself could provide them.

There was no response. She turned and went back into the news room, behind the clear glass barrier.

THREE

HE OPENED HIS EYES, LOOKED AROUND, AND CASUALLY WATCHED the strange woman slide out from under his crisp white sheets, stand and move to the wall of windows. English Bay stretched out far below, freighters all aligned in the tidal stream, sunshine beaming down ahead of dark mists hugging the far side of the strait. She quickly dressed, gathered up her things and left. When the door closed he began to stir. Someone had been with him but he couldn't remember her name. Huh, maybe she'd call him and self-identify, or maybe not. There were lots more in Vancouver.

Ted Murdoch sat up in the bed, ran a hand through his salt and pepper hair, and tried to clear his head from last night's indulgences. He surveyed his domain. A penthouse Vancouver West End condo, floor to vaulted ceiling windows overlooking English Bay, chrome and glass furnishings, all the latest touches. This was the life. He could smell the coffee, ready in the automated brewing machine he'd jammed a pod into last night. It was time to get up.

Prepped and ready, on the way out he grabbed another gulp of coffee, not taking the time to savour it. He knew Kaye would have another ready for him at the office. Ted rode the elevator to the parking garage where his trim black Audi sat.

He climbed in. The rush hour was over and he didn't have far to go to his next underground parking spot at the office on Alberni Street. He picked up a paper in the building lobby and rode to the 17th floor where his office had an excellent view over Vancouver Harbour, and the north shore mountains. Kaye brought him his coffee.

"Ted, do you need anything?" she asked, dutiful as always.

Ted looked at the oak desk, the black blotter over plate glass with one green file folder perfectly centred on it. Green meant money, revenue or financial annoyances. He wondered which.

"What is that?" He pointed to the file. "And why is it on my desk this early in the week, on a Monday morning?" asked Ted applying his usual aggressive manner and dismissive tone.

"Well, the contents came in by courier early this morning so I assumed it would be important and you'd want to see it right away," said Kaye, feigning a defensive posture, but she was used to his behaviour by now and the money he paid her was too good to pass up.

"How many times have I told you not to assume anything? Did you look at it?"

"I know it's from the bank but I didn't look at the contents. I know I'm not to look at the banking things."

"Damn right. That's my business. Mine alone. Well, anything else you want to lay on me this early?" demanded Ted bringing the Monday morning repartee to a close.

"No," said Kaye submissively backing out of the expensively appointed executive office and closing the door.

"Leave the door open," shouted Ted, and the door swung back, as if on its own.

Ted sat in his leather chair and opened the folder. He seized his monogramed silver letter opener and, holding it precisely between thumb and forefinger, slit the envelope the folder contained. Inside was a statement from the bank on the status of his company's financing. The penthouse condo, the Audi and the 57 foot yacht were all in the company name, all financed by loans to the company. He'd needed the boat for oceanographic work, as he told the bank and his employees who never set foot on it.

Ted picked up the bank statement, turned it over, turned it back, and then slid it into the inside breast pocket of his charcoal grey designer suit jacket. With authority he abruptly swivelled his chair around to gaze up at Grouse Mountain, sunlight catching the slash of white snow on it and the gleaming peaks beyond. He sat back and put his feet up on the window frame. The phone rang and he reached to grab it without otherwise moving to disturb the view. It was Kaye.

"Gordon's on the line from Stewart. Says he's been working up there in northern BC for a month now and his paycheques aren't being deposited in his bank account. He wants to know what's up and to talk with you. The apartment he's in is a dump and there's no money for rent even on that. Says he needs to talk to you directly and it's urgent."

"Tell him I'm in a meeting," said Ted dismissively. "Tell him the money was sent and there must be a mix-up at his bank. Tell him I don't need to be bothered about where he's living. He's a big boy and he can sort those things out. I don't ask him to deal with stuff like that for me."

"Okay boss," said Kaye as she switched to the other line to pass on Ted's message without questioning.

Ted turned away from the view and back to his desk and phone. He punched in the number of Ian Verster, the CEO over at New Discovery Gold.

"Hey Ian. How's it going? Just thought I'd touch base, see how you feel about maybe a drink and lunch."

"Ted, glad you called," said Ian with what sounded like relief mixed with enthusiasm. "We've had a bit of a situation out at the mine since you were there. I'll tell you about it over lunch. We can talk about what to do."

Ted confirmed a luncheon meeting at Ramparts and that his secretary would make the reservations. "Sounds good. See you there at 12:30." As he hung up the phone, his private cell phone vibrated.

"Hi, Ted?" came the sound of a breathy voice over the phone. "It's Lyla. Sorry I left in a hurry this morning. Last night you said to call if I wanted to, so here I am."

"Oh, uh, hello Lyla," said Ted, startled, surprised, remembering her smooth milky white skin, auburn hair and curves. Her sweet smell and the warm feel of her next to him. "Good to hear from you." A smile crossed his face, thankful he now had a name to go with the vague and fading memories.

"Again, sorry I had to leave. Had to get to work, you know," said Lyla obviously trying to engage him in extended conversation.

Ted couldn't remember if she'd told him where she worked. He was pretty sure he hadn't asked.

"Want to get together later?" Lyla asked in her smoky, sultry voice.

"Well I'm supposed to see my son after work, at the boat."

"Oh, you have a boat. I love boats."

"Maybe you'd like to join us then," said Ted, thinking the evening was shaping up just fine.

"Definitely," she said, leaving the last syllable hanging.

"OK then. Meet me at the Yaletown Marina at 5:00."

With his day planned, and a pleasurable evening in sight, Ted reached for capsules in the desk's top drawer to relieve his raging headache. For a fleeting moment he considered the wisdom of a lifestyle needing recovery medication on a Monday morning. Then he smiled. The price of his new post-divorce freedom.

*****

THE OAK PANELLED RESTAURANT WAS BUSY WITH THE USUAL
downtown Vancouver lunch crowd, even on a Monday. Ted
waved as Ian walked into Ramparts and past the men alone
in their fine wool suits at the bar. Ted already had a martini
and Ian shrugged and pointed to indicate to the waiter that
he would have the same.

"So, gold mining's good these days isn't. Price of gold is
up. Stock price is up. Everything looks good right now," said
Ted motioning to the empty chair opposite as he sat back
down.

"You'd think so, but you know it's always a struggle," said
Ian, settling in to his chair and surveying the assortment of
uptown women scattered about. "Workers always want more
money and benefits. Regulators come around, you know
Labour Board, Workman's Compensation." Ian winked as if
to seal their mutually beneficial arrangement before going
on. "The environmental guys could be a problem but
together we've had them under control for quite a while.
With the politicians we've got right now, nobody really wants
to push that environmental crap anyway. So all in all, I drink,"
said Ian raising the glass left by the waiter and taking a sip.

"Well the gold mining business looks good from where I
sit. As for the consulting business, my guys are always
wanting more money, wanting to get paid, invoicing,
collections, you know the drill."

Ian looked sideways at Ted when he heard the words
invoicing and collections.

"You know Ted," said Ian, casually picking up the menu
pretending to look it over. Glancing over the top he said, "I
think I may have some more work for you, if you can play
ball."

"Oh yeah? What you got?" said Ted enthusiastic,
immediately all in.

"Well after you were up at the mine, and by the way I'm
waiting for your report for the regulators, there was a bit of a
miss-step with some of that cyanide we brought in. Seems a

loader ran the bucket through a drum and there was a spill down into the wetland. Nothing serious but I'd like your guys to look into it."

"Sure we can look at it. Doesn't sound too serious. Cyanide volatilizes and breaks down relatively quickly. We can do something to prove that, if there's a budget for the work."

"Don't worry about the budget. We'll take care of you. Always have, haven't we?"

It was Ted's turn to look at Ian sideways. "There are a lot of outstanding invoices Ian, some for almost a year," he said, trying to appear as formidable as possible, but knowing it would have no effect.

Ian said, "Really? I just happen to have some cheques with me," as he pulled a business cheque out of his suit pocket. "How about one hundred and fifty thousand?"

"It's a lot more than that, but it's a start. We'll get on that cyanide thing right away," said Ted, thankful for the interim payment and the promised additional revenue, but always a bit leery about getting paid. Small mining companies were always a risk.

They talked and then Ian said, "Ted I gotta go. Flip you for the cheque?"

Ted agreed and won. Ian paid up at the bar, exchanging glances with a tall elegant brunette on his way out while Ted finished his drink.

He looked at his watch. It was 3:00 pm and Ted thought, 'Looks like Monday's shot'. Walking back to the office he decided to drive to Yaletown and pick up some deli-food for dinner with his son and this woman, who said she was Lyla.

*****

BACK AT THE OFFICE, WAYNE WAITED ALL AFTERNOON. IT WAS too quiet. The waiting was tense and the time dragged interminably. He was preparing to leave when a startling ring from the office phone broke the silence like a hammer blow. With resolute determination he turned away from the harbour, reached across the desk and answered.

"Oh hi Wayne. It's Susan. I just thought maybe I'd cook that salmon tonight. Want to come over and share it with me?"

Wayne was surprised, happy to hear her voice and relieved it wasn't Ted. The invitation was particularly surprising after the way Susan had been distant and a bit dismissive earlier. He gladly accepted.

As he walked back to the apartment the rain started up again. Not heavy, just enough to wet the streets and clothes, although his Floater jacket provided some protection, and a bit of warmth. At the liquor store he picked out a nice BC white, to go with the salmon.

The company apartment was cold and bare. This whole Prince Rupert north coast thing was just not working out as Wayne had hoped. There was time to kill so he took a shower, and decided to call home. 'What the hell, I haven't talked to them for a long time. Maybe they've got something to say. Maybe something reassuring, or even encouraging.' Wayne wasn't hopeful.

"Hi there you guys," he said when his parents picked up the phone.

"Wayne it's good to hear from you" said his father, sounding like he'd been caught off guard. "How's the consulting? Are you still up in Prince Rupert? I bet you're making lots of money up there."

"Yes. I'm still up here. It's been raining most of the time and the mine's a mess, but so far I'm still here."

"That doesn't sound too positive," said his father clearly not knowing what to say to his son.

"What does Kathy think of you being away? Poor girl on her own like that," his mother chimed in, sounding concerned, but not about him. "I guess you're making big money there anyway. You two will be able to afford a house soon, when you get back. You'll be able to settle down finally."

"Kathy's okay, I guess. She's mad at me for being away again, but we need the money."

"Ha! You've been making big money for years Wayne," said his mother, obviously not having any appreciation for what was really going on.

"Anyway, this job up here is really bad. The mining company is polluting the watershed and breaking a bunch of provincial and federal laws. I really don't know what to do."

"Well son, you have to do the ethical thing. Haven't the enforcement agencies done anything?" said his father, reverting to his usual deference to authority.

"My company's been fudging all the data since long before I got here and the agencies are just ignoring the place. They want me to fudge things too. But," he paused, the dead air hanging heavy as the weather. "I wrote a report this weekend that reflected the real situation." Wayne paused again to let that sink in. "Sent it to the head of my company, yesterday."

"Oh dear. Is that going to affect your position in the company? Maybe you should have toned it down a bit," said his mother, as usual more concerned about his potential for advancement, money and appearances than about Wayne. "You have to think about your future."

"I thought of that but there are some families that are going to be forced out the way things are going. I can't fudge things and look those people in the eye. I'll likely be fired." He ploughed on, determined to get the bad news out. "Thought that might happen today actually. Just thought I'd give you a heads up, see what you think, in case something happens."

"Well you did the right thing, I guess," said his father, echoing the view of a tenured ecology professor sheltered in

Toronto, away from such difficult realities. "You keep calling us if you need anything."

Wayne hung up and shook his head. It was like calling to outer space. He grabbed his Floater jacket off the railing and left in the truck. Out on Sixth Avenue East he parked in front of Susan's house. It was one of those houses built during the war that typically had two small bedrooms on the second floor, one on the first at the back. Over beers Susan had told him she bought it cheap and had done quite a bit of work to keep it fresh looking. It was getting dark when he arrived, holding the wine bottle up.

"Hey, good to see you," she said answering the door. "Oh thanks for the wine. White I hope, for the fish."

"Of course," said Wayne handing her the liquour store brown paper bag.

"Make yourself at home. The fish will be done soon. Hope you're hungry, I baked the whole thing."

"That's a lot of salmon," said Wayne. He sat on her couch backed up against the wall, beside the woodstove Susan said she installed herself. These houses were notoriously cold in winter. Heat from the stove was welcome at first but became a bit much, so he moved to the chair opposite.

His mind wandered as he soaked in the dry warmth like a soothing cocoon. 'Wonder what Ted's doing down there? Thought I might have heard something by now.' He snapped himself out of his reverie and asked, "You need any help in there?"

FOUR

SHE HEARD MARY CALLING TO HER FROM THE DOCK. "I'M coming," yelled Cedar yanking a rain jacket on over her quilted coat and jamming the homespun toque over auburn hair tamed with braided pigtails down to the shoulders.

"Hey Cedar, hurry up we're going to be late," Mary shouted up to her. "I've got a staff meeting and you have to organize the music and gym for the kid's choir thing."

Cedar tied a black woolen scarf around her neck to keep out the dampness and pulled on gumboots as she burst out the door. She was dressed for the harbour crossing to Fairview, her entire ensemble courtesy of the local Thrift Store. Sneakers and a snack were in her backpack.

"I'm coming. Just give me a minute," Cedar yelled, closing the wooden door that badly needed a coat of white paint, holding toast in her mouth and coffee in a thermos mug for the voyage over.

Mary already had the outboard running and Cedar untied the lines, tossed them into the open boat and stepped in at the last second, just as the boat and dock were parting company. She sat in the middle seat facing Mary in the stern, back to the wind and spray, holding a life jacket and her coffee, eating the toast. The dance was repeated every weekday morning, with precise choreography.

Anemones and purple starfish slid by underneath, visible through the clear aquamarine that gave way to deep black water as they rounded Hospital Island and entered the main shipping channel. A container ship was being unloaded on the opposite shore under the watchful gaze of Hay's Mountain stretching up behind. The two of them sat listening to the familiar drone of the outboard and splashing sounds as the bow cut through the water's surface. They had long since decided that in light of the wind and outboard, conversation on the trip should be limited to only the very necessary. The trip to town provided a time for quiet contemplation before the primary school chaos. Separation from town was both a gift to be savoured and a general annoyance on those occasions when something was needed right away, or in a medical emergency, or in really bad weather.

Cedar had been making this trip since her own days in high school after her mother decided that home-schooling would no longer suffice, and she had had been glad. She enjoyed living with Mary and Ray and the freedom she had in the big city. At least Prince Rupert was big for her, if only at first.

Approaching the Fairview wharf, Cedar readied herself as Mary steered into the slip informally reserved for Dodge Cove residents. She jumped out and secured the lines while Mary dealt with the outboard. They retrieved everything and hurried up the ramp to Mary's old Volvo station wagon. The car was rough and not meant for long trips but it got them where they needed to go around town, and could carry supplies protected from the rain.

By the time they arrived at school, Cedar was finally awake. She got right to work gathering sheet music and organizing the gym stage for choir recital. All the kids had been looking forward to the chance to sing in front of the full school and any parents who could attend.

After lunch duty, she walked back out to Fairview and went into the canteen there to kill time waiting for Mary. The canteen was a trailer type structure that had been there for years, since the Fishermen's Co-op was in business, before the big fire. As usual a varied collection of friends and acquaintances was there. She grabbed a coffee at the counter and paid for it. There was a vacant chair at the big table in the centre and Cedar sat, peeling off scarf and Gore-Tex. The homespun toque stayed in place. Mary would be along eventually, but Cedar always enjoyed the banter as people came and went while she waited.

The subject of New Discovery Gold came up often, with points of view passionately advocated. Many were opposed to the mine. A lot of people in town had been for the mine, done work for the company, and hadn't been paid. A few people continued to tout the benefits the company brought to town, although their numbers were diminishing as the unpaid bills piled up and the pollution risk increased. It was noticeable that the mine advocates had progressively moved to the periphery of their conversations, or just stopped coming in.

In her free time, Cedar worked hard to build opposition to the New Discovery Gold Mine. On this day, she managed to steer discussion around to ways they could ramp up their opposition. She explained that at her home next to the mine site, problems were increasing. "The tailings pond is leaking and the tailings dams look like they're starting to slump. We're worried they could breach in a heavy rain. There's obvious evidence of acid drainage. Even worse, cyanide drums are starting to show up on site. This company is just a bad actor." She took a sip of her coffee and surveyed people's response.

"But look at the jobs they've created," said Neil, taking a sip of his own coffee and playing with an unlit cigarette, on a break from the sea urchin processing plant. "I've got a friend,

Amar, who just got a job out there and he's making good money."

"Yeah, but they're makin' a helluva mess. I was up there on my boat checking out Mirage Inlet. Probably cost more to clean up the place than all the gold they've taken out is worth. Who do you think's gonna pay for that? Taxpayers, that's who. You and me," said Lloyd a fellow Dodge Cove resident with a gillnetter. "Geez Neil, would you either go outside and light that thing or put your cigarette away. I'm trying to quit and it's driving me nuts."

Cedar smiled at Lloyd's quick change of subject and his ongoing battle with the nicotine demons. "Well lots of people say they're about the worst in the mining industry out here. The last guy from their environmental consulting company was fired, for trying to tell the truth I guess," said Cedar passionately, putting her elbows on the table while she held the coffee mug in both hands to warm them up and take another drink. "That new guy they've got doing the monitoring, Wayne Dumont apparently, was parachuted in and Jimi says everyone knows he's a hard case corporate guy that's just a shill for industry."

"Huh, what's Jimi worried about? He doesn't pay any taxes anyway," said Lloyd, looking around and hunching his shoulders and arms for emphasis before laughing, along with the others.

"Anyway, things look bad out there. I think it's time for us to do something," said Cedar becoming more animated and looking around at the others to draw them in. "We need to get more people involved."

The metal door to the canteen opened and Mary came in, hearing the last of the exchange. Work was over and she was ready to grab the boat and go back to Dodge with Cedar. The conversation interested her though and she pulled a chair up to the table and sat. "Cedar. You need to organize a public meeting. Get some open discussion going around town. Stir things up a bit."

The others all nodded in agreement.

"I can try to get the Fishermen's Hall," said Lloyd right away, looking enthusiastic. "I'm fed up with the way these companies come in and push people around. Besides, if what you're saying is true Cedar, they could kill a lot of fish. Lord knows, Fisheries won't do anything."

"I guess we could do that. I've never really organized a public meeting." Cedar looked around the table, nervous and self-conscious, hoping someone would jump to the rescue.

"It's easy," said Mary putting a hand reassuringly on Cedar's arm. "Just like at the school. You get a place, print up some hand bills, post them around town, and get friends to do the same. Then you show up along with everyone else and lead a discussion. The people at the meeting will take over then and do the work for you."

"You could go to the newspaper too, if you really want to push this," said Neil, sticking the cigarette behind his ear and now fidgeting with his hands. "They're always looking for something to write about. Maybe they could do a story on the background of this new consultant guy too. That would be fun. Sort of an exposé. If you really want to do do some damage it never hurts to get personal, you know, put people on the spot, under the magnifying glass. But you have to know there are elements in town that will react, and maybe harshly. You'll need to be careful Cedar."

Cedar ignored the warning, knowing very well what those elements were like. "I'll talk to Susan at the paper. She could start with an article about the increasing opposition to the company and then tell people about my public meeting. Then she could do a profile on that new dirt bag, the consultant. That would be good for at least two solid articles for her, maybe a lot more. Good ideas people," said Cedar, gaining confidence.

They continued to kick around the idea of a public meeting and dates for the hall. Cedar went out and used the pay phone at the government wharf to call the paper. Returning she said, "I talked to Susan about doing a series of articles on the mine. She agreed that it was a good idea, but wanted to be sure that it's properly balanced. She said the paper can't be seen as a vehicle for any sort of anti-mining pressure group."

"Makes sense," said Lloyd nodding thoughtfully. "They won't want to alienate part of their market. Tough enough as it is for local newspapers these days."

"Susan agreed to get together with me to discuss it, when we've got a date for the meeting," said Cedar, adding that she would go and see about the hall the next day. She was starting to get enthused, but then the weight of the undertaking and her own insecurities tumbled back into her mind. She got up to leave, shaking her head and putting her scarf around her neck.

Mary followed her out the door with words of encouragement.

*****

NOTHING HAPPENED ON MONDAY. ON TUESDAY MORNING Wayne returned to his boat to carry on tracing the wiring and checking connections. He unlocked the hatch cover, lifted it off the fish hold and climbed down inside on the vertical wooden ladder. He surveyed the hold and everything appeared fine. The tarp had not been disturbed and the files and laptop were still safe underneath, untouched. He was just about to relax his guard when the boat rolled slightly and he heard footsteps on the deck overhead. He quickly replaced the tarp and looked up.

Gus' faced appeared over the hatch combing, looking down into the hold. "What the hell you doin' down there in the dark for?" asked Gus.

"Oh just spending quality time with *Molly B*," said Wayne looking up from the darkness. "I like to hang out on a new boat. Get the feel of her, you know. Look for trouble and hope I don't find any."

"She's not really a new boat but new to you I guess. Anyway, I know what you mean. I do exactly the same thing. Don't want to find out something's wrong out there in a Hecate Strait storm. That's a bad situation."

"Exactly," said Wayne climbing up and out over the combing. "What's up Gus? You checking up on us new people to see what we're doing wrong, so you guys can snicker and gloat and point it out?"

"Nah, not today. I can find lots wrong anytime, on any boat. No, today I'm just passing by on my way up town. Thought I'd be sociable. You not workin' today?"

"Yeah, I'll go to the office later. They owe me a ton of time off. And besides, they're way down in Vancouver living the good life based on the money I bring in. Wouldn't you slack off a bit now and again if you were in that situation?"

"Guess I would, but I've never been employed by someone else," Gus joked.

"You're a lucky man Gus," said Wayne with a laugh of his own. Then, pointing in the direction of the cabin, he added, "I'm going over the electrical system, checking connections. The connection to the light down there is a bit loose and corroded. I'll need to clean it up."

"I've got lots of tools on my boat. You just let me know," said Gus turning toward the rail. "I better keep on movin' now before I get too distracted and knocked off course."

Wayne watched Gus climb back over *Molly B*'s rail and step onto the float, nimble for his age, which was indiscernible. He considered how fishing either aged a person quickly or kept a person young.

Wayne finally relaxed after the Gus surprise. It didn't look like the old-timer had seen anything down in the hold, but he might have heard the tarp being pulled into place and ignored it. Hard to say with old timers like Gus. He replaced the hatch cover, locked it down with his new lock, and went into the cabin to look at the electrical terminal panel again.

As Gus left, a beat up old workboat pulled into the wharf. It was welded aluminium with a diesel engine powering a jet drive and looked rough but tough. Some prawn traps were on the stern, surrounding a towing bit. A guy with a thick black beard and dew-rag exited the wheelhouse and Starshine followed. They made the mooring lines fast and stood up to look around.

Wayne looked directly at them and said hello.

The guy stared straight back and said nothing.

"Nice boat," said Wayne trying to find the right channel for communicating with these people. "Looks like she can move when she's up and planing. You doing some prawn fishing?" In the ensuing silence he added, "Any luck?"

"What's it to you?" said Dave, trying to ignore Wayne. "You're that guy hooked up with those gold miners. You after our prawns too?"

Wayne was somewhat taken aback at the apparent hostility. "No, just trying to make conversation. I just bought this boat and I'm hoping to do a little cruising up the coast myself, maybe a little fishing. Maybe I could stop in sometime when I'm not working for them."

"You try it, I'll blow your ass off," said Dave. Starshine slipped into the background.

"Okay, just trying to be social."

"Well don't," said Dave, and he and Starshine finished securing their boat and left to walk up to town.

'Well that was unpleasant,' thought Wayne as went back into his own boat.

Later, around noon, he decided to go see Susan at the paper. 'That Vietnamese place might interest her for lunch and I could use someone to talk to.' He walked into the newspaper office and dinged the bell on the counter. Everyone looked up except Susan. She was on the phone. A couple of staff waved their arms at her and pointed so she turned and saw him through the inside window. She smiled and held up a finger that said, 'Wait a second.' She finished the call, and came out to meet Wayne at the counter.

"Hi there. This is a surprise," said Susan, friendly but reserved.

"I wanted to thank you for dinner."

"I should be thanking you for that beautiful Spring salmon."

"Anyway, I was wondering if you could get away for lunch. Maybe pHo?"

Susan looked at her watch, scanned her desk, hesitated and then said yes. "There really aren't any big stories breaking, so I Guess I can get away." She chuckled, adding, "Who knows, maybe you're the next big story."

On the walk over to the restaurant they chatted about day to day things, like the weather, people they saw on the street. Wayne told her he'd been down working on the boat that morning. At the restaurant they ordered at the counter and then sat. The usual small town crowd was there, a mix of small business owners, workers from City Hall, tradesmen and young people.

"So, what's on your mind?" Susan asked, putting down her menu to gaze around the establishment and then at him.

Wayne looked at her in surprise. Was he that transparent now? What happened to his iron clad poker face?

"Oh you know. This mine situation. I'm really having trouble with it. Can't focus on work. Not sure I want to work at all anymore." After a moment's contemplation he added, "At least not for those guys."

"Nobody wants to work, Wayne. We'd all rather be on a tropical beach somewhere. Maybe you really just want to spend your time on that boat you bought."

"Maybe," said Wayne, feeling like she was actually right.

"Look, you've been doing that crap for years without any pangs of conscience. Why the change?"

The hot broth and noodles arrived with spoons and chopsticks.

Wayne was pensive as he arranged the bowl and utensils. "I've never had to look directly at the people before. Into the eyes of those on the down side of development. They seem really nice, innocent and vulnerable."

"You mean Dave and Starshine. Believe me, Dave isn't all that innocent. Starshine is. She's younger and just got sucked into the escapist fantasy of Dave's, and now she's trapped for the rest of her life. But Dave, well that's another story."

"What do you mean?"

Susan changed the subject. "What would your family say about this potential change of heart you're having?"

Wayne shrugged as though he didn't care.

"Well, you know who you are. What you've done to get where you are. So, it's kind of set. I think maybe it might be too late," said Susan dismissively, retrieving a mouthful of noodles with her chopsticks.

Lunch with Susan, had ended strangely with her being a bit distant and evasive. Wayne went to the company's office on Third, a short walk down the main street. He couldn't avoid it any longer.

The office was the same as it had been, bare yellowed walls and cheap furnishings. He was the only thing that had changed. Wayne sat in the chair and turned away from the desk to face the window. The view was still the same. The harbour view was reassuring in its timelessness. There were no messages flashing on the phone.

Working was out of the question so he sat and waited, not knowing what to expect. About mid-afternoon, the call he'd been expecting came in from Ted and while the guy was stressed and not happy, it was not clear what would happen next.

FIVE

TED PUNCHED IN THE NUMBER AGAIN. "WAYNE, I'VE BEEN TRYING to reach you all morning," he shouted into the phone. "I got your report and it's not anything like we discussed. You were supposed to stick to the template."

"I know. Truck wouldn't start this morning. All the rain. We've got a real storm going on up here. Came in from the Gulf of Alaska overnight. I've heard that tailings dam is slumping more."

"I don't care about your little issues. This report has to disappear and be replaced by the kind of report we discussed."

"I'd like to Ted. Just send me an email directing me to do that," said Wayne with a bit of an edge.

Ted slammed his phone down. 'That son-of-a-bitch is documenting things.' He looked around his office, at the engineering certificates and commendations on his ego wall, and out the window. A massive container ship maneuvered into the Vancouver terminal for unloading. Those harbour and mountain views were his refuge. He'd worked hard and built his company from scratch and wasn't about to give it away now, especially because of reports coming from one of his own employees, like that snivelling little weasle Wayne.

He read the report again and knew all the identified issues could not be considered new. They'd been developing for some time but the reporting had been scoped to ensure the problems would never be documented. Now this. Ted ran his fingers through his trimmed salt and pepper hair, exasperated and very worried. He was in deep, really deep. 'What to do?'

"Kaye," said Ted into the intercom.

"Yes boss."

"Bring me a fresh coffee." It was a diversion, displacement activity, and they both knew it.

"Here's your coffee," said Kaye placing the cup on a coaster. "Anything else?"

The bank loan statement sat there on his desk, staring up at him like a living reminder of how tenuous the finances actually were. Without the work at New Discovery Gold, his company could be in trouble. In these tough times he had to hang onto the New Discovery account.

"Draft a letter to Wayne for my signature, telling him that due to a lack of new contracts, and that point is important, his employment is terminated immediately. Tell him he'll be paid out the required two weeks' notice in cash, and he is formally ordered to stop work immediately, vacate the office and company apartment, and get out of that town. Formally direct him to take nothing belonging to the company with him."

Kaye was shocked but not really surprised. She'd worked for Ted long enough to know the score and she was smart enough to look out for herself.

"Oh, and hire a security company in town to track Wayne down," continued Ted decisively, as he thought through his new strategy. "I want them to hand deliver the message to him and supervise his removal from the apartment and office."

That done, it was necessary to arrange for someone he could send up to the north coast to take over Wayne's job. There was only one person in the company, other than Wayne, who could handle this kind of situation. He picked up the phone and called. After a delay, a voice came on the line.

"Hello."

"You have to go up to Prince Rupert and take over work at the New Discovery Gold mine. I need you to do the inspections and work closely with the company. Make sure you work only with the reporting templates provided. It's sensitive. I need to know I can rely on you. Leave where you are on the next flight. Kaye will make the arrangements. Just get there."

"No problem," said the voice at the other end of the line. "I'll stop what I'm doing here in the Yukon and head there today. I think there's a flight out of here at 5:00 pm."

Ted placed the handset deliberately back on his desk telephone. "Kaye," he blasted into the intercom again.

"Yes boss."

"Work with Bruno to get him to Prince Rupert on the next available flights. He's Wayne's replacement."

"Yes boss. Right away."

*****

TED HAD BEEN COLD AND DISTANT ON THE PHONE, WHICH WAS not unusual. He was also obtuse and non-committal before abruptly hanging up. After the call, Wayne stayed where has was for a while confused by the conversation, not really sure about Ted and not really sure what to do next, so he straightened up the office and sanitized his email account. Those activities seemed advisable under the circumstances. Leave a clean slate if that's what's coming next.

At 4:00 pm he did a final pack up of the company laptop and his notes and files and headed for the door. Maybe things would be clearer tomorrow. Looking around the office, and out the window at the harbour view, was the opportunity to reflect on his history with the company and what the future might bring. He left, locking the door behind him.

Outside on the street a few people were walking, some were standing by the federal building seeking shelter from a cold wind. At the grocery store, a ready to eat dinner looked good and beer at the liquor store. His truck started right away, as it always did, and Wayne drove to the company apartment. Leaving everything under a tarp in the truck cab, he locked the door, stuffed the key into a crevice in the wheel well and walked over to the apartment building.

Unlocking the apartment door, he reached in and flicked the light switch. Light was fading under the late afternoon cloud cover. He turned on the television and cleared the table for dinner while he watched out of the corner of his eye. Just as the food and beer were ready on the table, there was a disturbance in the hallway outside the apartment. Loud voices and then loud pounding on the door. Wayne rushed over to look through the peephole and saw the image of a big guy standing there. The guy banged heavily on the door again.

Wayne's hiking pole leaned against the wall by the door, not put away after his last hike up Hays Mountain. He grabbed it, not really thinking about what he'd do with it, and opened the door a crack, bracing his foot behind the door in an attempt to limit its swing. Instead of the peephole guy, a bigger guy came at Wayne from where he'd been hidden beside the door, shoving the door wide open, snapping the pole in half and tossing it on the hallway floor. The peephole guy moved in behind.

"Hey, what were you going to do with that pole?" asked the first guy, who was obviously in charge.

Wayne stood back in shock, not knowing what to do, and said, "Can't be too careful when strangers start pounding on the door."

"Yeah, right. Maybe we're Jehovah's Witnesses, eh? What would you say to that?"

Wayne said nothing, startled and confused, trying to figure out where this was going and how to respond.

"Are you Wayne Dumont?"

"Yeah I guess. What's it to you?"

"There's a letter here for you. We'll give you a minute to read and digest it," said the guy in charge, handing an envelope to Wayne.

As Wayne ripped open the envelope and scanned the letter, the second guy started surveying the apartment and its contents.

"So I'm fired? Just like that?"

"Yup. That's it," said the guy in charge, handing Wayne a second envelope.

In it was enough cash to cover two week's pay.

"Now, the company says it's square with you and it's time for you to go. You pack up your clothes and personal stuff and get out. We'll help you. You have a vehicle?"

"No," said Wayne, stunned, and not wanting to reveal his limited last possessions. He had thought Ted might fire him but he had not thought through how the actual firing might unfold. Turned out pretty rough.

"Alright, we'll put your things on the curb then, and you can call a friend, or a cab, or whatever, we don't give a shit. But you can't stay here. Those are our orders."

"But it's cold and looks like a storm is coming in."

"Too bad. Our contract doesn't cover your transportation, accommodation, expenses or our sympathy. You'll have to figure things out on your own, but you need to get out of here and out of town."

The other bigger guy started hauling things out of closets and drawers. Wayne grabbed his travel bag and stuffed things in. He grabbed garbage bags for whatever didn't fit in that.

"You got any files, computers, discs here? The company wants all that kind of stuff seized."

"You can look around," said Wayne, still off balance and on the defensive. "But everything is at the office."

"Okay then, we'll go there next. Also, what about gear in a storage locker? We have an inventory so we'll have to check it out." The bigger guy stuck out a hand. "Give me your keys, now."

They carried Wayne's things down to the lobby, out of the building, and threw them on the concrete sidewalk in front. "Okay, let's go to the office and storage. I guess you'll have to ride with us. What a friggin' loser. Don't even have your own vehicle."

At the office, they went through everything. Computer, company laptop, files, desk. Wayne showed them where things were and they investigated well beyond that. It was obvious these guys had done this before. When satisfied they had everything, they took Wayne to the storage locker and went through the gear inventory. Wayne explained the gear to them and they checked everything off. Then they dumped Wayne back outside the apartment building where thankfully his bags still sat.

Wayne got out of their truck and closed the door. They said good night, and with more than a tinge of sarcasm thanked him for being cooperative. Sitting on the curb, he watched the two guys drive away into the dark. He was confused and wondering what to do.

When he thought the guys were gone, he walked to the furthest extent of illumination from the street lights to satisfy himself they were really gone and not watching from the shadows. He'd never seen these two in town before and had no idea how they might operate. They knew their way around like locals though. When everything looked safe, he took the bags over to his truck and tossed them on the front seat. Susan was the only person he knew who might be able to help. He called her.

"Susan. I just got fired. It happened. They threw me out of the apartment. I'm coming over."

"Gosh, Wayne, that's terrible. Who threw you out?"

"I don't know. Two big guys. I've never seen them before. They knew their way around town though. Said they were with some security company, I've never heard of. Ran me to the office and storage locker to make sure the company got everything I had. All my belongings are with me here in the truck, mostly in garbage bags. Can I come over and stay with you."

"I'd like that Wayne, but tonight's not good. Why don't you come by the office in the morning?"

That seemed like a strange response. He heard voices in the background at Susan's end and shrugged. Maybe she had people over for dinner. Still it seemed strange. He wondered who they were, but then thought, 'It's none of my business.'

Wayne had a sudden thought so he drove over to Susan's house anyway. When she answered the door he pleaded, "Susan, I'm not asking to stay, but here, keep this for me, please."

"What is it?" asked Susan, taking the envelope from Wayne's hand. "What am I supposed to do with this?"

"Just keep it safe for me tonight, okay? I'll get it from you later, over at your office if you prefer."

"Yes Wayne, that would be preferable," said Susan starting to close the door.

He backed away from the door stressing, "Please, just keep it safe. Very confidential."

Back in the truck, it was looking like the boat might be his only option for the night. It was late and the hotel would cost too much now that he had no income. He parked the truck away from the wharf and walked to the boat, carrying his travel bag and sleeping bag. He still wasn't convinced these guys wouldn't try to track him down and barge in again to see if he had company materials copied and hidden. As he walked he looked around, over his shoulders, constantly.

The *Molly B* was rolling gently at her slip. He stepped on board, unlocked the cabin door and entered. The other boats were dark except for Gus and Clarences', which both had lamps burning. His own boat was cold and damp, but the stove would take care of that soon enough. Wayne blocked out the windows to keep the light dim and lit an oil lamp, keeping it low to not attract attention. Leaning over the side rail, he unrolled his sleeping bag into the berth up in the port bow. The boat's fenders made soothing sounds as they squished and rubbed gently against dock.

Wayne sat in the forepeak for a while, trying to process his situation and think about what to do next. This boat was good for tonight, but regular activity over a period of time would probably attract attention. Better to get another place in town. He knew of a cheap rooming house, up the hill from the government wharf. He'd been by it a number of times but hadn't paid much attention. Maybe that would be a good place to stay, at least for a short while until he talked to Kathy and figured out his future. He felt lost and free at the same time and it was past time to set a new direction instead of just reacting to the next big ego building work opportunity. He'd try the rooming house in the morning.

SIX

CEDAR WALKED INTO THE CROWDED CANTEEN, UNWRAPPED HER scarf and went to the counter. The usual crowd was gathered around the central table. It was like any other construction trailer interior, beige vinyl but with the added smells of coffee, bacon and raingear.

"Coffee please." She inspected choices in the glass display under the counter. "And a glazed donut. I feel like a treat today."

She sailed across the canteen to add milk and sugar and surveyed the scene. The others shuffled their chairs around to make room and she grabbed one and sat.

"So Cedar," said Lloyd reporting in on his organizing efforts. "I talked to them down at the Fishermen's Hall. We can have it this Friday if we want. Won't cost a dime either. They're going to just let us use it. Think we can be ready by then?"

"That's great," said Cedar pulling some papers out of her worn canvas haversack and laying them on the table. "I drew up a design for the handbills. Just need to put in the date and time. What do you guys think? Can we be ready?"

"Nice handbill. Should do the trick. Sure we can," said Neil with enthusiasm, and the others nodded in agreement.

"Okay, it's a go then. I'll get Mary to run these off at the school," said Cedar, her tone displaying excitement at finally doing something concrete.

"How many copies you going to get?" asked Lloyd looking around the café and then at the others nervously. "I wonder how many people will come."

"I don't know, maybe fifty?" said Cedar with a shrug, her nervousness returning. "What do you guys think?"

Neil took a sip of his coffee and said, "Sounds about right. When you have them we'll divide the handbills up and get them posted and passed out to friends. I guess we'll have to think about covering some with plastic so they don't dissolve in the rain. How did it go at the newspaper?"

"It was good," said Cedar, straightening the handbill and biting into her donut. She drank some coffee to wash it down and swallowed before continuing. "Susan was great, really interested. She's going to write an article based on the information I gave her and the pictures my family's taken out there."

"She going to use your name?" asked Neil, showing concern. "Don't forget there are people in town that benefit from that company."

"Yeah, I guess she'll use my name. Don't see any reason why not. The mine already knows we hate them. Who else would be behind the article? I don't know what they can do to us that they haven't already done. Susan's going to do a bunch of research on that consultant guy too, for another article, an exposé on his background. He's been really aggressive advocating for other development projects in the past. Twists the truth all the time."

"I saw the guy walking around town. He bought that boat, *Molly B*, down in Cow Bay. It's still moored down there. He's been there off and on according to Clarence. But Clarence also said he checked into a rooming house this morning, which was weird. I thought that consulting company had an apartment in town." Lloyd looked around the table at the others and then out the window, first toward the fish boats tied up at the wharf and then up the hill to town.

"I don't really care where he is," said Cedar with an edge. "I don't trust him, the way he's been walking around out at the mine site, joking with the mine manager. I don't trust him at all."

Lloyd continued looking up the hill toward town and then partially stood for a better view. "Oh hey, isn't that him coming down the hill now? Walking out here to Fairview. See the guy in the Floater jacket over there."

"Not sure," said Cedar rising from her chair to look. "Oh yeah. That's him alright. You can tell by the shaggy brown hair sticking out from under his watch cap. I guess he makes so much money he doesn't have to work every day like the rest of us. Can afford to just wander around town like a homeless person."

"I thought he lived in a company apartment and figured he had a big per diem," added Neil fidgeting again, reaching for his pack of cigarettes and then catching himself. "Maybe he got fired or something. At least that's what happened to their last guy, Ron. Remember him? Fired and run right out of town, fast. Gone back to Newfoundland I heard."

"Yeah, I remember him," said Cedar sitting back down and drinking her coffee. "Used to see him out at the mine. He was a loser too, but not as shifty as this guy is supposed to be. That's what Jimi says anyway."

"Jimi," said Lloyd with a scowl. "Now there's a piece of work. Cedar I don't know how you people put up with that guy."

"Ah, Jimi's alright, once you get to know him. He and Chelsea were our alternate parents out there."

"Look, that consultant guy is walking right past here," said Lloyd rising halfway from his chair for a better view out the window. "He's headed for the dock. That's weird. What's he gonna do down there?"

"Watch he doesn't touch your boat Lloyd. Wouldn't want him to dirty it," added Neil, giving Lloyd an elbow jab in the ribs.

"He's going down to the floats looking at all the boats I guess," said Cedar, still standing and peering out the window.

They all watched him amble down the ramp and up and down the floats looking at fish boats. Eventually they saw him approach the float reserved for skiffs, where everyone from Dodge Cove and Crippen Cove tied up. He crouched down to look at the For Sale sign on one of the dinghies overturned on the float. He started to turn it over.

"Hey, that's my old dinghy he's looking at," said Lloyd getting up to go. "I'd better go down and see what he's up to. Hah, maybe I can unload it."

"I'll go with you," said Cedar putting on her jacket and scarf, pulling her toque down tight making her tangled hair jump out below. "Want to make sure he doesn't look too closely at Mary and Ray's boat, or even worse, touch it."

Cedar followed Lloyd as he walked down the ramp and over to the skiffs. Wayne had been crouching by the dinghy examining it but stood, turning to look at them, wearing a friendly smile.

"Hey sport. Wat'cha doin'?" asked Lloyd as they approached.

"Oh, hey there," answered Wayne nonchalantly. "I need a dinghy to go with a boat I just bought. This yours?"

"That's right, it's mine. What boat did you buy?" asked Lloyd, knowing the answer but wanting to see how the guy would respond.

"The *Molly B*. You know it?"

"Yeah, I know her. She's a sweet boat. It's a shame about old Sid passing away. He loved that boat and Molly his wife.

She passed away some years before," said Lloyd bending down so he and Wayne could turn the dinghy over.

Wayne held out his hand and introduced himself. Lloyd straightened up and stepped forward to shake hands but Cedar kept her hands behind her back.

"I know who you are," said Cedar standing erect, with thinly veiled aggression. "We've talked before and I've seen you around town and out at the gold mine."

"Oh yeah, that's right," said Wayne continuing his friendly smile. "Anyway, now you know my name. I like your dinghy," he added, turning his attention to address Lloyd. "I need one just like that, big enough for a small outboard but small enough to carry on deck."

"What for?" asked Lloyd with interest in making the sale.

"I'm going to be doing some cruising and fishing," said Wayne. "Normally I'd be working. I really should be doing another trip up to the mine, but ..."

"But what?" asked Cedar sharply.

"Don't know why you'd care," said Wayne clearly getting tired of the Cedar's thinly veiled hostility. "But if you really want to know, last night I got fired."

"Figures," said Cedar keeping up the aggression. "You look pretty incompetent."

"Look, I'm kind of in a bad spot right now. I'm just looking to buy a dinghy. Would that be okay?"

Cedar said nothing and looked down at the slick boards of the float, a little embarrassed at being called out, especially in front of Lloyd.

"In answer to your question though, as it turns out maybe I was too competent," said Wayne. "I sent in an accurate report from our last trip out there and the owner of the consulting company fired me. After all those years working for him, making him rich. I was just trying to do the right thing but I guess in this case he didn't want the truth being reported to the authorities."

"Yeah, and he made you rich too I bet," said Cedar, a bit mollified but not yet ready to let go. "All your deception, lies, manipulation, cheating. We know all about you. The paper's doing a feature article on you. An exposé on your past. I talked to them yesterday."

Wayne shrugged and appeared to give up, looked away from Cedar and said to Lloyd, "I'd like to buy your dinghy."

Cedar watched him pull cash from his jeans pocket and hand it over. Lloyd gave him the key to the lock and chain securing the boat to the float.

"I'll come by later and pick it up."

"It's yours now, so pick it up when you want," said Lloyd counting out the hundred and fifty dollars.

"I'll need a small outboard to go with it," said Wayne looking at both Cedar and Lloyd. "You guys know anyone wants to get rid of an outboard?"

Lloyd pulled out his wallet and stuffed the bills in. "I'll ask around. Come on up to the canteen, we can ask the other people there too. Hey, too bad about losing your job. We hate the mining company but everyone here knows what it's like to be out of work. Come on."

Cedar gave Lloyd a jab and a dirty look, and then followed them up to the canteen.

*****

WHILE WALKING BACK TO TOWN, WAYNE'S PHONE BUZZED. HE pulled it from his jacket pocket and answered. It was Kathy.

"Oh hi. I was going to call you. It's really good to hear from you.

"Oh sure you were," said Kathy with a hefty tinge of sarcasm.

"No really, I was. I'm pretty down right now and could use a lift from someone who cares. Someone like you."

"That doesn't sound like the Wayne I know."

"I know, but last night was pretty bad," said Wayne, his voice a bit shaky. The usual cocky confidence completely gone.

"How so? What happened?" asked Kathy, sounding concerned, like she might care.

"I got fired."

"What? You've got to be kidding." She sounded shocked, caught off guard.

"Wish I was, I guess, sort of. But no I'm definitely fired."

"What happened? What did Ted do? What did you do?"

"I went out to the mine site last week with Ted. Ted's been involved with this mine for a number of years, since start-up. And it's a mess out there. When I did my report for the regulators, I portrayed the real situation."

"That's not like you. Did you grow a conscience all of a sudden?"

"There are some back to the land people out there trying to hang on and there's a very high likelihood this mine will poison them, or bury them in tailings, or something. I just couldn't cover it up. Besides, if anything were to happen, and I was involved in a cover up, Ted would sell me out right quick. I'd be fined or in jail, or both."

"You're right about that. I never trusted that sleaze bag."

"Anyway ..." Wayne hesitated, trying to find the words. "I prepared an accurate, factual report and sent it to Ted. He lost it, I guess, his temper," said Wayne trying to rationalize the event as he spoke. "More like he buried the report. You know, I never even heard from him directly."

"How did you get fired then?" asked Kathy, starting to show some genuine interest, as though she finally realized she might be affected, herself, in some way.

"Ted hired some heavies who came beating down the apartment door last evening, while I was sitting down for supper. They hand delivered the termination notice from Ted. Gave me two weeks' pay and then tossed me out on the street, literally, with all my stuff in garbage bags. They were my own garbage bags even."

"Gosh Wayne, I'm sorry. That must have been awful," said Kathy as if she was making a serious attempt to sound sincere.

"They took me to the office and the company's gear storage locker to make sure I didn't steal any company computers, files, equipment or whatever, and then dumped me out, back at the apartment building. Left me sitting on the curb, in the dark and the rain."

"Wow, how are you? Are you okay?" Kathy almost sounded genuinely concerned.

"I'm not hurt, but I'm out of a job and pretty bummed out," said Wayne, again without the usual cocky confidence. "I didn't know what to do. Just crashed on the boat. It's a good thing I had it. This morning I got a cheap room at a rooming house, at least until I sort things out, figure out what to do. This is the first time I haven't had a job since grad school. It's the first time I've been fired."

"Oh yes, the beloved boat," said Kathy, returning to the sore point from their last telephone conversation, quickly moving beyond Wayne's crisis.

"I know you're mad about the boat, Kathy, but it really saved me last night. I hid my truck. The boat was safe, I think. These guys were big and rough Kathy. I didn't know what else to do. And maybe I can use the boat for independent consulting survey work and fishing to make money until I get another job."

"Why would Ted do that?" asked Kathy, apparently still trying to process the events.

"I just got here, just started working on this mine. But I think Ted must be in really deep. I think he's got money problems and by the looks of things probably has some legal liability problems with this mine. That's the only explanation for the approach he used. And I really don't know what else these guys, the heavies, will do."

Kathy was quiet at the other end. Then she said, "I'm sorry this had to happen to you Wayne. I really am. But I called about something else. Something that concerns us both."

Wayne's antennae went up, alert, waiting for something but not knowing what. "What is it?" he said, gazing up at the mist drifting over the town and the coast like a shroud crawling halfway up the mountain. He was nearing downtown and there was more traffic noise.

"Wayne."

"Yes?" Wayne answered, sensing the change in her voice and wondering.

"This is hard, and for you I understand the timing couldn't be worse."

"What is it?" asked Wayne, his voice becoming strained, impatient even. He looked at the sky, then at the ground, waiting, wondering.

"It's over Wayne."

"What? What's over?"

"I'm breaking it off. It's over."

Wayne paused, watching his feet move along the roadside, were they sinking into the wet ground or was he floating above it? He couldn't tell. "Just like that. Out of the blue?" asked Wayne, incredulous, beaten. He stumbled as he walked, like he'd been hit with a two by four in the gut.

"It's been coming for a long time. This last job you took, away from me, was the last straw. I don't want to be waiting for you all the time. Spending my life in limbo."

"But I'm out of a job now. I'll be home soon. I promise."

"I can't believe your promises. Never could. No one can. You're the master of manipulation. That's your job. That's your thing. That's who you've become."

"Kathy." Wayne paused before saying, "What am I going to do?" in hushed tones.

"I don't know. You lost all our money, actually your money I guess, since you bought a boat with all that was left."

Wayne sighed. The clouds darkened and the wind picked up. There was silence on the phone. He stood on the edge of a curb. He walked. He stood again, turning in circles.

"Wayne, you need to get your stuff out of my apartment. You haven't paid the rent so it's mine now and I don't want any reminders of you." She was cold and calculating now. She'd already moved on, leaving Wayne wondering what was actually happening there.

"What? Now? From here? How the hell am I going to do that?" demanded Wayne, quickly shifting from shock and dismay, to anger and frustration.

"Do it this weekend or its going to be thrown in the dumpster Wayne," said Kathy, keeping the pressure up, any previous hints of empathy now gone.

"I'll have to call someone I guess, get them to go over and pick it up for me. I don't know who yet. Will you co-operate with them?"

"Yes."

"Okay then. Expect a call. I'll have to find someone."

"Bye Wayne," said Kathy abruptly clicking off.

That click was so emotionless and final, like a toggle switch on a cabin light. Wayne stood on the corner at City Hall, looking desperately in every direction, but seeing nothing.

*****

THE PHONE RANG AT 10:30 AM AND TED ANSWERED. "KAYE. What is it?"

"It's Doug from the bank. He says he needs to talk to you."

"Tell him I'm in a meeting," said Ted, not wanting to talk to anyone, especially someone from the bank.

"He said that if you tried that excuse to get you out of the meeting. He says he has to talk to you right now. It's serious," said Kaye, pressing the point that this was something Ted really had to respond to.

"Alright," said Ted, resigned, but changing his tone for the bank manager. "Good morning Doug. Good to hear from you. Yes I am in a meeting but nothing that can't be set aside to talk to you. How are you? What's up?"

"I'm fine, thanks for asking. But you are not fine. Your payment was due yesterday but nothing came in," said Doug, professionally and dispassionately. "What are we going to do?"

"Gee I don't know," said Ted as his mind raced to come up with something. "I thought my office sent a payment over in the last day or so. I'll have to look into it. Somebody obviously messed up."

"You sent a small payment but you need to send a lot more. Consider this as our in person warning. You're not far away from the repo guy, and that would include a lot of the field equipment you use to generate revenue, in addition to the luxuries."

"Okay, I hear you. I have a delinquent client that owes me a lot. I'll chase that down and get you some money."

"That would be good Ted, and make it more than just some money. And I don't want to have to wait too long either."

As Ted hung up the phone, Kaye was waiting, leaning against the door frame. "Ted you have an 11:00 o'clock with Ian over at New Discovery Gold. He called while you were on the phone just now. Says it's important. You have to go over there right away."

Ted, impatient and frustrated, rose from his chair to leave, talking to Kaye on the way. "He's going to want that report for the provincial government guys. The one Wayne screwed up. Bruno will have to do a new report. Does Bruno know that?" Ted pushed the elevator button as they parted and Kaye returned to her desk.

"Actually, Bruno's on his way now. On a plane somewhere between Whitehorse and Vancouver. He'll probably get to Prince Rupert tomorrow." Kaye said she would contact the security company to make sure Bruno would get keys to the office and apartment.

"Alright," said Ted as the elevator doors closed.

Out on Alberni Street the sun shone brightly. It was a warm spring Vancouver day. Perfect. Blossoms would be out on the trees soon. Ted considered maybe it would be a good evening for a cruise. After crossing Burrard he turned right and entered the building housing New Discovery Gold. On the thirtieth floor he exited the elevator and turned left. The door at the end of the corridor was the one. He opened it and stepped into Ian Verster's bright and luxurious corner suite of offices.

"Ted, good to see you. Come in," said the secretary, as she ushered him in to see Ian. Moments later she returned with coffee, aromatic and strong. She turned and stepped slowly out on her spiked heels, closing the door softly.

After a few succinct pleasantries, Ian started right in. "So where are my reports? They were due at the province last week."

"I know. I know. Look, everything's fine up there at the mine. We had a bit of a hiccup internally, within our company."

"What kind of hiccup?"

"Well Wayne quit on me. Right out of the blue. Don't really know what happened."

Ian sat upright, fingers tapping gently on the glass covered desk. "What do you mean he quit? I thought he was your go to guy, the best." He stopped tapping and leaned forward, hands stretched out, flat on the glass, ignoring the fingerprints they left. "What exactly is going on up there?"

Ted shifted uncomfortably in his chair. "Quit. As I said, out of the blue he decided he didn't want to do the work anymore." He shifted again. "Strange I'll grant you, but there you have it. Some people decide they just want a change of direction, no explanation. Says he wants to take time off. Maybe he wants to travel, I don't know. Maybe his girlfriend's mad at him for taking off again. Who knows?" He smiled conspiratorially and added, "And who cares?"

"What's wrong with your people up there?" asked Ian as he leaned back in his chair, away from the desk, gazing toward the corner windows. "That guy Ron did the same thing only a few months ago. Does this mean you can't keep your people?" Ian rocked his chair back and waited for the answer.

"No, no, nothing like that. Ron just got homesick for the rock, went back Newfoundland." As he spun his explanation, Ted grew more confident and forthright. "A guy named Bruno is on his way up there now. He'll get that report done and to you right away. No problem."

"For the sake of both of us he'd better," said Ian, leaning forward again to stare directly into Ted's eyes. It was not a friendly look.

"Well at least your share price is up," said Ted, shifting the subject to something more positive. "You're making lots of money now in the markets."

"And so are you, on your shares in my company," said Ian, leaning back again with a smug self-satisfied little smile, stretching his arms over his head.

"Yes on those shares, perhaps, but Ian we really need to talk about the outstanding invoices. You have a lot of money owing and my bank is really pushing me. After all, those invoices are for work we already completed on your behalf, and they've been outstanding for months."

"Hah, you're just worried about losing your boat," chided Verster, showing that he understood Ted's vulnerabilities and how to use them.

"Well yes I am worried about that, and you like going out on that boat don't you? I'm worried about losing the whole company, and that would be bad for both of us. You'd have to find someone else willing to do the stuff I do."

"You threatening me?"

"No, no. Not at all. I'm just telling you how things are."

"Okay Ted. I get the message. You have a problem you think I can help you with. Well I have a problem you can help me with."

"What is it?"

"Get me my reports for the province," said Ian sharply, as he pulled out a cheque book. He wrote something, tore off a cheque, and handed it to Ted. "There that should get the bank off your back."

Ted looked at it and issued an unenthusiastic thank you before adding, "That should hold them until next month."

"Good," said Ian standing to indicate the meeting was over. "Now remember, I control the flow of the money to you. Get me that report."

SEVEN

ACROSS THE ROOM HIS BACKPACK LEANED AGAINST A WORN OAK dresser that was an artifact of another age, with stains from stubby beer bottles and cigarettes documenting its history. Wayne stared from the iron frame bed and wondered how many temporary workers, fishermen or transients had done the same before him, staring at the only other piece of furniture in the room. Some might have been exhausted from work, some might have been exhausted from their journey, and some might have been just hungover from the night before. He wasn't any of those. Wayne was emotionally exhausted.

He had checked into the Hecate Rooms the day before, after that first night on *Molly B*. Staying on the boat had been fine but he wanted more space than it could provide and a closer connection to town and his truck, still tucked away inconspicuously. There was no way of knowing what might happen next, or what he might want to do. Best to settle things down and see what might develop. That strategy had always worked before.

A steady rain drummed on the sloping roof right above his head. Rolling over, he could see big drops splattering on the old uneven window panes beside the bed. Yesterday's low pressure system had moved in and was drenching the town. It was going to be a wet day and he was glad to not be out at that mine doing field inspections. Why would he? He had no job now.

Getting up, he found the air was cold. The only heat came up the staircase from two floors below, through the wide gap under the door, on air that brought coffee and bacon smells with it. Heat rises, but apparently not well enough to shake the damp and cold from the fourth floor of an ancient wooden rooming house. Rent was cheap though and the term was short, and it came with a breakfast and dinner at the big communal table in the kitchen below. He washed and shaved in the old enameled basin bolted to the wall, pouring cold water from the pitcher perched on the adjoining shelf. At least the basin had a drain. Down the hall was the bathroom and shower that served the five other rooms on the fourth floor. Under that warm shower spray, his head started to clear.

Breakfast was bacon, eggs, fried potatoes and strong coffee. Ingrid served the welcome nourishment generously and precisely. She was apparently both proprietor and cook, a large woman of ambiguous eastern European heritage who tolerated no nonsense. It seemed to Wayne that all the residents liked her but were also a bit afraid. After eating and finishing his coffee, Wayne skipped the table chatter and went back up to the room. He lay down on the sagging bed. For the rest of the morning rain drops pummelled the roof and splattered the wavy glass window that afforded a view west up the hill into downtown.

Noon passed and Wayne decided he had to get moving. He walked up to the hotel at the top of a knoll overlooking rail lines and the harbour. On business and before getting fired, this had been his hotel of choice. This was the place where professional and government people always stayed, when they could get a room. If anything was happening job wise in town, it would happen here. He took a seat in the lounge, back to the wall, and ordered a BLT with fries and a coffee.

From this vantage point he was able to see Bruno coming through the entrance. His bulk and dark close cropped hair were distinctive. The jeans and workboots, while normal for the town, were not typical in this lounge. Wayne waved slightly and stood as Bruno approached.

As they shook hands, Wayne said, "This is a surprise. What're you doing in town?"

Bruno pulled out the heavy upholstered chair opposite and sat. "Just got in on the morning flight up from Vancouver. What a ride. There's a real storm raging out in the Strait. Anyway, made it here alive and now I'm in wonderful Prince Rupert. What a treat eh? What are you doing in here Wayne? Wasn't really expecting you."

The waitress brought Wayne's lunch and asked for Bruno's order. He shook his head no, saying he couldn't stay.

"Me? I'm just hanging out. Having a sandwich. Don't have much going on," said Wayne, taking a bite. Looking at Bruno and then looking out the big window, pretending to relax and take in the harbour view.

"That's strange," said Bruno, with a puzzled look, like he was trying to process new information. "I thought you were really over your head with work, you know, out at New Discovery Gold. That's why Ted sent me here, to help you out."

"And I thought you were in over your head in the Yukon," said Wayne, puzzled, dipping a French fry in ketchup and staring at it before casually sliding it into his mouth.

"Ted pulled me out of there two days ago and sent me up here in a rush. Actually, I never talked to Ted directly. Just Kaye. She gave me the orders and arranged everything. I'm here in the hotel today and go to the apartment tomorrow before I fly out to the mine."

"Oh, you're moving into the apartment?"

"I hope you don't mind sharing. I know it'll be tight, but I understand it's only for a short time."

"I guess," said Wayne, shrugging his shoulders, not giving away any information on his situation. "What are you doing out at the mine?"

"Helping you I guess. I was told you weren't able to get the monitoring report done and submitted. It's late going to the province Kaye said."

"Oh yeah, that's right. Good luck."

"Aren't you coming out with me? What will you be doing?"

"Nothing." Wayne watched carefully to gauge his reaction before turning his attention back to lunch.

Bruno looked at Wayne, obviously confused.

"That's right, nothing. Ted fired me," said Wayne taking another bite of the sandwich, holding the remaining quarter out for inspection.

Bruno looked shocked and said, "Geez you're kidding. Kaye didn't tell me that."

"I guess she was trying to smooth over Ted's latest mess, as usual."

"But you're the backbone of the company. What happened? What are we going to do?"

"Was the backbone of the company, I think you meant to say?" said Wayne, now looking beyond Bruno out into the hotel lobby to see who was coming and going. "I don't know what the company's going to do." He took another French fry and popped it into his mouth. "And I don't give a shit anymore. As to what happened, all I can say is, watch your step, carefully. This mining company is bad news."

"I assume the computers, files and digital records are all at the apartment."

"I guess. I didn't take anything. Kind of had to leave in a hurry. Cash for two weeks' pay and out the door with all my stuff in garbage bags. Two thugs tossed me out on the street in the rain and the dark. Kind of abrupt I thought. It was all a blur."

"Geez, that's harsh. You kept records to cover yourself I guess. We've all talked before about the need to do that when working for Ted. You were the one who told me to do that."

"Well, I didn't think I'd have to here, so no," said Wayne, looking down and focussed on pushing ketchup around his plate with another French fry.

"Well thanks for everything Wayne. You've been a good friend. Look I gotta go. Good talking to you. Hope I'll see you around. Where are you living?"

"It was a rush as I said and I don't know what's going to happen. I'm in a rooming house for now – Hecate Rooms."

"Geez Wayne, that's harsh" said Bruno again as he stood and walked out of the lounge, putting on his company Floater jacket.

Wayne finished his lunch and tried to pay with the company credit card. It was rejected. After using cash, he threw the card on the wet pavement outside, stepped on it, and walked further up the hill into town.

At the newspaper office, Wayne dinged the counter top bell. Everyone behind the glass looked up. Susan looked up. She had an exasperated expression and went back to her work. He dinged again, with the same response all round. On the third ding, Susan grimaced, pushed her keyboard away, pulled her sweater tighter around her shoulders and got up.

"What is it Wayne?" she asked as she emerged from the door behind the counter.

"I thought you might have a moment to talk."

"I'm in the middle of something now," she said looking back through the glass to her desk.

"So am I. I really need to talk to someone. What's so important that you're working on anyway?"

"News Wayne. It's news. That's what I do. News that's important to the people in this town."

"Like what?"

"Like the meeting on Friday night to organize against New Discovery Gold and its mine up at Mirage Inlet."

"What meeting?" asked Wayne, visibly surprised and shaken. "I didn't know the opposition was that strong, and organized."

"You've got a lot to learn, about this town, about people. The meeting's at the Fishermen's Hall on Friday night. Cedar and her friends are organizing it. I wouldn't go if I were you."

"Why shouldn't I go?"

"Cause of what I'm working on for tomorrow's paper. It's an exposé on your company and that means an exposé on you too."

"Why would you do that to me?"

Susan leaned over the counter, resting her head in upraised hands that ran through her straight black hair. "Cedar specifically asked me to because she's seen you out there working for them. She wants the people in town to know who they're dealing with. It's news and my company has to sell papers to make money. Not everything is pretty and not everything is about your interests Wayne."

Now he leaned on the counter, from his own side, head in his hands as well, and said, "Come on Susan. We're friends. Doesn't that mean anything? Besides, I don't even work there anymore. I did the right thing, wrote a truthful report for the government and got fired for it."

The others in the news room had their heads down, not looking out at Wayne.

"I might mention that in the article. I'll have to see how my editor wants to play this out to keep readers interested. I have a boss too, you know. Could be some great follow-up stories to write."

"Great, I'm just here to make money for your paper."

"Again Wayne, not everything is about you," said Susan as she turned to go back to her desk.

He turned away from the counter, pushed his way out the door, and walked through the downpour back to Hecate Rooms. As he entered the front door, a black pickup truck pulled away from the parking spot across the street, with the two occupants looking back.

"Hey fella," said the old timer sitting in the foyer watching an ancient TV sitting precariously on a rolling metal stand. "Two guys were here lookin' fer ye. Big guys too. Went up to knock on your door, which technically Ingrid doesn't allow but she was out and I wasn't about to stop them."

"Hey thanks," said Wayne, introducing himself.

"I'm Archie," said the old timer. "Used to fish but now I watch TV and look through these windows at the rain."

"Okay Archie. Thanks for the heads up. See you at dinner."

Wayne climbed the steep narrow staircase to the fourth floor. He put his key in the lock, but it was already unlocked. He opened the door.

The room was a mess. His stuff was spread all over, the backpack shredded by a knife. The mattress was stripped and tossed, dresser drawers were pulled out. A photograph was pinned to the dresser top by a mean looking tactical knife driven deep into the wood. Wayne stared at it. It was a picture of him talking to Cedar and Mary out at Fairview. On the picture was written, '*Wayne - We know you have the files and photos. They are stolen property. Give them back.*' He stumbled over the mattress, his head reeling. Wayne was stunned. He gathered up what things he could, jammed them into two pillowcases and left.

EIGHT

IN A DAZE, WAYNE HAULED THE PILLOW CASES BACK DOWN THE steep narrow wooden staircase and said, "See you around Archie," as he pushed past the foyer and out the door with the old glass window panes.

"Hey, what's the rush?" said Archie, one eye still on the TV. "Was it those fellas? Told you I didn't like the look of 'em."

But Wayne was gone.

Keys to the *Molly B* were in his pocket and hopefully those heavies hadn't been there too. He lugged his things down the street and worked his way down the steep slippery ramp at the government wharf. Gus and Clarence were visible on the dock below, talking.

"Wayne, glad you're back," said Gus, taking a drag on his cigarette, tossing the butt into the water between his boat and the float before stepping forward to meet him.

"Yeah," said Clarence, very agitated. "There were two big guys down here, lookin' at *Molly B*. They didn't look nice."

"What did they want?" asked Wayne urgently, even more concerned that his refuge on the boat might be at risk too.

"Don't know," said Clarence eyes downcast, fussing with his coffee mug. "I went over to talk but they weren't too sociable. They asked who the owner was though, and got kind of aggressive when I played dumb."

"Thanks," said Wayne, relieved to have at least some support.

"We need to keep to ourselves down here and take care of each other," said Clarence, nodding at Gus who reciprocated. "Those guys have been around town forever doing their stuff on the side, under the radar. When they're around, nothin' good happens."

"So did they just leave?" asked Wayne, looking up at the wharf above in some sort of desperate attempt to reconstruct their departure.

"They tried to go on the boat, speaking loudly. I started yelling and that's when Gus came out onto his deck."

"Yup," said Gus with solemn fortitude. "Grabbed my old shotgun that I always have on board. Got up on the foredeck there. Levelled the beast at one of 'em, right at the gut, the one that looked to be the leader. Told him to back off. Get away from your boat."

"Thanks," said Wayne, looking bewildered. "I don't know what to say."

"Well I would have blown his head off too if I had to. That's what I told him."

"I believe you Gus," said Wayne shaking his head in disbelief. "Are both you guys okay? I really don't want you getting any trouble because of me."

"More important, are you okay Wayne?" asked Clarence looking into Wayne's eyes with empathy and concern. "That's the main thing. What did they want anyway?"

Looking over his shoulder, all around and up the rain soaked ramp to the wharf, in a confidential tone Wayne said, "I got fired from my job. I think the company believes I stole records and pictures that could be very damaging to them, particularly the owner."

"Oh," said Clarence, shaking his head. "Did you?"

Wayne looked down. "There's something funny going on out there."

"Out where?" asked Gus.

"At the mine in Mirage Inlet."

Gus and Clarence looked at each other and said, "Oh?" in unison

"See you guys. We should all get out of this rain before we get completely soaked," said Wayne as he climbed over the rail of his own boat and fished his keys from a pocket. Looking back he asked, "Gus, why do you have a shotgun on your boat anyway?"

"Two reasons," said Gus with a swagger to his speech. "On a boat this size, sometimes a big halibut will do a ton of damage. Couple of hundred pounds flopping around could injure or kill me by knocking me overboard. I keep a shotgun handy when I'm hauling groundline and just blast the bugger in the mouth if I get a really big one that looks ornery. Settles them down right quick. Now the second reason. When I'm alone on the coast, or anchored, it's good security, just like today. Never know who might come along, especially when the fish are on and there's cash buyers out there. Bundles of cash everywhere. Have to be prepared."

"Oh," said Wayne, weighing this information.

"I've got a rifle too, and an old revolver ye can have if ye want."

"Are they legal Clarence?" asked Wayne.

"City boy," said Clarence with a smile. "We don't register nothin'. Never know. A gun could easily fall overboard if some enforcement guy starts snooping around."

"Anyways thanks a lot for your help, both of you. Really appreciate it. I'm not much of a gun guy Gus, but thanks for the offer. I'll keep it in mind."

"Okay, just say the word and you can have any one of these," said Gus nodding to them both and retreating to the wheelhouse on his boat.

Wayne surveyed everything on the *Molly B*, particularly the locks on the cabin door and the hatch cover. Everything looked fine, untouched. He turned his key in the lock and stepped into the cabin.

He heard Gus outside, saying, "Clarence, we'd better get in outta the rain," and they both went to their boats, their homes.

Wayne leaned out the cabin door, shook water off his jacket, hung it on a hook and went down into the forepeak. It was late afternoon and would be dark soon. His clothes in the pillow cases and garbage bags were wet so he rigged some lines to hang them, half wondering, "what's the point in this cold damp boat." He sat looking around thinking about the two visitors and that he had underestimated Ted's tenacity and viciousness.

After hanging the clothes and looking at his watch, Wayne decided it was time to get dinner. The afternoon had disappeared and the café up top, next to the wharf, looked the easiest. The food was usually okay.

As he walked through the café doorway, Wayne surveyed the situation. He was becoming more and more cautious, or maybe suspicious, or worse paranoid about these guys. The place was about half full, booths with orange vinyl benches and beige fake marble arborite table tops. Pictures from another time of famous salmon seiners, gillnetters and halibut longliners lined the faded and yellowing walls. In a booth on the opposite side of the centre divider, under the television playing the six o'clock news, was Cedar with her friends. He hesitated. Resigned and thinking things could not get much worse, he hung his jacket on the pole at the end of the first booth inside the door, on the right. He thought he could survive dinner and maybe leave before they passed by him on their exit path.

The clams and chips arrived with coffee, normally a favourite. But this time, they were tasteless to Wayne, and it wasn't the cook's fault.

There was animated discussion at the other end. He could discern that Cedar was making a point about the need to get rid of the mining company. He heard her raised voice saying, "With those crooked consultants, the government isn't even being made aware of the slumping tailings dams and acid."

As Cedar mentioned the word consultants, Mary made fleeting eye contact with Wayne. She tapped Cedar on the shoulder and pointed.

Cedar stopped talking, turned around and stared at Wayne. She turned back and said in a loud voice, audible throughout the restaurant, "There's one problem, and it's right over there. The consultant. That guy. He's the one who's going to get a big fine or a big jail term, for covering up. Sending misleading information to the enviro cops and Fisheries."

Wayne hung his head in despair. He had been wrong again. Things could get worse. He called for the cheque, paid and pushed the remaining clams and chips onto the paper placemat. Stuffing that into his jacket pocket, he left. The rain had let up but the square opposite the wharf was dark. After starting up the hill to town, he gave up, turned and walked back to the wharf and down the ramp to the solitude of his boat. *Molly B* rocked gently in the shining black water as he climbed aboard.

*****

THE BOAT WAS COLD AND DAMP SO HE LIT THE DIESEL STOVE AND oily black smoke belched out the stack, invisible in the darkness outside. The smell was there, however, and distinctive. Wayne blacked out the windows again and turned on a cabin light, which flickered before shining dimly. He put a headlamp in his pocket just in case and made a mental note of another detail to take care of, probably a loose connection. On a new old boat the list could be endless. He took the cold soggy clams and chips from his jacket pocket, sat on the berth opposite the stove, and finished them, one by one.

Bits and pieces of equipment and gear cluttered the forepeak berth. He cleared it, found his sleeping bag and spread it out. The forepeak had the distinctive smells of an old boat: rust; diesel; and, wood, with an underlying essence of mildew. Wayne didn't mind, with everything else going on he embraced it. This was his home now, his cocoon. He turned off the light, turned on a radio that came with the boat. He listened to a local station for a while, new country and classic rock with news and sports. Eventually, he turned the radio and light off, rolled into the comfort of the rail boards and drifted off to sleep, lulled by the gentle roll and the sound of wavelets slapping at the hull. Tomorrow would be another day.

*****

WELL INTO THE NIGHT, THE BOAT SUDDENLY ROLLED AND LOUD VOICES wakened *Molly B*'s occupant. Wayne sat bolt upright, hitting his head hard on the bulkhead above. Recoiling with curses under his breath, he put on the headlamp and slid out through the low point in the rail. He stood in underwear and bare feet on cold wood of the cabin sole. There were footsteps on deck. He heard them try the hatch cover lock, swearing when it wouldn't open.

"Damn, must have changed the lock. Try picking the cabin door."

Wayne heard the sound of metal entering the lock outside. He heard some clicking sounds and then the lock turned.

"Easy, got it," said another voice. "Let's check inside."

Wayne grabbed the fish club and gaff hook that hung just inside the door. When it opened, he yelled and stood as big as he could, his headlamp shining directly into the intruder's eyes. He swung the club and gaff aggressively. The intruder backed away, surprised, his face narrowly avoiding the gaff hook.

"What's wrong", said the first guy, who sounded like the one in charge.

"Looks like he's in there and ready for a fight. Should we continue?"

"Gotta get any copies of pictures and files he has, if we want to get paid," said the boss.

"Okay, here goes."

Wayne yelled again, louder.

At that moment, the distinctive sound of a shotgun blast ripped through the darkness. A spotlight drilled down from Gus's flying bridge.

"Get the fuck outta there," said Gus menacingly, with the shotgun aimed at the boss's gut. "I mean it. You got no business here. Unless you want a hole blasted through you, right through your gut." He shook the shotgun and sighted down the barrel again to emphasize his point.

The two big guys pulled their ball caps down low over their eyes, to shade and conceal, as they jumped off the boat and ran up the float and back up the ramp. They could hear a truck start and peel away from the square above.

"You okay Wayne?" Gus yelled across the way from his flying bridge. At least Wayne guessed it was Gus, given that he was being blinded by the search light.

"Yeah I guess," said Wayne, shaken and dazed. "What time is it anyway Gus?"

"Three a.m.," said Gus, turning off the search light. "Get some sleep."

Clarence stuck his head out of his boat. "What the hell's goin' on? Everybody okay?"

"We're fine," yelled Gus. "Go back to sleep Clarence. You too Wayne. We'll talk in the morning."

Wayne tried going back to sleep, but tossed and turned in the cramped bunk, on edge and anxious. Every roll of the boat and bump against the float felt like someone coming aboard. Eventually he drifted off again into a fitful oblivion.

In the morning, Wayne started working early to get his boat ready. He fixed the cabin light electrical connection first. That was easy. He tested the light, as well as the nav lights and the anchor light. Everything worked. The old diesel engine turned over and started with a belch of black smoke as usual. The anchor chain looked fine despite its age. Wayne turned on the VHF radio and radar, and both worked. Things looked generally pretty good, equipment wise.

Later in the day he waited in the cabin with the VHF radio squelching in the background. Clarence hauled himself over the rail and knocked. Wayne looked through the porthole in the door to see who it was and then opened the door to let him in.

"Saw you messing around over here," he said wedging his way into the cabin and perching himself on the skipper's stool behind the wheel. "Saw you bringing grocery bags from the Safeway down. See you went over to the fuel dock too. Fuel's important I guess, if you're goin' somewhere."

Clarence looked around the cabin, at the varnished mahogany dash and around the windows, the white paint on the bulkheads overhead, the tarnished brass gear shift and throttle, and the brass bell sitting on the dash near the compass with its soft iron adjustment spheres.

"I've spent a lot of hours in this wheelhouse with Sid," said Clarence rubbing the varnished mahogany and reaching to touch the wheel spokes, "talking, drinking coffee, drinking whiskey, smoking. Feels good. This boat's been through a lot and will take a lot more. She can handle foul weather better than the people she's carrying."

Clarence looked directly at Wayne and asked, "You okay Wayne? Gus told me all about it. That was some commotion last night."

"Yeah, I guess I'm okay."

"Them two fellas were pretty big I guess. Don't want to mess with that."

"That's for sure."

"Any idea what they were after?"

Wayne looked around and slouched against the dash. "Well, you know I got fired?"

"Yeah, I know," said Clarence turning on the stool that he had obviously occupied before.

"Well, they think I stole some documentation, files, pictures, stuff like that. Copies actually."

"Did you?" asked Clarence, intently studying the fancy cording on the centre top spoke of the brass wheel.

"No."

"Okay then. They're wasting their time, I guess."

"That's right." Wayne looked at him intently before asking, "Clarence, do you drive?"

Clarence looked puzzled by the question but let it go, just answering, "Yeah I can drive. Got a licence and everything, but no vehicle right now. Don't need one. Got everything I need right here on my boat."

"Well, here are the keys to my truck. It's parked out at Seal Cove by the curling rink. Gus can run you out there from time to time. Keep an eye on it for me, will you?"

"Yeah, sure Wayne. I guess I can try to keep an eye on it," said Clarence looking back at Wayne with questions in his eyes. "You got something in mind?"

"Maybe. Just take care okay," said Wayne solemnly.

"Sure Wayne." He tossed the keys in the air and caught them before stuffing them into his pocket.

After Clarence left, Wayne lay down in the forepeak berth. He heard Clarence talking with Gus out on the float, as he drifted off into a late afternoon power nap, preparing for what might lie ahead.

When he woke, it was dark outside. A moonless night, although the stars were countless and bright. A stiff wind was blowing in from the northwest. Wayne pulled his Floater jacket on and his navy watch cap. The engine started right away and sounded good. He was encouraged. This would be the first big test for his new boat. He cast off from the float and jogged the boat back and forth to escape the tight mooring spot. The wind kept pushing him back in so he had to go on deck and push his way off the neighbouring boats with a boat hook, using the outside engine controls and steering. Gus heard him and came down off his boat onto the float.

"Going somewhere Wayne?" asked Gus, loud over the thumping engine, showing interest and concern.

"Just taking her out for a run, to test things out."

Gus looked suspicious but said only, "Okay you have a good run. Might be a bit lumpy outside. Be careful."

"Thanks," said Wayne as he cleared the other boats. 'It's nice to have someone who seems to care about my safety,' he thought as he checked the nav lights and motored down the channel.

The water was black and rippled, it looked cold. Wayne ignored that. He focused on the light at the end of the floating breakwater. Once past that, he made a heading for the flashing red light over at Grindstone Reef. He had already decided to head north, out Venn Passage.

Wayne flipped the radar switch on. Comparison between the orange luminescent sweep on screen and the chart spread out on a board that passed as a chart table showed it was working fine. He checked the compass heading. Floodlights from the container terminal lit the shoreline and sky to the south where containers were being removed from a massive ship. Consumer goods from China. 'Those'll be in Alberta tomorrow night,' he thought, wondering if that wouldn't have been the smarter course of action for himself. 'But I can't leave. Can't run away like Ron did. Something's going to go wrong out there and that son-of-a-bitch Ted will try to pin it all me. That's what he sent me here for and I won't let him get away with it.' Wayne pondered the situation some more as he powered on into the night, finally admitting to himself, 'And I can't let something bad happen to Cedar and her family.'

The boat rounded Grindstone and Wayne set a course past the Tsimshian community of Metlakatla. He pondered all the schemes, pillaging and development projects that had been rained down upon these people, and they were still here, much more durable than the enterprises inflicted upon them. It made him reflect on his role in development schemes still going on and how ridiculous they ultimately were. The solitude of the wheelhouse, dull amber light from the compass, and the thrumming of the engine induced more solemn reflection.

Guided by the radar and the navigation lights marked on the chart Wayne steered *Molly B* past Metlakatla to starboard. Tugwell Island and open water loomed ahead. The wind quickly filled in and picked up to storm force as he cleared the sheltering islands. It was going to be a rough ride, one of those Easter storms that are so famous in Hecate Strait. He knew he really should turn back but also knew he had to try and disappear, to get away from the thugs trying to get at him. He had to think things through, figure out what to do. 'Come on. You're smart. You can do this,' he thought.

The bow dove into ocean waves that were steadily increasing in size. Spray coated the front windows, that he knew weren't built to withstand the full pressure of a breaking wave. As he eased to a more northerly heading the waves came on the beam and started a desperate rolling cadence. The boat dove into an extra deep trough and looking up, Wayne could see white foam above, luminescent against the blackness around him. *Molly B* rolled and the wave broke over the rail and the cabin, and then slid beneath the lee side in a shimmering rush of white foam. It seemed like the boat would never right itself, but it did. 'Those Japanese guys really knew how to build a boat, thank God.'

At that point, he decided not to push to extremes of the design and skills of the Japanese-Canadian boat builders of the north coast. He waited, and timed his turn on the crest of a wave. Once turned around, he began a crazy lurching run back into Venn Passage, past the rocks and breaking waves and into calmer waters behind the islands.

At Crippen Cove, Wayne dropped the hook onto a mud bottom, good holding ground. This would be secure for the night. He shut down the engine, lit an oil lamp, and turned off all the lights except the dim anchor light up in the rigging. To remain unseen he decided to risk getting hit by another vessel and turned that off too.

NINE

CEDAR LOOKED UP AND SAW MARY ENTER THE HALL. CHAIRS were being set up by the Fairview crowd, Neil, Cheryl and Lloyd. The head table was already in place.

She watched Mary approach. "So, what do you think?"

"I think you did it," said Mary, passing a satisfied look around at the hall. She smiled and added, "It looks like this meeting is actually going to happen."

"Yeah, I think so," said Cedar, organizing her notes. "I'm pretty nervous though."

"Don't be. When you look at them, see them as either the kindergarten children you organize every day or an enemy to be beaten at all costs and not worthy of your respect. You'll be fine."

"Thanks Mary."

"Are your parents here yet?"

"Haven't seen them. The weather outside has been bad, but the storm has passed. Could be a bumpy ride down from Mirage Inlet but they'll still make it. I think Jimi and Chelsea have been in town already, so they should be here too."

"I saw Jimi with some woman I hadn't seen before. She was all dressed in fancy new mountain casual gear. Who is she, do you know?"

"No idea. Haven't seen her. I guess we'll see when they get here."

It was six thirty on the Friday evening, and the room was starting to fill with a diverse cross section of town's people. Some were obvious environmentalists, the ones in hemp clothing that hung out at the Cow Bay coffee shop. The crowd that always showed up at meetings to stop development. Some were business types, always keen on new opportunities to expand, but possibly owed money by New Discovery Gold. There were fishermen interested in preserving wild salmon stocks. Native people from town and possibly Metlakatla and Lax Kw'alaams were coming in, the mine being located on land where they had never surrendered title or hereditary rights and obligations.

At about 6:50 p.m., some influential public voices started to show up. Susan was there from the paper. Her exposés on New Discovery Gold and its consultants had just been published and were the cause of much discussion. She was presumably there to report on events of the evening and to gauge the response to her articles and the mine. Construction types getting work at the mine entered, talking loudly and being belligerent about the environmentalists and back to the land people trying to stop development. Bruno slipped in, maintaining a low profile at the back.

Just before seven, Dave and Starshine entered the hall. They waved at Cedar and Starshine blew her a kiss.

Just as Cedar stood at the front and called the meeting to order, Jimi and Chelsea came through the doors at the back. With them was the new woman in town. They took chairs along the wall at the side, the only ones left.

"Thank you all for coming," said Cedar standing at the rough podium, looking nervously out over the crowd. "I was hoping to get a great turnout to get this mine shut down and you all came. Thank you."

The construction and development elements in the room started yelling and disrupting the applause of the people endorsing Cedar's introduction.

"I'll make a short presentation showing you all what is actually going on out at the mine," shouted Cedar into the microphone, seeing the enemy to be vanquished. "And then we'll have a discussion about what we can collectively do about it. We live out there and we're worried this mine will kill us. It's not safe. We may be the only people able to see this."

"You only see things 'cause you're out there trespassing," yelled a redneck from the back. "This mine complies with the regulations and you're just squatters with no business being there."

"You're just trying to cover things up for the company," shouted an angry environmentalist.

Discussion quickly accelerated to heated and antagonistic. This was not what Cedar had pictured for the meeting. She did not want these loud confrontational mine supporters at her meeting at all. She shouted into the microphone and held her hand up. The room became quiet.

"Yes," said Cedar pointing to the woman along the side with Jimi, "would you like to add something constructive to this discussion?"

The woman stood, looking like she had done this before. She was polished and looked educated. "I'm not from Prince Rupert," she said, eliciting a chorus of low boos. "I'm from Toronto." The boos got louder, turning into a spirited round of jeers from all sides. "Thank you," she said, giving a slight mocking bow. "My organization has studied mining companies like and including New Discovery Gold."

She went on to describe New Discovery Gold and other companies, their history of exploitation, destruction, unpaid bills, pollution and then bankruptcy when regulators caught up and the money ran out. "Even the investors get ripped off while the company executives live their lavish lifestyle for a few years. Then, after the bankruptcy or sale to another company, these same guys go and start all over again with another company, find some two bit mineral deposit already looked at five ways to Sunday, claim new information, go on the stock exchange and live off the capital they raise for another five years. It's a scheme for living the good life without working. And the kicker is that the Indigenous people of this country and the taxpayers are left with the costs of foregone opportunities and contaminated sites to cleanup."

"It's a formula, repeated time and again across this country and around the world," she said. The room was silent. Then cheers erupted from people opposed to the mine, and even from people who came to the meeting with neutral views. It was a powerful message, obviously workshopped, honed and delivered with experience.

Bruno slipped out the doors at the back. No one noticed but Cedar. Two large contractor types also left, followed a few minutes later by others of similar stature and demeanour.

Cedar started to wonder what was going on. She had noticed that Wayne was not in the room. He hadn't come to the meeting and she wondered why.

In the end, there was agreement among the remaining people that the mine should pay off its debts and be shut down. Since no one from government had attended, they agreed to write letters.

As the hall cleared, Jimi came forward and introduced the new woman, Caitlyn, to Cedar.

"That was some speech you made," said Cedar, greeting the woman after acknowledging Jimi. "Thank you."

"Caitlyn is from a large environmental organization back in Toronto where the big mining companies are," said Jimi. "It's called Sustainable People for Change. We've all heard of it."

"Hello, it's so nice to meet you," said Caitlyn standing relaxed and confident in her new Gore-Tex, like the perfect product placement model. "Jimi's told me all about you and your cause. You've done a lot of work organizing this meeting and we agree with you completely. We have our own Mining Action Initiative starting up and your efforts fit in perfectly."

"Thanks so much for coming," said Cedar, uncertain what else to say, wanting to be hospitable but not really sure about this new person. "Seems like a long way to travel for our little cause."

"Not at all. Every fight against injustice is important."

"Have you been to the North Coast before?"

"Oh yes," said Caitlyn with a satisfied smile. "My partner and I took a cruise up to Alaska a few years ago. It was wonderful when we were able to see the mountains. There was quite a lot of fog and rain though."

"Well you certainly got a genuine feel for the coast then, I suppose. Thank you for coming," said Cedar with a tinge of sarcasm, turning to walk away, and wondering about this newcomer's real knowledge and motives.

Jimi stopped her. "Caitlyn has a lot of good ideas for the next meetings, a series of meetings."

"Oh really," said Cedar turning back toward Caitlyn with feigned interest and real skepticism. "That's interesting."

"Yes," said Caitlyn enthusiastically, clearly pleased with the attention. "We could bring in some experts, have panel discussions, attract more media, put drone footage on television, that sort of thing."

"Wouldn't that cost a lot?" asked Cedar. "We really don't have any money."

"That's the beauty of it," said Caitlyn becoming more animated and speaking with her hands. "Your situation here is a great fund raising opportunity. With media attention and crowd funding this could be a whole new gold mine to build on."

Jimi was wearing a big smile as he watched Caitlyn explain what she was going to do.

"Okay, well I'm sure Jimi will know what to do," said Cedar, looking at him with narrowed eyes as she turned again to leave the two of them.

Loud noises, crashing and yelling erupted from outside. They rushed to the door, and there in the orange glow of the sodium vapour lights was a sizable brawl underway in the parking lot. Apparently the redneck construction workers objected to any efforts to have the mine shut down and they had attacked the environmentalists who fought back with matching enthusiasm. Just as Cedar and the others emerged through the doors of the hall, two police cars and a van rolled up, sirens blaring and lights flashing. The police began rounding up combatants and pushing them in handcuffs into the van. A pickup truck with tinted windows slipped away into the darkness beyond the sodium glare.

Dave saw her despondent look. He and Starshine came over and hugged Cedar, saying, "We're proud of you. Don't give up."

Caitlyn smiled and said, "I'll be staying at the Crest. Come on over and we'll talk."

"Pretty expensive," was all Cedar could think of to say.

Caitlyn guided Jimi and Chelsea to her rented SUV.

*****

"GOOD MORNING KAYE," SAID TED WITH AUTHORITY AS HE paraded past the office reception desk at nine thirty. It was another Monday morning after a hectic weekend. Kaye rose from her reception desk and followed him down the hall, as expected.

Ted yelled over his shoulder as he walked into his private office. "Get Bruno on the phone. I need to talk to him about that report for New Discovery Gold. He was sent up there last

Wednesday and I still don't have it. Ian is going to be all over me this morning."

"Yes sir. I'll get him," said Kaye, showing up at Ted's office door. "Anything else you need right away?"

"Yes, I need my coffee. It's supposed to be on my desk when I get here."

Kaye walked out of the office grimacing. Once again she had to pour out the cold coffee and pour another for Ted and call Bruno. Ted demanded coffee first, always.

"There's the coffee sir," said Kaye as she stepped gingerly into his office and set it on the coaster resting in its prescribed location at the distal right corner of the blotter pad. She returned to her desk to make the call to Bruno.

As Ted tasted the coffee, his phone rang. It was Kaye. "I have Bruno on the line."

"Bruno. How's Rupert and our little gold mine project?"

"Morning Ted," said Bruno matter of factly through the phone line. "It's a strange place up here. I was out at the mine and now I'm working through the report."

"Okay good. That's what you're there for. You know I need that report, needed it two weeks ago," said Ted, spinning his chair to admire the view. The view was larger than life and it always made him feel like he was too.

"Yes, I know. Like I said, I was out there and got new information and photos. I'm putting those together now. This morning. I think you'll like them."

"Good."

"Ted," said Bruno, pausing before adding, "Kaye didn't tell me Wayne was fired. I thought I was here to help him, not replace him."

"Oh, I guess Kaye screwed up. I'll talk to her about that." Ted spun the chair, sipped his coffee leisurely and started to check the markets on his computer screen.

"Ted, you know I've looked through the hard drives on the office computer and the laptop."

"Yes Bruno. What's your point?"

"Well there are lots of photos and data that show real problems at the mine. Problems since start-up that didn't get reported. Records that are not just from Wayne's work but from Ron's as well, and before Ron too. And some of the material in Wayne's last report is not on either hard drive."

There was a click on the line.

"Hello?" said Ted. "You still there?

"Still here. Bad line I guess."

"Anyway," said Ted, not wanting to bring attention to the interruption. He made a mental note to talk to Kaye about getting a tech in to check that damn call recording system again. "You don't need to look at those files from before. All the reports have already gone in and were accepted by the agencies. Those files are just redundant. You need to delete them now and that's an order. Don't keep copies."

"Do you think Wayne or Ron have copies?"

"No," said Ted, agitated, turning halfway to his view. "We had security lock things down tight and escort both of those guys out. Everything is secure. Wayne couldn't take anything, same with Ron. Don't worry about that. Just get me the report, today if you can." Ted hit the keyboard to bring up the current price of gold.

"Okay boss. I should be able to send it this afternoon."

"Good. Anything else, Bruno? You said it was a strange place?"

Bruno paused and then started to explain. "One thing. On Friday night there was a meeting, a public meeting. It looked like it was organized just by the squatters out at the mine site, but there was lots of attention. A reporter from the local newspaper was there."

"So?" said Ted, challenging any such questioning. "Just the desperate flailing of people who've already lost."

"I don't know. Last Thursday that same reporter did an exposé on the mine and its consultants. Our company really got trashed."

Ted became more agitated, but didn't want to draw attention to it. He wanted to make sure Bruno would stay calm and focussed. "That's crazy. Must be Wayne planting stories to get back at us."

"I don't know. She did another article. An exposé on Wayne's consulting past behaviour. It did not paint a pretty picture of our Wayne. They really did a number on him. They also talked about you, and your business record, but not as much. Whoever wrote those articles did some really good investigation."

Ted paused. He looked around his office and then out over Vancouver Harbour again. A tug was churning its way across his view, bow wave frothing like meringue over a lemon pie. "Sounds more like snooping, like invasion of privacy, than investigative reporting. Send me the articles."

"Okay boss. Oh and another thing."

"What now?" asked Ted growing more impatient.

"At that meeting there was a group of redneck construction guys that objected to the meeting and any people who spoke out against the mine."

"What do you mean? Were there any guys that looked like security?"

"Yeah, I guess you could call some of them that. I mean they completely disrupted the meeting and afterwards they started a major brawl out in the parking lot. A couple of the guys who looked like security were involved."

"That's good isn't it? And it's just the regular Friday night entertainment up there, right?"

"I don't know. This was pretty ugly. The cops came, broke things up, and took some people away in a police van."

"Did they take the guys who looked like security?"

"No, just run of the mill rednecks. There was a lot of yelling. It was dark. Those supposed security guys just melted back into the darkness."

Ted paused again and regained his composure. "Anyway, you don't need to get distracted by the local side shows. Just delete those old redundant records and get that report to me today."

"Okay boss."

"Thanks Bruno. I know I can depend on you. You're my best."

Bruno hung up the phone. That was exactly what Ted used to say about Wayne.

Ted's phone rang. "It's Doug from the bank," said Kaye. "He says he must speak to you. Now."

"Okay," said Ted into the speaker, his head in his hands.

"Hello Ted. It's Doug."

"Doug. What's up?"

"Ted, I've been re-examining your situation. I'm not really confident we'll be protected if interest rates change. We have to increase your payments. Remember, you opted for flex rates on all your loans. Well it's time for us to raise them. I know you made a payment last week, but it's not enough. You owe so much, across the board."

"I'll be able to make another payment this week," said Ted, with an imploring tone.

"That's another thing. Your clients make us nervous. A lot of shaky junior miners out there, and we're hearing rumours about this one on the north coast. Ted, maybe you should sell that boat and take the loan right off the books."

"They'll pay," said Ted sharply, offended and on the attack after being challenged. "You can depend on that. And I don't intend to sell the boat. I've worked hard for that and I deserve it."

"Okay Ted. You know your situation better than I. But you'll have to get us another payment, very soon or there will be consequences," said Doug hanging up the phone, clearly frustrated and not satisfied.

Late in the day, Ian Verster from New Discovery Gold called. He immediately started in by saying, "So, where's my report?"

"It's being finished now. Bruno said I'll have it by the end of the day. Do you want him to send it directly to you? We can do that, if it works better for you."

"No you review it. I want to see your signature on it before it comes to me, especially after the fiasco with that Wayne guy. When I get a good report, you'll get another payment."

"Okay, thanks Ian. I'll get that report to you as soon as I can."

"Tomorrow?"

"Tomorrow," said Ted with conviction, pushing down any potential doubts he might have, should have.

Ted put on his coat and walked out of his office. On the way to the elevator he said, "Kaye, I've got to go. I'm meeting my son down at the boat. We're going to spend some time together."

"Okay Ted. Have fun. See you tomorrow."

TEN

WAYNE WOKE IN THE FOREPEAK BERTH. WIND STILL HOWLED from the northwest through the rigging and *Molly B* tugged at the anchor rode like a roped mustang. In the shelter of the cove wavelets lapped at the hull, the pitch and frequency of the sounds changing as the boat charged back and forth.

Wayne extricated himself from the berth, dressed and lit the diesel stove. Black smoke outside was ripped away from the stack the wind, the only sign that life might exist within. He drew water and put the ancient kettle on the heat.

With instant coffee in hand, Wayne settled in on the skipper's stool in the wheelhouse. Looking out the surrounding forward windows he saw clouds breaking up and sun beginning to shine through. The cold spring day was brightened by a shaft of sunlight that made the small waves sparkle. Wayne took in the scene and his situation.

Yesterday had been bad, but he'd managed to get out of town unhurt. He'd been able to disappear and he still had the files and photographic defense evidence with him. Looking at his phone, he saw a missed call, from Kathy. He pressed to return the call.

"Oh Wayne, I was trying to reach you," said Kathy, answering as though Wayne had been a surprise interruption.

"Hi Kathy." Wayne tried faking pleasantries while inside he was distant and despondent. "I saw your call."

"Hey, no one showed up to get your stuff. That's why I called. What's up?"

"I called Stu and asked him to pick it up on the weekend."

"He talked to me, but then didn't show. He always was pretty useless. Total flake." The disparaging tone in her voice crackled through the air like an electrical storm on a hot humid unstable day.

"Thanks Kathy. He's my friend." Wayne was off balance, on the defensive, trying to gain some footing.

"Yeah figures. Anyway, one last chance. Get it out of here by Friday. I've got stuff coming in next weekend."

"New furniture? Where'd you get the money?"

"I didn't trust your money sense, Wayne. Especially when you started playing the stocks of those companies you were working for. I kept some aside for insurance."

"I wonder how much of that is mine?" asked Wayne, not expecting a straight answer. "And I wonder how much of that new furniture is actually yours?" After an empty pause he said, "I'll call Stu and get him to hurry up."

"Where are you anyway? You're hard to reach."

"I'm anchored in a cove. Had a bad Friday night outside the islands, in a storm. Waves were big, it was dark. I turned around and came back in. So I'm spending the weekend holed up in this protected cove."

"Be careful on that boat alone Wayne. You are alone aren't you?" The implied accusation again shot through the wireless system.

"Yes Kathy, I am alone." Wayne rolled his eyes to no one, throwing his hands in the air.

"Okay then. I'll see you sometime, maybe. If Stu doesn't show, I'll just pitch your things."

She clicked off. 'Well that was that,' thought Wayne with resignation. 'Things can't get much worse.'

He punched in a number. "Stu, what's going on? She's gonna pitch my stuff next Friday. Can you get it for sure this week? Sorry to put you through this buddy, but for all I know she's got someone else moving in."

"Yeah," said Stu. "I'll get it tonight. Sorry. Got busy over the weekend. You suspect someone else might be moving in"?

"Don't know what's going on with her, you, anybody. I'm holed up in some cove here on the run and totally isolated. How the hell would I know what's going on?"

Wayne clicked off and settled on his stool, leaning back against the bulkhead, feet up on the spokes of the locked wheel. Nothing he could do from here. Stu would get his stuff. Or not? He wasn't really sure he wanted that baggage tying him down anymore anyway.

Despite all the bad, Wayne was starting to enjoy this peaceful solitude. The wind, the waves, sunshine, salt water. The peacefulness was a new experience.

He puttered around the boat. The electrical system checked out. The anchor winch worked fine. He started the engine to check the hydraulics and they were fine. He used the hydraulics and the boom to hoist his newly acquired dinghy into the water. With the dinghy made fast, the oars were retrieved from the hold. While down there he checked the files and laptop. Everything looked good so he closed up again and locked the hatch cover. He locked the cabin door, zipped up his Floater jacket and pulled his watch cap down snug.

After dropping the oars into the dinghy, he climbed down, untied and pushed off against *Molly B*'s hull, deciding to go into the cove and see who lived in the houses there. He still needed a small outboard for the dinghy, and maybe someone in there would know of one for sale.

Wayne placed the oars in the oarlocks, settled himself in and began pulling with strong steady strokes. The wind came at him from the northwest, not strong enough to hold him back but strong enough to require frequent course adjustments. At the first and largest makeshift floating dock, he stepped out and secured the dinghy. The nearest house was nestled in rich green vegetation and surrounded by gardens that presumably produced vegetables in summer. As he made his way up the walk, someone emerged from the house, waved and came down to meet him.

"Hello," said Wayne approaching the person with a broad smile and extended hand. "I just anchored out in your cove and thought I'd come ashore to introduce myself."

"That's nice," said the stranger shaking his hand. "We've been watching you out there. I'm Ole. My wife's inside. Come on up."

"I'm Wayne."

Ole led the way up the path and the stone steps. "Looks like you have a nice garden in summer," said Wayne extending an arm in that direction.

"Thanks," said Ole as he opened the front door. "It's the long summer days, good soil, and obviously plenty of rain." Stepping through the door he said, "Greta, there's someone here. Let's put on some tea."

"I don't want to impose," said Wayne hesitant but exceptionally grateful for the warm welcome and hospitality.

"Nonsense. I'm Greta Gustafson," she said, entering the front room, wiping hands on her apron and introducing herself. "Come in. We don't get many new visitors over here, mostly just cove people we already know, only too well."

"Well thank you," said Wayne, picking a spot on the worn couch covered with an old style orange, brown and white crocheted affair thrown over the back. Like the

Gustafsons, the room was quaint and cozy. Linoleum over rough wavy floor boards painted grey long ago, wooden walls painted white for brightness, the wall studs exposed, no insulation, no panelling. A woodstove in the kitchen appeared to be the only source of the drying warmth that filled the room.

"I was heading into Chatham Sound on Friday night, but didn't get as far as Dundas Island, the storm was too much for my boat, or maybe just too much for me," said Wayne, trying to initiate conversation and explain his reason for landing in their cove and living room.

"I see your boat out there," said Ole. "*Molly B*, she's a tough old boat but, last Friday night, you probably had your hands full and made the right decision. I guess you just bought her after Sid died, did you?"

"That's right." Wayne accepted tea and homemade bread from the morning's oven. "So far she's running good."

"You new in town?" asked Ole taking a sip of tea, sliding into his recliner that looked like the original model, cracked vinyl showing ambiguous cloth beneath.

"Yeah, sort of. Came up here on a quick fill in job but got fired last week."

"What happened?" asked Greta settling into what was evidently her private rocking chair, her throne. Her long straight silver hair was pulled back, held in place by a blue elastic at the nape of her neck. "You really make a mess of something?"

"Yeah, I guess some people would see it that way. I was working for the consulting company doing environmental work out at New Discovery Gold, up in Mirage Inlet."

Ole and Greta looked at each other seriously, frowning. Ole said, "If you're that guy, then we saw the article about you in the paper last week. It didn't paint a very nice picture of you."

"Article? There's an article?" he asked in shocked surprise. "I've only been doing work out there for a short time," said Wayne, on the defensive, desperately trying to maintain at least some air of credibility, respectability. "I sent in a report for the company to send to the province. The provincial permit requires it. I wrote that report to tell the story of what's really going on at the mine site, and got fired for it. Looks like they've been bending the truth a lot out there over the years and I wanted no part of it."

As he said that, there was a knock at the door. Ole got up and swung the door open. In walked Cedar.

Ole and Greta greeted her as family. Cedar entered the room casually, until she saw Wayne. She responded like a cat cornered by a Rottweiler, focusing her hostile stare directly on him.

"What are *you* doing here?" asked Cedar, stopping in the middle of the room directly in front of Wayne. "Ole and Greta, how could you let this corporate leach into your house?"

"Come Cedar and sit," said Greta soothingly, with a sweep of her arm. "Have some tea and bread I baked this morning."

Cedar looked all around the room. The only remaining spot was on the couch where Wayne was seated. She accepted the tea from Greta, but hesitated, remaining standing for a moment looking derisively at Wayne. Tension continued to radiate, filling the room. Finally she sat on the edge of the couch, as far from Wayne as its physical boundaries would allow.

Ole finally broke the silent tension. "So Cedar, you just out for a run in Mary's boat? Nice morning for it."

"I'm following up from the meeting last Friday night, and to thank you for coming out and helping."

"We wanted to be there," said Greta, moving along in a less confrontational direction. "Who was that with Jimi? She seemed to really know her stuff and was very articulate. She could be a real help I guess."

"Yeah, I guess," said Cedar, in a monotone that continued to dampen the mood. She stared across the room at some imaginary spot on the linoleum.

"Do you know anything about her?"

"Not really. Jimi just showed up with her. He didn't warn me ahead of time. I don't know what to think of her. Sometimes Jimi can be duped by people like that. Sometimes Jimi isn't too bright."

"Well she sure stirred things up," said Ole heaving the recliner forward and jumping into the discussion. "That was quite a brawl at the end, wasn't it Cedar?" said Ole with a wry smile. "Reminded me of the heydays in this town, during the halibut and salmon seasons when the whole fleet was in on a Saturday night." He smiled reflecting on times past. "Those were some fights back then. What started the one on Friday night?"

"It was awful," said Cedar sounding discouraged. "Those rednecks started it, you know the guys. I guess they sensed opinion might shift against the mine and decided to disrupt the whole evening. They just wanted to remind people that they have a lot of power in town and make their money from projects like New Discovery."

"Well, they did that, for sure. It was quite nasty. Messed up a nice productive evening," said Ole sliding back into his recliner, taking a bite of his bread.

Wayne listened to the conversation, perplexed. Finally he said, "I saw the posters about the meeting, but I was on my boat in a storm on Friday night."

"Figures," said Cedar derisively. "Running away, when people call you out."

"Actually Cedar, Wayne was just telling us that he got fired last week," said Greta, again trying to smooth things over. "Wayne, maybe you could tell us more about that."

Wayne looked around the room, considering how much he should share. "I wrote a report for New Discovery to send to the province as part of its permit conditions. I wrote it depicting the whole story, not just the isolated bits required by the permits. To tell the truth about the mine. My consulting company quashed the report before even forwarding it to the mining company. The boss knew the company wouldn't want to see any bad news. Then he fired me. Threw me out on the street in the rain and now those rednecks, as you call them, are coming after me. I guess they're trying to run me out of town."

The room was silent. Cedar continued to bore a hole into her imaginary spot on the floor.

"I was trying to do the right thing," said Wayne, looking directly at Cedar on the couch to his right, desperately trying to clarify and remedy his situation. "When I came up here, I didn't like how things were being done out at the mine. Didn't like what I saw, photographed it, documented it and reported it."

"And now I suppose that's all lost," said Cedar, leaning away from him as much as she could without either spilling her tea or having to get up from the couch. "There was a new guy, some guy named Bruno, at the meeting. I guess that's why. I guess he's your replacement. He stayed at the back, keeping a low profile and snuck out when the rough stuff started. He'll never last in Rupert."

"Yeah, he's my replacement. Bumped into him by accident last week. I didn't know he was coming. Didn't know he was here. My company froze me out instantly. Even he didn't know what was going on. Thought he was just sent to help me out. Be my assistant." Wayne looked over his shoulder, directly at Cedar and said, "Cedar, I'd like to help you. I know how these guys think. I know how they work. I think that might be at least some value to you."

"Maybe Wayne could help," said Greta positively, trying to see a way to help Cedar and soothe the tension. "It's a big thing you're taking on. Trying to get rid of that mine. You're up against people with lots of money to lose and lots of money to hire experts and thugs."

"I don't know about him," said Cedar sceptically, looking Wayne up and down, and into his eyes. "I don't think he can be trusted. He's been nothing but a manipulator and a liar his whole career. What could possibly make him change so much all of a sudden, and now? He's just desperate right now and could change later."

*****

CEDAR STAYED SEATED ON THE COUCH WHILE THE OTHER TWO said good bye to Wayne and watched him row across the wind and waves to his boat in center of the cove.

Turning to Cedar, Greta said, "He seemed like a nice person Cedar. Not at all like that article in the paper."

Cedar grimaced. "I still don't like him. You just have to look at his history, his actions. I don't trust him."

"He did quit, and for some reason seems to be simply living on an old boat for now. Something must have changed him."

"Actually, he got fired. He wants people to believe it was because he chose to do the right thing, but I still don't trust him. How do we know it wasn't just incompetence?"

"He could really use an outboard for that dinghy," said Ole watching Wayne battle the cross wind and waves in the cove.

Cedar looked at Ole and Greta, shook her head, and said, "What am I going to do now? We had our meeting and there were lots of people there. But it ended in a mess. For a while I thought even I was going to be arrested, just for organizing the darn thing. I didn't do anything wrong."

Greta looked at her sympathetically, almost motherly. "Just have to keep going. Again, who was that woman with Jimi anyway? It seemed like she had some good ideas."

"Jimi thinks so," Cedar shrugged. "She's tried to stop mining in other communities, in Ontario, Quebec, B.C., the territories, you name it. She does it full time. Travels a lot."

"She seems to dress well," said Greta. "All the latest outdoor clothes, technical pockets, zippers, pulls and all that. Where does she get the money?"

"Maybe she's one of those Rosedale brats from Toronto," said Ole still reclined and pensive now. "Family makes a fortune and the daughter has the luxury of doing what she's doing."

"Maybe," said Cedar removing her homespun woolen toque and running fingers through hair tangled from the wind on the boat ride over. "But I think her organization does a lot of big fund raising with the Toronto rich people."

Ole rubbed his temples, blinked his eyes and said, "Maybe she looks for underdog causes like yours, and swoops in and pumps it up to raise lots of money. Sometimes those kinds of people pay themselves big salaries, have big travel budgets, everyone thinks they're experts cause they appear in magazines and on TV. They really like to jump on Native causes too and exploit them for their own ends."

"That's what I'm afraid of. I'm worried Jimi's getting taken for a ride, and taking us along with him. I'm worried she'll come in, use us to raise money for themselves and then leave us when the publicity dies down and the money flow stops. Then they'll be off on some other cause where the money's better and we'll be left with a lot of community division and animosity, which is bad in a small isolated place like this."

"That's true. Those kinds of people are good at stirring up a crowd for sure," said Greta shaking her head. "But that cuts both ways. Look at those fights on Friday night. They leave a torn community and we all have to live together up here on the north coast."

Cedar rose to leave. "Guess I'll go back over to Dodge Cove. Thanks for the tea and support you two. Please keep talking this up with the neighbours over here."

"Keep coming over Cedar. We love seeing you. Used to enjoy taking care of the two of you, when you were kids," said Greta, opening the door and giving Cedar a kiss on the cheek.

Cedar hung her head for a reflective melancholy moment and then looked up at Greta and said, "Both of us loved coming over here too."

As Cedar passed through the door and down the steps, Ole told her, "Cedar, be careful how you treat him. Wayne might be able to help you, even if you don't like him."

Cedar walked down the stone steps to where her boat gently bumped against the log float. As she motored out of the cove, Wayne waved from *Molly B*'s afterdeck. Cedar turned her head away, looking instead at the light marking Grindstone Reef.

Back at the house in Dodge Cove Mary greeted Cedar at the door. "Hey look, some people are here. They want to talk about the meeting last Friday and how to move forward. They want to talk to you."

Walking into the front room, she saw Jimi on a painted wooden kitchen chair beside Chelsea on its match. Caitlyn was seated in a big soft arm chair. It occurred to Cedar that she carried herself as if she were on a throne.

Cedar took her jacket and woolen toque to her room at the back, grabbing tea and a slice of Mary's corn bread on her return. The living room was warm and soothing after the chilling wind on her run from Crippen Cove. Caitlyn changed that.

"So Cedar, we've been talking about how to take your little initiative to the next level," said Caitlyn sitting erect in the arm chair, legs crossed, her arms resting on its arms, not leaning forward. "We thought it would be good to bring in a videographer. I know a really good one down in Vancouver. We bring her up. She does some interviews with you and the others. These cabins in the cove are perfect for getting the right look and feel. We have another public meeting. Get video of people speaking out against the mine. I would do a keynote on how mining is bad across Canada and how the government needs to do something about it, using the meeting as a backdrop. Then we get footage of the pro-mining people being belligerent. You know yelling, insulting you guys, starting fights. It would be perfect."

Mary and Ray were nodding enthusiastically in agreement. Cedar sat there, on her own hard wooden kitchen chair, dumbfounded.

Jimi, smiling broadly and looking silly, said, "Cedar, isn't she really something. Think of all the publicity."

Cedar stared straight at Jimi. "Yes, she's really something. That's for sure."

Cedar turned to Caitlyn, engaging her directly. "Who would organize all of this?"

Caitlyn was unfazed. "We'll be flying in a team of three. We have these response teams that can jump on an issue very quickly to optimize timing and benefits. They'll arrange it all and the videographer will come with them. I've already talked to her. She's a bit expensive but the best. She has the right philosophical bent and has never let us down."

"Really?" said Cedar with visible scepticism and some sarcasm. "What does she do full time?"

"She's a partner in a big advertising agency. They do ads for everybody. This kind of work is her passion though. What do you think Cedar?"

"Probably doesn't really matter what I think, I guess. I'm just wondering who's going to pay for all of this. Their travel costs for example."

Jimi smiled as he glanced back and forth between Caitlyn and Cedar. Caitlyn responded with a smug grin, "Oh, we'll cover the upfront costs, but the fund raising off this little initiative will make a fortune. We'll more than re-coup our costs."

Jimi nodded enthusiastically as he looked around the room smiling proudly at the others. Cedar hung her head so that her tangle of auburn hair fell forward and obscured her face. She looked up and said, "Who gets that money Caitlyn? And what will the pro-mining people do? The construction workers, the miners, the red necks? After you all leave."

"They'll be pretty upset," said Caitlyn with pride, ducking the question about who gets the money. "That's what usually happens when our initiatives get going."

"And then what?"

Caitlyn looked around the room for support with questions in her eyes. "The police will have to handle it, and civic authorities. If people assault others, break the law, they'll have to be punished."

"We'll still be living here, with them," said Cedar. She got up and went to her room at the back.

Caitlyn said to the others, "Those people will be even more cantankerous if she succeeds in getting the mine shut down."

*****

WAYNE WATCHED FROM OLE'S BOAT AS MARY GUIDED HER OWN boat in to the dock at Fairview, with Cedar in the bow. He greeted her tentatively as she stepped onto the float.

"Hello Wayne," replied Cedar into the distance, avoiding eye contact.

Wayne bent to secure Ole's lines. "I see you've been busy around the cove in Ray's boat," said Wayne trying to open up a conversation channel. He had seen Cedar going to and from Crippen Cove, her auburn tangle blowing in the wind.

"We're coming into town to go to work. What do you do? I see you're mooching rides from Crippen off Ole now. What's wrong with your own boat?"

Wayne had watched the activity in Crippen Cove from the wheelhouse and after deck as he worked around his own boat. *Molly B* was turning out to be a good home base once he'd moved things around to make room and started to clean up. He'd been hitching rides with Ole to pick up supplies in town. So far he hadn't seen anyone who might cause trouble.

"You look like you've been busy. Something going on?" said Wayne reaching to help secure Mary's mooring lines.

"Yeah, so what? You got nothing better to do than watch my comings and goings? You keeping a log book or something?" said Cedar grabbing the lines from him to secure them herself.

"Not really. Just staying aware of my surroundings. It's quiet living on the boat away from town. Not much else to do."

"That's the way we like it," said Cedar standing straight and stretching in the damp cold. "That's why we live over in Dodge Cove and up in Mirage Inlet."

Ole got out of his boat and stood on the float.

"You organizing another meeting?" asked Wayne, changing the subject as they followed Mary and Ole up the ramp.

"What's it to you?"

"Nothing. Just trying to make conversation."

"Well don't," said Cedar, turning away, and heading for Mary's old Volvo in the parking lot.

"Well you two," said Mary to Ole and acknowledging Wayne, "it's been nice chatting but we have to go to work so we'll say good bye here."

Mary got in and her station wagon started with a cough while Cedar walked around to the passenger side and got in. Wayne and Ole made their way over to the canteen. Neil, Cheryl and Lloyd were there as usual, sitting around the table having coffee and discussing the affairs of the day.

"Cedar's still mad at you Wayne," said Ole, pouring his coffee.

"I hoped maybe she'd come around by now," said Wayne getting his own and sitting at the table.

"Take longer than this, my friend. Her hatred for that mining company and anyone associated with it runs pretty deep."

"Seems pretty extreme. Why don't they just move?"

The others looked at each other in horror and then stared into their heavy ceramic mugs.

"Oh," said Wayne to the air. "It's like that."

"Don't ever say anything like that to Cedar, or even in her vicinity," said Cheryl directly to Wayne as he hid behind his mug, "if you want to stay alive." They all nodded sagely in agreement.

After a pause, Ole shifted the conversation. Wayne listened for a while, distracted, and then got up to leave.

"Guess I'll walk into town. Ole what time are you going back?"

"Five o'clock Wayne. Be there or you'll be swimming back."

Wayne considered the option of swimming in the dark cold water and quickly checked his watch. He left the canteen and went up the hill, past the ferry terminal and the container terminal security gate. He walked along the road into town, mountain to the right, harbour to the left, both obscured intermittently by the deep green of towering hemlock, fir and cedar. At road level the depths of the forest were dark, shaded by the heavy canopy above.

*****

As he approached the lower end of Third Avenue leading to downtown, a black pickup came thundering down the other side of the road headed for Fairview. When the occupants saw and recognized Wayne, the truck veered onto the shoulder, shot across the street, and onto the opposite shoulder in an aggressive U-turn. The truck slowly rolled up behind Wayne, nudging him with the front bumper. He looked straight ahead and kept walking but the truck kept nudging the back of his legs. Fed up and in self-defence, Wayne stepped behind a light standard and the bumper hit it, shaking it all the way up to the light at the top. It appeared as deliberate as Wayne's own action.

With the truck stopped, Wayne decided there was nothing else he could do. He walked up to the tinted driver side window, which powered down. Inside were the two big guys who had removed him from his job, apartment and office.

"What do you want?" said Wayne, looking from one to the other, trying not to appear nervous.

"Hello," said the leader from the driver's seat. "It's Wayne isn't it? Ah yes, I remember your name from the letter we so thoughtfully hand delivered to you."

"And the big payout too," added the other guy from the passenger side, wearing a broad sarcastic grin.

"We haven't seen you in town Wayne," said the driver looking straight ahead, holding the wheel firmly with both hands clenched and knuckles white under the strain. Turning his gaze toward Wayne he said, "Thought maybe you would've taken a bus out, or maybe the train. But no, we can see now that you're still here. Where you goin' to Wayne, on such a pleasant day?"

"Just out for a walk," replied Wayne, trying not to be intimidated. "Enjoying the sunshine."

"You still at the Hecate Rooms, Wayne? Haven't seen you there since last week."

"No, I'm staying with friends. Trying to save money. You know, since I don't have a job now."

"Yeah we know about your job situation," said the passenger laughing. "We handed you the letter and watched your face collapse when you read it. You remember? Those were fun times, eh?"

"Where's your boat, Wayne," said the driver, leaning an arm on the window sill like he might reach out to grab Wayne by the throat. "Haven't seen it at the dock since last week."

"Oh, I loaned it to a friend. Someone who wanted to do some fishing."

"You seem a very generous fellow, Wayne," said the driver extending his arm out the window and down the truck door.

"Oh, you know how it is."

"No. No I don't Wayne. How is it?"

"Look, I have to go," said Wayne, turning to walk away.

"Get in. We'll give you a ride," said the driver as the passenger leaned across smiling and opened the rear crew cab door.

"I'm fine. No thanks. Need the exercise you know."

"You know what I don't know Wayne?" said the driver with increasing menace in his voice. "I don't know what you kept."

"What do you mean?" asked Wayne as he started walking away.

"You know what I mean. I think you stole copies of materials that don't belong to you. What do you think of that?"

Wayne stopped walking and returned to address the accusation. "I think you're crazy," he said, looking straight into the driver's eyes and then pushing away from the truck again and turning toward town. "I don't know what you're talking about. Now, I have to get going."

Wayne walked quickly up the slope to downtown. The black bumper nudged him one more time from behind and then the truck roared off, black diesel exhaust belching out, kicking up stones and dirt.

Wayne cringed, thinking that had been unpleasant. He decided to visit Gus and Clarence down in Cow Bay to catch up on wharf news and gossip and then get his groceries before heading back to meet Ole.

*****

"BRUNO, HOW'S THE REPORT COMING? AM I GOING TO GET IT today? I have to send it to the client tomorrow."

"I'll send it down tonight. You'll be able to go through it in the morning," said Bruno responding to Ted's aggressive opening salvo. He was used to the approach.

Ted stared at his Engineering PhD and Professional Engineer Certificate on the ego wall beside his desk. He had worked so hard for these achievements. A photograph of his son stared at him from the left side of his desk, behind the phone.

"Is it going to be something the client can live with?" he asked sharply, wanting to send a message.

"I think so. I followed the protocol and templates you developed and the company and government agreed to. Had to leave information out to make the templates work, but that's what everyone agreed to."

"That's good Bruno. That's why you're there. You're reliable."

"You know boss," said Bruno a bit tentative and not wanting to upset Ted any more than he had to. "We should have some concerns up there."

"Yes, I know about the tailings dam and that Wayne saw what he thought was acid drainage, but I think he was just overreacting. Those conditions have been going on for a while and no one has complained, at least not the government inspectors. The engineers have provided everyone with assurances they'll be fine."

"It's more than that boss," said Bruno. He hesitated before pressing on, nervousness in his voice. "Some new equipment has shown up on site, and cyanide drums. Should we be doing anything with that information?"

"That's all news to me. I don't know anything about it," said Ted, thinking this must be what Ian had been talking about. Wayne had raised this in his last report. Ted was hoping there might be more money in the budget to deal with these developments. "It's not in the protocol, so we can't report it. Just keep an eye on it Bruno. Keep it in your notes and photos. But that's all you need to do for now."

"Okay Ted. I'll finish up the report and send it down," said Bruno, hanging up the phone.

Ted clicked off the hands free connection and leaned back in his chair, trying to estimate how much this cyanide dimension would increase his budget. He smiled, satisfied. Everything was going to turn out fine, just like it always did.

It was lunch time, and Ted had planned to go see his father. He walked down to the SeaBus and rode over to the North Shore. His father lived up the hill from the terminal in a small duplex on East Second, where Ted had grown up. His father had spent his life working in Burrard Shipyards at the foot of Lonsdale to put Ted, the special son, through school. Ted knew his father had sacrificed his health and his life to make a better life for him. Now Ted was making big money and his father was very proud.

Ted walked up to the dwelling and knocked. He noticed the grass had not been cut, and weeds were overtaking the garden. His elderly mother answered.

"Oh, Ted, come in," she said opening the door with a big smile.

Ted entered. "Where's Dad?"

"Oh, you know. He's in the basement," said his mother instantly disappointed that was all Ted had to say to her.

Ted descended the narrow steep stairs into the dark musty basement followed by his mother. The only light was from small windows set high in the concrete foundation. His father slouched in a worn old arm chair, one hand holding a cigarette, in the other hand a glass almost empty. A whiskey bottle sat upright at his feet. The man was watching a soap on an old black and white television.

"Hello Dad," called Ted as he descended.

"Is that you Ted?" He stirred, the only sign of life being an arm raising the glass to his lips. "So glad you stopped by. How are things? How's work? I bet you've got some big important jobs on the go."

"Oh well Dad, I'm working away. Things are really busy now."

"I bet they are son. Bet you're making a whole lot of money too. What do you think of that mother?"

"We're so proud of you Ted. Owning your own company. All that responsibility. I don't know how you do it," said his mother enthusiastically, even though she had been through this same routine many times before.

"Mom, why is Dad drinking again? I thought that was under control."

"I don't know why" she said with an anxious tinge to her voice along with arms raised in frustration. He just sits there. Can't seem to drag himself out of it. He keeps saying his life's been a waste. Except for you Ted. You're all he's got that gives him something to look forward to. You validate his life."

Ted grimaced and thought, 'Oh geez, not that again. Why did I come over here?'

Turning to his father he said, "Dad, you have to get out of that chair. Mom needs you. The yard is a mess. You need to go out and at least mow the lawn. Come on now Dad, pull yourself together."

The father just sat in the dim light staring blankly at the television. Ted threw up his hands and climbed back up the stairs with his mother behind him saying, "What are we going to do Teddy?"

On the SeaBus back to downtown, Ted watched the other passengers. There was an attractive woman getting off. He said hello and she smiled back. They chatted as they walked up the hill to Pender Street and Ted asked if he could meet her for drinks after work. She was surprised but agreed. He needed to clear his head and she was just the tonic he needed.

ELEVEN

WAYNE WALKED WEST ON THIRD AVENUE AND CUT OVER TO THE newspaper office. He pulled open the glass door and stepped in. Susan was visible in the newsroom, through the glass partition. He dinged the bell and she looked up. After finishing what she was working on she emerged through the news room door, with a look of surprise.

"So, I see now that you haven't left town. There have been lots of rumours around. One version says you were lost at sea in that storm, but I didn't believe that one. Why the low profile?"

"How much can I trust you Susan? With that article you wrote about me, you pretty much made it impossible for me in this town."

"Look Wayne, I was just doing my job. I was asked to do an exposé so I did it. I didn't enjoy doing it, but putting out real information for the public is what we do. I am sympathetic on how it might have affected you though."

"Yeah I know. It just means I have to be careful what I tell you though. I'm sure you understand." Wayne paused, looked away and then back at her. "Susan, you know I got fired for wanting to tell the truth about what's going on out at the New Discovery Mine."

"Yes, I know that. I know you're no longer working for the consulting company or the mine. I actually respect you for doing the right thing. I also know you've disappeared right off the radar, since last Thursday I think it was. I've been down to the dock looking for your boat and it's not there. Gus and Clarence aren't saying anything that's for sure. Either they don't know where you are or they're playing dumb. Hard to tell. Those guys are pros at keeping things to themselves. Old fishermen's habits die hard."

"Well when I got fired, Ted the company owner, sent security guys to deliver the news. Then they forced me out of the company apartment and the office, on the spot. They practically frisked me to make sure I wasn't taking anything."

Susan turned her head on an angle, cocked one eyebrow and said, "I remember you called asking to stay over. That was a surprise."

Wayne looked back at her. "Yeah I guess it was." He hesitated before adding, "I slept on the boat."

"Yes, I heard, from Clarence and Gus."

"And the confidential envelope I gave you that night?" he asked imploringly.

"Don't worry. It's safe. I haven't looked at it or told anyone. It's in a safe place."

Wayne heaved a sigh of relief.

"I won't even ask ..."

He managed a weak smile before saying, "Thanks. Those guys were definitely rough and have kept after me for some reason."

"Gus and Clarence told me that after you were fired some guys were down to the dock harassing you. Was that the same guys?"

"Yes it was. Two big thugs trying to pass themselves off as some sort of security company. They drive a black crew cab pickup with tinted windows. You know anything about these guys?"

"I know some guys that grew up here and have set themselves up like that. Could be them. Did they have hair clipped short, one blonde, one dark?"

"I think so," said Wayne. "It was hard to tell and I was focussed on self-preservation. They had watch caps pulled right down. Since then they've harassed me again, like just now when I was walking into town from Fairview, the same guys came after me."

"It sounds like guys I know. Be careful Wayne. Those guys are really dangerous and a bit psychotic. At least they were when we were in school. They were the kind of guys that were always in trouble, bullying everyone, pushing people around. And they were always mixed up in something illegal, you know like alcohol, drugs, knives."

"So how did they end up delivering a termination notice to a regular unsuspecting guy like me, just like a legitimate security company?" asked Wayne, leaning on the counter, trying to figure Susan out, where Susan was coming from.

"They couldn't get any real jobs. Didn't finish high school. They were just hanging around town and the receiver for the bankrupt pulp mill was looking for people to guard the place. There really wasn't much work for them at the time and the pay was good so they took it. An additional benefit was that they got access to all kinds of warehouse space and equipment. They did the job for a while and then proposed to the receiver that they form a small company and work directly under contract. The receiver liked the idea. Made life easier dealing with just one entity and reduced health and safety liabilities. So that's it. They had a security company, in the phone book and online. They got more and more small contracts but they're still the same loser thugs they always were."

"What were they using the warehouses for? Just for working on their trucks, or were they into something?"

"Nobody really knows," said Susan, shrugging her shoulders. "People just try to stay away from them. Nobody really wants to find out."

Susan reached across the counter, took Wayne's hands in hers and held them. Staring directly into his eyes she said, with concern and empathy, "You have to be careful Wayne."

Wayne was still weighing how much he could trust her. Susan knew the town and the coast having grown up here like her ancestors. And he was the newcomer. A newcomer with a past that she had just shone a spotlight on. "Okay Susan, I'll be careful." He disengaged and ran a finger across the counter. "They seem to want something from me. Wayne concentrated on the track his finger made as he added, "But I don't have anything."

"Okay, if they come around asking, I'll tell them that," said Susan shrugging again. Maybe she believed him, maybe not. She didn't mention the confidential envelope.

"What are their names?"

"The big blonde guy is Axel. The other guy is Cody. Axel's the smart one, the leader. Cody's not too bright but tough as nails and psychotic. They can both be dangerous as hell."

"Okay, thanks Susan. You've been a big help and I really appreciate it," said Wayne heading for the door.

As he pulled it open, Susan said, "How's it going with Cedar?"

Wayne turned back. "You know very well she hates my guts. Why would you ask that?"

"Just wondering if she's come around at all. See you Wayne," said Susan, smiling as she turned and walked back into the news room.

'So, Axel and Cody,' he thought to himself as he turned and pushed the door open. 'At least I know their names now.'

*****

THE CLIMB UP THE GENTLY SLOPING ROAD THROUGH THE MISTS was easy, but it was always the most difficult climb for Cedar, because of the destination. She often made this journey after finishing work at the school, on her own, alone, without parents. They were off in Mirage Inlet living out their utopian fantasies while her brother, their son, rested here in the cemetery.

At the fork in the track, just inside the cemetery entrance, she took the left hand option. Either way would work, but this was the longer route and she preferred the time with her thoughts and feelings. The silent peace of this place was soothing. She was confused and anxious about how her efforts to derail the mining company would work out. People definitely supported her, but there could also be a tragic reaction in town if the mine was forced out. There already had been a tragedy though, so why not?

As she approached the grave site, she hung her head low with closed eyes, visualizing her footsteps from memory. Opening eyes, there was her brother's headstone. Nathan. Dead at eighteen years of age. Rest in peace.

Tears flowed as grief washed over her, like it did every time. Only eighteen, he had his whole life ahead of him. And such promise. Nathan had been smart, athletic and tough. He was nine years younger than Cedar. She had looked after him while she lived at home in Mirage Inlet, being home-schooled by Starshine. He was her little project, snuffed out in an instant by falling rock at that godforsaken mine. The mine had to go. It had to be shut down. He was the source of her strength.

Cedar felt stronger on the way back down from the cemetery, strengthened by her brother's energy. But, as she walked back onto the main road there was Wayne, also headed for Fairview.

"Hi Cedar," he said, raising a hand to catch her eye, smiling pleasantly, trying to engage.

She kept her head averted. Looking toward the container terminal road and down to the Fairview wharf beyond, anywhere but at Wayne.

"Cedar, is everything okay with you?" he asked, merging his path with hers and falling into step.

"What would you care?" said Cedar, continuing to focus on the route ahead, down to Fairview. "You only care about yourself. You're in a tight spot now, but you'll change when this all blows over."

"You know, I'm in this tight spot because of you," said Wayne, trying a different tack.

"What the hell is that supposed to mean? Now you're blaming me for all your problems?"

"No, no. I'm not blaming you for anything. I mean, when I saw what the mine was doing out there, and I saw you and your parents, I had to write a report that included everything, the truth. The owner of my company suspected that and he warned me, telling me to shovel the same old crap to the regulators. But after seeing what the mine was doing to you, I couldn't do it."

"Aren't you the perfect little white knight then," said Cedar with heavy sarcasm.

"No not at all," said Wayne. "I know I've done things in the past that weren't perfect, but for me it was always abstract. I never had to look the affected people in the eye."

"So I guess this was a real revelation."

"Yes it was, for sure. Anyway, I knew I'd probably get fired if I sent in an accurate report." He paused before adding, "Which I did, and I got fired."

Cedar looked at Wayne intently. "That's quite admirable Wayne. But it doesn't really help us. They've already brought in another person to replace you. That Bruno guy. He'll just do what you wouldn't do, send in a misleading report."

"I guess you're right in some sense."

They walked on in silence. The ferry from Digby Island came in and the airport shuttle bus rolled up the ramp and past them, carrying passengers from the Vancouver flight into town. The airport crew followed in a van. That was all. Cedar watched them go by.

She knew Wayne was trying to reach out to her. She knew she needed help, at least someone to talk to. But most of all, she needed someone to trust and Wayne had not met that criterion. There was no way she could trust someone with such a long history of deception and manipulation.

Cedar considered Wayne for a bit, thinking, watching, and then asked, "Where are you from anyway Wayne? We know about your consulting work but not much about you. Wayne the person."

"Grew up in Toronto."

"That explains a lot," said Cedar with a bit of a smile, to which Wayne laughed.

At the canteen, Wayne held the door for her. It was mid-afternoon and there was no one else inside. Mary and Ole would be along later to take them back across the harbour. Wayne bought coffee for them both. At the table they each stared off into opposing ceiling corners waiting to see what, if anything, the other one had to say.

Eventually Cedar started. "Why did you do work like that Wayne? It must have bothered you. Must have been a pretty empty existence."

"It's sort of like a drug, Cedar. You get addicted to the rush."

"I don't understand. What rush? It's just work."

"Well you start off with a task to do, a job to complete. That was me at UBC Grad School, getting my PhD. When you succeed at that, it feels good. So you try again. The tougher the job, the better you feel, the bigger the rush. And it's always a competition with the other guys, the other grad students for grants and then the other companies for contracts. There's no option but to win. That's how you feel anyway."

Cedar looked at her mug, then at her ceiling corner again. "Don't blame me, but that seems pretty stupid and self-destructive. I never had a chance to enter that world, so I don't know. We've been living up here out of the mainstream my whole life, so I've been sheltered from those things."

"Depends how a person grows up I guess," said Wayne, relaxing and becoming more retrospective. "My father is a prof at U of T. My mother's in the society fund raising world. They have to impress people all the time. I wasn't overtly pushed to climb the system, it was just always there. No other options." Wayne stared out the window considering what he just said, then snapped out of it and shifted his attention to her. "Why were you coming down that road Cedar?"

She looked shocked at the question and then stared down into nothing. Tangles of hair shielded her face, her eyes. Without looking up, "How can you ask me that? Haven't you ever been up there?"

"No. I haven't. I don't know what's up there." After a pause Wayne said, "I'm very sorry if I've said something hurtful. If I've offended you."

Cedar raised her head, pushed her hair away from her face and with teary eyes said, "That's the cemetery."

Wayne waited. The question was there, hanging in the air between them, and Cedar knew it.

"My brother is up there," she said and hung her head again.

"I'm so sorry Cedar. I didn't know." Not knowing what else to do, he did nothing.

Cedar looked around, then at Wayne. "He died at only eighteen."

Wayne's eyes widened.

"I think I'm starting to understand you and your family more."

"No you don't. You don't understand the half of it." Cedar rose from her chair, to go. She had seen Mary's old Volvo drive in and park.

"Time to go Wayne."

"Cedar, I can help you with the mine. More than you know. More than anyone else can."

"Have to go now. I'm afraid I just don't trust you."

*****

"STU, WHAT'S GOING ON DOWN THERE?" SAID WAYNE, TALKING into the cell phone, looking around the cove from his skipper's stool.

"Oh hey Wayne. Glad you called," said Stu. "I'm over at Kathy's place right now. Your stuff is here. What do you want me to do with it?"

"Can you just take it and hold it for me 'til I can get back down there?"

"I don't know Wayne. It's a lot of stuff. I don't have room."

"Can you do anything? Maybe just put it in a storage locker for me for a month or so?" asked Wayne, his frustration and angst showing through.

"That's a lot for me to do Wayne. I don't have a truck. It's just a little Hyundai, the smallest they make. You know I prefer the small cars. Are you going to send me money to rent a truck and a locker?"

"Yeah, I know. I can't get money to you that fast. I've got a bit of a situation up here. Got fired. Bunch of nasty people trying to track me down. I'm living on a boat away from town." Wayne took a gulp from his morning instant coffee, black, thinking he really needed to get that background taste out of the on board water tank. Better add it to the list.

"Holy shit, Wayne. You're really in a mess. Look, most of this is just stuff. Why don't I get the things I think are important to you and keep them at my place for a while? And by that I mean small things. Like your degrees, letters, bank records, things that are financial, sentimental and, most important, portable."

"Yeah, that's the only thing we can do, I suppose. I don't really need the couch, the bed, the television, my office clothes, things like that." Wayne could see how things would turn out and finally just capitulated.

"Good for you Wayne. That's the spirit. You have to let go of that stuff. It can always be replaced. It'll just weigh you down."

"Why is Kathy in such a hurry anyway?"

"I figure she just wants to close that door, you know. I think she wants to move on."

"I guess. Is there someone else moving in Stu?"

"I didn't want to say anything buddy, but I think there might be."

"Who is it?" asked Wayne, grimacing, running the potential candidates through his mind, considering whether or not Stu was actually one of them. He tentatively dismissed Stu, on the grounds that Kathy had always found him annoying and disgusting. He recalled her saying something like, 'Stu's an idiot. Can't you get rid of him?' from time to time.

There was a long pause at the other end. "Not sure Wayne."

"Well whoever it is, I hope he enjoys my things. She doesn't make very much as an office assistant. Without my things the apartment would be bare. Maybe my clothes will fit him too."

"That's the spirit. I'll grab what I can and get you the hell out of here. You'll do better next time. Never liked her anyway."

Wayne clicked off and tossed his cell onto the dash where it landed with a dull clunk. He sat back on the wheelhouse stool, sipped coffee and surveyed his situation. The surface of the cove was glassy smooth. Current from the beginnings of a flood tide oriented the *Molly B* facing west and tiny surface eddies meandered listlessly past the boat.

He looked out the back of the wheelhouse at the dinghy lying on deck, with an outboard and tank lying beside it. Ole had dropped off the outboard, saying it was a loaner and Wayne didn't have to pay. He had left a full tank of gas too. Ole said he understood Wayne was going through a tough time and wanted to help.

The weather was calm. 'Why not do some exploring and try some fishing?' He reached for his phone and punched in Susan's number.

"Hey Susan, what are you doing?"

"Wayne, hello. I'm over at Metlakatla. Working on a story, but I'm visiting too."

"Oh." Wayne processed the information and adjusted his notional plans. "Oh well. I just thought ..."

"What's up Wayne? You sound a bit down."

"Oh nothing much. I had to get out of town so I'm over here anchored in Crippen Cove for now. I don't really know what to do. And my ex, down in Vancouver, is basically throwing all my belongings out on the street or in some dumpster or something."

"Geez Wayne I'm really sorry. What are you going to do?"

"I don't know," said Wayne in a low voice, tailing off into nothing. "Since you're busy, I guess I'll just go exploring in my dinghy."

"I could catch a ride back to town with you."

"Actually, I think right now it's better if I just avoid town. Thanks anyway though."

"Okay Wayne. Keep in touch. I wouldn't want anything bad to happen to you." Susan clicked off.

Wayne put the phone back down on the dash and to keep busy packed up the loose things in the boat to keep them secure for when he'd get underway again, sometime. He started up the engine and hydraulics and lowered the dinghy. Then he lowered Ole's outboard as the dinghy bumped up against *Molly B*'s hull. With the gas tank in place he was ready to go exploring.

He climbed down into the dinghy, untied the lines and pushed away from the *Molly B*'s wooden hull. Wayne pulled the starter cord and the old outboard sprang to life. He opened up the throttle and the dinghy climbed laboriously up onto the step and then onto a gentle plane. Wayne steered out of Crippen Cove, with the chart on his knees, and headed for a hidden cove that looked like it might be good for anchoring out of the way, and maybe to avoid detection. There was no way of guessing what might come next from those thugs in town.

*****

THE EMAIL NOTIFICATION CAUGHT TED'S ATTENTION immediately. He closed the file he was working on and opened the message from Bruno. There was a large file attached.

This was the report he'd been waiting for. The email message was short and inconsequential, other than to document the source attribution. Ted opened the file.

He read through the report quickly. It was the usual information, basically a reworked version of the previous reports, with updated data and photos. They showed everything functioning as planned and in compliance with provincial permits. Wayne's incriminating information and photos no longer appeared.

Ted was pleased. This was how things were supposed to work. Churn out the same old information over and over again, and get paid a fortune for it. He thought to himself what a great gig he had. What a great way to make lots of money. Then he got to the new section Bruno had included. The section documenting new equipment and cyanide drums on site. He read through the section. It was still pretty high level, not a lot of detail that could hang him. Suddenly his state of consulting euphoria began to fade, like a balloon with a slow leak, like an addict coming down from a high. The worry began to creep in again.

"Kaye."

"Yes boss," said Kaye back into the intercom.

"Get me Ian on the phone. Ian over at New Discovery. I need to talk with him right away."

"Okay boss"

The call came back connecting him. "Ian, good morning."

"What is it? I am going to get my report today, yes?" Ian was direct, to the point, curt.

"I have it right here. It just came in from Bruno. I have a question for you though. What's happening with this cyanide and equipment showing up?"

"What do you mean Ted?"

"Well, this is new, and Bruno refers to it in his report. What are you guys doing up there? And what should I do?"

"This is what I mentioned the other day. Our ore grades are diminishing. The gold vein we started with is being exhausted so we have to start mining and processing ore with lower gold concentrations. To do that we have to start an on-site cyanidation process so we're not shipping out so much material for off-site gold recovery. You know all about cyanidation, we've done it before at other mines."

"Right," said, Ted tentative but noticeably frustrated. "Does the province know about this? Has this been approved?"

"Those provincial guys know the mining world. They know something like this is always the inevitable next step as the hot spot is mined out and some capital is built up from initial mine production."

"Yes. I suppose you're right. It's just that I'm feeling a little exposed here."

"This is just a pilot-scale operation, to see if we can make cyanidation work and to see what it might take to scale up. If this is successful then we'll expand it and everyone will make money. You'll make money Ted. There's more work for you in this and your New Discovery Gold shares will go up. Good things for everyone."

"So what do you want me to do Ian?"

"You're the consultant. What do you think you should do?"

"I'll take out reference to the cyanide and the equipment from the report. We'll just include the right camera angles to miss those items. How's that?"

"Whatever you think is best. Just get me that report today."

After the call, Ted recorded the conversation in his journal and called directly to Bruno in the Prince Rupert office. "Bruno, thanks for the report, it's great."

Bruno waited for the next thing Ted would say.

"Thanks boss."

"Look Bruno, I just got off the phone with the client. He wants us to remove the references to cyanide and the equipment. If you could delete that information and only include photos from camera angles that avoid those items that would finish the report so I can send it."

"Okay boss. It's your call. I'll get right on it."

"Good. Send it to me early this afternoon. It has to go to New Discovery this afternoon.

"Okay, I'm on it. Anything else?"

"No that's it."

There was a pause at the other end. Ted was about to hang up when Bruno said, "Ted, what's up with Wayne and these security guys? The whole thing is kind of creepy."

Ted was surprised and disturbed by the question. No one had ever asked him about the security tactics before. "Don't worry about it Bruno. It doesn't affect you at this time. I'll let you know if I need your help with that."

The revised report came in at one o'clock on the dot. Ted quickly read it and signed off for Kaye to send it to Ian Verster. He waited half an hour and then called over.

"Ian, you have the report now. Everything okay?"

"Got it Ted and its perfect. I'm sending it to the provincial regulators now."

"Ian, any chance of getting our invoices paid up?"

"This is your lucky day Ted. I'll have a cheque this afternoon."

"That's good news. How about we get together for a drink? Four o'clock at Ramparts?"

"Sounds good. I'll bring the cheque, but you can buy the drinks."

"Done," said Ted.

TWELVE

A MUFFLED CLANG FROM THE BOAT'S RELIC ALARM CLOCK RATTLED from where it was jammed between mattress and rail. It was dark in the boat and, rolling out of the berth, Wayne fumbled around before finding his head lamp. Up in the wheelhouse he pushed the switch to turn over the engine. The diesel coughed and wheezed and then sprang to life, the thumping heartbeat of *Molly B.* It was pitch black in the pre-dawn, the darkest, coldest time of the diurnal cycle. He descended back into the forepeak to dress and put on deck boots.

Outside, Wayne flicked on the hydraulics and edged forward along the side decks, slippery from the moisture of low hanging mist. Looking around from the foredeck, there was no sign of morning light behind the mountains to the east. There were no signs of any boats either, no running lights. He reached down and engaged the anchor winch that sprang to life with a whirring noise, the hydraulic fluids waiting for his command.

After confirming the chain was free, he drew the hydraulic control back and watched as the winch turned. Chain clanked through the bow chock, over the capstan and down through the hawse pipe to its locker below. Wayne grimaced at the noise, but there was no choice. He couldn't move the boat without incurring that awful noise. It was one of the many trade-offs he seemed to be making.

With the anchor raised and secure, Wayne shuffled his way back down to the after deck and the external controls mounted on the rear of the wheelhouse. He put the small outside wheel hard over and engaged the prop. A current of prop wash boiled up from below the stern and the boat moved forward, angling to starboard out of Crippen Cove. Grindstone light was the only visible feature ahead until he cleared the rock that the concrete and steel tower was anchored to. He kept it to starboard. The lights of three freighters anchored in the harbour came into view, and beyond were the bright lights of Prince Rupert. The container terminal lit up the shoreline southwest of Fairview, floodlights blazing, working around the clock to turn the huge ships back to China, or Japan, or wherever. The *Molly B* displayed no lights, invisible as it skirted along the harbour's north shore through the oily black and cold North Pacific water.

Once clear of Grindstone, Wayne stepped inside the wheelhouse and flipped on the radar and depth sounder. The cove he had checked out was small with a restricted entrance, perfect for hiding but tricky to get into in the dark. He slipped along the shore, unconcerned by the morning mist that clung there, low to the water, watching the radar and sounder displays.

The cove entrance glowed orange on the radar screen. He made the turn north, to port, and throttled back. The engine revs dropped and the bow wave disappeared as the boat's fine entry cut through the water like a sharp knife. The cove entrance was invisible but he cruised ahead confidently following his reconnaissance the previous afternoon, revelling in the feel of cruising in the pre-dawn darkness, the primal solitude. The bottom came up fast on the depth sounder as he slipped over the low tide shallow sill of the narrow entrance to the greater depth inside. He shifted into neutral to allow *Molly B* to glide into a perfect anchoring spot.

Wayne threw the gears into reverse and revved the engine to stop the boat on a dime. Throwing it back into neutral he hurried forward and lowered the anchor. Chain rattled through the hawse pipe and bow chock as the anchor dropped, splashing into the water and descending to its muddy repose. He went back to the controls and reversed thrust again, setting the anchor flukes in the primordial clay below.

Molly B settled happily into her new, temporary home. She languished close around the slack anchor chain, suspended on a ghostly surface in the pre-dawn calm. Wayne crouched, sitting on the winch, and from the foredeck surveyed the eastern sky where faint light was beginning to show grey through the cloud cover. The light would be coming soon and he had moved the boat, seemingly undetected.

In the early morning grey, Wayne launched the dinghy with boom and hydraulics, checked the outboard again and loaded the gas tank. He zipped up his Floater jacket and stepped down into the dinghy. On the third pull the outboard started. He pushed off and headed back out the cove opening barely visible through the dim light and mist. He wanted to run directly across the harbour to town in the dark, undetected, so no one would know where his home in *Molly B* was cached away.

The Rushbrook government wharf was beginning to stir when he arrived. Full dawn had finally arrived and some fishermen were starting out. He pulled into a spot on the floats near the ramp up to the wharf above, steep in the low tide.

Walking over to downtown he saw that only a few people were up, construction types. Wayne didn't recognize any of the trucks or occupants that passed by. He stopped in at the coffe shop that was just opening, for breakfast and a coffee. Inside was Bruno, sitting in the back corner by himself. Wayne picked up coffee and a huckleberry scone and went to the chair Bruno pushed out with his boot. He sat.

"So Bruno. How do you like it?"

Bruno looked at him. Trying to appear puzzled by the question. "Like what?"

Wayne took a bite and a slow draw on his coffee. "You know, my apartment, Prince Rupert, New Discovery Gold, the new Ted. Any one of those or all together, your choice. How do you like it?"

"Oh that. It's good. You know. It's a job. I guess I like it."

"All of it?" asked Wayne, taking another bite and drink, staring steadily into Bruno with a grin, baiting him.

"Yeah sure, why the hell wouldn't I? Pay's good. I'm on my own. No one to bother me," said Bruno, now avoiding Wayne's stare.

"You're really something aren't you Bruno." Wayne finished his scone and took another pull on the coffee. "I'm surprised you even come into this coffee shop. The vibe and clientele here are pretty back to the land, environmentalist even, wouldn't you say."

At that moment, as if on cue, Cedar and Mary entered. Wayne turned his head and looked as they ordered coffee and yogurt with granola. He gave a slight wave to which Cedar responded with a sharp turn of her head, away. The two women sat by the windows on the opposite side of the shop, their attention focussed on the few passersby outside.

"I like to check out the hippie chicks," said Bruno with a wry grin. "It's like travelling back in time. I see you do too."

"Shut up Bruno," said Wayne, finishing his coffee. "They're nice people, those two."

"Yeah, well, that younger one, she's the one that organized the public meeting. She's trying to get the mine shut down. So she's the opposition. She's basically trying to take my job away, her and her friend there. So, I don't really think they're all that nice."

"Maybe they think that you're not very nice."

"I don't really care what they think. I just don't like those back to the land hippie squatters."

"Well that younger one, she and her family live out there in Mirage Inlet. They're the ones that'll be ruined if the tailings dam breaches or worse poisoned by cyanide."

"Not really my problem," said Bruno, pushing back his chair to leave.

"Well they're the reason I'm fired," said Wayne turning on his chair to watch Bruno.

"What?" said Bruno sitting back down. "You mean they got you fired."

"No you idiot. I mean that after looking them in the eye, and knowing what's happening at the mine, I just couldn't send in another one of those stupid bogus reports Ted insists on. I sent in a good professional report and got fired."

"That's not why he fired you is it? I thought you were just slacking off, riding your reputation and Ted didn't think he was getting his money's worth anymore."

"Open your eyes buddy boy. Same thing happened to Ron. Ted's in deep on this one. He's been covering for that mine since the beginning and now things have gone so far he's really in a bind. He could be fined or go to jail if things go really wrong."

"That's bullshit, Wayne. You're just bitter. He thinks you kept copies of everything, you know. Did you?"

"No, of course not. That would be unethical, maybe even illegal. You know me better than that," said Wayne, as Bruno stood again to leave.

"See you later buddy boy. I've got to go to my job at the office," said Bruno stepping away from the table. He left, staring at Cedar on the way out.

Wayne went up to the counter and bought another cup of coffee. On the way back to sit down he stopped by the table where Cedar and Mary were seated. Cedar looked at him with a hostile stare.

"Hello Wayne," said Mary trying to be hospitable. "We didn't seen you over at Fairview this morning."

"Yeah, I've been busying myself on the boat," said Wayne, looking at Mary and avoiding Cedar's icy stare. "I see you stopped in for coffee before going to work."

"Yes, we're early today and Cedar took the day off to plan the next meeting."

"What's wrong with you?" said Cedar, finally exploding. "You were just talking to that consultant jerk, the guy who replaced you. I was beginning to think you might be okay, and then I see you conspiring with that guy. Just get out of here. Get away from us and leave us in peace."

She was furious and getting more and more upset. Wayne could see that there was nothing to be done so he went back to his table and sat down, to try and enjoy what was left of his coffee.

*****

CEDAR AND MARY, CHATTING AND DRINKING THEIR COFFEE, looked blankly out the window. There were no passersby. The table between them, an old slab of sawn fir worn smooth by time and customers, served as a resting place for coffee cups and elbows.

"That guy Wayne is such a jerk," said Cedar, gazing out through the myriad of individual panes, the frames needing a fresh coat of red paint. "He was being nice the other day. I was almost starting to think he cared. But then, today, he's sneaking in here early in the morning for some sort of breakfast meetup with his replacement. Probably telling the new guy how to isolate us. How to make sure we leave the property out there."

"Maybe," said Mary raising a questioning eyebrow.

"Well we're not going to leave, and that's that. We're going to get that mine shut down." Cedar slapped her hand down on the wood for emphasis.

Mary raised a hand to calm Cedar and said, "Look Cedar, just because he was talking to the guy, doesn't mean he's plotting with them. Maybe he just came in for coffee and the new guy was there. We don't know."

"That's just too much of a coincidence. And the way that new guy was looking at us, at me and then talking about us. It was just creepy," said Cedar shivering.

"I know Cedar. I know you're upset. But maybe that Wayne guy actually wants to help. Just don't completely close your mind okay."

"Are you turning on me too?" said Cedar sharply and then with regret she added. "Oh sorry, I didn't mean that Mary. You know that right?"

"I know you didn't," said Mary, changing her attention to focus on a group coming up to the café door. "Look here comes Jimi with that woman from Sustainable People or whatever that group was called. I think Caitlyn was her name. I'm going to leave you now, have to get to work. Hope you have a productive day and I'll see you out at Fairview after work."

Cedar watched Mary leave and Caitlyn, Jimi and another new person step through the door. Jimi brought them over to her table. She greeted Jimi and acknowledged Caitlyn. The new person didn't register. Jimi collected chairs from the other tables and the group circled Cedar's table.

"So Jimi, how's the opposition going?" asked Cedar trying to manoeuvre herself and her chair to avoid being encircled.

Caitlyn answered for him with a big smile. "Well hello there Cedar. I'm really glad we can get together again. We've raised a few thousand already on our crowdfunding site and luckily our videographer was available this week. This is Shannon, she came up on a flight from Vancouver last night. She's staying with me at the Crest Hotel."

"Hello Caitlyn, so nice to see you again." Cedar nodded acknowledgement of Shannon. "What's the name of your GoFundMe campaign?"

"The name of the initiative is 'Stop Mining from Destroying Communities'", said Caitlyn smiling proudly at Cedar and then at Shannon.

"That doesn't mention our little community that I'm trying to save. It doesn't mention New Discovery Gold, Mirage Inlet, the North Coast, or even British Columbia," said Cedar, looking at Jimi questioningly. "What's up Jimi?" Jimi shrugged and passed off to Caitlyn.

"Well," said Caitlyn still smiling and talking fast, "the people back at headquarters told us it would be more effective to leave it broad, to capture as many donors as we can. This is a real opportunity and they didn't want anyone to feel left out."

"It's just very vague," said Cedar, agitated and perplexed, still trying to make room for herself and avoid being encircled or smothered.

"Well we ran it by Jimi. He's very excited about the whole plan. And Shannon likes it," said Caitlyn, connecting directly into Shannon's big blue eyes with familiarity. "Shannon's onside and ready to roll, as they say."

"They don't really say that crap Caitlyn," said Shannon gently laughing and touching Caitlyn's hand. Cedar noticed these were the first words she had spoken.

Cedar also noticed that Wayne was still seated in the opposite corner.

"I can't believe the people up here allowed this mine to go ahead," said Caitlyn looking around the café to assess the local people. "Boy the locals really got sucked in."

Shannon jumped in saying, "Yeah, you'd think they would know what's going on. Doesn't anyone up here read the paper, look at the news on television? It's everywhere what these companies do."

"I guess no one up here knows how the environmental assessment process really works" said Caitlyn, clearly talking down to any locals that might be listening. "Kind of crazy don't you think? What happened here Cedar?"

Cedar was taken aback. On the one hand she didn't approve of the mine but on the other hand she didn't like outsiders treating people of the north coast like they were idiots.

"They came in here promising all kinds of money and jobs. We just lost the pulp mill and the fishing, and people were desperate for something to pin their hopes to. Those of us who opposed it didn't really have a chance to speak up because of the way the process was railroaded through." Cedar paused for a moment, looking around the table and finally back at Caitlyn. "But I don't really appreciate the way you're talking about the people that live up here, my neighbours and friends. We don't need to be told what to do by a bunch of know-it-alls from Toronto, or Vancouver, or wherever else your people are from."

Cedar shifted in her chair, pulling her homespun toque down over her auburn tangle, looking out the window and then around the café. She noticed that Wayne was watching from his corner, eyebrows raised, and quickly looked away out the window again.

"Anyway," said Caitlyn unfazed by the push back, "we need to get going to undo this. Shannon wants to interview people in town."

Shannon leaned forward and jumped into the conversation. "That's right, I'd like to get footage of local people, mainly those who are opposed to the mine, but maybe some supporters as well, to show what they're like and just to leave the impression that this is a somewhat balanced piece."

Caitlyn nodded, adding, "We would logically start with you of course Cedar, and work outward from there."

"My parents should come first."

"Of course, if that's what you'd like. Have they done any on camera work before? This can be a bit intimidating for anyone not used to speaking in front of people," said Shannon becoming animated over the work.

"They're not inarticulate idiots if that's what you mean."

"No not at all," said Shannon, sitting back again and pushing blue tinged bangs out of her eyes. "I'm sure they're fine. We could start with them. Let's do that."

"When can we get started?" asked Caitlyn. "We only have Shannon for a couple of days so we'll have to move quickly. Cedar, when can we interview your parents?"

"You can do that any time. You'll just have to book a charter plane." Out of the corner of her eye Cedar caught Wayne smirking as he winked at her. "Do that as soon as possible. It's coming up to herring season and the planes get booked up by the fishing skippers."

Shannon looked at Caitlyn. Now she was confused. "You mean they don't live here in town?"

"No they live out at Mirage Inlet, that's the whole point of our initiative. They live downslope, downstream from the tailings pond," said Cedar impatiently. "What did you think the point was?"

Shannon looked over at Caitlyn, playing with the printed Haida motif silk scarf around her neck. "Caitlyn, I thought we were just on an anti-mining campaign? That's right isn't it?"

"Of course that's right," replied Caitlyn, fussing with her own scarf and fine wool sweater. "This mine is the start and it's very important. Cedar, when can your parents come in to town for an interview?"

"I don't know. Maybe you should call them on the short wave radio," said Cedar matter of factly, taking charge to demonstrate how things were done in her world. "That's how they communicate. They have a sat phone for emergencies but it's not usually turned on."

"You mean there's no cell phone service?" asked Caitlyn, incredulously. "Jimi this is getting complicated."

Cedar laughed derisively and caught Wayne's wink out of the corner of her eye before turning away again, quickly.

"You mean to tell me that you have no plans to go out to the mine site?" asked Cedar who was now the incredulous one.

"Jimi didn't tell us we needed to. There's no money in our budget to fly the team out there. Doesn't anyone have pictures?" she asked looking at Jimi who shrugged and then at Cedar.

At this point, Wayne got up to leave. Passing Cedar's table he said, "I've got pictures. Lots of them. Some video too."

Cedar looked at Wayne and said, "I don't care what you say you've got. You're just a shill for industry. Anything from you would just hurt us. Why don't you get the hell out of town, or better yet go kill yourself, drown or something."

The others looked away, uneasy with the confrontation and embarrassed, as Wayne calmly pushed his way out the door.

"What was that?" asked Shannon looking at Cedar. "I don't know if I can work with so much hostility.

Caitlyn added, "It's so important that everyone in this project is professional and measured in their communications. Audiences for our funding programs tend not to respond to this kind of emotional outburst, unless it is from the general crowd at a demonstration or on a blockade."

"This whole thing is getting weird," said Cedar as she shrugged her shoulders and looked at Jimi with exasperated questions in her eyes. "Dave and Starshine would not be happy. I know that. You know it too." She started to leave. Jimi did not move.

"You know Cedar, we are your best hope," said Caitlyn, as Cedar walked to the door. "We're professionals in this business. We do this kind of thing all the time. We know what we're doing."

"I don't know if you've ever fixed anything," said Cedar pushing on the door. "You raise lots of money for yourselves, but you depend on the mining industry for it. Without fundraising based on the industry you might have to get a real job somewhere. What does that make you?" The door closed behind her.

*****

"HEY CLARENCE, YOU IN THERE?" YELLED WAYNE, POUNDING ON the hull.

"Yeah, yeah I'm here. Just a minute. Geez, I wish people wouldn't pound on the hull like that. Never know what might happen. Could have a heart attack or somethin'." Clarence's grumbling complaints emanated from somewhere deep within the bowels of the boat.

Wayne hauled on the mooring line, pulling the boat closer and climbed aboard. He was sitting in a moulded white plastic patio chair on the cluttered afterdeck when Clarence emerged from the deck house.

"Geez Wayne, you scared the hell out of me. I was really concentrating. Doing my income tax on the paper forms, you know what a mess that is. Damn government trying to take my pogey back. Anyway, how the hell have you been? Where the hell have you been? Haven't seen you for days."

"I've been around. Let's go inside," said Wayne rising from the chair and setting it back in place on the deck.

"So, you don't want to be seen on my deck, eh?" said Clarence moving inside. "Don't blame you. It's a mess. Wayne are you trying to stay low? After those guys came onto your boat?"

"Yeah, I am," said Wayne, trying to clear off space for himself in the galley. "I feel like they've been following me around. They threatened me again a few days ago. Pushing me around with their truck, if you can believe it. Bumped me from behind so I had to step behind a light post."

Clarence grimaced and shook his head. "You feel like coffee?"

Wayne looked into Clarence's own mug of acrid black liquid, the congealed can of condensed milk on the table, and declined. "Nah, thanks anyway. I just came from the coffee shop. Had enough for a while," said Wayne trying to be polite and respectful. "Hey Clarence, what do you know about those guys anyway? The guys that tried to break into my boat?"

"Oh those boys. They've been around town for a long while," said Clarence leaning up against the bulkhead. "Grew up here. They were terrors in school. Always gettin' in trouble with teachers and even the police from time to time. Go by Axel, he's the leader, and Cody, he's the follower."

"Yeah well they're the guys that delivered the notice firing me from the consulting company. Said they were from a security company hired by my boss."

"Yeah you told me and Gus. That's a pretty rough boss."

"For sure. He didn't even have the guts to fire me on the phone. Let alone look me in the eye. Those two guys have been after me ever since. When they threatened me, they accused me of having stolen materials from the company. Copies of records, and such."

"Did you?"

"Nah, I didn't steal anything," said Wayne, dismissing the notion as nonsense with a flip of his his hand. "Just took my own stuff." The boat rocked a little as Gus climbed over the rail. He entered the cabin and pushed Wayne over as he slid onto the bench at the galley table.

"So Wayne, you takin' good care of my rifle and pistol?" asked Gus as he settled himself on the bench, placing his elbows on the galley table.

"You bet. They're stored safe on the boat."

"Good, you keep 'em close. Should be carrying the pistol on you if you ask me. Don't know where you're holed up. Don't want to know."

Wayne chatted back and forth with the two men. He learned that the two security guys were based out at the industrial park, using an old shipping container converted for an office and storage. Gus said now they provide security for business people out there, all very sketchy.

"They're in the phone book," said Gus accepting the steaming cup of coffee proffered by Clarence. "That's probably where your boss got their company name and number."

"The whole thing is crazy," said Wayne starting to extricate himself past Gus on the bench. "Well guys, I think I'm going to push off. I've got the day to kill. I don't want to go back until dusk, til it's dark. Don't want people watching where I'm going."

Gus rose to let him wedge his way out. "Good plan".

The museum was interesting and Wayne killed time there looking through the exhibits of Tsimshian artifacts and art. The history of developers raping and pillaging the waters, the landscape and the culture was laid bare in detail.

Up the hill, he found the library was basically empty, with the exception of a primary class on a reading field trip from school down the street. Wayne disappeared into the stacks upstairs, browsing for books with photos showing local history. He found photos of Crippen Cove, the quarantine hospital at Dodge Cove, boatyards, hippies from the seventies. He half expected to see Dave and Starshine in that book but didn't. So much to consider and he had been part of the ongoing destruction, not here specifically but in so many other projects across the country.

People did not look up when Wayne entered the waterfront bar late in the day. He didn't recognize anyone and that was the way he wanted it. Sitting on a bar stool he ordered a draft beer, whatever was on tap, and fish and chips. The menu said halibut and he ordered it. A basketball game was on one television above the bar, and hockey on the other. Wayne stared at them without caring who was playing or the score.

"Hey, you're Wayne aren't you," said the guy sitting on the stool next to him who said his name was Jeff. "I have the office across the hall from yours." He was an accountant or bookkeeper or something. Wayne had never paid much attention to him.

"Yeah," said Wayne, thinking 'what's it to you?'

"I'm just taking a break. It's tax time and this shit just kills me. Needed a drink before I go back for the rest of the evening." Jeff ordered a double Scotch on the rocks.

"I won't be in the office anymore," said Wayne, taking a long pull from his beer and staring straight ahead at the multi-coloured liquor bottles behind the bar. "Got fired."

The guy looked over at him, eyebrows raised in questions. "Thought I'd seen some new guy going in and out of that office. Door's closed all the time so it's hard to tell. Don't even really know what you guys do."

"Environmental consulting. Mining company work in that office right now," said Wayne as his fish and chips arrived. He shook salt over the potatoes and squeezed ketchup into a mound in the centre of the plate.

"Wow that's a drag, getting fired. What'd you do? Really screw something up, I guess."

"Yeah I guess some would look at it that way," said Wayne, taking a bite of the halibut in beer batter and savouring it. The beer and talking to someone, effectively a stranger, loosened him up. "You always drink Scotch when you do peoples' taxes?"

"Yeah, clears the head," said Jeff smiling grimly, ordering another.

"You gonna eat?" asked Wayne crunching down on a French fry.

"Nah, why bother? What's your deal anyway Wayne? What're you gonna do, leave town?

"Good question I guess. I'm going through a bit of a retrospective phase right now. Thinking about making some changes," said Wayne, cutting off another piece of halibut and sliding it into his mouth. The fish was delicious. He washed it down with more beer.

"How so? Sounds a little new age doesn't it. Wouldn't have expected that from a guy like you."

"I had plans Jeff, back at UBC in grad school. Thought I'd get a PhD and then go on to some tenured research position at DFO in Nanaimo or the Institute in Pat Bay, or maybe even at one of the west coast universities.

"Department of Fisheries and Oceans, yeah. Good plan. Everybody hates them," said Jeff taking a drink, leaning on his elbows propped on the bar.

"Didn't work out," said Wayne, savouring another French fry. "I got lured into consulting. You know some valuable one-off contracts, lots of money, fast. People thought I was smart and I got hooked. The consulting rush was addictive. But that rat race wears you down, always hustling for the next contract, doing as little work as possible for the most money and never getting ahead."

"Sounds like an accounting firm," said Jeff with a weak chuckle, leaning his head on one hand.

"Yeah I guess. Anyway, that was that. Years of hard work and stress only to be fired by a slimy loser like Ted Murdoch."

"Screw Ted," said Jeff, raising his glass high and taking a drink.

"I've been on the move from one project to the next for years. Never settled enough to have a serious relationship. The last one, Kathy, was the most serious. Who knows who's moving in with her now," said Wayne, draining the last of his beer, waiting for the dregs to drip into his mouth, ordering another.

"Screw Kathy," said Jeff taking another drink.

"Maybe. Someone else is, I guess," said Wayne, pausing again and staring at himself in the mirror behind the liquor bottles opposite.

Jeff finished his drink and said, "Time to go back to work," as he slid off the stool.

*****

WAYNE FINISHED HIS FISH AND MOPPED UP THE REMAINING ketchup with the last chip. He drained the beer glass and ordered another.

Leaving the bar, he noticed the light had faded, but there was still a bit of brightness in the western sky, and some reflected illumination on the far shore. Looking carefully all around, there was no sign of a strange vehicle, especially that black pickup that had bumped him. 'Must be getting paranoid.' He walked along the waterfront, past the fish plant and over to Rushbrook where he'd tied the dinghy that morning. He looked all around again, confirming his own paranoia, before descending the ramp. He pulled the cord and the outboard started.

Before clearing the Rushbrook breakwater, Wayne looked back and saw a black pickup under the light, high up on the government wharf. When he looked back again after clearing the breakwater, the truck was gone. There were no running lights on the dinghy.

Wayne strategized the crossing back to his boat. It was imperative not to reveal *Molly B*'s location. He decided to motor along the Prince Rupert shore, down to Fairview and then cut across to Dodge Cove. Hand on the outboard tiller, Wayne pulled his watch cap out of a pocket and pulled it down tight over his dishevelled hair with the other hand. He hunkered down into the collar of the Floater jacket and settled in for the ride. The night air was damp and chilled his body right through as he watched the shore and steered toward the dim light in the western sky.

At Fairview, a crab boat pulled away from its government float and moved through black water of the fishing harbour. It cleared the floating breakwater behind Wayne. Wayne could see the running lights and the phosphorescence of the bow wave, reassured by the presence of another boat on the water.

He made the turn to take him west over to the cove on Digby Island. From there he could either make his way along the island shore to the other side of the harbour, or wait in the cove. He looked back but couldn't see the crab boat. He thought nothing of it. Vision and perspective played tricks at dusk.

Approaching Dodge Cove he had a decision to make. Go into the cove or continue toward Grindstone light and maybe *Molly B* on the far shore. While he weighed the options, the crab boat suddenly appeared. It had been travelling fast with its running lights off. Suddenly the running lights were turned on. Bow mounted headlights flashed on and Wayne was fully illuminated.

The crab boat came at him from a forty five degree angle off his bow at full speed, its radar turning on top of the deck house. He held up a hand to shield his eyes from the glare. It was perhaps ten boat lengths away, charging out of the darkness. Wayne tried to avoid it. It clipped his dinghy on the starboard bow. Wayne thought he saw a dark figure on the afterdeck. He thought he heard yelling, "Get out of town," but couldn't be sure. He was gone.

Salt water struck his face like a plank when he hit. Black and cold it welcomed him in, wrapping tight like a black shroud, shocking lungs and heart. Stunned he sank into its depths.

THIRTEEN

THE BOAT WAS DAMAGED IN THE BOW BUT PLOWED ON, THE outboard unaffected by loss of a hand on the tiller. Wayne had been thrown clear.

His Floater jacket brought Wayne to the surface gasping for air, sliding up over his head and entangling his arms. He heard the outboard and as he wrestled to pull the jacket down he could vaguely make out a silhouette of the crab boat disappearing into the darkness. Panic. He was alone in the dark, cold water, away from shore. 'Get hold of yourself Wayne,' he said to no one. 'You can do this.'

He forced himself to be calm. The lights of Dodge Cove were ahead and didn't look too far off. The current was carrying him, but he couldn't sense which way. Fish and whales and seaweed grabbed at his feet and legs, in his mind. Swimming for the lights he angled off the current toward Hospital Island, the old quarantine hospital back in the early 1900s. Wayne didn't know much about it but now felt a kinship with any other lost souls that might have become lodged there like the drifting flotsam that he was.

Some distance past the channel buoy, his feet tested for bottom. He thought he felt something, but there was nothing. Wayne swam and tested again, with a more positive result. The next test was even better. Slowly he worked his way up onto the slippery mud, sand, gravel, rock, eelgrass and rockweed on the shore. '*Fucus* species' he thought. 'Why do I even care about the fucking seaweed nomenclature right now?'

Losing his grip on reality, he hauled himself up the shore and over the barnacles and slippery rocks, his cold hands not feeling the damage being done to them. The logs at the top of the intertidal were both a barrier and a refuge. He let his own mass wedge his body between them. Sweet unconsciousness.

*****

CEDAR HEARD MARY SHOUT FROM THE FLOAT DOWN IN THE cove. "Come on Cedar, we're going to be late, hurry up. Why do we have to go through this every morning?"

"I'm coming. Just a minute." Cedar grabbed a biscuit from the table and her mug of coffee. She stepped into her boots, passed through the door and closed it behind her.

Mary started her outboard and guided the boat away from the dock. As they entered the channel, Mary saw a damaged boat on shore, stranded by the tide. She pointed it out to Cedar.

"What's that Mary?" asked Cedar as she turned to look.

Mary throttled back and steered in for a closer view, saying "Cedar, whose boat is that? It doesn't look right. Look the engine is tilted up and has gouged the mud on the way in."

Cedar stared at the boat and the engine. "Isn't that Ole's old engine?"

Mary paused. "You may be right. Did Ole have an accident?"

"No I don't think it was him. Remember he loaned it to that jerk Wayne. Actually I think that's the boat he bought from Lloyd, that day at Fairview."

Mary throttled back and slowed the down. "This doesn't look right. We'd better go in and see what's going on." Cedar set her coffee down on the seat and reached as Mary said in a low voice etched with concern, "Cedar, better get the oars out." She cut the outboard and tilted it out of the water.

"We'll be late for work," said Cedar inserting the pins into the oar locks.

"Cedar, how can you say such a thing? He could be lost, drowned, or dying of hypothermia on the shore," said a concerned Mary sitting in the stern and surveying the shoreline.

"He could be," Cedar muttered dispassionately as she rowed the boat in. It touched bottom and they got out.

Walking up the beach, Cedar said, "Look the boat's been damaged on the bow. I wonder what happened."

"I don't know, but I don't have a good feeling about this," said Mary, walking over to inspect the dinghy more closely. "I guess we can look around this little island. If we don't find anything it'll need a bigger search, with more people and more time."

"I'll go this way," said Cedar, taking the side where the dredged channel passed beyond the red navigation buoy.

Cedar walked up the shore, slipping over cobbles and boulders covered in rock weed and stepping on eel grass in the sandy muddy spots. The drift logs above the high tide line interested her. Her father, Dave, would like these for salvage. She'd thought that every time they went past in the boat on the morning pilgrimage to town.

At a spot between the ends of two massive cedar logs, she caught a flash of orange that disappeared right away. Maybe it was imagination. She looked again. Nothing. She cautiously approached and peered over the log.

*****

WAYNE HAD HEARD NOISE ON THE BEACH, FIRST AN OUTBOARD, then voices. He lay still, not sure if he was alive or dead, unable to raise himself to look. At first he was afraid it might be the thugs from town, but then realized the voices were female. 'Maybe this is how it ends.'

Through his hypothermic stupor he thought he saw a pretty face framed by tangled auburn hair peering over the log, and then he heard the sound of Cedar yelling, "Mary, there's a body here. Come quick."

Wayne felt himself being lifted into a boat, the two women talking in low, serious tones.

"Do you think he's okay?" Cedar asked ambiguously, as though not sure if she cared one way or the other.

"He's hypothermic. We'll have to revive him. Ray will help us get him up to the house."

When they arrived at the float, Mary shouted and Ray appeared at the door. The next thing Wayne knew, he was out of his clothes and wrapped in blankets by the woodstove. He couldn't move, and didn't fight it.

Wayne heard Mary say, "Okay Cedar, I'm going to work. You stay here with Ray and I'll tell them that you won't be in today. I'll tell them there was an accident in Dodge Cove and you're looking after someone. It'll be fine."

After Mary departed, Ray looked the situation over, and seeing there wasn't much more he could do, said, "I'll go check the state of that boat."

Wayne heard Cedar complain, saying, "Don't leave me here, alone with him," but the door closed and they were alone.

He gradually warmed up. Wayne opened his eyes and there was Cedar sitting at the kitchen table listening to the radio, the local news. "Thank you," he said in a weak shaky voice.

Cedar turned, shifted her gaze away from the window and looked at him, a look of pity mixed with disdain. Hard to read. "So you're starting to stir," she said matter of factly. "What happened?"

Wayne just looked at her and closed his eyes, too weak to talk. They remained in their respective positions for the duration of the morning.

He started to stir again in the early afternoon, as feeling returned to his limbs and awareness to his mind. He tried to talk. In a shaky voice he said, "I was coming across in the dinghy and a crab boat ran me down. At least I think it was a crab boat. I tried to avoid it but it was too close and too fast." Wayne paused, collecting his thoughts and his strength. "It rammed my dinghy and threw me into the water. That's all I know. My boat kept going without me."

"Who was it," asked Cedar, beginning to show some empathy and interest.

"I don't have a clue, but I thought I saw a dark figure on deck and thought I heard someone yell 'get out of town,' but I'm not really sure."

"That's terrible. So you were in the water for a while? How did you get to the island?"

"Swam I guess," said Wayne, still not moving. "Angled off the current aiming for the light on the red marker buoy and swam, then I felt the bottom and hauled myself up on shore. I don't remember anything after that."

"We should call the police," said Cedar, reaching for a phone.

"Please don't," said Wayne raising himself and putting up a hand as if to stop her. "I don't think they can or will do very much. I want to investigate this myself before that happens. Calling the cops could just amp up the aggression from these guys."

"Maybe they were just out in their boat and didn't see you," said Cedar, trying to sound positive. "Maybe it's not a big conspiracy."

"Yeah, maybe."

Ray came through the door, parking his jacket on a chair. "I got the boat. Needs repair but it can be salvaged. It'll float fine for now. The motor still works alright. Shakes a bit with the chewed up prop, but it's fixable. It'll run."

"Thanks Ray," said Wayne. Looking at Cedar he asked, "What's going on with this mining company? It must have been them. I don't know who else would do this."

"You worked for them. You tell me what's going on, said Cedar, her distant dispassionate tone returning.

"I know their operation is a mess. They're out of compliance all over the place and those tailings dams are a huge risk," said Wayne, reaching out for validation from the other two. When none was forthcoming he added, "And there's acid drainage coming off the site."

No one spoke.

FOURTEEN

MOLLY B TUGGED AT THE ANCHOR RODE LIKE A COHO ON THE line. Catspaws scattered across the water's steel blue surface. A breeze filling in from the southeast foreshadowed clouds and rain of the predicted low. The last of the bright sunlight still streamed in through the forward windows of the wheelhouse as he sipped instant coffee and listened in on VHF Channel 16. Tug boat skippers, the harbour pilot, and others engaged in clipped communications before switching to their own channels. Fishermen, heading out for the start of herring season, talked on the VHF worried about timing of the opening, where the fish would be, the weather, prices for the herring roe they all sought.

Cedar and Ray had dropped him off with his dinghy. They did it at dusk like he'd asked, to avoid drawing attention to his boat's location. The boat had, miraculously, been untouched. His place of refuge secure, for the moment anyway.

He plucked his cell phone from the dash, where he'd tossed it before going over to Rupert. Before the collision. Before the night of terror. His dinghy was hauled on board, okay but in need of more fibreglass and resin to seal up the foam core in the bow.

"Hi Susan," said Wayne into the phone.

"Wayne. How are you? Are you okay?" asked Susan, sounding genuinely concerned. "Mary came in yesterday and told me what happened. At least what she could glean from you when you were still out of it. That's terrible. Are you okay?"

"I've survived, I guess. Ray and Cedar took care of me, got me warmed up and gave me hot food and drinks. They brought me back to the *Molly B* last evening," said Wayne, pausing for a moment before carrying on. "If they hadn't found me in the logs on that beach, I'd have ......"

"I know," said Susan, empathy and a hint of emotion in her voice. "I feel awful. Can I do anything? What can I do?"

"Are you going over to see your family? Are you going to Metlakatla? Can you meet me there?"

"I could do that. Can't you just come over here to town?"

"The boat's hidden over on this side. I'm trying to avoid those guys and I don't want them seeing where my boat is coming from and going to. They're obviously watching me. I'll go back and forth to Metlakatla at night. Can you come over?"

"Yes, I'll come over tonight."

"Great. Can you pick up some fibreglass cloth and resin? I need to repair the dinghy," asked Wayne standing up from the stool and leaning on the dash, staring at Gus' Colt 45.

"Okay. No problem. I'll see you over there."

"Oh and another thing."

"Yes," she said, hesitantly.

"Can you pick up some 30-30 ammunition? Gus loaned me his rifle."

"Why do you need that?"

"Insurance. These guys are coming closer and getting more aggressive and violent every time," said Wayne turning the pistol over, checking the bullets in the cylinder. "And Gus also loaned me what I think is an old Colt 45 too. I need ammunition for that as well."

"Okay Wayne. I'll catch the last water taxi over, it leaves this side at four fifteen."

"I'll run over to Metlakatla after dark. Where should we meet?"

"Just come up to my parent's house. You know the one. I showed you."

"Okay. Thanks so much Susan. I can't tell you how important this is," said Wayne relieved. He really needed the supplies but he also needed someone to talk to.

"Okay. See you later," said Susan, signing off.

After talking with Susan he scrolled through his contacts, found Charles and called him.

"Charles, it's Wayne here, up on the north coast. You know that thing we were talking about, with the New Discovery Gold stock." He waited for Charles to check his account.

"Oh yeah," said Charles. "That one's a real dog. You want to dump it?"

"I don't work for them anymore and I've got a bad feeling about it. You know what to do."

"Sure Wayne. Right away. Hope you know what you're doing."

"Yeah well, that would be a first, eh?" Wayne punched the screen and cut the call.

Later, at dusk, Wayne powered up the engine and flipped on the radar and sounder. On the VHF he'd heard Prince Rupert Coast Guard Radio broadcasting the weather, but didn't need the radio to know that the predicted low pressure trough had moved in. It was now misty and a soft drenching rain was falling. He flipped the switch on the wiper to clear the forward centre window, before going onto the foredeck and using the winch raise the anchor and secure it. He backed the boat up, put the wheel over hard and engaged the prop. Turbulence boiled up from under the stern and *Molly B* inched forward in the darkness, Wayne watching the instruments and chart.

The sounder told him when the shallow sill at cove entrance had been cleared. He turned northwest toward Venn Passage. Across the water there were no vessel running lights visible, and no vessel showed up on the radar, except the freighters anchored in the harbour centre, their mercury and sodium vapour lights showing outlines of the ships. *Molly B* was running dark. 'So far so good,' Wayne thought, settling in for the short run, the wiper swishing back and forth partially cleared rain off the window.

He was looking forward to seeing Susan. She had been cool lately but maybe he could at least trust her, he thought. 'She was just doing her journalist job when she wrote that exposé on me. And unfortunately those were the facts that she reported. Wish they weren't, but can't undo the past.' Gliding in toward the dock at 9:30 p.m., Wayne could see Susan standing there in the illuminated cone under the wharf light, wearing rain gear with one foot on the rail.

She walked down onto the float and stepped forward to take the mooring line Wayne proffered. She made it fast as a spring line while Wayne reversed the engine and spun the wheel hard over to bring the stern snug to the float. Susan made the other lines fast while Wayne cut the engine, and shut down the electronics.

"Hey, thanks a lot," said Wayne as he stepped out of the boat. "And thanks for coming over here. You didn't have to stand out in the rain though."

Susan acknowledged. "I got here on the four fifteen water taxi, so I've had time for a nice visit with family. I knew you'd be along about now and thought you might like to see a welcoming familiar face on the dock, especially after your ordeal."

"I really appreciate seeing you here believe me," he said, spontaneously giving her an emotional hug, which she responded to with a quick step back in surprise.

She patted him on the shoulder saying, "Come on. Let's go up to the house. Bring your rifle and pistol, my dad can help you with the ammunition. He knows a lot more about those things than you, I imagine."

"Wouldn't be hard," said Wayne, retrieving the guns. He locked up and shielded them from the rain, under his Floater jacket. "Let's go."

Susan led the way as they walked along the paved road spanning the Metlakatla waterfront, where a Tsimshian village had existed for thousands of years. At her parents' house, she turned right and led him up the walkway. Inside, her father greeted Wayne from his big arm chair.

"Wayne, this is my father Steve. Dad this is Wayne," said Susan, stepping into the living room and leaning over to give her father a kiss.

"Heard you had a hard time of it the other night," said Steve, acknowledging Wayne but staying comfortably rooted in his chair. "You didn't need to bring all your guns though did you?"

Wayne sheepishly set the guns down by the door. "Someone loaned them to me. Susan was helping me with them."

"Yeah," said Steve, putting the hockey game on mute with his remote.

"Wayne, here's all the fibreglass stuff I bought for you," said Susan handing him a bag from the marine supply store. "I hope that's what you need."

Wayne looked through the bag, finding cloth, resin and hardener. "Perfect."

"Good," said Susan smiling. "You can pay me when you get back on your feet. Need anything else?"

"This will be great," said Wayne, "unless there's an old disposable aluminium pan around, you know sort of a takeout thing, or from a frozen cake or something. I could use something like that to mix the resin in."

Steve waved his arm and said, "Think there's something like that in the kitchen."

"I'll go look. Meanwhile Dad maybe you can show Wayne what to do with these." She popped two boxes of cartridges down on the table, one for the rifle, one for the pistol.

When Wayne brought the guns over. Steve leaned forward from his arm chair and took up the boxes in his large right hand. He motioned for Wayne to sit and proceeded to go over the basics of safety and reloading.

"What'cha gonna use these for?" he asked finally.

"Hopefully nothing, but I want to be able to defend myself if those guys come at me again."

"You be careful," said Steve, sitting back in his chair. He flicked the TV remote and turned back to the Canucks game.

Susan returned with a pan and an old wooden spatula. "Here," she said. "Thought you could use this spatula too."

"Great. Thanks."

They watched the game for a while with Steve and then, thanking them both, Wayne said he should get going.

"I'll walk you back to the boat," said Susan reaching for her rain gear. "Don't want you getting lost."

She helped him gather up the guns, ammunition and fibreglass supplies. "Bye Steve," he said, "Thanks for your help. You've got quite a daughter here."

Steve nodded without taking his eyes off the game. "You be careful. Don't shoot yourself or put a hole in your boat."

Susan closed the door behind them. Outside, the rain had let up and a breeze gently wafted through the overhead cedar boughs. They walked along the waterfront, street lights shining down through a cold heavy mist.

"What's going on Wayne?" asked Susan, not really expecting an answer. "Those mining guys sure seem to be worried about something. Why else would they be doing the crazy things they're doing, coming after you?"

"I really don't know," said Wayne obviously evading further disclosure. "What happened to Cedar's brother anyway?"

"He was killed out at the mine. The police investigation said he was trespassing, shouldn't have been on the property. Anyway he got caught in a rock slide." Susan turned to face him and looked deep into Wayne's eyes. "Do you think there's a connection?"

"It's really hard to say. They're in violation of so many permit conditions and laws there could be other reasons too. What do you think of Cedar, her parents and the others out there?"

"I have mixed feelings about them. Cedar's really nice, but you know, they're squatting on what is really Tsimshian territory."

"They'll say its Crown Land," said Wayne, wading into the mine field of historical fact.

Susan looked away throwing her hands up in the air and then back at Wayne. "That's the typical colonial response and you don't even realise it Wayne. Right now they're useful to us though, if they can protect the land by getting rid of that mine."

"I can see that."

"Problem is, we can't forget that while they may be helping us now, they came here with the logging companies that completely raped all those valleys up there."

They arrived at Wayne's boat and he stepped onboard and started the engine. "I understand what you're saying."

"You think you understand, but you've been part of the problem too, without even knowing it." She bent down to untie his mooring lines.

Wayne leaned over to say good bye. She touched him lightly on the shoulder, looked into his eyes and said, "Be careful and good luck," before turning to walk away. She disappeared behind the orange pool from the wharf light at the top of the ramp.

*****

"MORNING TED," SAID KAYE, GREETING HIM AS HE CLEARED THE elevator doors.

Ted turned and walked straight down the corridor, checking behind he could see Kaye was following closely.

"What is it?" said Ted as he unlocked his office door and entered.

"You want to get your coat off first? Sit maybe?" asked Kaye, standing in the office doorway.

He complied and sat and looked up. "What?"

"Wayne called in this morning. He wanted to talk to you. You weren't here so he put his questions directly to me. The questions went along the lines of: 'Why is Ted having me followed and harassed? Is Ted trying to have me killed?' He also said, 'The guys from that security company you hired have been behind this.' He summed up with, 'Tell Ted it's on now. I'm his worst nightmare. Let's see what he says to that.'"

Ted looked up at the ego wall, at all his engineering certifications, awards and achievements. He said, "Kaye, you hired that security company, remember?"

Kaye asked, "Ted, why did you give me the number of that security company in Prince Rupert to handle Wayne's firing? Why that company?"

"Ian gave me the name."

"Oh, you mean the Ian from Johannesburg?"

"Yes, Ian Verster. New Discovery Gold Inc. Our client," said Ted brusquely. "The guy that pays our salaries."

"When he pays. He's still way behind on our accounts payable."

"I know. He likes to play the big guy, getting leverage and all that, but he's been a good client for us over many years."

"I wonder if we'd touch him at all if ...," Kaye mumbled as she turned to leave.

Ted heard the coded message, ignored it.

Later Ted entered the dark wood paneled extravagance of The Exchange on West Pender. The ray of daylight following him narrowed and was extinguished as the heavy wooden door closed behind. Ian was waiting for him at the bar. "So, what's so urgent?"

"Call came in from Wayne up in Rupert this morning. He talked to Kaye, not me. Says some security company is harassing him. Says those guys tried to kill him. What's the deal Ian?"

"How should I know?" said Ian shrugging his shoulders. "You fired him. That's your business, your company. Run it any way you want, I don't care. I didn't even know you did it or how you did it."

"Kaye got the name of a security company from you. She hired them, they did the job. Now according to Wayne they won't leave him alone. Do you know these guys?" asked Ted, signalling to the skinny, pale, middle-aged bartender that he wanted the same as Ian.

"No," said Ian, raising the glass to sip his Scotch, looking at himself, and Ted, in the mirror behind the bartender. "The mine manager up there hired them a couple of years ago to watch some equipment in their warehouse out at Port Edward. That's all I know."

"Well Wayne's understandably pissed. Told Kaye to tell me that, and I quote, 'It's on.'"

"What the hell does that mean?" said Ian shrugging again and laughing. Answering his own question he said, "I guess you got a problem brother, no?" his Afrikaans accent slipping out.

"We've got a problem," said Ted, turning to talk directly to Ian. "I'm working hard on this to cover your ass."

Ian continued watching him in the mirror, and said, "Ted, it's best for you if you just stick to the environmental and engineering details. You leave the big picture mining to me." He reached into the pocket of his finely woven wool suit coat and pulled out an envelope which he slid along the bar to Ted with a wink.

"Ian, we have an understanding," said Ted his face growing tighter as he peeked in at the cheque.

Ian tipped his head far back finishing the Scotch. Putting his glass down with authority, he winked at the bartender as he nodded his head in Ted's direction. He slipped off his stool, leaving Ted sitting there, watching him in the mirror as he wove his way through people and out of the bar.

Ted shook his head slightly and grimaced. This was getting beyond his depth. In the mirror he watched a tall woman with straight platinum hair pick the stool Ian had vacated. He turned to her as he gently nudged the finger bowl of complimentary cocktail olives in her direction. She nodded and ordered a vodka martini. Ted caught the bartender's eye and ordered another Scotch for himself. He paid for both, and for Ian Verster's.

"My name's Ted."

"How nice for you," she said, avoiding the mirror view of him.

They talked, with Ted telling her about his business and the boat, alluding to the large sums of money he made. She gave him her number.

Back at the office, Ted followed up with a call to Bruno to make sure the next report would be coming. "Bruno, what's happening up there? Did you get out to the mine site for the next monitoring run?"

"Oh hey, it's Prince Rupert, nothing's happening here. It rains, the wind blows, the fog moves in and the fog moves out. The only thing going on is the casino," said Bruno. He was clearly not thrilled with this posting.

"You'd better stay out of there. Don't want you to throw away all that money you're being paid."

Bruno chuckled slightly. "Yeah right. About the money, I haven't seen a cheque for a while. Is there anything I should know about?"

"I'll talk to Kaye. Don't worry," said Ted confidently. "Again, did you get out to the mine site for the next monitoring run?"

"Yeah I was out there for a couple of days. They had a lot of rain and those tailings dams are looking worse Ted. Erosion channels down the face are getting deeper and the water levels behind the dams are dangerously high," said Bruno emphasizing concern and caution. "What do you want me to do?"

"Just follow the monitoring protocols and reporting template, everything will be fine. The rain won't last. You didn't take any additional pictures did you?"

"No, of course not. I'm not crazy. I know what happened to Ron and I figure maybe the same to Wayne."

"You watch it Bruno," said Ted sharply to nip in the bud any hint of doubt or questioning on Bruno's part. "Don't get smart."

"Bye the way, I ran into Wayne the other day. Had a coffee with him."

"What did you do that for?" barked Ted, telegraphing his level of concern.

"Well I was sitting alone, as usual in this place, having a coffee. And Wayne came and sat right down at the same table. What was I supposed to do, just get up and leave?"

"All right," said Ted, starting to probe the dialogue for hints and information. "What did he say? What did you guys talk about?"

"He told me how he was thrown out of the apartment and office when he got fired, and how his room in a rooming house was ransacked with a threatening note left, stuck with a big sharp knife jammed into the furniture. And we talked about old times, working together, how he used to be your go to guy, that sort of thing."

"You need to avoid him. He's become bad news since he went up there. I don't know what happened. Maybe some woman got to him or something, I don't know. Anyway stay away from him, and is that report going to be coming soon?"

"Yeah sure," said Bruno somewhat dismissively. "In the next day or so. And yes, I'll follow the templates, religiously. Could you please make sure Kaye deposits a cheque in my account? My funds are running low."

"That's good. And send your timesheet with the report so I can invoice New Discovery."

Ted signed off and leaned back in his chair. Done. He got his coat from the rack and said to Kaye on the way out, "Please make sure Bruno gets a cheque. We don't want him turning on us too."

"Right boss. I'll get on it right away."

"I have to go pick up Jamie at school and keep him with me until his mother gets off work."

Later in the evening, after dropping Jamie off, Ted arrived back at his penthouse overlooking the lighted ships in English Bay. She said her name was Sheila as she draped her coat across a chair. "Thanks for calling Ted. After talking at lunch I didn't know if I'd hear from you. Thanks for the great evening too. Dinner at Mulvaney's was fantastic."

"It's always great there, isn't it?" said Ted preparing a fresh martini. "Sorry I was late. I had to pick my son up at school and amuse him until his mother finished work."

"That's okay, we all have our own albatross. Gosh, this is a fantastic place you've got here. Must cost a fortune," said Sheila, accepting the drink and kicking off her shoes as she settled on the white leather couch facing the wall of windows and English Bay.

"It's worth it, don't you think?" he said, sitting down close to her.

"Oh definitely," she responded, moving closer and placing a hand on his shoulder.

*****

"MARY, I THINK I'LL STAY HOME TODAY," SAID CEDAR STIRRING her coffee. "Can you cover for me at school?"

Mary was busy packing up her lesson plans and lunch. She was just about to leave. "I know you've got things on your mind and things to do, but you shouldn't skip work like this too often. People will start to question your commitment," said Mary putting her jacket on.

"I know," said Cedar, making no move to leave, pushing her biscuit around the plate with a finger. "But talking to mom and dad on the radio last night was really upsetting. I need to do something about it."

"Like what?"

"I don't know, maybe I'll go over to town. Start organizing another meeting."

"You could do that after school," said Mary starting to get impatient. "You've got something else in mind, don't you?"

"Do you think we should go over and see if that Wayne guy has recovered alright?" said Cedar to Ray, who had been sitting at the kitchen table with her, but trying to stay out of the fray. "I'm a bit worried. That was quite an accident he was in."

"That was no accident," said Ray pouring another cup of coffee, "but yah we should probably go see if he's still alive. And I can run you over to town later."

"Okay Mary, I'll take another day off. Sorry."

"That's okay. I guess I would too after that call last night and everything else that's happened. You two be careful and I'll see you tonight," said Mary, grabbing her things and opening the door to leave.

"I didn't hear your parents last night, what did they say?" asked Ray after Mary had left and he'd plunked himself back down at the kitchen table.

Cedar nudged the sugar over to him. "Oh they were talking about how the people at the mine are always hassling them. And they're getting more and more concerned that the tailings dam will break."

"That's a big concern," said Ray, grabbing a spoonful and tilting it just enough for the sugar to slowly slide into his coffee. "I've seen the pictures."

Cedar spread butter on her biscuit. "There were more erosion channels in the dam after the last rain, and the water level behind the dam has gone way up again. They're worried that if there's another really heavy rain storm the whole thing could fail. That valley collects a lot of water fast, especially after the logging companies clear-cut the slopes. The spring snow melt this year will be really scary too."

"Won't the mining company do anything?" asked Ray after taking a sip of his coffee. "This has been developing for a while, why aren't the provincial enviro cops doing something about it?"

"Cause they've all had their budgets cut. They're a long way off and rely on what the company's consultants put in their reports. And those guys will do anything to avoid reporting a problem."

"That was that Wayne guy, right?" said Ray. "Is that why you hate him so much?"

"Yes, that's why," said Cedar taking a bite before carrying on. "But he said he got fired for trying to send in a real report, a report that would show everything. So now I really don't know what to think Ray. It's all so confusing. I'd really like to get up there and see them, and see what's going on."

They left the house and walked down to Ray's boat. He steered it out of Dodge Cove, across the channel and along the north shore to the cove where Wayne was anchored. Rounding the small island guarding the cove entrance, noise from Wayne's diesel may have been shattering the peaceful serenity there but it was drowned out by the noise from their own outboard. They saw Wayne hurry out of *Molly B*'s deckhouse, then step back inside for a split second when he saw who it was. It might have been a pistol that they'd seen him put back inside, it was hard to tell in the distance.

"Good morning," said Cedar matter-of-factly as they pulled alongside *Molly B* and she passed mooring lines to him.

As she came over the side, Wayne said, "Morning to you too. Thanks for coming by. And thank you for everything you did for me."

She scowled at him in response to a comment that she was looking nice. "Not sure that's much of a compliment coming from a man who's been holed up alone in an old boat, after almost being killed."

She scowled at Ray too, when he muttered, "Probably better to just take the compliment Cedar."

"What's up guys?" asked Wayne, trying to be cheerful, but staying a bit wary.

"I thought we should see if you're alright, still alive you know," said Cedar, still with an edge. "And I need to talk to someone who knows what kind of reports New Discovery has been sending to the environmental protection people. Since you were one of the guys preparing them, I kind of thought you might be someone to talk to."

"You know I got fired because I sent an accurate report to the consulting company owner," said Wayne. "So shouldn't I kind of get at least a bit of credit for trying?"

"Maybe," said Cedar cautiously, but starting warm up slightly. "But you were part of the system of lies for so long it's hard to tell."

Ignoring her jab, Wayne said, "So the way it works is this. A protocol and reporting template are developed when the mine first starts. That gets approved by everybody, and gets followed no matter what's happening on the ground unless something changes and someone says something. With budget cuts, nobody from the regulators ever has time or money to go out and check, unless people like you and your parents do and notify them. That's when the mine people get antsy, and start going after those people to intimidate them, stop them from reporting." He watched to see how Cedar would respond.

"Well obviously that's where we're at," said Cedar, sitting down on the hatch cover. "They're intimidating my family out there. I don't know what to do and I'm not sure if I can even trust you to talk to." She stared a hole into the deck, and then looked away to the bald eagle perched high atop a cedar tree on the island at the cove entrance, to Ray, anywhere but at Wayne.

"I organized that public meeting." She paused before carrying on. "I know you didn't go."

Wayne stepped back and turned his head to look at the eagle. "Yeah I kind of avoided it after I got trashed in the paper." He watched as the eagle lifted off and flew out of sight on the other side of the island.

"Oh yeah, sorry about that. That kind of resulted from me pushing the idea on Susan."

"I know. She told me." Wayne paused and thought for a moment before going on. "Anyway, guess I'll have to live with it, just my entire career laid bare for public criticism and ridicule. But I was about to make a big change anyway. When I saw what was going on out there and the look in the eyes of you and your family, I knew I couldn't do that job anymore."

Cedar looked down again, and Wayne thought for a moment he might have struck an empathetic chord.

"Don't know if you're aware, but someone trashed my place at the Hecate Rooms too. Left a note pinned to the dresser top with a big knife. That's when I moved onto this boat. Those two guys came down to the boat and tried to rob me at the dock. Gus scared them off with his shotgun."

"Yeah I know, I guess," said Cedar looking back up at Wayne. "But anyway. There was a big brawl outside the meeting hall."

"I heard about it."

"Yeah, it didn't really hurt us, but it created a lot of negative feelings in town and with the police. People who've worked for the mine, and people owed money by that company, they really don't like us. Shutting down the mine could put them out of jobs or mean they don't ever get paid. So we're getting a lot of friction in town."

"Kind of to be expected when people's money and future may be on the line." Wayne stepped aft from the wheelhouse and sat opposite Cedar on the rail.

"I know, but there it is. Anyway on the other side of this mess, Jimi brought along this environmental group from Toronto to the meeting. A really arrogant woman, urban environmentalist, you know what I mean. They have some national anti-mining campaign and say they want to help."

"That's a good thing for you, no?"

"On the face of it you'd think so, but I think they're just using us. We all think they're just jumping on New Discovery as a big fund raising opportunity for themselves," she added and glanced over at Ray.

"They need to pay their own high salaries and it seems to us they think this might be a good way for them to do it," added Ray from his perch on the far rail where his boat was tied on.

"This group, they call themselves Sustainable People, is hijacking our whole initiative. They don't give a shit about our problems with New Discovery and Jimi's too stunned to see it," said Cedar taking the lead again.

"Is that it?" said Wayne, to which Cedar nodded.

"Something else?" asked Wayne. After no response, he said, "Then you should do something about it. Taking apart money sucking groups like that isn't very hard."

"Maybe not for you, but what can we do?"

"You could ask for my help?"

"I don't know what I'm doing," said Cedar, looking down again and shaking her head so a tangle of hair spilled down to hide her face.

"Maybe you should figure that out then."

"My parents are also trying to figure out what happened to Nathan," she said softly. "They went up to look around the mine and take pictures."

"I bet that got the mine guys worried. They don't like people taking pictures."

"You took pictures out there didn't you?" asked Cedar looking up again.

"Yes I did. I took lots of pictures."

Finally Cedar blurted out the question she had been harbouring since she woke up, "Wayne, will you take me up to the mine to see if my family's okay?" She looked over at Ray who was as stunned by the request as Wayne.

Wayne looked at Cedar, over at Ray, and again at Cedar. "Gee Cedar, I don't know. I need more fuel, don't have any money, I'm out of a job because I felt bad about your family, you had me trashed in the paper, and you've told me so many times that I'm a horrible person who can't be trusted."

Cedar looked down at the deck again, paused for an eternity, then got up and climbed over the rail to Ray's boat.

Ray untied the lines and climbed into his boat. He pulled the cord and the outboard started. The boat cleared Wayne's guardian island, and serenity returned to the cove, but not to Cedar.

*****

"IAN, GOOD TO HEAR FROM YOU. WHAT'S UP?" SAID TED SETTING his cup on the mirror polished desk top. He had been finishing his second coffee and going over Bruno's latest report. "I've got your next report here from Bruno. Reviewing it now, but so far it looks good. I think you'll be pleased."

"That's good," said Ian brusquely. "But that's not why I'm calling."

"Okay then, how can we help?"

"We're ready to run some tests with the cyanide we've brought in. I'd like you guys to do the monitoring."

"Sounds good. When will this be happening? I'll get Bruno on it."

"Day after tomorrow."

"That's very short notice. What exactly do you want us to do?"

"Just be there. Take the right pictures and collect the right notes. Klaus will tell Bruno exactly what to do."

"Okay, I'll call Bruno right away. Do you want a quote from us?"

"No just go ahead and do your thing, Ted. I trust you'll bill the hours fairly and at the usual rate."

"We'll bill," said Ted, pausing a moment before adding, "It's the payment that I sometimes worry about."

"Just gave you a cheque. Don't worry so much Ted. You'll live longer," said Ian dismissively. "Now, do me a favour and get Bruno out there."

"Sounds good, thanks," said Ted, clicking off and taking another slug of coffee, spilling and leaving a ring on the desk.

"Hey Kaye," shouted Ted from his chair behind the big desk. "Get me Bruno on the phone."

"Bruno, Ted here. Just got off the phone with Ian Verster over at New Discovery Gold. They want to run some tests on the ore using cyanide gold extraction. We've got the go ahead to do the monitoring. I need you to fly up there tomorrow. The tests will start the next day. So pack up everything you need and book a charter."

"Hey Ted. How's it going? The extra work is good, but do you know what we're actually supposed to be monitoring? What I'm supposed to do?"

"Not really. Ian was pretty vague, just talking about notes and photos. Kind of an inspection report using our templates I guess."

"Do they have cyanide permit terms and conditions we have to fulfill for them?" asked Bruno trying to be professional.

"He didn't mention anything like that."

"Are we taking any samples?"

"Good point. Take some sample bottles and we'll send them out to the lab. At least we'll have the information on file if we need it."

"Okay. I'll organize that today and go tomorrow."

"Good. We'll talk when you get back. I know I can rely on you Bruno."

Ted sat back pleased. He had some cheques flowing in and additional new work with new revenue from the cyanide test. Things were looking good. He had to pick up Jamie after school. His son had a soccer game Ted agreed to drive him to. He'd be free after that and maybe he'd hit the clubs.

Gathering up gear after the soccer game and putting it in the Audi, Ted said, "That was a good game Jamie. You played well."

"Thanks Dad. I'm glad you could come." A strained smile crossed his face.

"Where do you want to go for dinner? How 'bout that Chinese restaurant in Dundarave before I drop you off?"

"Sure Dad. Unless you've got work to do this evening. I'd actually like to go home if that's okay. I've got some things to do."

"Sure, I'll take you home. Your mom will be glad to see you."

Ted dropped his son at the apartment building off Seventeenth in Ambleside. It was close to the soccer pitch. He went up to the door with Jamie and pushed the intercom. Ted's ex-wife answered curtly and buzzed Jamie in. Returning to his Audi, Ted checked his watch. 'Time for a drink and dinner. Where to go?'

Driving over the Lions Gate Bridge, Ted revelled in the glory of a west coast early spring evening. He took the route through Stanley Park and ended up at his condo on Beach Avenue. Time for a run before having a drink. He parked the Audi in his underground spot and rode to the penthouse, greeting and chatting with people getting on and off the elevator as it floated upward.

After changing clothes, Ted exited the building in the latest technical gear, and jogged along the seawall toward Third Beach. At Second Beach he lost interest and took a trail that lead him back to Barclay Street and then to his condo building. 'Enough for today,' he thought. In the penthouse he showered and prepped for drinks, dinner and the clubs.

Starting in the comfort of the panelled Sylvia bar just up the street he waited for the cute server to fill the order, while watching the sunset over English Bay .

Next morning, Ted entered the office at nine thirty hungover and tired. The night had been good. Kaye greeted him, brought coffee right away and left him alone to get his bearings. After a time, he pressed the intercom. "Kaye, have we heard anything from Bruno?"

From the speaker on his desk, Kaye answered, "Nothing yet boss. Should I call him?"

"No it's okay. He'll call when he needs to."

*****

NEXT MORNING WAS THE SAME. "KAYE, GET BRUNO ON THE phone," said Ted into the intercom.

"Bruno, Ted here. How was the test? Did you get everything recorded?"

"Oh they went ahead with the test alright," said Bruno, with an edge of hesitancy. "It was a bit messy but they ran the test. I got back just before dark last night."

"What do you mean 'a bit messy'?"

"Well there was a bit of spillage."

"Cyanide?"

"Yeah."

"Not much though, right?" asked Ted, a bit concerned, trying to be positive.

"Yeah, I guess," said Bruno, stumbling over the words.

"Okay Bruno. You send me that report tomorrow. Just make sure you follow the protocol and templates."

"But those templates were for routine monitoring, not this cyanide business," said Bruno sounding concerned and uneasy. "Do I still use the same ones?"

"Oh for sure," said Ted, projecting confidence. "There's no need to re-invent the wheel, right?"

"Yeah, I guess. It'll take some creativity to make this fit. I've got it though. I'll work on the report right away and send it to you tomorrow."

The next morning Ted greeted Kaye when he came off the elevator and into the office, late and hungover again. "Good morning Kaye. Did we get that report from Bruno yet?"

"Not yet," said Kaye, heading for the coffee machine. "I'll get your coffee right away. Do you need anything for a headache as well?"

"Yes Kaye. I definitely need something for this headache. It was a really late one last night."

"I can see that, Ted. This divorce is really taking a toll on you."

Ted smiled and said, "Yes it is. The price of freedom."

Kaye disengaged. The 'price of freedom' line came out virtually every morning since the divorce and it had grown very tired.

Mid-afternoon Ted saw the report from Bruno show up in his email. He opened and read it. Everything looked in order. There had been no adverse effects associated with the test. There was passing mention of minor spillage, but a conclusion that the any adverse effects had been negated by presumed cyanide volatilization. Ted inserted his digital signature and forwarded the report on to Ian Verster.

He sent Bruno's timesheet and expenses on to Kaye and immediately punched the intercom. "Kaye, do up an invoice for Bruno's latest work and send it to New Discovery Gold."

"Right boss."

Ted saw the invoice email go shortly after the report. An email came back from Ian Verster right away, saying, "Drinks at Ramparts. Five o'clock. I'll bring a cheque."

Ted smiled. All was good. At four forty five he said good night to Kaye and left the building in the black Audi.

It was happy hour and Ramparts was boisterous, filled with young professionals. Ted grabbed a table in the centre of the action. 'Easy pickings if you have money,' he thought and ordered a Scotch. He watched Ian enter the bar and caught his eye. Ian pulled a chair out and sat opposite. The waitress took his order.

Ian flashed a big smile, saying, "Here's your cheque. Our share price shot through the roof in today's trading. I sold a ton of stock. There was a rumour floating around the exchange today that New Discovery Gold was planning enhanced gold recovery out of the Mirage Inlet site and that profitability would go way up."

Ted smiled thinking about his own shares. "How would such a rumour get started I wonder?"

Ian shrugged and they clinked glasses and drank. Ted began looking around to see what attractive young professionals might be there in the bar tonight, which ones would be the most likely targets for his attention.

FIFTEEN

"HELLO, IS THIS WAYNE DUMONT?" SAID THE VOICE AT THE other end. "It's Constable Stasiuk of the RCMP in Prince Rupert." It was dark outside, and Wayne was down in the forepeak getting ready to contort himself into *Molly B*'s forepeak berth.

He held the phone away for a moment to verify the attribution and then brought it close, trying to think what this call might be about. "Hello, yes?"

"Mr. Dumont do you own an old faded red Ford F150 pickup truck, licence plate 241 EKA."

"Yes I do," said Wayne sitting down on the opposite berth.

"Well I regret to inform you that it's been found abandoned down in Seal Cove. Do you know where that is?" said Constable Stasiuk curtly, without emotion.

"Yes, I do," said Wayne, worried and trying to figure how best to respond and ultimately opting for the plain truth, the police clearly having more information than he did.

"And the windshield has been smashed by a large rock that is now sitting on the front seat. Someone from the Curling Club called it in."

"Oh damn," said Wayne, his head in his left hand, elbow wedged against the bulkhead, desperately trying to process this new information.

"Now Mr. Dumont, I would like you to come and claim the truck. You need to take it away for repairs or whatever you'd like to do, and sign our police report."

"I'll do that first thing in the morning. I'm on a boat out of town at this moment and will come right over as soon as I can tomorrow."

"Alright then Mr. Dumont. Please come in to the detachment office as soon as you get back to town and we'll take care of this."

"Yes, I'll do that," said Wayne, disconnecting and solemnly putting the phone down. "What next?" he yelled at the bulkhead as he struck it with a fist, immediately wincing in pain.

Before dawn Wayne started the engine and weighed anchor to leave his quiet, secluded cove. 'Should be okay as long as no one sees where I'm coming from,' he thought. As before, the radar and sounder guided him through the cove's narrow entrance in the dark and through the early morning shroud of fog. He increased the engine revs to drive the boat at seven knots across the harbour to the docks at Cow Bay.

The space opposite Clarence on the same float was free so he nosed in there, reversing thrust to draw the stern in to the dock. He stepped off the boat and secured the mooring lines. The dawn was just breaking, sending faint pink streaks into the clouds of the eastern sky above the mist on the water. Lights on pilings brightened the float and deck of Clarence's boat. A dim light glowed within. The boat belonging to Gus was gone.

Wayne looked all around, and went up the ramp to the wharf deck above. There was no sign of anyone waiting or watching. Descending the ramp again he went over to Clarence's boat.

"Clarence, it's Wayne. You up?" said Wayne in a low voice, tapping gently on the hull.

There was rustling and cursing from within the vessel, before the top half of the wheelhouse door swung open and a dishevelled head popped out. "Jesus Christ Wayne, you have to stop scaring me like that. Where the hell you been to anyway? We heard you drowned but then came back to life. Good Christ don't just stand there gawkin' at me in my long johns, come in and I'll make coffee."

With considerable trepidation regarding the coffee, Wayne climbed aboard and entered the wheelhouse. Clarence put water on to boil and threw in a cupful of ground coffee.

"That's Mocha-Java Wayne. The best," said Clarence. Wayne was unconvinced. "You watch the coffee and I'll go below and get dressed." He crab walked down the short companionway muttering something like, "What you doin' up so early anyways?"

Wayne slid onto the bench and leaned elbows on the galley table, watching his boat through a porthole opposite. Clarence returned just as the water boiled. With a heavy mitt he picked up the pot, stepped outside and swung his arm and the pot around in a windmill motion. He brought it back inside and poured the liquid into two heavy porcelain mugs that, at some time in the past, might have resembled a shade of white.

Clarence shoved a mug in Wayne's direction pointing and saying, "Sugar and milk are there."

A can of evaporated milk sat on the table, congealed yellowing clots stuck around the triangular holes on both sides. Wayne said, "Thanks. I'll take it black." He took a sip, straining the grounds with his teeth. He grimaced and said, "That's some good coffee Clarence."

"So what's up," said Clarence looking at him seriously. "Really, where the hell have you been?"

Wayne recounted his activities and those of his tormentors. Then he said, "You know last night, as I was about to get into the berth, I got a call from the RCMP, a Constable Stasiuk."

"Don't know the man. Heard of him though. What about?" asked Clarence, wide-eyed and questioning.

"He said my truck had been trashed."

"I didn't do it Wayne. You know that."

"Yeah, I know you old cuss." He laughed at Clarence's default response. "But somebody did. I have go with him to retrieve it."

"What did they do?"

"The Constable said they threw a boulder through the windshield."

Clarence was silent. "I'm sorry. I should have been watching it more carefully."

"Relax. I know it's not your fault. But that's why I'm here. I have to go get it and I wanted to come in the dark in case anyone's watching my comings and goings. Don't want anyone knowing where I've been holed up."

"Good plan Wayne."

"Where's Gus anyway?" Wayne asked, looking out the window at the float.

"He's out on the herring for a bit. Wanted to make some money. Told him I didn't feel like it this week."

"Figured." Wayne took another sip, applying maximum will power to avoid another grimace.

They chatted for a while, finishing the coffee, which really wasn't too bad despite the grounds. With the arrival of full daylight he retrieved the truck keys from Clarence and walked up to the RCMP Detachment.

Constable Stasiuk drove him out to Seal Cove to retrieve the truck.

"That's sure a mess there," said Stasiuk as he parked the police cruiser and opened the door to get out. "What do you want to do?"

Wayne opened the driver's side door of his truck and with his sleeve pushed broken cubes of glass off the seat. He tossed the boulder and inserted the ignition key. It started.

"Well at least it runs," said Stasiuk, encouragingly. "What now?"

"I'm going to drive it to the wreckers and leave it there," said Wayne, resigned to what had happened, too beaten down to fight it.

"It's just a windshield Mr. Dumont. I'm sure the vehicle's worth the repair."

Wayne looked at him and said, "It's been a rough week. I've got the boat. I don't need this baggage. I'll drive it right to the wrecker's."

"You're having a tough day, and I don't have any active calls right now, I'll follow you out there and give you a ride back."

"I'd really appreciate it," said Wayne.

At the wrecking yard, Wayne signed over the papers, the final tie to town and his past life. He had already mentally written off his things at what was now Kathy's apartment in Vancouver. As he climbed into the police cruiser, he saw a black pickup cruise by. Cody rolled down the passenger window and waved, ostensibly at Stasiuk, but Wayne knew it was for him.

Constable Stasiuk gave a familiar nod and a wave back.

*****

CEDAR WATCHED WAYNE ENTER FROM WHERE SHE SAT AT THE back of the coffe shop. He looked around before spotting her. With a subtle nod, he went to the counter and came away with coffee and two donuts. She stared as he walked over to her table and with his eyes asked permission to sit. She didn't say no.

"What brings you to town, Wayne? I thought you'd be staying low over in your nice little cove," she said in a neutral tone, not engaging but not aggressive either.

"Here, have a donut. I owe you that at least, for saving my life."

She looked up and smiled. "A lot more than that, but thanks."

"What's up? When's your next meeting?" Wayne was trying to find an avenue that might open up conversation.

"Who cares? Caitlyn and that group from Toronto have taken over the whole thing. I just want to get out of here."

"Same here. I have to get out before I get hurt, or killed apparently. They wrecked my truck. Yesterday I guess. That was the last connection I had to this place."

"What happened to your truck?"

Wayne explained what happened and that he had left the truck at the wrecking yard.

"Sorry about the truck," said Cedar and she commented that he must be wondering where he would go. "Wayne?" She looked at him with deep imploring eyes.

"Yes?" said Wayne sensing the question, and uncomfortable with the wait.

"Will you take me out of here? Up to the mine. To my family." And there it was. The question had been asked and it was clear from the look on her face she wasn't confident in the answer.

Cedar watched him look at her, as he paused and considered his response. She wondered if he was thinking, 'Why the hell should I?' She took a bite of the donut and a sip from her coffee, and studied the old postcards and photos pinned to the coffe shop wall.

He put down his coffee and donut. Leaning his chin on interlaced fingers he said, "You know you've treated me like shit."

She gazed straight back into his eyes and said, "I know. But I saved your life too. That counts for something, doesn't it? Will you help me?"

He relaxed his face and body and smiled. "Oh what the hell. I'm leaving today anyway, as fast as possible. Tried before but ran into a storm and I was single-handing. Could use a deckhand. I'll take you on. We'll go north instead of south, if that's what you want. Doesn't really matter that much to me. I just want out of here as soon as possible." He held out his hand.

Relieved, she shook his hand to close the deal. "When do we go?"

Wayne stood and began putting his jacket back on. "Right now, partner. We'll go get groceries, then fuel."

"We can get them in Lax Kw'alaams. Let's just go. Now," said Cedar, smiling and then frowning as she watched a black pickup drive by outside the windows. "Can we get some of my things over at Dodge on the way?"

After stopping at Dodge Cove, the run up the coast was rough. The wind was up, cold and in their faces. White crests of breaking waves shone against a deep blue background. In the wheelhouse, Cedar perched on the stool, hanging onto the bulkhead while she watched Wayne at the wheel, knees slightly bent, swaying back and forth with the roll of the waves. *Molly B* appeared to love the ride, diving into troughs and launching off crests. The wiper could not keep up with the salt spray but they didn't care. Headwinds slowed progress so it was dusk when they pulled in behind the Lax Kw'alaams breakwater, tired but relieved to be away from Rupert. As they passed the breakwater, she saw Wayne tracking a sea truck passing by, running east out on the open water. It appeared to carry a cylindrical tank and drums as pay load. He shook his head and guided the boat to the nearest available mooring spot.

Once tied up they went into the small community to buy groceries and see about fuel. The Band Office was closed so fuel would have to wait. They both wanted to stay in Lax Kw'alaams overnight anyway.

Cedar led the way to a store tucked behind an unmarked ground level entrance, in the basement below a raised bungalow. No need to advertise, everyone in town knew it was there. She went to talk with the cashier, while Wayne collected groceries.

"Hi Ida. How's things?" said Cedar approaching the counter.

"Hi Cedar, haven't seen you for a while. You goin' up home?" asked Ida, straightening snacks and confections on the counter.

"Yeah, I'm really worried about my family."

"Whose the k'amksiiwaa?"

"Oh that's Wayne Dumont. He's giving me a ride up home. He used to do environmental monitoring for the mine but got fired."

"Don't tell me," said Ida with a wry smile and shaking her head slowly. "He was doing his job too well."

"You got it. You always were a good judge of people," said Cedar, feeling like it was good to be with an old friend and away from Rupert.

"You watch yourself anyway. I'm not always right, remember that. You be careful with him." Cedar knew Ida was watching Wayne the whole time, not yet ready to trust.

Wayne pulled some canned ham and a bag of Mocha Java coffee off the shelf, a couple of frozen stir fries out of the freezer and brought the groceries over to the counter. "Well Cedar, how does this look?"

"Should be okay," said Cedar, "at least until we can get some of my mother's good cooking when we get up there."

Ida smiled. "She makes really good bread and corn meal muffins too. Wayne is it?"

Wayne introduced himself. He added two bags of chips and two slushies to the order and paid. "Treats?" said Cedar smiling, and he nodded in reply. Returning his attention to Ida, Wayne asked, "What time does the Band Office open in the morning? We'd like to buy some fuel."

"Opens at eight," answered Ida as she packed the purchases into a bag. "You be careful," she said to both of them, as she slid the slushies across the counter, but really directing her message at Cedar.

Cedar walked with Wayne back to the harbour, bracing against the northwest wind. The quiet fish plant with a dragger secured to a piling below, and the smell of fish and low tide, suggested a busy day tomorrow. She held the groceries and treats as Wayne opened up the boat and checked to make sure everything was okay before entering. No tampering was apparent. Cedar hadn't expected any in this small community. The wind was cold off the water so they chose to make do cramped inside. Cedar sat on the skipper's stool in the wheelhouse and they chatted while Wayne heated a generic prepackaged stir fry on the diesel stove down below. She could see him sitting on the berth opposite the stove, and she relished the warmth rising into the wheelhouse.

Cedar listened patiently while Wayne told her about growing up in Toronto in a privileged neighbourhood with high achieving parents. The expectations were high, and had not included a scenario that even remotely hinted at his current circumstances. He hadn't called home for a while. They wouldn't understand and would worry, but mainly they would think he'd failed. As he talked, she appeared to ponder the privileged life he'd squandered, and her own challenges.

Cedar told Wayne about growing up back to the land style in Mirage Inlet. At first her father was working for a logging company and, when the loggers left, the family just stayed and occupied the property. Her father and Jimi had built the cabins they lived in. Growing up had been free and happy. She'd watched over, and played with, her younger brother. The one now dead. Nathan.

Out of the blue Wayne asked her, "Cedar, can I trust you?" as they ate sitting side by side on the lower berth opposite the stove.

"That's a stupid question," said Cedar, the sarcasm clear in her voice. "You're the one in control right now, here in this boat. You're the one working for the mining company. How can I trust you?"

"I guess we're going to having to get past this. I really have turned my back on that world. I'm starting to question everything about what I was doing. Can you tell me what happened to your brother?"

"I guess. A little bit," she said, changing to hushed tones. "You saw how things are out at the mine site. He was up there looking things over, they called it trespassing and snooping, and he got caught in a rock slide. A boulder caught him on the head and that was the end."

"I'm so sorry Cedar. That must have been a terrible blow for you and your family. Such a loss." The boat rocked, gently bumping against the float.

"It was. It was the end of our peaceful life. Now my parents are a wreck, empty shells compared to before."

"What did the mine people do?"

"Well that guy, Klaus, he came over and told mom and dad about Nathan, what happened to him. I was in Rupert. They called me at Mary's place on the shortwave. The company arranged a plane to take my brother's body to town. My mom rode in the plane, but there wasn't room for my dad. He came down in his old jet boat. It was crazy. I met the plane and had to go with my mom to take Nathan to the coroner's office.' Cedar paused, reflecting on the story, "She was a complete mess as you can imagine, and it was the first time I'd felt that weight of responsibility. The police never came out to investigate and the coroner just concluded Nathan had died from the head injury. An unfortunate accident. No one ever investigated the causes. Just a bunch of useless hippies out there where they had no business being, that was the general sentiment."

"That's awful Cedar."

"Nathan is buried in the Prince Rupert cemetery out by Fairview. You saw me walking down from there the other day."

Cedar sat in silence, staring into the void in her head. Wayne sat looking across at the stove, eating.

"Cedar, are you serious about shutting this mine down completely? I can help, you know."

"Of course I'm serious. It's my reason for living right now. How can you help?"

"Well we can make sure some real reports get sent to the province. That would stir things up to start with."

"But you don't work for them anymore."

"I know. But I feel like I can trust you now, after what you've told me," said Wayne, putting his empty plate on the galley sink and turning sideways to look directly at her. "So, here goes."

She looked at him and said, "What, why so dramatic?"

"Look, I have all the records. The notes, the draft and final reports, and the photos. All the material collected and produced by my company since the mine started. After I saw you guys living up at Mirage Inlet, I decided I had to set things right, with a proper truthful report. I knew I was going to get fired so I copied everything and kept it. I have the whole story. The evidence needed to shut them down."

She looked at him in disbelief. "So that's why they've been coming after you so hard. I never could figure that out. You've got the keys to their future."

"They're not sure," said Wayne nervous now that he'd told her. "But my ex-boss, the consulting company owner, knows what I'm like because I learned it all from him. He just assumes I would act like he would and have taken the copies."

"They want to get you away from here, and recover the copies," said Cedar pondering the new information.

"That's right. That's why I'm on the run and living on this boat."

They talked some more, and then worked out the sleeping arrangements. Cedar surveyed the situation and said she would take the berth with the rough weather safety rail on the port side bow, the bunk that had been Wayne's. Wayne got the low berth along the starboard side, opposite the stove.

After he turned off the light, Cedar said into the darkness, "I wonder if we'll ever get an even break?" The boat softly bumped the float in response to subtle movements of the water beneath.

SIXTEEN

WAYNE WOKE WITH A START FROM A DREAM, BEING PULLED under in black cold North Pacific water. He could taste the salt. Gradually clearing his head and looking around, he saw Cedar was there, sleeping quietly in the other berth. Her breathing was soft and regular. Her head was buried in a wavy auburn shroud. He sat up and leaned over to the galley sink, pumped water into the coffee pot and set it on the oil stove. He turned up the heat.

Today was going to be pivotal, a change of life. He dressed hunched over with the lack of headroom, went outside to pee over the rail. He filled a bucket for her. Back inside Cedar was stirring.

"So sleepy head. How was the night?" asked Wayne as he tossed scoops of ground coffee into the pot.

"Surprisingly, I slept okay," said Cedar. She dressed horizontally, behind the bunk rail before emerging. "Cowboy coffee, eh?"

"Sorry, they took my cappuccino maker when they kicked me out of the apartment," was Wayne's sarcastic response.

"So skipper, what are the plans for today?" asked Cedar, climbing out of the berth to sit close beside him so she could warm up next to the stove.

"We run up to your place at Mirage Inlet, I guess," said Wayne moving over a bit to make room. "What's it like at the narrows there?"

Cedar looked at her watch and went up to the wheelhouse. Coming back down, with the tide tables open, she said, "By the time we get to the narrows it'll be mid-afternoon, and the tide through there will be in full ebb. That means a current flowing out of the inlet against us at somewhere around five to seven knots, with lots of overfalls and whirlpools. Not good."

"Hmmm, what should we do then?"

"There's a sheltered cove just this side of the narrows. We can hole up there tonight and leave in the early morning after maximum flood tide. It will be less violent then and we'll get a bit of a free ride on the current."

"Perfect, we'll get a quiet night to relax, unwind and think things through." Wayne stepped outside to windmill the coffee pot and back inside he poured. "We just have to get fuel before we go."

They walked along the floats, slippery with the morning damp, and up the ramp. At the top they parted company, Wayne up to the Band Office and Cedar to the fish plant. She knew people there and wanted to pick up something fresh for dinner.

As Wayne was filling the tank with diesel, Cedar rounded the corner of the fish plant building, from where a dragger was unloading. She had two bags in hand.

She held them high coming down the ramp, waving to Wayne. "Hey I got some fresh grey cod." As she approached she held the other plastic bag, open. "And look at this."

Wayne looked inside with a smile. There were strips of kelp, thick with a white crust of herring spawn. Cedar smiled and said, "Arnold's boat just came in. He picked it early this morning and gave me some."

"That's fantastic. We'll have a great dinner tonight. You know what you have to do now, while I fill up the water tank." He watched as Cedar walked over to town, the first time he'd seen a jump in her step.

When he'd finished with the diesel and filling the water tank, he moved the boat back over to the moorage float. Cedar wasn't back yet, and when his phone rang he picked up the call.

"Hi, it's Kathy here," said the voice at the end of the line.

Wayne hesitated, shocked that she would be calling. "Hello?" he said tentatively, dragging the word out.

"I need to talk to you," she said in a rushed manner, agitated.

"Okay, but I can't talk long. I'm just about to leave."

"Sorry, I should have asked about you. Where are you anyway? Are you okay now, after that bad incident?"

"I'm okay. I'm up in Lax Kw'alaams. And I'm recovering from the incident as you call it, thank you for asking. I just have nightmares about it, where I'm being pulled under the surface of dark, cold water."

"What's Lax Kw'laams? Why Lax Kw'laams? Where is that anyway?"

Wayne smiled to himself at her confusion. "You might know it as Port Simpson, north of town. Anyway, I just had to get out of Rupert after they trashed my truck so I'm kind of on the run as they say."

"Oh," said Kathy hesitantly.

"What do you want Kathy? I assume Stu didn't pick up my things and you're going to tell me you pitched them," said Wayne in an exasperated, resigned voice. He found he didn't care anymore, about his stuff, about her.

"Uhmm, not really," said Kathy and she broke down crying. Heavy wracking sobs. "Things haven't worked out Wayne."

"That's a shame Kathy," said Wayne, dispassionately. "Did you call just to tell me that?"

"Wayne?"

"Yes"

"Wayne, I want to get back together again."

Wayne held the cell phone away from his ear. This was unexpected. He looked around at the boat, at the town, at the fish plant, at Cedar skipping down from the wharf with her woolen toque and tangle of auburn, and back at the phone. "Uhmm, Kathy. I've made a lot of decisions in the past week, and getting back together wasn't on the options list at the time. I've pretty much moved on and I'm very comfortable with that."

"What does that mean, Wayne?"

As she said this, Cedar stepped onto the boat rocking it slightly. "Hey Wayne, I got the soya sauce."

There was dead air and then Kathy said sharply, "Who's that?"

"That's Cedar," said Wayne. He smiled at Cedar and said, "We're on a little boat trip."

"Oh," was all Kathy could say.

"As you can see, I've moved on."

The line went dead.

"Who was that?" said Cedar, her smile and jump fading but only slightly.

"My old girlfriend. She called, crying cause she's having trouble. She dumped me and now she wants me back."

"And?"

"As you heard, I told her I'd moved on. I regret a lot of things in my past, but I don't regret making a definite break with that," he said pointing at the phone as he set it down.

"Oh," said Cedar, with a slight smile. "Ida says hi, by the way."

"She doesn't like me, does she?" said Wayne with a return smile. "I can tell."

"Well, as a rule, she's cautious around your types. With good reason I would say. She did give me a word of caution, but in the end thought you might be okay. She told me to just watch my back at all times."

"Not exactly a ringing endorsement, but I'll take it I guess. Guess we can go now?"

Cedar acknowledged it was time to go, and began releasing the mooring lines. The engine sounded good. She jumped back on board as Wayne, standing at the outside steering station, reversed the thrust and put the wheel over. The stern eased away from the dock as prop wash boiled to the surface between the boat and the float.

Molly B rounded the headland outside Lax Kw'alaams and Wayne set a course for the channel leading to Mirage Inlet. At the channel entrance, steep slopes jutted up sharply from the water on both sides. Rock and old growth, with high tide marked by the downward extent of overhanging branches. The day was generally clear. Clouds with the temerity to form latched onto mountains above, halfway to the summits. Looking up, the boat seemed small but with an egocentric view focussed on the water ahead, that scale did not register. Cedar pointed out some sea lions lounging on rocks along the shore.

Up ahead, Mirage Inlet narrowed where cliffs squeezed the passage on both sides. Progress over the bottom was slowed by the opposing current and the outflow breeze coming down the mountain gap.

Cedar pointed to a dip in the shoreline elevation on the inlet's north side. "There's the cove," she said. "We should pull in there for the night. A stream comes down there."

Wayne turned to port, onto a northerly heading, watching the bottom rise sharply on the sounder right at the inlet edge. He guided *Molly B* between some submerged rocks and behind a small point of land into the cove beyond and shifted the prop thrust into reverse to stop in the centre. He tossed Cedar a key as he headed up to the bow winch to drop anchor. "Here," he said, pointing to the hatch cover in the middle of the afterdeck. "Open that up, there's a couple of crab traps down there. Could you get them while I set the anchor?"

While Wayne released the anchor, Cedar lifted the hatch cover and climbed over the edge and down into the hold. As she emerged, Wayne was at the outside controls putting the boat in reverse, setting the anchor in the mud bottom.

When he shut the engine down and turned to face her she said, "Wayne, is there anything I need to know about the mine? About your last report?" asked Cedar, looking at him intently, her eyes boring into his soul.

"What do you mean? I thought we'd been through all that."

"I found the crab traps down in the hold. That was easy. But in the corner there was a tarp."

Wayne froze. "So?"

I looked under it. I saw the paper reports, CDs with files, a laptop, and other things. The report on top was very recent so I peeked. In the summary, was reference to cyanide at the mine site and poor handling practices." She glared at him, accusations in her eyes. "You didn't tell me they have cyanide up there now," she said, striking him in the chest with her right fist and breaking into tears. "How could you not tell me?"

"Cedar, I tried to report it and got fired. It seemed like everyone in town was out to get me. I guess I just didn't think of it. Cyanide is often used to extract gold from the ore. It's an old process. But it breaks down naturally and goes into the air pretty quickly."

"It could poison my family," she screamed at him, hitting his chest with both fists now.

"Look, if I thought it was an immediate hazard to your family, don't you think I would have done something. It's because I was starting to really care about your family that I'm in the mess I'm in."

She collapsed on the hatch cover, sobbing. "What do we do now?"

*****

"TED, WHAT THE HELL'S GOING ON UP AT MY MINE?" SHOUTED Ian Verster into the phone.

"What? What's happening? What's happened?" Ted responded, caught off guard and momentarily floundering.

"There's a real mess up on the north coast. The media's reporting a cyanide spill at the mine. Why didn't you include that in the report you just sent? I paid you for that report."

Ted held the phone away from his ear and in his mind ran through the report and his conversations with Bruno. There had been some mention of a minor cyanide incident, but Bruno had concluded the cyanide would volatilize quickly with no adverse effects.

"Bruno told me the spill was really small, minor, and the cyanide volatilized right away, broke down and went into the air. Bruno said there were no adverse effects."

Ian paused, started to say something then hesitated before revealing the truth. "Ted, I should have mentioned this before but we've started milling the ore and it has quite a high copper grade."

"Oh shit," said Ted surprised and getting very worried. "Copper cyanide complexes don't readily volatilize, they're quite stable and more toxic than free cyanide. What actually happened?"

"You'd better call Bruno and find out. Get the full report," said Ian, still the aggressor.

"Why didn't you tell me about the copper? This could be really bad."

"For you maybe. You're the one doing the monitoring," said Ian hanging up the phone.

"Kaye, get me Bruno on the phone," Ted leaned out his office door and yelled down the hall.

"Hello," said Bruno. "What's up?"

"Bruno," Ted yelled into the phone. "What the hell's going on up there? I just got off the phone with Ian Verster. He said the spill was getting picked up by the media."

Bruno was calm. He'd followed his instructions. "The pipeline to the tailings pond had a non-catastrophic failure and spilled into the brush. The slurry ran down into the wetland and creek."

Ted yelled, "Why wasn't that in your report?"

"You ordered me to use the existing reporting protocols and templates. I asked and you cut that discussion off. So I did exactly what you said. Wayne, and Ron before him, were fired for not following those, so I did."

"Well you should have used your head. What's the situation up there?"

"I came back right away after the test. The cyanide was supposed to breakdown and volatilize, so I didn't think too much about the spill anyway and you had ordered me not to include anything negative, so I left it alone."

"Ian Verster says the media's making a big deal about it. Apparently there's a fish kill?"

"I didn't see any dead fish," said Bruno still confident, "but, as I said, I left right away, confident that the stuff would breakdown quickly. Can't see why there'd be any dead fish."

"Ian told me now there's copper in the ore, a lot."

"Oh shit. It would have been nice if they'd told us."

"I know. He never said anything about the copper before," said Ted agitated and thinking fast, trying to save himself. "It makes you look pretty bad for not reporting it."

"Fuck you Ted. I was doing exactly what I was told to do."

"Oh well. I'll always have your back. Don't you worry," said Ted to reassure Bruno, but it sounded hollow, even to him as he said it.

"Should I be going up there? Should I be doing something?"

"We don't have a contract for anything like that, so I guess you'll have to sit tight."

"I'm pretty uncomfortable doing that. It's like just by being here, I'm a sitting duck."

"Don't worry Bruno," said Ted again, "we'll always have your back."

Ted got off the phone thinking, 'This whole thing is very dicey.' He checked in on his New Discovery stock. It was way up again. Apparently news of possible high copper grades had hit the market and people were anxious to get in on the action.

"Kaye," yelled Ted, "get Ian Verster on the phone, right now."

Ted's phone rang. "Ian hello. I talked to my guy Bruno up there. He says he was aware of the spill, but didn't think too much of it because the cyanide would break down. Not his best decision but there you have it. Like me, he wasn't told about the copper. He didn't stick around so he didn't see any evidence of a fish kill."

"Is he going to go back up and deal with it?"

"That's something we could do if we get the go ahead from you."

"Oh for Christ's sake Ted," said Ian exasperated and impatient, "Tell him to get the hell up there. I need someone on site who knows about this stuff. Someone who can at least talk to the media. Don't worry about the money."

"Okay. I'll call him now."

"Hey Ted, did you see the stock price today? That's speculation on the copper information. Great isn't it?"

"Fantastic. I'll make sure Bruno gets up there right away," said Ted, preparing to hang up.

Ian carried on, becoming more serious. "Ted, I've been hearing that your boy Wayne has disappeared. Had his truck hauled to the junk yard even though it was still basically fine and no one's seen him since. You heard anything?"

"No," said Ted, surprised at the question. He'd gotten rid of Wayne, as Ian had expected and that was considered a closed case. "I wonder why he hauled the truck to the junk yard."

"Word around town is it got vandalized. A big rock, boulder actually, through the windshield. Kids I guess. Ted you really need to track that guy down. He could be serious trouble for us, for you."

"I'll ask Bruno when I talk to him," said Ted, pausing perplexed, before hanging up the phone.

After hanging up he shouted, "Kaye, get Bruno on the phone again."

"Bruno," said Ted when the call came in, "Ian authorized you to go back out to the mine site. Get yourself a charter and fly up there right away. Stay as long as you need to."

"Okay," said Bruno, with a hint of consternation and concern in his voice. "Anything I need to know, or do, Ted?"

"Ian wants you to be the guy talking to the media about the fish kill. You know enough to just downplay everything and deny everything you can. By the way, have you heard anything new about Wayne? Or seen him around?"

"I ran into him a couple of days ago, but not since then. What's up?

Ted gazed up at certificates and awards, momentarily wondering what it had all gotten him and then banished any doubts. "Oh Ian Verster was asking. He'd heard Wayne had kind of disappeared and his truck was vandalized. Said Wayne just dumped it at the wrecker's even though it was still working fine. No one's seen him since."

"I haven't seen him," said Bruno flatly. "Why is Ian so interested in Wayne anyway?"

"I don't know. Anyway, just thought I'd ask. Now you get out there and see what's happening. Call me from there." Ted started to hang up but was stopped when Bruno carried on.

"You know there's no cell phone service out there, and the VHF radio doesn't work because the mountains cut off the line of sight."

Exasperated, Ted said sharply, "Take the sat phone then. Use that. Do I have to spell everything out for you?"

"Ted, hate to tell you but I didn't find any sat phone in the office, the apartment or in storage."

"That bastard Wayne did steal stuff," said Ted, frustrated and angry.

"If they let me use their sat phone I'll call," said Bruno, trying to move things along, avoiding any conflict between Ted and Wayne.

"Okay," said Ted curtly. Then, trying to put a positive spin on the end of the conversation, he added, "Good luck, and remember, we'll always have your back."

Ted hung up the phone angry at first but then smiling happily, thinking only about the increase in revenue from this incident and the increasing value of his New Discovery Gold Inc. shares.

*****

"THE CRAB TRAPS ARE SET," SAID WAYNE BEING POSITIVE, TRYING to turn things around. "Look, everything will be fine. We'll catch some crabs and have some dinner. That herring roe looks really good. I'll pull the traps while you get plates and soya sauce."

Wayne returned to the boat with the crab traps and two Dungeness crabs.

"We need rice," said Cedar truculently from the forepeak as he climbed aboard.

"There's some stowed in the compartment under the starboard berth. I'll get it." He entered the cabin and went down into the forepeak motioning for Cedar get up. He lifted the panel, reached under the berth and the rice was there, wrapped in a plastic bag to keep out the moisture. Extending his right arm further, he pulled out a bottle of Sauvignon Blanc with a flourish. Replacing the panel, he motioned for her to sit back down.

Smiling Wayne passed two mugs from the rack and said, "I picked this up in Rupert for an emergency. So let's enjoy it shall we?" He twisted the cap.

She nodded and savoured the wine.

"You pour and I'll finish with the rice," said Wayne, cranking up the stove.

They boiled up rice and the crabs and fried the cod in a frying pan. With that and the herring roe they were stuffed. Sitting back and savouring the wine, Wayne was content but still wary of Cedar's attitude toward him.

"Cedar, we'll go up there tomorrow and see what we need to do to help out your parents. They have a boat so they're not stuck there, and they've got their shortwave radio. I'm sure they're fine."

"You'd better hope so," said Cedar defiantly. After a long pause she quietly said, "I'm sorry. I know you're trying."

"I'm sorry too Cedar. But, you know you're family is changing my life."

She smiled. The sky was clear and a galaxy of stars shone overhead.

"If you look up, it's almost like you can touch the heavens," said Wayne stretching his arms out on the afterdeck and leaning back against the hatch, almost touching her. "It's unbelievable out here."

"This is what we love," said Cedar leaning back as well, head resting against the hatch. "Why we live out here the way we do. It's so much more peaceful and beautiful than in any city." She took another sip from her mug and snuggled in close, resting her head on Wayne's shoulder.

In the distance a wolf howled and a response came from farther away. Wayne reached for the bottle, poured more wine into each of their mugs. Later they slept, in the same arrangement as before but with a new closeness between them.

The grey light of morning lit the wheelhouse, just visible to Wayne from where he lay in the starboard berth, looking up and thinking, studying the brush strokes in the white paint on the underside of the deck above. They were a testament to the hard work and care for this boat over the years. Years when Wayne had been travelling around the country working to promote big development projects. Maybe the painter had actually accomplished more. For sure the painter was probably more content.

No need to get up early, they had to wait for slack tide at the narrows. He listened again to Cedar's soft breathing as she slept, so apparently peaceful under a rumple of sleeping bag behind the rail of the forward berth. He had no idea what they would find at Cedar's family home or at the mine site.

When she began to stir he got up, turned up the stove and put the coffee on. With the first essence of coffee aroma her head rose to peer over the rail. Her blue eyes looked out at him, bright under tangled tendrils of auburn hair.

"Morning Wayne," said Cedar in a soft, somewhat hoarse voice.

Wayne noticed she spoke first. While he went out to swing the coffee pot, she dressed horizontal in the bunk again, trying to comb out the tangle with her fingers, using a scrap of mirror she'd brought. They drank coffee in the wheelhouse, looking across the mist shrouded cove. It was cool out, about 5 degrees Celsius but the stove kept the cabin cozy.

Cedar was first to initiate conversation. "I wonder what kind of new discovery we'll uncover today," she mused gazing around as if something might reveal itself in the mist.

"I don't know," said Wayne lazily, "but together we'll figure it out."

She smiled a half smile.

Wayne tried listening in on the VHF but in the cove, isolated by surrounding mountains, there was no radio traffic. He watched the time during the morning, while he pumped the bilge, checked the engine oil and washed down the decks. Cedar straightened up the forepeak and helped scrub the decks.

"Should be about time to get moving," said Wayne finishing up his lunch of leftover crab and rice. "The flood tide will be easing so it should be getting safe at the narrows. We can get a bit of a ride on the last of the flood."

The diesel started up with a growl and a belch of black out the stack. While that warmed up he went forward to haul the anchor. Cedar showed she was a natural, by taking the wheel and shifting into forward to take up slack on the rode. With the anchor safely secured, Wayne came back to the wheelhouse.

"Hey, thanks for helping pick up the anchor."

"No problem. I've been around these things more than you think, doing log salvage with my dad and all."

"You're right. I guess I overlooked that," said Wayne with a sheepish grin.

They exited the cove and turned for the narrows. Remnants of the flood tide were still on, and the water became more and more active as they approached the narrows. At least it was going their way, pushing them forward. At the tightest spot, dark whirlpools formed all around and water boiled up beside them. Ahead were some remaining standing waves. A log shot up from nowhere off the port bow. A seal watched from a back eddy along the shore. And then they were through.

"We should hug the north shore from here on up the inlet," said Cedar pointing and giving directions. "The mine is on this side and we'll want to stay as close to shore as we can so we won't be seen."

Wayne checked the chart. "Okay, it's deep right up to the shore." He edged the boat close in.

Cedar went over to the chart and pointed. "See this cove, here. That's where we'll anchor."

Wayne looked at the chart. "Looks like a tight entrance with elevation all around."

"That's right. No one can see a boat in there, even from the air it's hard unless you're directly over top. A plane can't get close enough though because of the mountains behind it."

"The mine people must know it's there?" said Wayne.

"They do, but they never go there. It will take them a while to figure things out if they want to find us. Besides, those guys don't really go poking around the bays. They're working all the time and then they go in and out on the fast crew boat.

Wayne threaded the entrance and dropped anchor as close to shore as possible. He launched the dinghy from the after deck using the boom.

"I guess we should row up to the cabin before dawn tomorrow. Just to be on the safe side. Knowing your history with these guys, I think we're better off if they don't know we're here."

Wayne's alarm went off at five the next morning. He got up quickly and dressed. Cedar was awake and waited until Wayne went up to the wheelhouse to change.

"You want coffee or anything?" asked Wayne from the wheelhouse.

"Nah, don't need it. My mom'll give us something when we get there."

The morning was dark with a heavy downpour. It might have been misty if there'd been enough light to see it. In his rain gear, Wayne climbed down into the dinghy and reached up to help Cedar. Then as an afterthought he said, "Hey, Cedar, better toss down those life jackets and a bailer, just in case."

"Okay, here."

He reached up to help her into the boat and with her body language she indicated that the assistance had not been needed.

Wayne rowed, leaving Ole's outboard turned off to stay quiet, while Cedar gave directions out of the cove and down the inlet. They stayed close to shore, almost within touching distance. The tide was low and there was a slight adverse current to row against. A breeze from the west had brought rain from the outer coast funneling up the inlet and it helped push them along. Wayne rowed silently, thankful he had thought to duct tape the metal on metal of the oarlocks to dampen the sound. As they approached, they reduced cummunication to head nods and hand signals from Cedar sitting in the stern.

The cabin Dave and Starshine had built was located at the mouth of the creek Wayne noted in his report. The report that got him fired. Jimi and Chelsea's cabin was nearby. They glided shoreward until the sounds of sand and gravel scratching at the fibreglass of the hull signified the shallows of the creek's small alluvial fan. Cedar stepped out into the shallow water and dragged the boat up the shore. Wayne stowed the oars and followed. Together they hauled the boat farther up the shore to conceal it in underbrush above the tide line.

Cedar was excited to see her family. She rushed up to the door and knocked, calling out in the darkness.

"Don't want to get met by a shotgun in the face," she said to a startled Wayne.

Dave opened the door. His beard broke to reveal the white teeth of a smile as he greeted his daughter.

"Come on in, Cedar. It's so good to see you. How did you get here?" Looking beyond Cedar at Wayne he muttered, "Oh, I see."

Wayne steeled himself and stepped forward to shake hands. Dave turned away and, putting his arm around Cedar's shoulder, announced, "Starshine, look who's here, our little girl."

SEVENTEEN

CEDAR GAVE HER FATHER A BIG HUG AND WATCHED HER MOTHER emerge from the cabin's rear bedroom, combing her long salt and pepper hair.

"Cedar, darling, it's so good to see you. Thank you for coming," said Starshine as she dropped the comb and rushed across the main room. They hugged before Starshine looked over Cedar's shoulder at Wayne and said pointedly, "Who's he?"

"Mom, you know who this is," said Cedar, breaking away and stepping back. "You've seen him in town."

With a sweeping motion of her arm, Cedar turned and suggested to Wayne that he come in and sit down at the table, rather than attempt shaking hands with her parents. She watched her mother stare briefly at Wayne and then go to make coffee and breakfast.

"We left Rupert a couple of days ago and spent a night at Lax Kw'alaams and then in the cove waiting for slack tide at the narrows," said Cedar explaining their presence. "We snuck in late yesterday to hide Wayne's boat and then came over here before first light."

"Probably a good plan to stay out of sight," said Dave, turning and fidgeting with his hands, his burning dark eyes fixed on Wayne from under hair hanging loosely over an inclined faced. "There's weird shit going on up there at the mine. But I thought this loser you brought with you worked for the mine."

"Dad, he brought me here," said Cedar imploring, caught between worlds and perspectives. "I practically begged him to bring me up here and he did it to help me, to help you guys." She glanced at Wayne, trying to relieve his anxiety and then sat down next to him, backed up against the log wall. "Anyway, he got fired from his consulting company cause he tried to do the right thing and report all the environmental problems up there."

Dave, still standing over Wayne and staring, cracked a weak smile, looked at Cedar and said, "Well maybe, just maybe, we'll give him a second chance." Looking menacingly back at Wayne, he said, "Just remember, I've always got my rifle and shotgun handy."

"Dad!" exclaimed Cedar. "You don't need to try and scare him. People from the mine side of things already tried to kill him last week. They ran him down in the harbour at night and left him in the freezing dark water. He managed to swim and drag himself onto Hospital Island where Mary and I found him the next day. He was hypothermic and practically dead."

Dave looked threateningly at Wayne again and said to Cedar, "You didn't strip down and get in a sleeping bag with this guy did you? To warm him up?"

Cedar and Wayne both laughed and she said, "No I did not. We wrapped him in blankets while Ray stoked the woodstove. We gave him hot tea and soup."

"Oh," said Dave mollified a bit. "I see. Well that's good, I guess." He stared daggers at Wayne again.

"So you guys, what's the latest up here?" asked Cedar trying to get her parents to move onto another subject. "What are those bastards doing over there?"

"There've been shipments coming in again," said Dave sitting down at the table across from Wayne and starting to open up. "Barrels and stuff. A sea truck came in yesterday with a load that included a big tank. Don't know what it's for."

"Wayne does, doesn't he?" said Cedar motioning to Wayne, encouraging him to speak. "Actually he tried to include that in his report for the province and that was what got him fired. Tell them Wayne."

Wayne leaned forward, arms on the kitchen table to explain. "It wasn't just the drums," said Wayne, "but that was part of it. The drums contain cyanide."

"Fuckin' eh," said Dave shocked and angry. He stood up again and started pacing across the main room toward the door, rage in his eyes. "You mean they've got cyanide up there? That explains the fish kill we just had in the creek. I was worrying about that."

"Yes Dad, they do. I saw the report." Cedar did not mention the other things Wayne had stashed aboard.

"Aw shit man, we gotta get rid of those sons-a-bitches," said Dave clenching and unclenching his fists as he paced back toward the kitchen. "They're like a blight, a cancer, a plague on the land."

"That's all Dave," said Starshine wringing her hands, visibly uncomfortable with the overall situation and what it was doing to her family. "Cedar how's it coming along in town. Your efforts to get rid of these guys through civilized means."

"Mom, I feel like I'm being hijacked," said Cedar, starting to tell them. "Jimi's gone and brought in someone from Toronto...."

"Goddam that Jimi. If he screws things up ...."

"Dave, let her finish," said Starshine, putting a hand on his arm. "Go on now Cedar."

Wayne stayed seated on the hard wooden chair, leaning back, watching.

"Well this women from Toronto is from some group called Sustainable People. They've started a big fund raising campaign on the internet and they brought in a videographer to make a video supposedly to help get rid of the mine."

"Don't tell me," said Starshine. "They're going to use it on their website to raise lots of money for the crowd back in Toronto."

"To pay their own salaries," chipped in Wayne. Everyone turned to stare at him and he shrugged.

"They don't even plan to come up here to see the mine first hand and interview you two. Jimi said he'd take care of it in Rupert. I'm really discouraged. That's why I left." Cedar carried on. "Wayne had to get out of Rupert to save himself after they tried to drown him. So I got out too. I'm not going to help raise money for a bunch of uppity eco exploiters from Toronto."

"That's my girl," said Dave sitting back down and pounding his right fist into his open left palm. "Fuckin' eh."

Starshine brought out coffee and corn bread.

"So here we are," said Cedar reaching for corn bread and breaking a piece off. "We thought we'd come up and poke around, see what's going on. Right Wayne?"

"Yeah, maybe we could gather some information and photos that could help put these guys away. I know they're way out of compliance, so that's a good place to start. Send the info to the province and Fisheries, and if they don't do anything go to the papers and tell them what the regulators are not doing."

Cedar looked at Dave, and then at Starshine smiling. "This jerk actually knows how to do this. He knows the soft spots and the levers to pull."

"Spent his career pushing the system, he should," said Dave setting his coffee cup down and smiling back. "Don't like his type, but I like him on our side."

At Cedar's request, Wayne talked about the findings from his last trip out, mentioning the acid runoff, silt erosion, high water level in the tailings pond and slumping tailings dam.

"That tailings situation is getting worse, isn't it Dave?" Looking over at the others Starshine elaborated. "Dave and I were up there after the last big rain storm. The water level's higher in the pond and there are more slump cracks in the dam. The wetland is right below and you can see the seepage into it."

"Be gettin' worse after the rain we're getting now," said Dave. They looked out at the rain now visible in the early daylight. They heard it on the roof like a drum roll.

"And there were drums of cyanide, right Wayne? When we pulled in to Lax Kw'alaams we saw that sea truck go by, quite fast, carrying a big tank or vat or something. Wayne thought it might be for mixing cyanide to get more gold out of the ore slurry."

"So what can we do? Do we stick with the evidence using the regulators and courts, go to the media, or do we do something else as well? More coffee you guys?" Starshine reached over and poured coffee into Cedar's cup and Wayne's.

"What are you suggesting Mom?" asked Cedar, looking surprised and shocked that someone as meek as Starshine would be contemplating other options.

"Oh, I don't know," said Starshine, her moxy fading as fast as it had come. "Maybe there's nothing we can do."

"What we should do is go up and get the evidence and pictures when this rain stops," said Dave decisively. "Wayne, you up for some hiking?"

"For sure," said Wayne relieved at finally being asked to help, especially by Dave. "Out of interest, what have you got for communications here?"

"Well, we've been using a field short wave setup for years but not that many people have short wave these days. To talk to others I picked up a sat phone a short while ago. Keeps me in touch with people I need to be in touch with, and it's essential for emergencies. Got a marine VHF on the boat, but of course range is limited by the mountains. What about you?"

"I've got a VHF on the boat too, but it's no good in here. And I've got the company's sat phone if I need it. They're suspicious but there's no way they can know for sure that I've got it. So I can always call someone."

"Like who?" asked Cedar quickly.

"Oh Susan. I know you know her," said Wayne without thinking about why Cedar had asked so quickly. "I told her to watch for any distress call from me. I didn't tell her where I was going though, didn't have time."

"Why are you asking this Dad?"

"Just need to know what we've got available for emergencies. You know just in case. Never know when things might heat up."

"There's a rifle and pistol on board as well," added Wayne. "Gus loaned them to me."

"Good old Gus," said Dave, smiling to himself.

"Well, I don't know what's going on here, but we're sticking with the evidence gathering idea, right?" said Cedar, with Starshine nodding her muted agreement.

"One more question," said Dave his black eyes burning straight into Wayne's. "Ever used dynamite?"

*****

RAIN CONTINUED TO FALL ALL AFTERNOON AND INTO THE evening. The atmosphere was heavy and grey. A steady thrumming on the roof, drips falling onto the ground below the eaves. Starshine shuffled around the cabin doing chores, while Wayne watched. Cedar strummed Dave's guitar in the background. Dave paced back and forth, and went out to his wood shed from time to time. There was homemade beer and the dope Dave grew, up in the clear-cut. They went to bed early, with Dave saying he wanted to get a good start in the morning and show Wayne a few things.

Wayne was wakened next morning by the sounds of Starshine stoking the woodstove and the smell of coffee. Cedar had slept in her own bed and Wayne in Nathan's old bed, in an area partitioned off at the back of the cabin. Starshine served eggs and toast on the roughhewn kitchen table. It was tight but cozy, made even tighter when Jimi showed up at the door.

"Come on in Jimi," welcomed Dave from the kitchen table as the door opened. "Have some coffee. We're almost ready to go."

Removing his camo rain jacket, Jimi said, "So what's the plan? It's pretty wet out there. Think we'll be socked in for the whole day." He hung the jacket on a hook by the door to let the water drip off.

"In this weather, with the low ceiling, there won't be any plane," said Wayne craning to look past Jimi and out the windows at the cabin front. "I guess that's a good thing. Let's go up below the tailings pond to check the base of the dam. Then we can go up by the pit area and the portal, see what they're up to. I'd like to see what happens with the acid runoff in this heavy rain."

"The wetland's below the dam so we'll have to work our way around and then walk along the base of the dam itself," said Dave biting off a mouthful of toast and washing it down with strong coffee. "And, we need to find out what's going on with this cyanide. Find out where it is and where they're going to use it."

"Sounds good to me," said Jimi, pulling up a chair and spooning some sugar into the coffee Starshine placed in front of him.

"The cyanide's over by the mill halfway up to the portal," said Wayne sopping up the last of his eggs with toast and pushing back from the table. "There were barrels down by the barge landing too, where they've been unloading from the sea truck. It'll be wet in this rain."

"That's fine. You can borrow my extra set of rain gear," said Dave pushing away from the table as well.

Wayne, Dave and Jimi donned camo rain gear and went out. They left the log cabin, stepping onto the gravel yard. Last summer's sedges to the right, growing out of the sand and mud above the high tide line, bent over in the rain. For the first time, Wayne was gaining an appreciation for the setting of this tiny homestead. He knew the gravel base was from the pad of an old log dump, but he hadn't seen the old boom log loader rusting away over at the edge. Two goats roamed the yard around the loader and down on the foreshore, grazing the grass that grew up through the gravel. Wayne realized that the eggs had come from the chicken coop behind the cabin. The only neighbour was Jimi, his log cabin located obliquely behind and to the west, in the direction of the inlet's narrows.

Rather than risk being observed along the shoreline, Jimi led the way up the old gravel logging road that the rain forest had begun to re-claim. Grasses and budding willow shoots grew from the middle of the road where there had been no vehicle tracks for years. There were also the bare thorny stalks that Wayne assumed produced raspberries and blackberries in the summer. Similar undergrowth crowded in the track from the both sides. Passage was easy on foot but would have been tight for any vehicle larger than an ATV.

The thorns on last summer's devil's club lining the roadsides were light beige and threateningly visible. Beyond the underbrush, forest was reclaiming the area with what Wayne figured was a mix of trembling aspen, poplar, fir, hemlock, and cedar.

Walking north away from the inlet, the creek was to the right. From the slope of the terrain to the left, Wayne imagined the high snow-capped peaks he had seen on previous trips, but right now they were completely enveloped in thick black water-laden clouds. The mist started halfway up. There was not even a hint of the peaks that Wayne knew loomed over the opposite side of the valley as well. About a kilometre up the road, the vegetation to the right opened up into a wetland of water, sedge, and muskeg with small cedars sparsely interspersed on moss and sedge hummocks. Further up the valley was a large steep gravel slope, the tailings dam.

"There it is," said Dave, stopping to point out the dam and a very faint hint of a trail skirting the wetland's edge.

It was wet, and Wayne jumped from mossy hummock to hummock to avoid sinking into muskeg and getting completely soaked. The trail eventually led up a perceptible slope to the base of the tailings dam.

"Look," said Jimi pointing to the discoloured wetness at the dam's base. "And there's the emergency decant structure," he said pointing into the distance along the dam.

They all knew the decant structure fed a pipeline that eventually discharged straight into the ocean.

Dave turned to Wayne and asked, "Is this a problem? The dam I mean. Sure looks like it to us."

"I'm no geotechnical engineer," said Wayne bending down to examine the discoloured wet area, "but I've been around these structures for a while. Looks like seepage to me."

"What does that mean?" asked Dave as Wayne stood up again.

"The seepage itself could be contaminated. Plus, it could show internal erosion progressing, unseen, back into the core of the dam. If that's happening, the whole structure would be weakened, from the inside." Wayne bent again to examine the ground and said, "The foundation materials themselves, the natural ground underneath the dam, could be weakening as well. Either way, it's not a good sign, especially with all this rain."

"You mean this seepage could be contaminated?" asked Dave, starting to really lose his cool. "We're right down there in this watershed. Our animals drink the water in this creek. Our own water has always come from the watershed. You mean we could be poisoned?"

"It shouldn't be too bad, unless they're using chemicals to dissolve gold and other metals in ore body."

"Like cyanide type chemicals? What do you mean Wayne?" asked Jimi who was now really starting to worry.

"That's right. Even that isn't necessarily a big problem because cyanide's unstable, unless there's other metals in the ore like copper. Copper reacts with the cyanide to become very stable and even more toxic."

"Oh shit," said Dave, suddenly realizing what was going on. "Of course there's copper. Before this damn gold mine was set up, we had some other exploration geologists through here checking for copper. They thought there might even be enough for a big mine. But they went away and no one heard anything more about it."

Looking up into the cloudy gloom, Jimi said, "Can't see it today but there's so much snow way up high on the peaks that still has to come down. All the snow up there ends up as water down here, fast too if there's a big melt."

"It was a heavy snow year too," said Dave, directing his eyes up toward the shrouded peaks as well. "Can't see it now, but the snow's up there alright."

"Let's go take a look at the water level at the top of this dam." Wayne started to walk back along the base of the dam, and then stood aside so Dave could lead.

"We'll have to stay out of sight," said Dave as he made his way along the base of the dam. "Someone could see us up on top. They're always looking."

They walked back down the trail and around to reach the end of the dam. The end furthest from mine activities, and mine people. To get there they ducked back into the second growth forest, fighting through a thick understory of aspen, poplar, evergreens and the ubiquitous devil's club and thorns. Once around the end, they ascended to the top of the dam.

Jimi swept his arm along an arc tracking the length of the dam. "Look, that water level is really high for the time of year. I don't like the look of that. What do you guys think?"

"I reported the water level as too high in my last report," said Wayne following Jimi's view.

"The one that got you fired?" asked Dave.

"That's the one," said Wayne with an edge. "Look, over there is the water level gauge. The level is higher than the dam's design limit."

"Anyone can see the level's too high. It's common sense," said Jimi authoritatively, as if he was an expert. "I wonder why they don't release it through the decant structure?"

Wayne shook his head and raised his arms in exasperation. "They're keeping it there cause they cheaped out on the treatment. They won't release cause the effluent would be out of compliance and they'd get a big fine and probably be shut down."

"That'd be good," said Jimi with a smile at the idea of getting the mine shut down.

"You'd think so, but the water would still keep building up behind, and someone would have to deal with it eventually" said Wayne.

"So we're fucked," said Dave throwing his hands up into the air, frustrated. "We can't win."

Wayne attempted to explain the inexplicable, the vagaries of regulating a mine. "It's tricky for sure. The province would have to take over management and cleanup using money in the company's performance bond, and then tax payer money when that runs out. The public would end up with the problem."

"Probably cost more than the gold was ever worth," said Jimi, shaking his head. "Good thing we don't pay taxes."

Wayne laughed, saying, "That's a definite possibility." Then he added, "I haven't done the math but I'll bet there are many cases where the cost of cleanup is more than the value of all the gold taken out."

"With what you've seen," said Dave, growing more analytical and serious, "what do you think could happen Wayne?"

"To me, it doesn't look very good. Worst case scenario is a catastrophic dam failure."

"What the hell does that mean?" Dave blurted the question out, desperate and shocked again. Things weren't looking good.

"The dam turns soft, the face of the exterior slope sloughs down, and everything starts to pour over the top until it breaches. Then everything pours out in a massive slug of tailings slurry and water that flows downslope." Wayne pointed in the direction of Mirage Inlet with a sweep of his arm.

Jimi was getting more and more angry. "Into the wetland? That's part of our watershed."

"It was Jimi. Looks like that could be the past tense," said Dave solemnly, as if accepting defeat. "It was our watershed until these bastards took it and destroyed it."

They left the dam, heads down, pensive and despondent as they walked further up the old logging road. On another faint trail, they crossed over the creek and climbed far up to where the mine portal cut into the mountain. They stayed off the roads, fighting through the new growth on the old clear-cut landscape. Wayne wanted to inspect and get pictures of the acid runoff.

As they emerged onto the mine yard, someone shouted out, "The fuck you doin' here?"

The crew worker ran toward them yelling and a mine truck driver got out to do the same. Wayne, Dave and Jimi backed away. Cyanide drums were visible. It looked like they might be transporting them to storage.

From nowhere, a shot rang out in the mist and rain. Coming around the corner of the cyanide truck was Jack, the site manager. With his rifle trained on them, he walked forward. Recognizing Wayne, he broke into a broad smile. "So Wayne, it's you. What ya doin' up here with these dirty hippie squatter thieves?"

"Came up here for a visit with them. We're out for a walk, okay?" said Wayne with a heavy emphasis on the 'okay'. "We noticed the water level in the tailings pond is pretty high. Maybe dangerous even. What's Bruno doing with that?"

"Fuck you. I was wondering if you'd show up after you got fired trying to rat me out. You goddam environmentals, never know which way you're gonna turn. Can't bloody well be trusted. None of you," said Jack, still smiling, moving laterally to gain advantage. "But I've got you now. All of you."

Wayne smiled. "Are you planning to add kidnapping and maybe murder to all the convictions coming your way for the pollution mess you've got here?"

"Geez Wayne, don't make it worse," said Dave, worried about what Jack might do. "We live here you know."

"You sons-a-bitches," screamed Jimi, as he shocked everyone by lunging at Jack in a rage. "I'll kill you myself. I've had all I can take of your bullshit."

G . A .   P A C K M A N

Two big miners lunged forward to intercept. They grabbed Jimi, pinning his arms behind his back.

"That's it," said Jack with a firmness that indicated room for discussion had disappeared. "You're trespassing and you're gonna pay for it." To the two miners he said, "Put him in the portal. There's some zip ties in my truck, use them to keep him in there. I don't care how." Looking at Jimi he said, "I'll deal with you sometime, when you're more malleable."

"That's kidnapping," said Wayne standing his ground.

"He's a trespasser on private property, threatening assault. Now get the fuck out of here."

Wayne turned to go. "I'll come visit you in jail, Jack. After this tailings dam breaches and destroys everything," he yelled back over his shoulder as he took Dave by the arm and walked away.

"Don't bother," yelled Jack.

*****

"TED, BRUNO'S ON THE PHONE. HE'S CALLING FROM THE MINE site on a sat phone."

"Tell him I'm in a meeting," said Ted, short and dismissive.

"He sounds pretty anxious. You might want to take this one."

"I don't want to hear anything from up there Kaye. And don't ever question me again," snapped Ted, betraying a nervous edge.

"Yes boss. I'll tell him you're in a meeting," said Kaye turning off the intercom.

Ted shuffled some papers on his desk, looking at the company financial statements. This last bit of work on the cyanide issue was going to be very lucrative. Brochures from the car dealer sat on the desk edge. His Audi had been looking like it needed an upgrade.

The intercom buzzed again and Kaye announced another call when Ted responded.

"I'll take the call," said Ted.

"Hello Ted. It's Klaus here. Up at New Discovery Gold."

"Klaus, how are you. Good to hear from you," said Ted turning his chair leisurely to gaze out at the harbour view he valued so much. The sun shone bright on the white slash down Grouse Mountain. Ted always enjoyed mixing with the working level at client projects. Made him feel connected. "What's up? What can I do to help?"

"Ted, we've got a bit of a problem up here," said Klaus.

"Is Bruno being a problem?"

"Nah. Nothin' like that. He's a good fella. Those damn hippie squatters are the problem."

"Again?"

Klaus launched into an overview of events. "Yep. Caught three of 'em snoopin' around the site. They were right up at the mine portal, and before that I think they saw us moving the cyanide around. Not sure though. Until now, I don't think they knew we'd started up a cyanidation program."

Ted turned away from the view and back towards his desk. "Well hopefully not. What did you do?"

"Jack caught one of them long haired bastards. Got him zip tied in the mine right now. The others got away. Told 'em they were trespassing."

"How many altogether?"

"Three altogether counting the one we caught." Klaus hesitated before adding, "The third one was your employee, Wayne."

Ted's reaction was immediate and forceful. "Wayne? I fired him. He doesn't work for me anymore."

"Well he's here, that's for sure. Snoopin' around. He knows about the cyanide and might have had a camera under his rain gear. Don't know. It's fuckin' pouring up here."

"How are the water levels Klaus?" asked Ted switching the topic to one of even greater concern.

"They're bad and gettin' a lot worse with this rain. We'll be screwed when the snowmelt hits."

"Okay Klaus. I guess you're going to keep the hippie under wraps for a while? Maybe scare him, rough him up a bit?"

"That's the plan. Just thought I'd let you know, and about you're guy Wayne."

"He's not my guy," said Ted with definitive emphasis.

Klaus laughed and signed off.

Ted spun his chair lazily, thinking through the situation, the new information. "Kaye, get me Ian Verster. I need to talk to him now. And do you still have the number of that security company up in Rupert?"

"Right away boss," said Kaye. "Everything okay?"

"Ian, hello. Ted here."

"I know it's you," said Ian, impatient. "What's up?"

"Klaus just called. Did you know those hippies were up on the site again? They caught one and they're holding him."

"Why would I want to know that?" said Ian dismissively. "I don't micromanage everything up there. Is there a problem that needs an executive decision?"

"No. I guess not."

"Say it again, Ted. I didn't quite catch that. What did you say?"

"No. There isn't a problem up there that requires you to make an executive decision," said Ted, carefully repeating what he'd already said.

"Now, up there means what?"

"At the New Discovery Gold Mine in Mirage Inlet," said Ted capitulating completely.

"Very well then, was there anything else?"

"Just one thing," said Ted, seizing the opportunity.

"What?"

"My former employee, Wayne, you know the guy. The mine people saw him, talked to him up there. We still don't know what files and photographs he has. And he's always dangerous, with what he knows."

"Dangerous for you maybe."

"Maybe dangerous for both of us."

Ian assumed a more magnanimous demeanour. "Hey, don't worry Ted. Everything will be fine. You know I've always got your back."

"Okay, sounds good. I'll keep you posted."

"No need," said Ian. "You know I trust you."

Ted hung up the phone thinking that the call had been very strange. Ian distancing himself so much, so quickly.

Kaye came on the intercom. "I found the information for the security company."

"Good. Call them."

Kaye was on top of the situation. "Already did. Told them Wayne is now up at the mine site. They said they'd take care of it. I don't know what that means but I assume you do, and it's what you wanted."

Ted was noncommittal. "That will be all Kaye."

He turned back to the harbour and the gleaming spring snow on the mountain tops, confident things were under control. After some time contemplating his situation, he rose, put on his coat and picked up his brief case.

"Think I'll leave early today Kaye. I'm sure Bruno has everything under control."

"I'm sure he does. Good night boss."

Ted noticed her look at her watch and raise her eyebrows. It was only two thirty in the afternoon but, 'Hey, it's my company,' he thought.

He drove over to Yaletown, to the marina. Ted parked, slipped his card into the security lock and entered through the gate. The company yacht was there, gleaming white. He went aboard, puttered around and waited for Lyla. He hadn't seen her for a while and was curious to see if they would pick up where they'd left off.

EIGHTEEN

CEDAR HEARD THEM ON THE GRAVEL AND OPENED THE DOOR. AS she helped them in she asked, "How was it? Come on in, it's pouring. Where's Jimi?"

Dave was first through the door, followed by Wayne. "The bastards came at us with a rifle and they've got Jimi," said Dave charging through the door upset, furious, water dripping.

"What do you mean? That can't be." Cedar was confused and anxious.

"Well it's true," said Wayne, resolute, starting to take off his own dripping jacket.

Cedar waited while they peeled off the rain gear and then she hung it to dry. "Come on guys. Come and sit down. Just relax a bit and tell us. You must be cold and hungry." She poured coffee from the stove top and set bread and jarred salmon on the table for them to eat.

"Tell me what happened." Cedar sat down at the table and waited for them to speak.

Starshine sat at the table as well.

Dave and Wayne told them everything and that the mine people had Jimi tied up. Starshine crossed the room and put on a rain jacket. Putting the hood up she said, "I have to get

Chelsea. She's on her own over there and will want to know what's happened to Jimi." She closed the door behind her as she ducked past the drips from the roof above.

Cedar was worried. "What are we going to do? What will they do to Jimi? We have to go up and get him."

She watched her father sit pensively, eyes glazed, fixated on his coffee mug. She knew his deep side. Had seen it many times before. Some would call it dark. His fists clenched and relaxed repeatedly, white skin on the knuckles. She watched him rise and go to the back of the kitchen, returning with the rifle and shotgun, boxes of cartridges and shells tucked under his arm.

"Oh shit dad, has it come to this?"

Starshine and Chelsea came in and saw Dave with the guns. Chelsea had thought ahead and brought Jimi's pistol with her and a stick of something.

"So when do we go?" asked Cedar. "Do we leave him over night and go in the morning? Or do we go now?" She watched Starshine sit down in the corner playing with her hair, while Chelsea put the gun and stick on the table.

Pointing to the stick, Chelsea said, "Jimi's been stealing dynamite from them for years, since the exploration camp first showed up."

"That looks dangerous. Should you guys be having that?" said Cedar pushing the gun away. "I thought you were working with that trendy crowd from Sustainable People? The environmental saviours. What happened?"

"Oh they finished all their interviews and videos and then they all went back to Vancouver and Toronto. Probably never see them again, but they'll make lots of money from our sad little story. Jimi finally got disillusioned and parted company. We're on our own now," Chelsea said pushing the stick and gun further across the table. "We'll have to take things into our own hands now that Jimi's being held captive. Who knows what they might do to him."

Dave finished his coffee, bread and salmon. He grabbed the stick as he stood and said, "Let's go. Have to go get Jimi and deal with these bastards." Wayne did the same.

Cedar stood. "I'm going too. Time for us to take some real action." Starshine buried her face in her hands.

Cedar, Dave and Wayne followed the same route as the morning trek, up to where Jimi had been taken. The mountains were still shrouded in clouds and mist that was unable to support the weight of the moisture that just seemed to drip out of the air. Thorns and devils club tried to tear at their clothes but slid off the raingear. Dave carried the rifle and dynamite, Cedar the shotgun. Wayne had his camera.

From the underbrush, behind an old growth stump, Wayne gathered evidence. Photographs and video. The movements of individuals and the cyanide drums.

"I think we're okay here. We're safe," said Dave crouching behind a massive stump, a small fir tree growing out of its mossy top. "Are you getting the pictures you need Wayne?"

"Look," Cedar whispered as she nudged her father. "That's Jack supervising the cyanide transport. That guy's always been a bastard." She looked at Dave who nodded in agreement.

Wayne fiddled with the camera in the wet. "My lens isn't that powerful. I need images and footage of the cyanide handling that would stand up in court."

"Let's move closer then. So a jury can easily identify their faces and the labels on the drums." Cedar started to edge forward in the underbrush with the shotgun.

Dave touched her arm whispering, "I'll go first. To that stump over there."

Wayne followed behind the two of them, camera shielded under the rain gear.

Half the distance to the mine, they crouched behind another old growth stump. Cedar noticed that this one did not have a new seedling growing out the top. Probably killed by those jerks at the mine she thought. She watched as Wayne crouched and readied his camera.

"That belong to the consulting company?" asked Cedar pointing to the camera Wayne was aiming at the mine workers and Jack.

"You bet," said Wayne with a wry smile, clicking the shutter.

"Might be more effective if dad shot the stills with this," she said, patting the rifle Dave cradled in the crook of his arm.

"Might be," Wayne agreed, snapping another shot, a close up of Jack's face.

"I guess they'd like their camera back," said Cedar.

"I guess," said Wayne. Staring into the camera image he said, "Oh shit. Jack's seen us. Run."

Cedar stayed crouched. Wayne startled and stood up. Dave raised the weapon, sighting down the barrel.

"There's that guy over there. The consultant that got fired." shouted Jack running for his truck and his own rifle. "Go get him, he's just got a camera."

"Let's get the hell out of here," said Cedar, turning to hurtle back down the slope, staying hidden in the underbrush. Dave did the same. "Come one Wayne. Hurry up."

Wayne turned and ran through the underbrush. He tripped and fell. Cedar saw the miners quickly on him.

"The fuck you doin' here?" asked a rough looking miner, looking back to see if Jack was coming.

Cedar and Dave stood, emerging from the underbrush. "He's with us," said Cedar, the shotgun aimed at the closest miner.

Dave had his rifle aimed at the one confronting Wayne. "Back off," he said. "We've had enough of you fuckers. Two seconds I'll blow your fuckin' head off."

"We came looking for our friend Jimi," said Cedar. "You've got him held up here, against his will. You kidnapped him."

It was a standoff as Jack approached from behind the two miners. He had his rifle cradled, pointing down.

"We don't know what you're talking about. This Jimi? Who the hell is that?"

"It's the guy you kidnapped this morning," said Dave.

"Don't know what you're talkin' about. Now get outta here before someone gets hurt."

"Yeah, like you," said Cedar, brandishing the shotgun, before firing just over their heads.

As they ducked and exclaimed surprise, Jack made a move with his rifle.

"I've got more shells," said Cedar. "You want one? Or maybe you want my dad to shoot up that ANFO truck over there. That'd make a nice boom, no?"

While Cedar talked and fired the shotgun, Dave had moved downslope and taken up a position, rifle squarely pointed at Jack's expansive gut. "I got him sighted. Good old gut shot."

"We're leaving," said Cedar. "Don't try to do anything. We've got lots more of this nastiness back at the cabin. Come one Wayne, let's leave these fuckers. They'll rot in hell anyway." Turning back she screamed at Jack, "Don't you dare hurt Jimi. We know every inch of this place, and where your family lives in town."

All three were silent walking back down the old logging road to the cabin. Opening the door, Chelsea was right there. Cedar shook her head saying, "Sorry Chelse, we couldn't get him. Couldn't get near the mine. They saw us and were armed." She put her arm around the poor woman's shoulders.

*****

DURING THE EVENING WAYNE OBSERVED THE OTHERS IN THE light of a couple of oil lamps. Starshine was trying to console Chelsea, while Dave sat in his corner chair, cleaning and oiling the rifle. He had already finished with the shotgun. Cedar stared at the stick sitting on the table. They listened to the faint static of the CBC on the portable radio. It was the only station even remotely reachable.

"This rain has been coming down hard, even for here," said the weather guy, "and it's going to continue for the week. Another low has moved in from the Gulf. The Forest Service issued warnings to all people thinking about venturing into the backcountry. Avalanche risk is extreme and there are severe risks of rock and mudslides affecting roads and trails. Be careful out there."

Starshine had asked whether they should call the police on Dave's emergency sat phone. They all quickly dismissed the notion. Every one of them had some reason for not wanting to involve the police, except Cedar, and she was leaning sharply toward frontier justice anyway. Wayne began to realise that his indiscretions in stealing records and some equipment were the most minor of the group.

Raising his head from lengthy contemplation Wayne said, "I know Dave and Jimi's trails now. I'm going up there tomorrow to see if I can get Jimi out of there. I used to work for them. I know the miners. They'll talk to me."

"I'll go with you," said Dave, rubbing oiled cloth on the rifle. "I need to go."

"No. I'll go alone. I feel bad that the company I used to do work for has put you in this position. I'll do this alone and we'll see what happens."

Starshine walked Chelsea back to her cabin and said she would stay with her through the night. As they all retired into a restless, sleepless night, wolves howled in the distance.

Wayne got up at first light. He'd been lying awake listening to the steady patter of rain on the roof and outside on the gravel yard. He sensed the others were awake too. Cedar got up and made coffee for him along with eggs and toast, again. She tried to hand him the rifle but he declined saying, "Not really my thing, Cedar."

"City boy," was her condescending response.

She helped him with the raingear and binoculars, and ushered Wayne out the door saying, "Good luck. Hope you do better than yesterday. We'll expect you to be back by three o'clock, at the latest. Hope Jimi's okay."

Wayne stepped out into the morning air. There was mist that enveloped everything and heavy rain, still. He had hoped for a nice sunny day, but knew the mist worked in his favour, as long as he didn't get lost. Trudging up the road thoughts of the past filled his head. He had to do this, but he was worried. Scared, even though he'd never admit it to anyone, including himself. In a flash he wondered what Kathy would be doing this morning. 'Having a leisurely coffee and watching the news before walking to work I guess.' Then he pushed it out of his mind. 'Hell with her,' he thought.

Wayne turned onto the faint trail past the tailings pond, and ascended the incline, fighting through vicious clawing underbrush again. The raingear served as much to fend off the brush and devil's club as to keep him dry. Mist began to clear and that was raising the ceiling. Wayne heard the familiar sound of a Cessna coming up the inlet. At first it was hard to see against the cliffs at the narrows, but the sound of the engine echoed off the surrounding peaks.

From the trail he watched the plane swoop in and drop to the water, a streak of white spray streaming in its wake. The reversed thrust created an enveloping cloud of mist as the Cessna slowed and settled into the water. The pilot taxied over to the camp barge. Through Dave's binoculars Wayne saw two figures get off. He recognized them immediately, even at a distance.

At the top of the slope Wayne walked right out onto the gravel pad at the ore processing area. Two workers operating a crusher saw him and approached.

"Hey Wayne. You alone today?" asked the first one, who Wayne knew as Stas. This one was gruff and could be confrontational, although he had been helpful to Wayne from time to time.

"Yeah, I'm on my own," said Wayne, putting out his hand and then greeting the second miner, Amar. "Hi Amar, how's it going? How's the new baby at home?"

"Oh just fine, Wayne. Thank you for asking," said Amar, reaching to shake hands. Amar was always gracious, and even tempered, a stark contrast to Stas.

"So what are you doing here? Where are the others? Where's that bitch with the shotgun?" asked Stas, looking around suspiciously, like he might get ambushed at any time.

"I told you I'm on my own Stas," said Wayne. "I want to see about Jimi. You guys can't keep him forever, and I'd just like to see us end this thing peacefully. There's no reason for violence. No need for anyone to get hurt."

"Tell that to your friends, coming up here with guns and all." Stas' radio squelched and he talked into it.

"I think it was Jack that started with the guns, but let's not quibble over it. Let's just get Jimi and I'll be on my way."

A truck pulled up spraying mud from the potholes. "Hold it," said Jack getting out. He walked over, puffed up chest to look authoritative. "So, it's our buddy Wayne again. Where are your friends Wayne?"

Another truck rolled up, Axel's arm hanging out the rolled down window. As it slowed, the passenger side door opened and Cody was out immediately, even before the wheels stopped rolling.

Jack turned to acknowledge the two newcomers and then back to Wayne saying, "I think you know these two fellas?"

"Oh fuck," said Wayne under his breath.

"What did you say?" said Axel approaching Wayne aggressively and getting right up to his face.

"I said 'It's so nice to see you two again'," replied Wayne.

"Well we're happy to see you too, Wayne. It's been a while since we've had a chance to talk. We've missed you haven't we Cody," said Axel. Cody walked up and nodded in agreement, wearing a big silly smile.

"Now that we're all re-acquainted, I'll ask again. What the fuck are you doing up here? I thought I told you and your hippie friends to stay off the property," said Jack aggressively, his gut protruding.

"You did suggest that Jack, but those people down there are concerned that your property, and by that I mean your tailings, will end up in their property, and by that I mean their homes. Anyway, I came up this morning to see about retrieving their friend Jimi. I think you have him on deposit here, maybe in the portal over there," Wayne said. Pointing to the mine opening.

Axel stepped closer. "You're being pretty smart ass for a defenceless guy talking to five other guys. Don't you think you should show some respect, given your circumstances."

Wayne looked around at the group, took a step back from Cody and said, "You're right. I apologize. If I could just collect Jimi, we'll both get right out of here and you all can have a good day."

"Sure," said Axel menacingly. "Maybe Jack will take us all over and show us where Jimi is." He motioned to Jack and they all started walking across the yard to the portal.

As Wayne approached the blasted cavern, an underground mine truck emerged from the depths of the dark hole the miners had clawed into the mountain. The operator turned his engine off. Wayne could hear groans emanating from within, not just from the machine.

Stas said to the truck operator, "Want to see the captive."

The man went into the adit and came back with Jimi, dragging him on the rough rock and broken stone surface. He was still restrained with zip ties and looked like he had been subjected to cranial and full body beatings.

"This the guy?" said Stas, giving Jimi a sharp poke with the steel toe of his boot.

Wayne started to bend down to help Jimi, and that's when Axel caught him with a fist in the back of the head. He crumpled and fell to the ground. Then both Axel and Cody were on him.

"Been waitin' a long time to get a piece of you mister," said Axel, pulling zip ties from the chest pocket of his work coat. Cody had zip ties in his teeth like a rodeo cowboy.

"So Wayne, what've you got to say for yourself now?" asked Axel. "It's not quite so sophisticated out here is it? Now what have you done with the files and disks you stole?" he starting dragging Wayne to the portal and Cody dragged Jimi back there as well.

Wayne heard Jack tell them, "Rough him up Axel. But make it look like an accident."

"You mean just like that stupid hippie kid?" asked Cody.

"Yeah, like an accident. Come on Stas and Amar, let's get back to work. We'll go down to the barge landing where we won't have to listen to this shit."

Wayne saw them leave and wondered what would happen. Cody was clearly enjoying this.

*****

WAYNE LAY ON THE ROCK OF THE MINE FLOOR, NEXT TO JIMI. They both had hands bound behind their backs with zip ties and ankles bound the same way. They could see in the distance faint diffuse light from the portal entrance reflected off a slight bend in the adit. He kept thinking 'So maybe these guys did kill Cedar's younger brother Nathan. They tried to kill me, so they probably did kill him and covered it up to look like an accident.' Now he knew what he was really dealing with. Another reason why everybody up here had been so sensitive. He started wondering if there might be something in the photos that Ron had taken. The ones that would be in all the digital files he'd copied and stored in *Molly B*'s hold.

"Jimi, you okay?"

Jimi just groaned. It seemed he'd been beaten pretty bad.

Wayne kept on talking, to himself for all he cared. "Jimi, I was supposed to be in Vancouver with Kathy, she was my live in girlfriend until I came up here. I took this job for New Discovery just to make some extra cash. It was a stupid little job. Supposed to be short term. In and out. And here I am. If only I hadn't lost so much in the stock market I wouldn't have been so desperate for the money. I wouldn't have even come up here. Shit Jimi."

Jimi just groaned from the gloom. Wayne didn't know if Jimi'd heard him, or understood. He could barely make out his crumpled form lying on the damp stone floor.

"Who you talkin' too?" yelled Axel, as the forms of he and Cody blocked the light when they entered the adit. Their faces were shadowed against the backdrop of bent daylight from the portal entrance and blocked out by the glare from their headlamps shining on Wayne. He came right up to Wayne and gave him a sharp kick, in the kidney area for special effect.

"Just talking to Jimi," Wayne stuttered the words out. "He's not answering though." Wayne slumped against the cold jagged wall of the adit, motionless.

"Well you shoulda' stayed right away from this place," said Cody giving Wayne a tap with the steel toe of his boot, in the ear. "I heard you talkin', to yerself I guess. You definitely shoulda' stayed away."

"What're you going to do with us? Jimi's in pain. I think he needs medical attention. We both need water."

Axel crouched down in front of Wayne in the dim light, his headlamp blinding Wayne's eyes. "Oh Jimi's fine. You should just worry about yourself. It's not really going to go easy for you I think."

"Hey Axel," said Cody, as he checked on Jimi. "This one doesn't look too good. Should I just finish him off? Save us lots of bother. We could just burn him and be done with it right here."

"Okay, go for it," said Axel, watching for Wayne's reaction. Then he burst out laughing, joined by Cody. "Just screwing with your head there Wayne, boy. Cody, stop making our guests feel uncomfortable."

"Okay Axel, you always know best," said Cody laughing. "These two sure make a pathetic pair don't they? Should we beat the shit out of them now, or let them soften up overnight."

"Doesn't really matter to me. What would you prefer Wayne?" asked Axel as he poked Wayne hard in the forehead with his forefinger. "But we have something we have to discuss, don't we."

"I've got nothing to discuss with an asshole like you," said Wayne. He spit at Axel's face but missed, and it landed on his rain pants and slid slowly down.

Axel laughed. "See Cody. This one still needs to soften up. Now Wayne, you know you've got things that don't belong to you, they belong to the company."

"Oh yeah. Like what?"

"Like files, records, copies off the computers, pictures, those kinds of things."

"What makes you think I've got those?"

"Because you're a smart guy. Smart enough to know you'd be fired and smart enough to grab whatever you could on the way out the door, eh? It's just logical."

"Sure using you're kind of logic. But I'm not like you. I don't use that logic. I don't have anything. You made sure I took nothing."

"I guess maybe you're not as smart as everyone thinks then. You either don't have anything, which is dumb, or you won't give it up. That's also dumb because giving it up is the only way to avoid what's gonna happen to you."

"What about Jimi? What's going to happen to him?"

"Oh he's finished anyway. Nobody gives a shit about dirty squatter dope growing hippies like that. We can make him disappear and no one will ever care."

"His friends down there will care."

Axel thought for a moment before saying, "They won't be there long."

"Whatever, Axel, if that's even your name," said Wayne with a shrug before disdainfully adding, "Do what you're gonna do or just get the fuck outta my face and stop irritating the hell outa me and Jimi. Okay?"

Axel looked at Wayne and stood up. "Okay Wayne, if that's the way you want it, we'll go. Have a nice night." He turned and walked away.

"What about some water?" Wayne shouted after them.

"Room service is closed," shouted Axel over his shoulder. "Try licking some off the rocks."

In the gloom Wayne surveyed his surroundings. The rock wall of the adit was biting into his back. There was the mine truck nearby and some drill equipment. As he sat leaning against the wall, he thought through his options. None looked promising.

Jimi was clearly a mess. "Jimi, did you think they actually killed Nathan and staged it as an accident?" Jimi shook his head and groaned. Wayne could barely see the head shake but heard the groan and didn't know what to make of it. He knew he had to get them both out of there but had no idea how.

Wayne talked to Jimi to pass the time, a one way conversation. "Don't know what we're going to do Jimi. This whole thing is a lot more serious than just pollution or getting you guys to move out. Someone here committed murder, and the rest have been covering it up. And now we know, and they know we know."

Silence and dim light enveloped them and, given the alternatives, he was thankful. Jimi was quiet and Wayne dosed off.

After a time Wayne heard footsteps, boots crunching on rock and stones. A headlamp.

Wayne shouted out, "Who's there?"

"Hello Wayne. It's Amar," came a gentle voice from behind the headlamp.

Wayne watched him approach. Amar held a bottle of water to Wayne's lips. He drank as much as he could, water spilling down his chin. "Thank you Amar. Thank you. You're a good man."

Amar then went over to Jimi.

"Amar, how is he?"

Amar shone the headlamp on Jimi and Wayne could see blood from cuts and scrapes on his head and face. "They beat him a lot," said Amar, giving Jimi water. Jimi drank weakly, the water spilling down over his chin and shirt. Amar put some water on a rag he found on the mine truck and wiped the blood off Jimi's face. "This is terrible Wayne."

"We know it's not your fault Amar. You're a good man, a good worker and honourable," said Wayne. "We could really use your help though."

"You know I can't really help you, Wayne. I would lose my job and that would be the easy part. I don't know what Axel and Cody would do to me."

"Yeah, I know you're caught in a no win. It's going to be a long night. So how is your family Amar?" said Wayne changing the subject to relieve both of them.

"Oh very well," said Amar, touched that Wayne cared enough to ask about him and his family, especially at a time like this. "The baby is growing every day. It's very exciting. I hope he will have a better job than this."

"This mining company's bad, isn't it?" After a pause Wayne asked, "Amar, what's going on here?"

Amar shrugged. "I don't know Wayne. They don't tell me anything. I guess they just want to get rid of the two families down there."

"But why me. Why are they coming after me? Have they said anything?"

"I don't know. Maybe because they think you're one of them now." Amar thought some more before saying, "Bruno says you're going to expose the pollution violations up here."

"Bruno told you that?"

"Yeah, that's what he said."

"Is he here now?"

"Yes, he's right down there at the barge camp. I don't think he knows you're here, trapped in the mine though."

"Would you please tell him Amar? Please, for me."

"Yes, I'll do that for you Wayne. You've always been fair with me."

"Amar, are you getting paid regularly?" asked Wayne with compassion.

Amar hung his head and shook it. "Wayne it's worse than you think. We have no money at home because they haven't paid me for more than a month. I don't know what to do. There's nowhere else to work. We'd have to move to get another job, but don't have the money to do so."

"Well, my company was bad too. I didn't realise it until I came up here to work on this," said Wayne, starting to open up. "You know I worked for them right out of school when I really needed a job. I just kept rolling along and now look at me."

"That sounds awfully good from over here," said Amar, not particularly moved.

"Yeah, you'd think so," said Wayne shaking his head, "but nothing's ever as it seems, is it? To do the work you have to bend information to fit the need. First you bend a little bit, and get rewarded for it. Then you bend some more and get rewarded even more. You end up being a success, but all that bending stuff stays in your head, your legacy."

"And then you're so far in you take on a shitty job for quick money and end up zip tied in a mine in a rained out inlet in the middle of nowhere talking to some guy from Jaipur. Is that it?" said Amar, chuckling quietly.

"Yeah, kinda," said Wayne with a bit of a laugh. "Thanks for that bit of clarity and for lightening things up Amar."

"No problem."

"But you know, this job here made me realise how far down I'd gone. I just couldn't do it anymore. I needed the money cause of stupid investments and now I don't have anything. Just my small savings and my knowledge. Is karma real?"

"Oh yes Wayne. Karma is very real. I'm sure things will turn around, if you make the change" said Amar being positive. "They always do."

"Karma's a bitch, isn't it?"

"Oh yes Wayne. It surely is."

*****

"WAYNE IT'S GETTING LATE," SAID AMAR SHIFTING POSITION AND flipping his headlamp on. The lamp illuminated portions of the cavern creating obscene shadows from the equipment, the jagged rock walls and Jimi. "My shift is over. You're safe here and immobilized, and no one's come to relieve me. They've said they're not paying me overtime money, so I'm going."

Amar rose and stretched out to relieve his cramps and pains from sitting on the cold damp stone. Wayne watched him leave, around the bend in the adit. Looking back, Amar yelled, "It's really dark out here and still pissing rain Wayne," as he disappeared into the night.

Wayne heard a truck start and drive away. He sat there in the dark and wished he could stretch the pains out too. Jimi lay motionless on the floor over by the mine truck, and Wayne hoped for his sake that he was sleeping. He couldn't see.

The direction and approximate location of the mine truck were pictures in Wayne's brain, from the images Amar's headlamp had illuminated. He eased himself down into a prone position and wriggled over to where he thought the truck was. After some trial and error, he found the truck and a rough edge where steel had been cut with a torch. He turned and backed himself up to it and began a tedious process of wearing a break through the zip ties holding his wrists behind his back. Finally, he broke through. With his hands he found a sharp shard of rock and used it to wear a cut through his ankle restraint.

Wayne stood, unsteadily, and stretched out the cramps before getting back down on his knees. He felt his way in the general direction of Jimi, eventually finding him.

"Jimi, can you hear me?" said Wayne as he began to cut through Jimi's zip ties with the rock shard.

Jimi made a deep groaning noise, barely discernable as, "Yes Wayne."

"Okay Jimi. Listen to me," said Wayne as he finished cutting. He slid the sharp rock into his pocket and said, "Jimi, I'm going to get us out of here. Can you get up on your knees?"

Jimi flexed his legs that had been restrained for more than a day. They worked, more or less. He rolled onto his stomach and summoned the strength to get up onto his knees.

"That's good Jimi. Take a bit of a rest. We'll need to get going soon though, in case someone comes back." Wayne put his arms around the man's chest and said, "Okay Jimi, time to get up. I'll help."

Wayne lifted and Jimi slowly stood. He stretched out his legs and became a bit steadier.

"Okay Jimi. Time to say good bye to your nice home here in this wretched mine."

Jimi managed to squeak out something like, "Fuck you gold mine." It really didn't make a lot of sense but seemed to give him strength.

"Okay let's go now. It's dark, I'll lead. We'll hold onto each other," said Wayne, putting an arm around to help him walk.

They felt their way along the adit with feet and hands. The rocks were cold, damp and slippery. Eventually they reached the portal.

"It's dark and pouring rain," said Wayne checking outside. "Good thing you wore rain gear yesterday."

"It might have some holes in it from the beatings," mumbled Jimi, not caring at all.

"Okay Jimi, time to make a run for it. You okay with that?" asked Wayne as he ventured out. "We'll have to be careful of potholes in the gravel yard out here."

"The trail is over there. I know it like the back of my hand," said Jimi as he stumbled along weakly. His mobility improved slightly as circulation returned and his legs started to work again.

"Good," said Wayne, helping him along. The rain water streamed down on the two of them.

Feeling their way across the wet gravel and potholes of the yard, they stumbled, and even fell a few times in the darkness.

"Here it is," said Jimi, feeling ahead with his foot. "This depression in the grade. This is the start of our trail."

"Are you sure? I'm not doubting, just want to be as sure as we can before we head down. It's slippery and we don't want to fall."

"Yeah, this is it. We've been up here before in the night, stealing equipment and dynamite sticks, you know." Jimi started down and Wayne supported his shoulder. They stumbled repeatedly but made it into the underbrush below, where they would be hard to detect.

It was vicious, fighting in the dark through the underbrush, the thorns, the unseen devil's club. Their hands were cut and full of spikes. The slope steepened to where they had to traverse a rock incline. Together they slipped and fell, sliding down the slick face into scrub below.

Lying in the underbrush, Jimi said, "I think we'd better wait here. There are steeper rock patches on this slope, some with a vertical drop. Too dangerous in the dark. Below this rock, they won't see us when we get moving as the morning light dawns." He settled in, rain running off his hood and jacket.

"Alright," said Wayne, settling down on the soft organic ground under the brush. "You're the boss. I don't know these trails at all. How do you feel, anyway?"

"I'll survive," said Jimi, begining to relax. "Hey Wayne, thanks for getting me out of there. I wasn't really thinking. Don't think I even realised Amar had left."

"You were in pretty rough shape alright. How badly did they beat you?"

"Yeah, they beat me. Pretty good too. Don't really know why, though. Intimidation I guess. Mostly just the rage of violent people. They want us out of here and haven't been able to get us to leave."

"Why haven't you guys left already?" asked Wayne, venturing into uncharted personal territory. I know it's none of my business, but I'd be interested if you feel like talking about it."

"Well, after the logging quit we did log salvage along the beaches for a while and some tree planting. While we were tree planting, we started planting some dope plants. You know, just for fun, for ourselves. Then we started selling product to the other tree planters. The pulp mill shut down so the log salvage was more of a bust. We planted more dope in the clearcuts, harvested more, sold more. Our spots are all here in this valley."

"You could still have moved?"

"Nah, we put too much into it here. It's a lot of income on the line here, and no one even knows about it. And fuck them anyway. They'll be gone before long. These companies always come in, screw up an area and leave a mess. The whole thing's a rip off. The only people getting rich are the guys mining the share price on the stock exchange and getting their cash out before the bust."

"Yeah, you're right. The gold grades in the ore here are going down already. That's why the cyanide, but that's just a ploy for optics and share price. When this reaches its inevitable conclusion, they'll just move on and rape another valley."

The two of them dozed occasionally in the cold and the rain. A wolf howled in the distance. They heard a large animal moving in the underbrush making huffing noises not far away.

"Griz," whispered Jimi. "They're just waking up from winter, hungry and ornery." They lay still and it moved off downslope.

Wayne's pulse raced at the presence of a grizzly so close, with them completely unprotected. He calmed himself and dozed again, thinking, 'At a certain point, when there's nothing you can do, you just don't give a shit anymore. It can't get worse than this.'

The underbrush started to become discernible through the gloom as the light of dawn increased. It became apparent they had slid down a smooth rock incline, made slick by the rain, onto a small shelf area. There was a drop of about ten feet below them. 'Close but manageable,' thought Wayne. "It's starting to get some light in the sky Jimi, you think we can move on now?"

"Yeah, I'd say so." Jimi brought his body up into a crouch. "I'll lead. I'm feeling better after the rest. Cold, wet and starving but at least I know the way."

"Okay, I'm right with you."

They worked their way around the drop, found the trail again and inched down hill, staying low in the underbrush, out of sight. When the miners showed up for work, there was a commotion, but they couldn't see Wayne and Jimi in the underbrush well down the slope.

Eventually they came out at the old logging road, and behind the cover of second growth were able to walk freely along it, past the tailings dam.

"That water level's gotten higher," said Wayne looking over at the dam top and the staff gauge. "Maybe the decant can't keep up with all the inflow from the runoff this whole valley is sending into it. Let's check out the seepage below."

Walking further along, they came to the trail leading along the base of the dam. "There's more seepage," said Wayne. "Shouldn't happen that fast, unless there's a problem.

This doesn't look good Jimi. Looks like it might be starting to slump too, on the face of that dam. Let's get going."

NINETEEN

THE OLD LOGGING ROAD WAS LIKE HOME AFTER THE STEEP overgrown trails up at the mine. As they struggled along, Jimi limping badly, the façade of safety and security grew. The smell of smoke from the woodstove was fragrant and reassuring. Wayne helped Jimi round the corner of Dave's cabin and pushed open the door. Everyone, including Chelsea, looked up from their coffee and breakfast, shocked and grateful.

Wayne's hands and face were cut and scraped from the trek down the mountain in the dark and the slide down the rock. Jimi's rain gear was ripped and torn and his face was a mess of cuts, abrasions and contusions. Both eyes were blackened and he had a limp.

Wayne watched as Chelsea ran over to Jimi, who collapsed into her arms. He smiled at Cedar who surprisingly came over and hugged him, appearing not to care at all that she was getting wet from his rain gear.

"Morning everyone," said Wayne nodding to Dave and Starshine, and removing the rain gear. "We both need water and Jimi hasn't had food for a long time."

The cabin scene looked like a First World War bunker with exhausted dirty wet soldiers languishing and regaining their strength and will for the next assault. Wayne and Jimi were the soldiers.

"What the hell happened?" asked Cedar desperately. She helped Wayne to a chair at the kitchen table while Starshine put water, coffee and biscuits in front of him. Starshine brought a cloth and wiped Wayne's face.

Wayne watched as Chelsea gave Jimi water to drink and wiped his face gently. He winced with each stroke, and she cringed and cried.

"Wayne got me out of there," said Jimi nodding gratefully at Wayne to show his thanks. "Without him I think they'd have beaten me to death."

Wayne looked over at Jimi, directly into his eyes, and shook his head slowly to signal it was too soon. There would be a better time. Both Wayne and Jimi drank their coffee and slowly ate. Starshine brought ham and eggs, and they ate that too. Everyone peppered the two soldiers with questions but they just stared blankly and ate and drank, gaining strength from the fuel.

"We've been up for a long time," said Wayne as he pushed his plate to the table centre. "Jimi a day longer than me."

Chelsea slid her chair back and stood, moving to rub Jimi's shoulders from behind. She gave him a hug and when she kissed him on the temple he winced involuntarily. "Sorry hon," Wayne heard her whisper into his ear.

He watched as Chelsea fetched Jimi's rain gear and helped him climb into the jacket. "Have to put this on again," she said. "It's still a monsoon out there."

She got Jimi mobile and took him across the yard to their cabin, through the ever present rain.

As he watched them, Wayne shivered and thought, 'When will this low pressure weather system ever move on?'

While Starshine cleared the table, Cedar led Wayne to the bed that had been Nathan's and lay him down on it. Dave went out, down to the water to check on the boats, his and Jimi's. They were anchored out in the inlet, beyond low tide, moored at big orange floats and accessible from shore by clothesline systems. The moorings and anchors had to be substantial enough to withstand the outflow winds that often ripped down the inlet, especially in winter.

Cedar helped Wayne as he undressed and put Dave's dry clothes on. She gave him a quick hug as he lay down on the bed, and then bent and gave him a light kiss on the forehead. Wayne watched her, warmed by her presence and signs of affection. He quickly fell into a deep, fitful sleep as she gently pulled Nathan's blanket over him. As sleep's dark shroud closed in on his consciousness he thought, this is the second time Cedar has revived me. He smiled.

Wayne and Jimi slept through the morning. At late lunch they all got together again for a meal of fried potatoes, and grey cod and spot prawns that Dave had caught.

Wayne started by saying, "I think it's time to go you guys. You need to leave this place. Things don't look good. I know you don't want to but ..."

"No fuckin' way," said Dave in a booming voice, almost shouting. "Jimi?"

Wayne looked over at Jimi who shook his head, before saying, "I hear you Dave. This is our home. We've invested a lot of ourselves here."

"A lot of money too," said Dave angrily. "What about that?"

"One thing I know though, I can't do that again Dave," said Jimi, tilting his head in the direction of the mine. "They'll kill me next time, that's for sure." He looked questioningly to Wayne.

"There are some harsh realities," said Wayne steeling himself before stepping into the middle of this maelstrom. "The miners are getting more aggressive and the tailings dam is getting worse. Much worse. With all this rain anything could happen. Dave, let's go look at that dam. You have to see it. Then we'll talk again."

Wayne looked back at Jimi, as he'd done earlier that morning and nodded his head in agreement. Jimi said, "Dave, Starshine, Cedar, we learned something up there that we don't want to tell you but we have a duty to. We heard those thugs from Rupert talking. About Nathan."

Jimi, rubbed his hands over his face, parted his fingers and peered around the room. The others watched, in expectation and denial, Starshine turning her own face to the wall.

Wayne nodded to Jimi who stumbled over his words. "They beat him and staged it to look like an accident."

Starshine screamed and Dave yelled as he reached for his rifle. "Sons-a-bitches. I'll go kill them right now. All of them."

Cedar put a hand on Dave's arms and said, "Dad, you know we always suspected something. It just didn't make sense, the explanation they gave."

Wayne reached out and gently took the gun, as Dave crumpled into his easy chair heaving in inconsolable grief.

Wayne leaned in and said calmly, "Dave, it's time to go to the authorities. This valley will always be here but this mine will be history when our stories are told." He rose to put on his rain gear again. "Dave, you and Cedar come with me. I need to show you that dam. It's really very dicey. We'll talk again after you see what it's like today."

They slogged through the rain and wet scrub along the logging road. No one talked. There was nothing to say. Dave was bitter and remorseful, wanting to lash out at anything, and kill it, beat to a pulp, to death. Cedar was quiet, sad, within herself. She had become closed off to the world around her.

Wayne stayed watchful for people from the mine, but none appeared. He wondered what they were up to after yesterday and finding they'd gone over night. Cedar led the way when they got to the faint trail choosing a branch along the wetland perimeter and up to the base of the dam. They remained concealed in the vegetation at the wetland edge. From the shelter of the brush, it was clear that the sloughing on the dam's face had advanced during the day. The never ending rainfall doing its job.

"When these dams give way, it happens very quickly," said Wayne trying to explain the risks. "All at once. It's always like that. There will be a slug of contaminated water and tailings that will rush down here. An unstoppable wall that will tear up this wetland and coat it with tailings that will lie bare for the next hundred years or more. That wall will blast right through your cabins Dave." Dave was silent and Wayne waited a moment to allow the true impact to sink in. "It's not safe at the cabins," Wayne implored him. "This thing is ready to go and will destroy them, and you too if you're there."

Dave looked at the dam and at Cedar, and turned to go. Despondency and mixed feelings were etched all over his face. He looked in the direction of the snow-capped pass at the head of the valley, shrouded in deep dark cloud cover. Cedar held his arm. He was both about to explode in rage and beaten into submission. Wayne could see this condition would not last. Dave was going through something very deep, or maybe he was thinking through other matters, his contingencies.

"I don't think it will happen," Dave said finally. "I watched them build that dam. It's keyed into the sub-grade, nothing could move it."

They turned and began to walk back to the cabin. Wayne looked over at Cedar and shook his head. Degradation of the dam could not be stopped now. He saw Cedar acknowledge the meaning with a grimace.

At the cabin, when Cedar went inside, Dave went to the covered area out back to check his seedlings for the spring planting season. He had worked hard to develop this system for germinating and starting his plants. Wayne followed and could see him weighing his inputs of time and effort against the threats they had just seen up at the tailings dam.

As they walked, Wayne said, "Dave, you can always plant again. It's not the end of the world. The most important thing is the safety of you and your family."

Dave started to lash out with, "You. You work for them. Why should I listen to you? You're as bad as they are. I saw you up there looking down on us like we were nothing and you acting so superior. You're doing their dirty work getting us to leave. I should just beat the shit out of you right here. Right now."

"I'm right here whenever you want," said Wayne, signalling his own capitulation. He could see there was nothing to be done with Dave. This would not be easy.

*****

WHEN WAYNE RETURNED FROM THE SHED, CEDAR COULD SEE things had not gone well with her father. Dave was out talking to his seedlings again, an annual ritual that was going to have to end. From her position at the kitchen table Cedar watched Wayne shed his rain gear and hang it next to hers. She saw her mother sitting in her usual spot in the corner by the kitchen window, now shrunken to half her usual size, hands passing over one another repeatedly.

Pushing a chair out so he could sit near her, Cedar asked "So what happened with Dad? Is he coming around?" She had been worried ever since their return from the walk up to the tailings dam. She'd never seen his brooding get this bad.

Wayne shook his head. "I think we've lost him. He's out tending his seedlings. Talking to them."

"He does that every year," Cedar brushed the observation aside. "It's kind of his thing. A ritual before planting season. All of the family's money, except for the welfare, comes from those seedlings. Dad built all of this with his bare hands." She spread her arms to encompass the cabin, emphasizing the point.

Starshine shook her head, her long salt and pepper hair, partially concealing her face. Cedar heard her saying things she'd never heard before. "I should have gone back to school instead of staying to work at the canneries and getting wrapped up in this back to the land bullshit. Smoking and dreaming all day, all pointless. I could be living back in West Montreal working and making lots of money. Thought I'd become a lawyer, and look at me now. Out of touch, out of money, out of everything."

"But you wouldn't have had me," said Cedar, shocked and hurt. "And I love it here. We don't need all that stuff Mom. Not when we have family."

"Huh, family. We've lost Nathan and what the hell's this guy doing here anyway," she snorted derisively and pointed at Wayne. "All the problems started when he showed up."

Cedar crossed the room to put an arm around her mother's shoulder. "That's not right Mom. You know he didn't make this mess. He didn't even know about Nathan."

"Yeah I know. You're right," said Starshine holding onto Cedar's hand. "And I wouldn't have missed out on having you for the world. It's all so confusing right now."

"I know Mom. We'll get through this. But we have to stay alive first. We won't be doing anything if that wall of water and tailings comes down on top of us."

The rain poured down like it would never stop. From across the valley came the sound of a blast up at the mine, the sound of ammonium nitrate and diesel fuel coming together with oxygen in a massive exothermic reaction. They all looked up startled and then shook their heads in disgust at the activities of the mining company.

A few moments later, like an echo, came a sound like another explosion, from their side of the valley. They looked at each other all visibly shaken and wondering what the second sound had been. It wasn't from the direction of the mine.

"What the hell was that?" asked Cedar anxiously standing from her chair. "Are they going to try to blast us out now?"

Before she could get the words out, a sound like a runaway freight train could be heard up the mountain. It was very close.

Cedar grabbed her rain gear and headed out the door, followed closely by Wayne. As they went by Dave and his plants, Cedar said, "Dad, we're going to check things out. See what happened. See what that noise was." It was as though Dave hadn't heard the sound or seen them, or heard Cedar. He was hunched over, talking to his plants and puttering around the shed, like he was looking for something.

Cedar led the way up the old logging road. "You know Wayne, that sound was really weird. I'd like to say it was the mine. That would be simple. Blame them as the common enemy. But I'm not so sure. It was too big and long to be an ANFO explosion."

"Yeah, I know what you mean," said Wayne, walking along behind her. "Sounded different, and not good."

They rounded a bend in the logging road and there it was, a mess of rock, mud, broken evergreen branches and tangled tree trunks. The road was impassable. Looking up, there was a swath cleared down to glistening bedrock extending up the mountain into the rain laden clouds.

"Holy shit," said Cedar looking up at the cleared chute extending vertically to oblivion. "That rain soaked into the ground and turned the soil to muck. Anything not solid rock has come away. That's what we heard."

"Look," said Wayne, directing his gaze to the right, "it's gone down to the creek too."

Cedar started climbing over the mass of tree trunks, rocks and mud to continue up the road. "Where are you going Cedar?" he asked anxiously.

"Farther up, to see what happened. See if anything happened to the dam."

She looked at Wayne and he shook his head. "You know there's no point, Cedar. All the soils here are obviously saturated. The dam will be the same."

"You're right," said Cedar turning back. She climbed down from the debris pile and headed back to her home. I guess we have to get out of here right away. Is that what you want to say?"

Cedar walked quickly, almost running, in silence. Wayne followed behind. She walked past Dave and said, "Dad we're going in the morning. No questions, no discussion, no objections, no staying behind. Get yourself ready, and the boat."

"What happened up the road?" asked Dave, looking up from his plants.

"Half the mountain came down across the road and into the stream and wetland. The ground is saturated. Everything is about to give way. There's no way that tailings dam is going to hold any longer." She caught her breath and in a new authoritative tone gave her father his orders. "Get going old man."

Dave shook his head and smiled slightly at the change in her. "Okay, we'll go."

"Wayne, you tell Jimi and Chelsea, I'm going to get our family packed up," said Cedar striding quickly over to the cabin.

She flung the door open and startled Starshine who was still sitting in the corner hunched over. "Come on Mom. Time to pack up."

Looking up, Starshine said, "What was that noise? Was it the blasting again, over at the mine?"

"No Mom. It was a big slide, right across the road and into the creek and wetland. If the ground is so saturated that it gives way, then the tailings dam won't last long either. Come on, let's get going."

*****

TED LOOKED AROUND AS HE USED HIS ACCESS CARD TO OPEN THE locked marina gate. There was no pressing need to go to the office this morning. Kaye would let him know if anything needed his attention. Walking along the slip, he sized up his boat up against the others and was well pleased. Things were going great. They would be even better when Ian paid the remaining outstanding invoices. Between that, and the money he'd make on increases in the New Discovery Gold share price, he'd be clear.

His boat stood out above the float. He climbed up the dock steps to deck level and stepped aboard. The morning was sunny and warm, with spring in the air. It was a great time to be out of the office and Ted wanted to catch up on some things on the boat. He had a crew coming down to polish the cabin and topsides and oil the teak. He looked forward to getting away for a week in the Gulf Islands over Easter.

Sitting in the skipper's chair with coffee he'd just made, his cell buzzed and jumped across the galley table. He looked at it and after a moment of indecision, punched the keypad to answer.

"Bruno, what's up?"

"Ted I'm up at the mine."

"That's good. Good for your billable hours. How can I help?"

"Yesterday there was a spill. A drum of cyanide got knocked over and the cyanide ran down toward the water."

"Yeah I know about that," said Ted, taking a sip. "Didn't that get dealt with?"

"Well some of it hit the water and there were some dead shiners and herring and stuff, but that's all dissipated now."

"Any evidence?"

"Nah, there's nothing remaining."

"Those hippies see anything?"

"I don't think so. But they went by in their boat around that time, so it's hard to say."

"Well you know what to do about the reporting strategy, right? No questions on that?"

"No I got the message last time."

"Pictures of dead fish? Any questions?"

"No pictures of dead fish, right."

"Okay then, anything else."

"Just one thing Ted." Bruno hesitated, leaving a pause for the coming message to sink in. "There's more weird shit going on up here. Two guys showed up from Prince Rupert. They say they're security guys just checking things out, but to me they're just a couple of thugs. Intimidation guys."

"So, that's none of your business really, is it? I guess they're doing some work for New Discovery Gold. Just stick to your job, everything will be fine."

"I don't know. Like I said things are getting pretty weird. Those hippies were up here snooping around and guys from the company caught one of them. Had him zip tied in an adit."

"So?"

"So Wayne came next and was caught. And they zip tied him in the adit too," said Bruno, his voice becoming strained.

"Wayne, what's he doing anyway?" asked Ted, paying more attention now and becoming more edgy.

"I don't know, but the whole thing makes me really nervous."

"Relax. None of that concerns you. Just do the job you're hired to do and everything will be fine."

Bruno hesitated, like he was focussing on something up there. "Who do these guys work for Ted?"

"I don't know. Maybe Klaus hired them for security if those hippies are creating problems. They're probably trying to steal gold or something."

"Yeah, maybe. I don't know," said Bruno with skepticism clear in every syllable."

"Anyway, just do your job and you'll be fine," said Ted, trying to wrap up the call. "I've got to go now, there's another call coming in."

"Hold on a second. It's been raining like crazy up here, for days and days. Water level in the tailings pond is really high and there's some noticeable slumping on the face of the dam."

"So? That's all standard for the North Coast. What do you want me to do about it? Make the rain stop?"

"No. That's not the point. The ground is saturated. There was a big slide last night, over on the opposite side of the valley. It's getting dangerous."

"I have to go now," said Ted.

They signed off as Ted saw his crew at the gate. As he let them in, Ted motioned to the boat. He explained what he wanted done, scrub the decks, polish the fiberglass, clean the windows, oil the teak. He wanted the boat to be in tip top condition for the weekend.

Perched on the skipper's seat, Ted punched in a number on his phone. "Hello Ian. Ted here. Just checking in. I understand the cyanide spill was contained and cleaned up."

"Oh hi. Yes, things are okay. Klaus says the spill was all cleaned up. And we did some bench scale gold extraction with the cyanide. Just enough to support the press release we sent out today. You should be glad. Our share price shot up on news of the enhanced extraction potential. We're all making money."

"That is good news, on both the spill and the share price. And yes, on your recommendation I did buy a lot more stock a few days ago. Made money already. Regarding the spill, I'll send an invoice over today."

"Sure Ted, send the invoice. Everything's looking good." Ian hesitated, in a pause that had Ted shifting in his seat. "Except for your guy Wayne."

"Like I told you before, Wayne doesn't work for me. What's he doing now?"

"He and those damn hippies have been snooping around. Axel and Cody took care of them, for a while."

"What do you mean, 'for a while'," asked Ted rising from the seat and pacing the bridge deck impatiently.

"Had them trussed up in the adit, but they got away in the night. Damn slippery those bastards."

"I hope Klaus has everything under control. We don't want another incident like the one you had with that hippie kid."

"Ted, that was your incident. I'm just the money guy. Axel and Cody work for you, remember that."

Ted gazed south into the distance, at the condos lining the far shore of False Creek and up the slope to West Broadway. Ian was being difficult again. "Okay Ian. I'll talk to them."

Ted signed off and sipped his coffee, watching the blonde in his service crew polish the windows. He punched numbers into the sat phone he kept on board for business up the coast and got through to the camp barge in Mirage Inlet. They found Axel.

"Axel, this is Ted."

"Hey Ted. What do you want?"

"I'm calling to see if you've recovered those materials yet."

"Not yet. This Wayne guy's a real piece of work. He's got them stashed somewhere, I can feel it. He's up here now but we don't know where those files are."

"Can't you squeeze the information out?"

"Tried, but it ain't that easy with this guy."

"Well get it done. I don't care how. Those files could ..., well you know what's potentially at stake. Just do it."

"Okay, gotta go now Ted." Axel hung up and Ted felt pleased with himself. He was taking control now.

The morning passed pleasantly as he puttered about in the sunshine while his service crew worked on getting the spring yacht cleanup done. As he watched them work, he thought, I should really take someone besides Jamie with me over to the Gulf Islands this weekend. He called Lyla, who readily agreed.

TWENTY

WAKING UP TO THE SOUND OF RAIN AND SLEEP, WAYNE THOUGHT again, 'This is the day'. The rain was coming down harder than ever and now an outflow gale was howling down the inlet. He had to get these people out, before it was too late.

He leaned over Cedar, and gently nudged her, brushing her cheek lightly with finger tips he talked calmly in low tones. "Cedar, time to get up. We have to get moving. Need to get everything packed up now. We don't know how long that dam will hold."

He watched Cedar get up, pushing auburn hair off her face. Wayne looked at her thinking that even in the grey morning light she looked beautiful. Dave was snoring. Starshine was already up and fussing in the kitchen.

Emerging from the back room, Wayne said, "You guys need to pack up some things you want to take. I'll go tell Jimi everyone has to leave. Cedar, you get your Dad moving."

As Wayne went out the door, Cedar started packing things to go: clothes; books from her childhood; and, family memories. A picture of Nathan going off to school in Rupert for the first time.

When Wayne returned, Dave scowled at him. Wayne said, "Come on Dave, I'll help you get the boat ready."

They both went down to the beach where the gale was blowing strong. Whitecaps stretched across the inlet. It took the power of both of them to haul Dave's boat in from its mooring and secure it at the beach. Jimi joined them and they brought the boat in as close as its draft allowed. Wayne helped Jimi bring his dinghy down to take their things out to his boat.

Cedar, Starshine and Chelsea brought the first loads down and everyone joined in for the rest. When they were ready to go Dave, Starshine and Cedar went back to close up the cabin, not knowing if they'd ever see it again. They looked around at their lonely paradise, the end of escapist dreams, delusions from the seventies, home brew and dope filled memories. Suddenly, Dave and Cedar ran back into the cabin. She emerged with Dave's guitar, almost forgotten in the chaos. Dave lingered and when he finally emerged he was flustered and had a heavy metal box that took both arms to carry. Cedar sheltered the instrument from the pouring rain the best she could with her jacket.

The sound of a large blast over at the mine echoed across the valley.

"That was a big one," said Wayne ominously. "Extra charge. They're getting greedy. Come on you guys, let's go," he yelled, loud and urgent. "I'm getting really nervous. That blast could ..."

Out of nowhere, suddenly they could all hear the sound, like a massive freight train roaring down the valley, through the bush, through the wetland, over the stream.

"Cedar, hurry, run," yelled Wayne, releasing Dave's boat and starting to push off.

They could see a progression of trees falling and ravens rising in a cloud to circle above, making their loud alarm calls. Cedar ran for the beach and they all jumped into the boats. As they cast off and backed away from the shore, a wall of grey death rushed toward them. It hit the chicken coop,

Dave's plants, Jimi and Chelsea's cabin and then her own. Her home, Nathan's home, crushed under the grey slurry, splintered wood tossed insignificantly. She saw the two goats scramble up to higher elevation into the bush, up the mountain, and said a silent prayer for their safety.

The tailings streamed into the ocean in a semi-liquid flow, creating a tsunami that pushed into the gale tossed inlet and sent out a grey cloud of turbidity that grew like an evil force across the water and down into the depths. Cutthroat trout from the creek washed out to sea, dead. The vibrant intertidal community of rockweed, shore crabs, barnacles and anemones instantly suffocated under a coating destined to become cement-like. Death reigned supreme. The gale force winds and torrents of rain could not disperse that much destruction.

Everyone was awestruck, shocked and terrified at once. What had just happened? How could this have happened? Their valley turned into a wasteland. They consoled each other. Dave and Starshine on one boat, Wayne and Cedar with Chelsea and Jimi on his boat. No one spoke. The members of this former community cried, burying faces into wool and Floater jackets.

After a moment Wayne asked, "Chelsea do you guys have a camera on the boat?"

Chelsea produced the digital camera Jimi sometimes kept on board and passed it to him. While they quietly mourned, Wayne took pictures of the destruction, all of it. In the distance they could all see the frantic activity on the camp barge. Klaus and the other miners were in a panic. None of them saw Dave and Jimi's boats leave except, through the zoom lens of the camera, Wayne could see one person on shore, Axel, looking back at him through binoculars. Wayne knew Axel could see him taking a picture of him looking back through his binoculars. 'Good,' he thought. Axel fired a round with the rifle he carried, but missed all of them.

The powerful diesel engine of Dave's jet boat roared and a torrent of salt water jetted out the stern. Jimi secured Wayne's dinghy to his towing bit and threw the drive into gear, moving forward down the inlet to the narrows at a slower and steadier pace. Cedar watched as Dave and Starshine roared down the inlet in the fast jet boat bouncing off waves, spray flying skyward. They saw the jet boat stop just before the narrows to wait at the cove, the one where Wayne had anchored *Molly B*. Cedar and Wayne sat on the afterdeck leaning against Jimi's dinghy and watched Wayne's dinghy ride the wake crazily, constantly on the brink of disaster.

When they dropped Wayne off, he rowed into the cove where *Molly B* was hidden. He climbed aboard and went below into the hold to retrieve his files, laptop and digital copies. He passed them to Dave saying, "Your boat is fast. They won't catch you. Wrap these up and keep them dry. Whatever you do, don't let anything happen to these. These are the evidence that will ruin the company and put those guys away. You can out run any boat they have. Get these to Rupert, and Jimi's camera with the pictures I just took. Hide everything at Mary and Ray's place."

Dave took the materials and wrapped them in garbage bags he kept in the cuddy cabin. "It'll be fine Wayne. So where's the newspaper and the cops you talked about."

"They'll be along," said Wayne from the rail of the *Molly B*. "They should be here today. Do you want to hang around and tell them what happened?"

"No way. I'm getting the hell out of here."

"Good. We can talk to them on the radio. We should pass them on our way."

Wayne watched Cedar sitting on the afterdeck of Jimi's boat as they navigated out of the cove leaving him alone with his boat. He fired up *Molly B*'s engine and it coughed into life with a belch of black from the stack. Wayne went up to the foredeck and raised the anchor. He reversed to get the bow swinging, then put the wheel hard over and gunned the engine to turn. He throttled back and slid out of the cove that had kept his boat hidden so well.

Jimi's boat was up in the narrows. At the beginning of the flood tide the current was against them but manageable. The problem was the waves coming from behind kicked up against the opposing current. *Molly B* pitched fore and aft in the steep chop but luckily kept moving forward.

It was slow going in the narrows. *Molly B* was the slowest boat of the three, but Wayne was confident he'd get through. As his boat laboured, in the distance he thought he could see the mine's crew boat pull away from the camp barge. 'Oh shit,' he thought.

Crew boats are not small, but they are designed to transport people quickly. Wayne knew that boat would catch up before long.

*****

WITH ONE LAST FOLLOWING WAVE *MOLLY B* CLEARED THE current in the narrows. Two eagles peered down from the tops of their weathered cedar monuments to old growth. Wayne hugged the shore picking up back eddies and avoiding the main current, watching the sounder and radar. He hoped to blend into the shore but knew whoever was in that crew boat would find him. He checked the rifle and the revolver. They were close at hand. The flares were nearby. There was nothing else he could do. Chances were that this was going to end in a fight. The others were all gone.

The crew boat gained steadily. With its semi-planing hull there was no chance for the *Molly B* displacement hull. Wayne knew that, had known it all along. He called out on the radio and Chelsea responded, and passed the mic to Cedar.

"Cedar. Wayne here."

"Right Wayne."

"There's a crew boat following me, gaining fast. It will catch up soon."

"Okay. Should we come back to get you?"

"Negative. Keep going. Just call over to whatever boat Susan and the cops are on if you see them go by and tell them what's happening."

"Okay Wayne, I'll call the press and the cops."

All of a sudden, a third voice cut into their radio conversation. "Wayne, you'll never make it. This will be the end for you. You need to give us those records you stole. The cops can't help you now."

"Who was that?" demanded Cedar anxiously.

"Must be Axel or Cody in the crew boat. I guess they've been listening in on this VHF channel. Are you recording this at your end?"

"Absolutely. I got it," said Cedar. "Fuck you Axel. I'll get back at you yet."

"Ah Cedar. So nice to hear your voice. Those were good times weren't they, back in high school. I dream of you every night," said Axel as the crew boat came charging up to *Molly B*. "Gotta go now beautiful. I got business here with my friend Wayne."

"You leave Wayne alone. He doesn't have anything," Cedar yelled into the microphone.

"That's where your wrong beautiful. Wayne doesn't tell you everything. You should know that," said Axel, his voice oozing insinuation.

"Don't listen to him," said Wayne as the crew boat edged ahead and started to cut across *Molly B*'s bow. The two boats crashed together, aluminium on wood. Wayne heard Cedar scream into the radio airwaves.

He throttled back and *Molly B* slowed to a stop, drifting with the wind and tide broadside. Turning to look aft, through the glass in the wheelhouse door, he saw Cody jump over the rail onto *Molly B*'s deck and fasten a line. Wayne reached for the revolver and stuffed it and some flares into his pockets. He stood in the galley facing aft, toward the wheelhouse door grabbing the rifle.

The door opened. Cody began to step in and Wayne thrust the rifle up, cold steel against the pock-marked skin of his face.

"What the hell do you guys want with me anyway?" asked Wayne, prodding his face with the muzzle.

Cody smiled. "We want those things you stole from your company. Just give them to us and we'll leave you."

"The mine's finished anyway," said Wayne, his eyes never moving from Cody's. "Anything I might have is useless now. And I don't have anything."

"We know you've got something. Maybe you don't even know what you've got. I don't know."

"Well I don't know either," said Wayne, jamming the rifle further, forcing Cody's head back. "All I know is that I don't have anything here. You could search the boat, but, oh yeah I forgot, you've got a fuckin' rifle up your nose."

Cody quickly ducked his head to the left and brought his right arm up to deflect the rifle away. Wayne stepped back to re-aim the gun, but Cody grabbed the barrel and threw it to the deck. "There, that's a lot better," said Cody. He stepped back and stood beside Axel who had joined him on deck.

"Okay Wayne. So you think you're a tough guy, eh?" said Axel with a derisive sneer. "Office boy with some big education. You don't know what you're up against out here. Just let us search this tub and we'll be on our way. Cody you search the cabin and engine compartment, I'll look in the hold."

"Go ahead and look," said Wayne acquiescing, realizing that any other response would be fruitless. Axel was right, this kind of confrontation wasn't his thing at all. "Go ahead.

I really don't want to shoot you anyway, and you won't be satisfied until you see for yourselves there's nothing here."

Cody stepped past Wayne into the cabin. Axel put out his hand and said, "Key Wayne. Give me the key for the hatch cover."

Wayne handed over the key and stood back out of the way. He kept the revolver hidden, knowing they wouldn't find anything and hoping they'd just leave when they didn't. He waited on deck, while they searched.

"Hey, don't make a mess down there," yelled Wayne at Cody as he went through belongings in the forepeak. The search continued.

Climbing out of the hold, Axel yelled, "You find anything Cody?"

"Nope," said Cody, emerging from the wheelhouse.

"Okay, we know you had stuff and we have to get it back or we won't get paid. Where is it?" demanded Cody, raising a fist and pushing Wayne up against the rigging.

"Well I did have a few things," said Wayne, acting more relaxed and shifting into story-telling mode. "Personal kind of stuff. You know, my 'Employee of the Month' coffee mug, shit like that. Nothing really."

"Where is it?"

"Well, after you threw me out of the apartment I put some personal things on the boat, in the hold down there. You know, like my pay slips, dismissal letter, that kind of stuff. Then you trashed my room and wrecked my truck and I figured I should just get out of town."

"We don't want a history lesson. Where's the stuff?" said Axel, impatient and aggressive.

"Damndest thing. When I came up here to Mirage Inlet I put that stuff in Dave's cabin. I needed a place to store my belongings and they generously offered. And then when the tailings dam failed, and we all had to leave in such a hurry, there wasn't time to pack up much. I guess my stuff is still there. Bottom of Mirage Inlet right now I guess. Nothing of interest to you though."

"Bullshit, you're lying," said Axel, looking over at Cody who shrugged his shoulders as if to say 'What can we do?' Axel looked uncertain as to next steps.

"The only way to find out would be to go dig it out of that pile of shit the cabin's under or go diving in the inlet," said Wayne seeing their confusion on learning the new unexpected information. "The tailings pond wiped everything out. You know that."

"You blew up the tailings pond," said Axel, finding his footing and the confrontational high ground again.

Wayne recoiled at the new accusation. "What the hell are you talking about? That dam was on the brink of giving way. Had been for weeks. That's why I got fired. For trying to report it."

"There was a big explosion just before the tailings pond breached. That had to be you guys."

"That's bullshit and you know it. That was the miners getting greedy and using too much charge."

"If they'd used too much charge, then they'd have a pile of broken rock in the mine, wouldn't they?" said Axel, backing up his position. "Well they don't."

"How would you know? You're out here hassling me."

"You just have to go look. Why don't you come back with us?"

Wayne chuckled and said, "Fat chance of that. Never going back to that place with you two and New Discovery Gold there. I guess it's time for you guys to go, eh? Like I told you, there's nothing here on this boat." He wanted to say, 'And you don't want another murder on your hands,' but he decided it would be better not to make his dangerous situation worse.

"You know what they do have, Wayne," said Axel continuing to describe results from the blast, "is a pile of rock that came down the mountain, right over the portal."

"Was anyone hurt?" asked Wayne with genuine concern.

"Wouldn't you like to know," sneered Axel. "Come back with us and find out."

Wayne shook his head and said nothing.

"Okay Cody," said Axel breaking off discussion and moving to the rail. "Let's leave this pathetic loser. Looks like the stuff isn't here. I guess we'll have to just get him for blowing up the dam. This Wayne guy thinks he's some sort of eco-guerilla now I guess. But he's going down. Going to go down hard."

"It was the miners that wrecked the dam, when that huge blast shook everything. That dam was teetering on the brink and the tremors from the blast were the last straw."

"Tell that to the cops that are coming. The ones you called. And to the judge," said Cody, laughing as he climbed back over the rail to the crew boat. "We're still comin' for you Wayne. Never forget that. We're always comin' for you."

*****

IN THE STRONG WINDS AND FOLLOWING SEAS, CEDAR WATCHED Jimi wrestle the wheel of his log salvage boat, a boat best suited for work in tight, hauling logs off the shore. A boat not designed for strong winds and big waves. She and Chelsea stood beside him in the wheelhouse, holding onto the dash and peering out through the rain smeared windscreen. White caps churned by, not big swells like on the open coast, but short steep waves needing constant attention. They'd made this trip down the inlet many times over the years, never comfortable in such weather.

In her head, Cedar was reminiscing about all the good times in Mirage Inlet. Playing with Nathan along the shore and in the forest. Taking care of the chickens and goats. Studying the lessons Starshine gave them. Isolated but idyllic. Jimi and Chelsea had taken care of them too, whenever both Dave and Cedar were away doing business in town. Then along came New Discovery Gold Inc. That's when everything started to go wrong. The boat rocked and pivoted in the waves and Cedar's mind did the same.

Out of the mist, ahead off the port bow, they saw a fishing boat emerge and slowly angle toward them. As it closed in, Cedar recognized Gus' boat from Cow Bay. She grabbed the microphone and called over on Channel 16. Gus responded. Then Susan came on the radio.

Jimi altered course across the inlet and the waves toward the oncoming boat, and it did the same. They met in the middle.

Cedar greeted Susan yelling across the gap between the two vessels. When the yelling proved fruitless, Cedar made the dangerous transfer to Gus' boat.

"Where's the RCMP?" asked Cedar. "Wayne said the police were coming."

Susan put an arm around Cedar's shoulder and guided her into the wheelhouse where they could talk. "There wasn't enough information for them to go on. They only do marine calls on their own boats and there wasn't enough information to justify a whole crew."

Cedar broke down in tears saying, "Susan, it's awful. Our home is gone. Jimi's home is gone. Everything is gone."

Susan hugged her and said to Gus, "Tell Jimi to continue on. We'll go see about Wayne and what's happened up at the mine. I've got a camera and sat phone. We'll get the information out and we'll be okay. The police know we're here and why."

Gus made the radio call and Jimi's voice came back. "That's okay with us, but only if it's okay with Cedar." Gus looked over at Cedar and she nodded, 'Okay'.

"She's says she's okay with it," said Gus into the microphone. "You guys be careful on the outside. There's a real stinker blowin' out there." Gus signed off and steered his boat to pull away from Jimi. They carried on up the inlet to the narrows, with Cedar onboard.

Cedar was first to spot the *Molly B*. Through Gus' binoculars she could see two men climbing back onto the rafted up crew boat. 'So they did catch up to Wayne,' she thought. Cedar pointed and said, "We need to go over to Wayne's boat and see what's happening. See if he's okay." She watched as Gus altered course heading for the *Molly B*. The crew boat accelerated in a fuss of spray and a huge wake, and roared off, headed back toward the narrows.

As they motored over to Wayne's boat, through her tears Cedar explained to Susan what had happened. How the wall of liquid mud had raced down and wiped them out. "Susan, you have to get pictures and report this disaster."

Susan kept her arm around the sobbing Cedar and whispered, "I will Cedar, and this will go right into the paper, I promise. Don't forget my clan has a stake in this mess too."

Cedar said, "I know," as she tucked her head into Susan and cried. Susan stroked her hair.

As Gus pulled alongside *Molly B*, Cedar rose and went out onto the afterdeck to look for Wayne. He was on deck and looked fine, no worse than when they'd parted. When Gus came along side, she passed him a line.

"Hey are you okay? I saw the crew boat. Did they hurt you?"

"Nah, I was okay," said Wayne with false bravado. "Thanks to Gus' friend here," he said as he pulled the revolver from his pocket and showed her the flares in his other pockets. "They demanded and I let them search the boat. There's nothing here as you know. It's with Dave and Starshine."

"What did they do?" asked Cedar. "Why did they give up so easily?"

"Cause I told them everything was lost. I told them the files and everything they thought I had was in your home when the wall of tailings hit. I told them everything was either under ten feet of tailings or out in the inlet. They weren't so demanding after that. Guess they didn't want another murder on their hands, at least not yet. When they saw Gus' boat coming they decided to get out, in a hurry."

"Still," said Cedar "those guys are dangerous. Wonder what their game is now?"

""I'll tell you what they're doing now," said Wayne shaking his head and looking away to the waves coming down the shrouded inlet. "They're trying to pin the blame for the dam breaking on us, on me."

"How could they do that? It was an accident waiting to happen."

"With all the real records gone, their response plan would be to doctor everything up and say I or you guys planted dynamite and blew up the dam. Remember the big blast just before the dam gave way? They plan to spin it as eco-terrorism or something like that. Should be interesting when the records show up in Rupert though."

"Everything will work out then," said Cedar, trying to be positive, "cause Mom and Dad have the records."

Wayne nodded and said, "I hope so."

"Why don't I go with you, back to Rupert" said Cedar. "Keep you company. Susan and Gus can go up to the mine and get the pictures and report on things. I don't want to go back there and see the disaster right now."

"Sure," said Wayne. "Everything up there is pretty self-evident. Someone just needs to officially call it in to the police, the provincial environment guys and Fisheries."

Cedar followed Wayne into the wheelhouse as they pulled away from Gus' boat. She was still upset about losing her home, but growing more concerned all the time. She saw Wayne watching her but avoided his glances.

Eventually Wayne said, "Is there something else bothering you Cedar? You're upset and that's natural, but you seem to be concerned about something else as well.

Cedar looked over at Wayne. "Well, I guess I'd better spill it," she said.

"Spill what?" asked Wayne, puzzled, confused. "What are you talking about?"

"Well," started Cedar, and then she hesitated. "About that blast before the tailings dam gave way."

"What about it?" said Wayne, growing even more concerned. "What's going on?"

"Well my Dad and I, with help from Jimi sometimes, we were stealing dynamite from the mine, and stockpiling it."

"What do you mean stealing dynamite? What are you talking about?"

"Stealing, over a period of years. We had quite a bit stashed away. We didn't really have any plans for it, but knew at some time we'd probably have to defend ourselves. So we stole it and stashed it in a sort of a cavern in the rocks on a slope above the mine yard."

"So," said Wayne becoming uneasy. "It couldn't go off by itself."

"We stole wires and detonators too, and a switch triggered by a radio signal. Dad had the radio," said Cedar, putting a fist to her mouth and pushing. With gravity she said, "Wayne, there was a lot of dynamite in there."

"That's a bomb, Cedar. Do you think ...?" Wayne stuttered, unable to finish the question. "Do you?"

"He might have done it," said Cedar very agitated and sucking the fingers still in her mouth. "I don't know. He was really upset about Nathan and having to leave. Never seen him that bad."

"Yeah, really upset."

"I hope it wasn't him."

"You know," said Wayne pounding on the dash, "if they find those wires and the triggering device ... Well let's just say, it won't go well for me."

"Wayne, I know," said Cedar, grabbing his arm to hold it and comfort him.

Wayne shook from her grasp and pushed her away. He stared out at the mist and the rain through the streaked window.

*****

RAIN PELTED DOWN AS WAYNE PEERED FORWARD AT THE OCEAN saying, "Can't see anything. The shore's over there to port but I can't see it."

"Maybe we should duck in to Lax Kw'alaams and wait out the weather," said Cedar, trying to be helpful, and not sure where she stood with Wayne after her revelation about Dave. "The wind is from the southeast so we'll be heading into it the whole way south to Rupert once we get outside. A guaranteed bumpy dangerous ride that'll take forever."

"Maybe," said Wayne, wondering where all of this was going. "Do you think Dave and Starshine went in there or straight down in this storm?"

"They're in Dave's jet boat which isn't much good in heavy seas. I bet they turned in and I think we should too."

Wayne said nothing. He continued to stare forward into the mists and rain. He wasn't sure what to do or where to turn. Everything had gotten a lot more complicated with the revelation about Dave's dynamite and the possibility, even likelihood, that he had set off the explosion.

Cedar moved closer to Wayne and put her arm around his waist. He stretched out his arm and put it around her shoulder. Reaching with his hand to stroke her tangles. She looked up into his eyes and despite the puffiness from crying she looked beautiful. He shook his head. This was a real mess he'd gotten into.

When they reached the harbour entrance at Lax Kw'alaams, it was decision time. For a moment he thought of heading in, but then thought, 'What the hell, things can't get much worse.' Instead of heading in, he held true to his course and rounded the headland into open water. Dundas Island further west seemed a long way off and was invisible in the mist and rain.

As soon as they cleared the headland, the wind picked up to about 35 knots, driving rain into the forward window like pebbles on glass. They were still in the lee of the mainland, but could see big waves further out, breaking into white foam.

"I thought we'd turn in," said Cedar, not sure what was going on. "It'll be getting dark soon."

Wayne bent down and flipped on the running lights. "I need to get back to Rupert, before too many rumours and stories start circulating about me."

Cedar looked away. "Wayne, you didn't do anything," she said, imploring him with her eyes. "Don't make this day any worse."

"It'll be fine," said Wayne projecting confidence he wasn't sure he really had. "These old trollers don't look like much but they're a helluva sea boat. You just have to hang on. These hulls roll a lot but there's nothing to worry about."

They powered on into the storm, ploughing into troughs and launching off oncoming wave tops. Everything in the boat shook and anything not secured flew into the air, projectiles in the forepeak below. Wayne tried to take the waves at an angle, meaning every third or fourth wave was a near disaster experience of rolling and righting, the rail scooping up black seawater and then shedding it foaming through scuppers. He focussed on the compass course, occasionally checking his position on the radar. Eventually the light faded to darkness and the waves were unseen, just the luminescent foaming crests breaking above the wheelhouse.

"I'm scared Wayne," said Cedar, no longer holding onto him but clinging to the dash instead. "We should go back, and spend the night at Lax Kw'alaams. This is crazy."

"Maybe I am crazy, Cedar." Wayne stayed focussed on guiding the boat, a smile growing from deep inside to become a slight upturn of the lips. "I need to get back to Rupert and right now, this minute. I need to battle something that's real, like this weather. Instead of shadow boxing everything. I'm sick of that."

"Wayne, you're talking nonsense."

"I went to school to be on the ocean, so here I am," the smile breaking full onto his face, faintly illuminated by a low amber glow from the compass light and radar screen. "This is a southeast wind, we can always get a bit of shelter at Georgetown Mills if we have to."

"I don't think we can go in there at night in a storm. There are rocks and shoals, besides, I don't know how sheltered it will really be, unless you go right in tight to shore and that could be disastrous."

"So we tough it out running down the coast I guess."

"I guess so. Wayne, what's up with you anyway? You come up here for work, on some crazy no money excuse. You're a complete industry shill with an absolutely evil consulting record, and then you get a crisis of conscience. You're on the run and trying to help us out. I mean who the hell is the real Wayne Dumont anyway?"

"As they say in the movies Cedar, it's complicated."

"Well why are you alone? Don't you have someone? Don't you have a life somewhere?"

"I thought I'd told you, my long-time girlfriend just threw me out and maybe hooked up with someone new. I don't know who, maybe one of my good friends, eh? Who knows?"

"Sounds like nice friends you've got."

"Then she calls me. You were there. Says she wants me back cause it didn't work out for her."

Cedar mulled this over for a bit before asking, "You gonna go back to her?"

"No way. Once it's broken, it's gone. She's bad news anyway, really flaky and just interested in money. You know the type."

"Where's home?"

"Right now I really don't know. I was living in Vancouver, but Kathy took the place and threw all my things out, while I'm up here trying to make more money for the two of us. So ... you know. That's not really my home."

"Where were you from before Vancouver?"

Wayne explained his parents and Toronto origins summing up by saying, "A person can never go back to Toronto after spending time on the west coast. You know that, don't you?"

"Not really. I've always lived up here on the North Coast."

Tell me more about your life and parents. I don't really know much beyond the superficial stuff.

Cedar turned quickly away pretending to look out the side window, but there was only rain and foam and blackness beyond. The boat rolled hard to starboard and she was thrown into the bulkhead, jamming her arm hard. She let out a slight cry of pain, but that was all. She continued pretending to look out the window.

Wayne watched out of the corner of his eye and said nothing.

"My parents are crazy, mental," she said finally, in a faltering voice. "They lived in isolation, kept us in isolation, until high school. Then we were thrust into the larger society in the city, Rupert, and expected to survive."

There was silence again, only the waves crashing into the bow, the wind, the rain and the diesel engine. She stared out the black window, leaning on the dash. "Dad started as a wild eyed idealist with an escapist dream. Back in the seventies there were lots of those, a lot ended up in Rupert. You know the old end of the road thing. My mother came out for the summer to meet up with friends and make lots of money in the fish plants, before going back to Montreal to law school."

"I guess she didn't go back."

"One thing led to another and she was pregnant before the summer was over. And that was that. She stayed to have me and raise me. She didn't go back to school."

There was silence again.

"I think she always resented that. Having to raise me. Having to stay in Rupert and miss out on a whole career, a whole life. She was a good mother and loved me, but you know when you can feel it. It's just always there, but maybe I made it up a bit in my own mind. Who knows? I just don't know about anything anymore."

"What about your dad?" asked Wayne, maintaining a watch on the compass and radar. "What's the story with him? The relationship?"

Cedar was quiet for a long time. "I love my dad, but, you know ..."

"What?"

"He isolated us. It was selfish. He's been operating outside the law his whole life. Stealing logs. Growing and dealing dope. Stealing dynamite. He's been going up the valley alone for years, without saying anything. He's always been there, but not there in my life. I don't know. Just not a lot of love there."

"He does care about you though?"

"Yeah, I guess. More Nathan than me, cause Nathan was a boy. He could groom Nathan to carry on with his activities."

"Anything else?"

Cedar turned her head away from Wayne, silent.

TWENTY-ONE

TED ROLLED OVER AND PUT HIS ARM AROUND LYLA, DRAWING her close, smelling her hair and everything about her. He looked around the owner's stateroom on his boat and at the woman on the bed beside him, and relaxed in perfect harmony. This world he'd built.

He went up to the wheelhouse, where Jamie could be seen on deck leaning over the rail, in a jacket and toque against the cold March breeze. The sun was shining, and wavelets in Silva Bay sparkled. He waved at Jamie, and Jamie nodded back. 'Good enough,' thought Ted. He went into the galley and began making bacon and eggs and coffee for breakfast.

The aroma of coffee soon wafted out of the galley and Lyla emerged from the stateroom, wearing tight jeans and a loose t-shirt. She helped set the galley table while Ted did the eggs. Jamie came in when everything was ready, sitting at the spot furthest away from Lyla.

Ted's cell phone rang.

"Ted, its Ian. Kaye told me to call your cell phone," said Ian, sounding more serious than usual.

"Morning Ian. I'm surprised you're calling on a Friday. Thought you'd be off to Reno or Las Vegas or someplace warm and sunny. Must be something up," said Ted as he scrambled the eggs. "Maybe you want to tell me my last invoices have been paid.

"Ted, this is serious. The shit hit the fan up at the mine." Ian paused. "Ted, the tailings dam burst."

"What the hell? That can't be right. Everything was fine," said Ted, shaken and setting the eggs down, moving to his skipper's chair. On his way Ted caught Jamie look at him, at Lyla and back, with a smirk on his face.

"That's right Ted. The tailings dam burst. I don't know what happened yet, but it's been raining hard for days and the spring thaw has started."

"What happened?" asked Ted, turning white with shock.

"The dam burst and a wall of tailings went right through the wetland. Right through those squatters' cabins," said Ian, matter-of-factly.

"Was anyone hurt?" asked Ted, worried.

"No. We don't think so. We think the squatters all got away. Your guy Wayne too, by the sounds of it. I'm going on second hand information from Klaus though. Ted, it was your job to monitor that dam to make sure it would hold. What the hell happened?"

'So this is it,' thought Ted. 'Here comes the blame.' He almost wished Ian hadn't or wouldn't pay those last invoices.

"I'll talk to Bruno. Find out what happened. It must be that Wayne guy that didn't report things to me. And maybe that Ron guy before him," said Ted, desperately. "I'll call you back. By the way, has this hit the news yet?"

"Hasn't hit the news yet but I'm sure it will, and soon."

"That won't be good for the share price, will it," said Ted, thinking about his own fortunes, and how much of his life might get re-possessed. "Look Ian, I've got some calls to make and then I'll get back to you."

"Damn right you've got some calls to make. So do I," said Ian, slamming down the phone.

Ted turned his seat to look back at the galley table where Lyla was still seated. He could see that Jamie had left and was out in the cold wind leaning over the rail again. He reached for the sat phone and punched in the number of the New Discovery Gold camp barge up in Mirage Inlet. Ted asked to speak to Bruno.

"Bruno, I just got a call from Ian Verster about the tailings dam. Did it really fail?" asked Ted, unable to conceal his concerns and fear.

"Yes. It really did fail. It's a hell of a mess up here everything between the tailings pond and the ocean is completely covered in mine tailings. Those cabins are completely gone but I think the squatters all got away. Three boats went out of here right after it happened, and it's impossible to get over there to look because it's all covered in tailings. Like quicksand, that stuff. It's still pouring rain and storm force winds are blowing," said Bruno. Ted could hear the panic in Bruno's voice.

"Are Axel and Cody there?" asked Ted, trying to sound off the cuff, but sounding very scared and concerned.

"Yeah, they're around but they took off in the company crew boat after the squatters left. Looked like they were chasing after them for some unknown reason. Should I get them to call you?"

"No I'll call them. They should have a sat phone with them. Don't worry about it."

"You know Ted," said Bruno, getting more expansive in his dialogue, "it's been raining here like crazy for a long time."

"I know. Everyone keeps reminding me of that. The dam should've still held."

"Well I was going to say that, just before the dam failed, there was a huge explosion that really shook the ground. Rocks were flying high in the air and coming down everywhere. By some miracle, no one got hurt, but rocks came down the mountainside and partially closed the portal to the main adit. Right after that, the dam just turned to liquid and everything flowed out."

Ted considered this information. "Sounds like the explosion shook the dam, turning it to liquid slurry and causing the failure," he said. "Why else would it fail?"

"The monitoring was showing a lot of seepage going back up into the base and slumping on the face," said Bruno, apparently sensing he needed to start covering his own potential liabilities. "Ted you knew that. And with all the rain the decant structure couldn't keep up and the water level in the tailings pond was way beyond the design limit."

"I was not aware of that," said Ted, emphatically, even aggressively. "Remember that Bruno. You remember that."

"Yes Ted," said Bruno apparently capitulating. "What do you want me to do now? There are no planes flying in or out of here. We're weathered in."

Ted thought for a moment, looking out at the sunny Silva Bay morning and the comely Lyla at the galley table eating scrambled eggs. "I guess you'll have to just hang in there for a while. Nothing else we can do. You said those guys Axel and Cody took off in the crew boat. They coming back?"

"I don't know," said Bruno, sounding frustrated with the whole business and guarded since the changes in Ted.

"Okay, Bruno, I guess I gotta go now. You hang in there." Ted punched the button to disconnect.

He stared at the sat phone, looked up the number for the sat phone Axel was carrying and pushed the button to call.

"Yeah, what?" said the voice at the other end, the high whine of a turbo charged diesel in the background.

"Axel, it's Ted here."

"What? What do you want?"

"What are you doing? Where are you?"

"We were trying to chase down your boy Wayne. We caught up to him, dodged a rifle and searched his boat. There were none of your stinking files on board. Says he stashed them all in the hippie cabin that got smothered. You want them you can come up and look through about ten feet of fucking mine tailings, or go diving for them at the bottom of the inlet."

"You mean Wayne's still out there and we don't know where the files are? You really think he stashed them in the hippie cabin?"

Axel responded saying, "Don't worry Ted. We've got something for you. First you get to blame him for not reporting problems. Second, there was a big blast before the dam gave way. Everyone here is going to blame that on Wayne, or maybe the hippies. Either way, you're covered. Pretty cool eh?"

Ted thought this new information through for a moment and then said, "That's good Axel. Better than the original plan. Did you guys do the blast? Where did that come from?"

Axel laughed. "Actually we have no idea. Could have been the miners, this place is run so bad, or could have been the hippies. Who knows? The facts don't really matter when things are this chaotic. Anyway you're covered, and we get paid a big bonus, right?"

Ted hesitated on mention of a big bonus.

"Right Ted? You're not getting tight with me are you?" said Axel with menace.

"That's right Axel. I'll just have to figure it out and get the money to you. Let me know when you're back in Rupert."

*****

WITH WAVES BREAKING OVER THE BOW, WAYNE KNEW HE shouldn't continue on, but it was too late now. He'd committed to the run and turning back could be more risky. The turn and following sea might be even more dangerous. Besides, the *Molly B* was handling the weather despite her size and limited power. Cedar wasn't talking as she stood staring into the darkness, the only thing visible through the starboard window was the flashing light at Greens Island. He steered a compass course for the faint flashes of Lucy Island light station far ahead.

Finally, the waves diminished as *Molly B* entered Venn Passage in the sheltering lee of Digby Island, after he picked his way in darkness through the outer rocks. Inside, Prince Rupert harbour was blustery but without the big waves. The lights of the city and the container terminal were a welcome sight, despite being obscured by mist. Eventually *Molly B* rounded Hospital Island and Wayne dropped anchor in Dodge Cove while Cedar still remained motionless at the window. When Wayne returned from the foredeck, Cedar had descended to the forepeak and climbed into the berth. She hadn't spoken. Wayne shut down the engine, electronics and all but the anchor light, before going down to collapse into the other berth. It would be dawn soon, and the past day and night had been exhausting, emotionally and physically.

Too soon he was awakened by pounding on the hull. He sprang to life grabbing the pistol and rushed outside. There was Mary in her boat looking concerned.

"Wayne, when did you get in? We've been worried sick ever since Starshine called from Lax Kw'alaams."

Wayne concealed the pistol. "We came all the way down last night. Cedar's with me," explained Wayne but he didn't have to as Cedar burst out of the wheelhouse and leaned over to greet Mary.

Cedar climbed down into the boat and they hugged. Clinging to Mary she looked back at Wayne and said, "I'm going to Mary's." These were the first and only words she'd spoken.

Mary looked at Cedar and back up at Wayne and said, "Do you want to come in with me?"

Wayne shook his head. "Not now. I need to clean up the boat and sort some things out. I'll come over later in the dinghy."

Mary pushed away from the *Molly B,* started her outboard and guided her boat across the cove to their float.

Wayne shook his head, trying to make sense of his situation. He went back inside and climbed into the berth Cedar had just vacated. Her faint scent lingered there among the musty boat smells. He fell into a deep sleep again.

When he woke at noon, the rain had eased. A stiff breeze was still blowing but had begun to break up the cloud cover. 'Maybe today will be better,' thought Wayne, as he turned up the stove to generate more heat and dry out the damp.

In the wheelhouse he turned on the local radio station to catch the news. His attention galvanized when he heard the names New Discovery Gold Mine and Mirage Inlet in the same sentence. 'So Susan's broken the story,' he realized. The news reader told the entire story, including new information Wayne was not yet aware of. The police and environment cops had arrived on the scene that morning. Wayne was glad to be out of there, but he realized that planes must now be able to fly in and out of Mirage Inlet, meaning the Axel and Cody might be out now too, and soon prowling the town.

He had two things to do. He had to retrieve his documents and laptop and secure them somewhere, and then had to call his broker. He decided to call his broker first.

"Hey Charles," said Wayne after punching the number in. So much easier to communicate now he was in cellphone range and not relying on the sat phone. "Did you short the stock?"

"Got your weird phone call. You just signed off with no discussion and thought about it for a minute. I know you're strapped and I worried about you putting all your money on one lame horse," he responded.

"Shut up Charles," said Wayne, impatient. "Did you do it?"

"Yeah, I did it. Wish I'd trusted you and done the same for myself."

"What's it doing now?"

"Just started to drop. The downside momentum's building but it's not quite there yet. How did you know it would drop?"

"I was there. When I called you, it looked like the tailings dam would go at any minute."

"Insider info Wayne?"

"No. Not at all," said Wayne, launching into a more extensive explanation of the circumstances. "They fired me a while ago for wanting to report the mess up there. I went back up on my own. There was this big rainstorm all over the North Coast and that tailings dam was showing signs of failure. With the rain it just couldn't hold all the water. I don't want to get technical, but the material making up the dam was saturated with water and over time was eroding internally. The company just didn't want it reported."

"Crazy. Their share price shot up in the last few trading days because they were reporting enhanced gold recovery with tests on a new process."

"That was all BS, just to pump the up the share price."

"Well, you got in at the top Wayne, lucky play."

"Yeah, for once I got lucky."

"What do you want me to do," asked Charles, his voice revealing a complex mix of empathy, concern and enthusiasm. "You have everything on the line."

Wayne hesitated, thought for a moment, considering his situation. "Let's hang on. I'll call you later. I'm anchored across the harbour right now and have no way of checking the news and share prices. I'll try to get Wi-Fi this afternoon in Rupert."

"Okay, you're a genius on this one. I should have followed your lead."

"Bye. Call me on this cell phone number if there are any changes," said Wayne pushing the End Call button and sitting back to survey Dodge Cove.

Wayne went aft into the stern cockpit. He looked around the cove. There was no one. Crouching down he disappeared from sight, and reached up under the combing. Feeling around, he found the false panel, where he figured the original owner had stored hundred dollar bills from the cash buyers on the fishing grounds, back in the days when cash was everywhere. He turned the screws and drew out his package. The envelope containing his failsafe compact external hard drive with all the electronic file copies was safe, dry within the watertight bag. He thought for a moment. Cedar would be staying with Ray and Mary for a while. He could leave it with her but they would get the files and laptop from Dave when he arrived. He trusted Gus and Clarence, he could leave it with one of them. Then there was Susan but she was already okay. Or, he could just leave it on the boat. He opted for the status quo for now, and sealed everything back up behind the panel.

He called over to Mary's cabin. Cedar told him her parents and Jimi and Chelsea would be coming down to Rupert on the Lax Kw'alaams ferry. Still too rough for the jet boat. They planned to go over and meet the ferry in the late afternoon.

"I hope they brought the package I gave them," he said with a tinge of anxiety in his voice.

"I didn't ask them specifically," was Cedar's response. Then she added, "But I'm sure they did. Why wouldn't they?"

"Please make sure you get that package. It's really important for me."

Cedar promised she would and he started up the engine, raised the anchor and powered over to the fuel barge where he filled again with his credit card. When he approached the float in Cow Bay, he found his spot opposite Clarence was clear so he slid in and tied up. As soon as the boat was secure, Clarence came out.

"Did you see Gus?" he asked, anxious for information about his friend.

"Yeah, I saw him, and Susan from the paper as well," answered Wayne. "I guess they're still up there."

At Clarence's invitation, Wayne went onboard and into the galley. He watched with trepidation as Clarence poured coffee, but he accepted it gratefully despite its age and tarry aroma. Wayne went on to explain the whole situation while Clarence listened intently.

"I'm worried," said Wayne, taking another sip and wincing reflexively.

"About those two guys again?" asked Clarence.

"Yeah, about those guys. I don't know what to do."

"You still got the rifle and pistol don't you?"

"Yeah, I do. Had to threaten those guys with them a couple of times too."

"It's good you had them," said Clarence and then sounding concerned he added, "You know I'll help out any way I can."

"Yeah, I know," said Wayne thankfully. He finished his coffee with a grimace and said, "I'm going up to the café to get something to eat. Haven't eaten for a long time. You want to come?"

"Nah. You go on. I'm more comfortable here on my boat. I'll keep an eye on things for you. Better pass those guns over though. Don't want them gettin' into the wrong hands while you're away."

Wayne went over to his own boat and climbed aboard via the stern cockpit where he tripped and fell down on the cockpit floor. Eventually, he climbed stiffly out and walked forward to open the cabin. Once inside he gathered up the guns and ammunition, stuffing them into a duffle that he passed over to Clarence. He left and went up the dock and the ramp.

*****

THE MOLLY B WAS HIS ONLY HOME AND WAYNE RETURNED TO IT after eating, not really sure if he'd had lunch or dinner. Exhaustion from the mine disaster and escape was extreme. Running down the coast in that storm through the night had pushed body and mind beyond their limits. He went below and lay down in the forward berth. Thinking he'd read for a while, he fell asleep almost immediately.

In the afternoon, he was awakened by the sound of a boat coming in to tie up. Groggy he extricated himself from the berth and looked out. It was Gus, back down from Mirage Inlet. Susan was with him, handling the lines.

Wayne went over to help secure the boat. "You guys got the story out," said Wayne, taking a line from Susan. "It's all over the radio. Haven't seen the paper yet but I'm sure it'll be there." He gave Susan a hug, and shook Gus' hand.

"We got there just in time," said Gus, coming over to Wayne from the outside steering station. "You were lucky to get out. The authorities are there now doing their investigation. Must've been a rough ride coming back down to Rupert last night though."

Wayne went aboard and they talked into the evening. Clarence joined them later. Susan eventually left and Gus heated up some beans and made toast. After going back and forth on the problems at the mine, Wayne eventually gave up and called it a night. Back on his boat, alone, he climbed into the forward berth and turned in.

In the midnight darkness, a boat bumped the *Molly B*. Wayne heard voices, low and muffled. Then the sound of breaking glass, as a flaming bottle flew though the wheel house window smashing on the cabin sole. Flames shot across the floor spreading immediately through the wheelhouse, a wall of heat and light. Wayne dove out of berth in shock. He grabbed an old blanket and using it for cover made a dash up to the wheelhouse and broke through the door. Out on deck with singed feet and clothes, the situation was desperate. *Molly B* would be a loss. Oak, and fir and yellow cedar and mahogany. Strong Japanese-Canadian craftsmanship and heritage incinerated.

Suddenly a wall of flames burst hot and bright out of the wheelhouse as the oil stove exploded. Wayne looked around and the only way out was the harbour. He jumped. Just in time as flames enveloped *Molly B*'s topsides. Fuel tanks full.

Gus and Clarence quickly emerged from their own boats. Gus started up his engine and manoeuvered to put a line on *Molly B*. Clarence used his fire ax to cut the mooring lines. The flaming *Molly B* was towed out to open water as burning fuel spread across the surface forcing Wayne to dive into the darkness below. He held his breath, afraid to surface into the flames. He couldn't see anything. It felt like blackness and icy cold were finally enveloping him in their deathly embrace.

Eventually he could hold his breath no longer and Wayne surfaced, spewing air and fuel. Looking around, his boat was silhouetted in the darkness, burning to the waterline. He swam through the scum. As he climbed back onto the float, he watched *Molly B* sink into a sizzling, steaming hole in the deep black ocean, out of sight, another relic on the harbour floor. Cold, wet and destitute, Wayne collapsed on the float, head in hands.

Clarence approached, put an arm around Wayne's shoulder and helped him onto his boat.

"It'll be okay, son. You'll see," said Clarence as he pulled dry old clothes out of somewhere. Wayne changed and Clarence sat him down at the cluttered galley table. He passed Wayne a mug of his tar like coffee, pouring in the whiskey in one smooth motion.

Wayne took a drink saying, "Geez Clarence, that was a hell of a thing," as he sat still shaking from shock. He took another drink.

Clarence reached over, topped up the mug with whiskey and said, "Give it time. Give it time."

Gus came back to the float to tie up, arriving at about the same time as the fire inspector and the police. It was Stasiuk, and he did not look sympathetic. At the sight of them, Gus called Wayne out onto the float, saying. "Cops are here Wayne."

"Oh, so it's you again," said Stasiuk approaching Wayne and blocking any potential access up the float, out of the marina. "You're really getting to be a pain in the ass up here on the North Coast. First it was the truck with the smashed windshield, marooned on Hospital Island, and now the boat. What's next?"

The fire inspector backed away from what was apparently becoming a tense situation.

"Actually, I know what's next," said Stasiuk as he reached around, took out a pair of hand cuffs and slapped them on Wayne's wrists. "I need you to come with me up to the Detachment for being a public nuisance, and that's just the start of your problems. We'll see what else you've been up to. There are lots of rumours and stories about you around town."

Wayne's face froze and he lurched forward in response to Stasiuk's push from behind. Stasiuk returned to Gus's boat and boarded it. Wayne saw him re-emerge and climb back down onto the float, carrying his wet clothes, his only belongings.

"What's this all about? Someone just fire bombed me and my boat, and now you're arresting me? What the hell?" he yelled in desperation, trying to free himself.

"Take it easy," said Stasiuk pushing him along. "Don't add resisting arrest to your problems."

Wayne tried to look back over his shoulder but was stopped by another rough shove, so he yelled out, "Clarence, Gus, go tell Cedar what's happened. Tell Susan."

Clarence and Gus stood on the float, looking on in shock, unable to move. To break the stunned silence, Gus said, "At least I got my guns back." He reflected a moment before adding, "That was a stupid, insensitive thing to say." As he was hustled away Wayne, saw Clarence nod in agreement.

Wayne took one last look down over the floats where *Molly B* had been tied up, before he was pushed into the squad car. At the Detachment, he was ushered in to stand in front of the main desk where he was booked into the criminal justice system, for the first time in his life. At the same time Wayne was being processed by the desk sergeant, he saw Axel and Cody in the office with Stasiuk and Inspector Campbell, giving statements. Wayne realized they were carrying through on their threat to pin responsibility for the explosion on him. They were the likely fire bombers too, trying to destroy the company records they thought he still had, even if they couldn't steal them. He collapsed in despair when Stasiuk shoved him into the cell, after relieving him of his pitiful remaining belongings.

When Susan arrived Wayne was sitting in a corner on the cell floor, still in the old clothes Clarence had given him, rubbing his wrists. She came in to talk and he explained what had happened and how Axel had promised to pin the whole tailings dam failure on him.

Susan said, "Well at least you've got witnesses. I'll call Cedar over at Mary and Ray's place. Gus and I will go get her and bring her over here. She'll help you."

Wayne looked up in despair, "I sure hope she will."

Susan left and the Inspector opened the holding cell and guided him to a small enclosed room for questioning.

"Well Wayne. I'm going to ask questions, and you're going to answer. Okay?" said Inspector Campbell without a shred of empathy.

"Can I make a call? Have a lawyer?"

"We'll get to that. I see you've been a busy little beaver since you got back to town."

"I don't know what you're talking about."

Stasiuk held up his cell phone. "We recovered this and salvaged the records." He smiled a thin smile. "You've made calls to a certain stock broker in Vancouver. Care to tell me about it?"

Wayne slumped. 'They've gone through my cell phone. How could things get any worse?' And yet they were getting worse. "I want a lawyer. Now. And what am I supposed to have done, anyway? I haven't done anything."

"We'll see about that," said Inspector Campbell, his hands clasped in front of him on the table, looking at Wayne with an expressionless face. "We'll see. Overall your behaviour is very suspicious and your reputation isn't good. People we've talked to say you have quite a history of manipulation. Bending the truth was a recurring theme. Those must be some acquaintances you've made. Do you have anything to say?"

"I want to see a lawyer."

"Who's your lawyer then?"

"I don't have one."

TWENTY-TWO

STASIUK LED WAYNE BACK TO THE HOLDING CELL, REMOVING handcuffs and locking the door. He slumped again into the corner. Maybe he'd get to make a phone call, maybe he wouldn't. Maybe he'd get a lawyer, maybe he'd be left to fend for himself. Stasiuk was definitely not on his side. Nothing looked good, so what was the point of thinking about potential actions and outcomes.

He'd had a great future when he left grad school. Top of his class, in demand, he'd been making good money, great money actually. Ted had offered him a dream job and he took it, without looking too far under the hood. There'd been the girlfriends, women, lots of them, when he was leading the fast life. Late nights working, late nights drinking, and the cocaine had helped to focus the work. He'd never even thought about the feelings, the lives, the futures of the people he'd passed along the way.

The public profile of the big projects had been great too. He'd never thought about the people on the other side of the projects he'd helped sell. He thought, 'That's it, isn't it? As a consultant I was nothing more than a salesman, cloaked in the guise of science and truth.' It had never occurred to him to worry about the people displaced by hydro dams, people's farms flooded, sacred sites and burial grounds destroyed, fishing and hunting grounds ruined, all in the name of Return on Investment, Capital Appreciation, greed. Investor greed and his own.

He'd never had to look those people in the eye, bear witness to the destruction of lives, families, relationships, communities. He'd been sheltered from it all, isolated in metropolitan Vancouver, so self-righteous about its environmental image, living the good life, living the lie.

Now he was on the other side of the karma ledger. It was all coming back and he was being tossed aside. What was the point of it all? Wayne looked around the cell and thought, 'So this is it. Time to make my world small.' He focussed within himself thinking, 'In reality I'm in here, out of the never ending wind, rain and cold. I'm dry and warm enough. I'll be provided with food and a place to sleep. Everything else is beyond my control. I'm okay.' Small reassurances. Then he thought, 'And I have a woman who I think cares about me and I hope she will come to my rescue. She knows the truth.'

Time passed slowly and the more time passed the more worried he became. Maybe Cedar wasn't coming to explain what really happened. Stasiuk came back, and lead him to the little room again where somebody who introduced himself as Dean Smith sat. Smith said he was from the enforcement arm of the provincial environment department.

"Mr. Dumont, I'd like to ask you a few questions about New Discovery Gold Incorporated and its Mirage Inlet mine. As you know, the tailings dam failed causing catastrophic environmental and property damage. I believe you worked for the company and you were there when the dam failed. Care to tell me about it?"

Wayne recounted the story and the history of his involvement.

"Mr. Dumont, you prepared a number of reports preceding the incident. It is my understanding that those reports did not provide any indication of current or impending problems."

"That's because I was not allowed to file fulsome reports. The reports that were filed only addressed the protocols your agency approved."

Mr. Smith shook his head as he wrote in his notebook. When finished he raised his head and asked with a tone of incredulity, "Did you not think to expand on those most basic requirements to provide a more accurate and truthful picture of the state of affairs?"

"Yes I did. But, when I filed a more complete report with my company, the boss fired me on the spot, and I presume my replacement went back to the more restricted reporting protocol."

"I see. Do you have any proof?"

Wayne hesitated. Things were getting very complicated and there were loose ends he didn't understand. Cedar being one of them. Bruno being the other. "Well I did get fired for trying to do the right thing," he finally said.

"Not exactly an endorsement, Mr. Dumont," said Dean Smith sarcastically.

"I discussed this with my replacement," said Wayne, quietly, looking directly into the officer's eyes, trying to appear as honest and forthcoming as possible. He wondered whether his nervousness would show. "I don't know what his reporting was like, or anything about his experience with the boss. I was no longer employed there."

"There are people saying you were at the mine site when the dam failed."

"Yes I was. And I'd like a lawyer before saying anything more."

"Why do you need a lawyer? Is there something you're trying to hide?" asked Smith, like he was trying to bait Wayne into admitting something.

"No. I just don't want to get led into a trap on something I didn't do."

"Alright then, Mr. Dumont." Smith closed up his notebook with a flourish and stood. As he turned to leave the little room he said, "We'll be in touch. I'm sure Constable Stasiuk will have more questions later."

Stasiuk led Wayne back to the holding cell. He didn't know what to think. His mind raced, burning circuits in his brain. Suddenly Cedar appeared outside the cell.

*****

WHEN STASIUK LET HER IN, WAYNE MOVED QUICKLY TO GREET HER, throwing his arms around her. "I'm so glad you came," he said, barely keeping his emotions in check. At first she was cool and stiff, and then she reciprocated the hug, but with much less emotion.

"They're blaming that explosion on you, just like they threatened. What are you going to do?" she asked, showing some empathy and interest but remaining guarded. After a pause she added, "Is there something I should do ...? To help?"

Wayne looked directly into Cedar's eyes, saying, "Somebody set off the explosion. It could only be someone at the mine. Or, it could also have been one of you guys. Cedar, look at me." She avoided his questioning eyes. Wayne shook her shoulders. "Look at me and tell me truthfully."

"Like I told you, we did stash dynamite and a detonator. Dad had a remote radio switch. That's all I know."

"Was it your father?"

"I don't know Wayne. I just don't know." Cedar broke away from his grip, stepped back and turned away. "You're asking about things that are very close to home and difficult for me. I thought you knew that by now."

"Yes, I know that, but I'm the one in a jail cell for something I definitely didn't do. We both know I didn't do it."

"I asked him. My father. He said no, but I just don't know."

"Was it Jimi? He was really losing it after his capture. Do you think he did it?"

Cedar turned back to face him, still avoiding his eyes. "I don't know Wayne." She closed her eyes momentarily and shook her head. "Maybe it was Jimi."

"He was mixed up with those enviro bitches. Could they have put him up to it?"

"Maybe. I don't know. That wouldn't make too much sense because they were just using the mine to raise lots of money for themselves. That would be killing their golden goose."

Wayne squeezed his fists in anger and rubbed his eyes in frustration. "You know I could go to jail for a long time over the explosion, and the false reporting that my company did is being blamed on me too."

"I thought your documents and records had the reporting stuff covered."

"The only records I had went down with the *Molly B* when they torched it."

Cedar looked shocked but not as much as Wayne might have hoped. "You mean you don't have any of the records?"

"Like I said Cedar, they went down with the boat. Can you help me? Somehow? Dave has all the other records."

"What can I possibly do?" asked Cedar, looking blankly at Wayne and then away again.

The sergeant came to the cell door and indicated there was another visitor. Susan had come to see him.

Wayne thought Cedar seemed lost when Susan arrived. She appeared confused and overwhelmed, and looked conflicted all of a sudden.

Cedar looked at Susan, back at Wayne and said, "I think I have to go now. You hang in there Wayne. I'll see what I can do." She left the cell quickly, without looking back.

With the acknowledgement of the sergeant, Susan entered the cell. She looked around and down at Wayne, slumped again in the corner.

"Well Wayne, you're in a shitload of trouble here."

"Hi Susan, thanks for pointing out the obvious."

"You know Cedar's not going to do anything, don't you? Her family's too far into this."

Wayne wondered how things could get any worse and now they had. "What do you mean?"

"She'll never tell you, but that family's got lots of its own skeletons in the closet. She can't go against her family."

"Did Dave set off the blast?"

"I don't know, but wouldn't be surprised."

"Susan, I'm done, aren't I?" said Wayne hiding his face in his hands as he sat on the floor in the corner of the holding cell. "They're going to pin everything on me and there's nothing I can do about it. All my files are gone. People are framing me. I'm completely done."

Susan slid her back down the wall and sat on the floor beside Wayne. With sympathy she asked, "What are you going to do?"

"There's nothing I can do. But I'll tell you one thing, if I do get out of this, I'll never be the way I was before. I'll do what's right. I'll devote my life to it, and to standing up for other people against these greedy bastards that take everything and leave such an unforgivable mess behind. I will."

"Sounds like a typical gallows promise, Wayne. Do you mean that?"

"Yes I do. I'm done with the life I was leading. Look where it got me."

"Do you have a lawyer?"

"No."

"Know a lawyer?"

"No, just the ones I worked with for industrial clients."

"They're not likely to help you now."

"Yeah, I know.

*****

THE POLICE SERGEANT LED CEDAR INTO THE HOLDING CELL, closing the door as he left them. The steel lock clicked into place.

"Good morning."

"Hello Cedar," said Wayne, getting up to greet her. "Did you make any progress on getting me out of here?"

Cedar looked at Wayne and then back towards the locked door like she wanted to leave.

"I guess not," said Wayne, desolate and sliding back down the wall to the floor. "Did you get a lawyer?"

Cedar hesitated before saying, "We don't know any lawyers. We've always avoided the law."

"Didn't you go see the one in my old office building, like I asked?"

"I went there but he was out."

Wayne could see by the way she spoke that she was lying. "Can you do anything? To get me out of here?"

Cedar broke into tears. "I feel so helpless Wayne. I don't know what to do and my family and friends aren't helping. I don't know anything about this kind of thing and I'm all on my own."

"What's your father doing Cedar?"

"He doesn't want to get near this at all. Neither does Jimi."

"Are they avoiding talking to the police about the explosion?"

Cedar nodded her head before burying her face in her hands, crying.

"It's your family, isn't it?"

"I don't know Wayne. I just don't know. Maybe it could be but it could also have been Axel and Cody."

"What do you think Cedar? I need to know," said Wayne urgently, peering directly into her eyes, pleading in desperation. "If you don't speak up to defend me then I've got no one. I'll go to prison."

Cedar turned and knocked on the door. When the sergeant opened it, she said, "Family is the only thing I've got."

As Cedar left she saw Wayne put his head in his fists, screaming his frustration and rage in silence.

*****

HEAD DOWN, OUT OF THE CORNER OF HIS EYE, WAYNE WATCHED Susan sit down on the floor beside him. She didn't say anything, waiting patiently for him to process his situation and her presence, and open up.

"You know what's going on around this town, the North Coast. Where can I go from here? Without those records and Cedar's testimony, I've got no way to defend myself. I don't even have a lawyer."

"Look at me Wayne," said Susan placing her hand under his chin and turning his face toward her. "Look at me."

Wayne slowly raised his gaze and she looked deep into his eyes, like she was inspecting his soul. Then Susan said, "You know I'm a reporter, right? Investigation is what I do. It's what I love. Finding out the truth. Telling the story. I've loved that since high school."

"So?"

"So when you first came to my place after they fired you, remember? It was late in the evening, pouring rain. You didn't know where to go or what to do. You left an envelope with me for safe keeping over night until you figured things out. Remember?"

"Yeah?"

"I copied everything. Was up all night copying. I copied all the files on that hard drive and gave it back to you when you came to the office. You looked pathetic then and you do now. But a copy of all your records is in a locked cabinet in my basement. It's all there. Everything from your computer hard drive and the discs. All the reports, photos, emails, everything."

Wayne's eyes opened wide as he stared at her in disbelief. "You mean you got everything?"

"Yup, copies of everything. I've got it all. In my basement."

Wayne threw his arms around Susan's neck, burying his face in her straight, dark, fragrant hair. He just hung on while she held him close and stroked his head that still smelled of harbour and diesel.

After a time, he raised his head and said, "Susan, you're wonderful. How can I thank you?"

She pushed his head back down and continued holding him tight.

"You know that won't help me with the explosion they're trying to pin on me."

"I know," said Susan, still holding him tight. "But don't worry. It will work out. I know it will."

Wayne relaxed for the first time in a long time. The sergeant came in and told Susan it was time to go. The two of them stood. Susan gave Wayne a hug and a soft kiss on the cheek and left. He was left there, alone, for the night.

Wayne sat in silence. There was nothing he could do. He passed the time counting marks on the floor, in imaginary quadrants, like the diving surveys he used to do, measuring changes in biota from pollution. That was the kind of work he really loved.

Susan appeared at about mid-morning the next day, accompanied by a man Wayne recognized.

"I'm so glad you came, thank you. I'm going nuts in here."

"Did Cedar come?" asked Susan in a way that suggested she already knew the answer. "Did she do anything to get you out of here?"

Wayne shook his head, and as he did, saw the man open the door and enter the cell.

"Wayne this is Ranjit."

"Hello Ranjit. I recognize you from the building. Was meaning to say hello."

"Hello Wayne. Pleased to meet you."

"Ranjit is a lawyer. He can help. Do you want him to handle this for you?"

Wayne looked from Susan to Ranjit and back to Susan. "Should I?"

"Yes. He's one of the best in town."

"Okay then yes. Ranjit would you please handle my case?"

Ranjit smiled and nodded his head. He stepped back and tapped on the door. The sergeant opened and Ranjit motioned to someone. In walked Amar.

Susan spoke. "I talked to Ranjit and he spoke with his friend Amar. He knew Amar worked out at the mine so he asked him about the incident reported on the news. Amar, could you please tell us what you saw out at the mine."

Amar stepped forward and said, "Hello Wayne. It's good to see you again. I hope you're doing okay."

"Hi Amar."

"I saw a lot of things out there at the mine. I saw those squatters stealing dynamite and hiding it in a cavern above the portal. I saw them steal detonators too. When I went and looked at the cavern I saw they had rigged it with a radio receiver. I'm pretty sure they set off the explosion. I know Wayne had nothing to do with it. He wasn't there long enough and had no reason to."

"Tell us what else you've seen," said Ranjit.

"Well I saw them kidnap Wayne and Jimi and hold them in the mine, until they escaped."

"What about the other thing?"

"I saw Axel and Cody beat up that boy, the son of the squatters. They caught him up on the property and beat him to send a message. They wanted the squatters out of there."

"And?" said Ranjit.

"They killed him. They beat him so hard he died. Then they staged everything to make it look like an accident, a slide. But there was no accident. I was so scared for myself and my family I couldn't say anything. I saw that guy Ron, the guy Wayne replaced. I saw him take pictures of the beating, of Nathan and of people staging the accident. He was very careful so no one saw him take the pictures. After a while he couldn't stand working up there anymore and he left. He was scared too. Too scared to say anything I guess."

"He was fired just like me," said Wayne. "For trying to do the right thing."

"I guess he did that to get the hell out of there," said Amar, indicating with a flourish of his hands he was finished.

"So, will you testify to present this information? In court?" asked Ranjit placing a hand on Amar's shoulder. "It could be dangerous for you."

"Yes, I'll testify. These are bad people that need to face justice. I'll leave town anyway since my job is gone. This mine is finished now."

TWENTY-THREE

HEADLIGHT BEAMS FROM THE NEW RED PICKUP FAILED TO PIERCE the blanket of thick fog obscuring the road. Wayne went to catch the plane he'd chartered. He parked, in the charter company's parking lot, facing the spot where his old truck had been trashed. Susan opened her door and got out. He grabbed his camera, voice recorder and note book, stuffed them in a day pack, and stepped out onto the wet gravel. The harbour at Seal Cove was thickly shrouded. Hints of blue sky poked through the mist directly above.

Down on the dock, Wayne paced back and forth by the plane. They should have taken off by now. The pilot watched him and for the tenth time said they'd go as soon as the fog burned off. Wayne couldn't wait. The cell phone in his pocket rang and vibrated simultaneously.

"Hello Wayne. It's Ted here."

Wayne was dumbfounded. He held the phone away from his head and looked at the attribution. It really was Ted. "The fuck you want?"

Ted waited a moment before saying, "I've been arrested Wayne. I really need your help."

Susan looked on, signalling questions with her eyes, hands, arms, and raised shoulders.

Again dumbfounded, Wayne paused before saying, "You want my help?"

"Yes. I'm being charged for pollution violations at New Discovery Gold and they're investigating me in connection with the dam failure and the death of that hippie kid."

"Oh gosh Ted, that's really tough. How are you doing?" said Wayne with sarcastic empathy.

"I'm doing awful. Can you help me? Can you testify on my behalf?"

"What could you possibly want me to say?"

"Say that the dam failure could not be predicted. That it was an accident, an act of God, force majeure. Something like that. Say as far as you know the hippie kid thing was an accident."

"Gee Ted, I'd really like to but we both know that would be lying. And, you know, you were pretty hard on me at the end, what with the zip tie kidnapping, trying to frame me, firebombing me and my boat, and all that. You know."

"That was those crazies Axel and Cody. Not me. Please Wayne. I'm desperate. I lost all my money on that stock. I can't afford a lawyer. Ian Verster's acting like he never met me. And those bastards, Axel and Cody are saying they only did what they did because I ordered them to. They're lying."

Wayne smiled and shrugged as he looked at Susan, who was listening. She shook her head looking down, dark hair hiding her face, before she raised her head with a big smile.

"That's a tough situation Ted. By the way, I made a fortune shorting that damn New Discovery Gold stock. So I guess everything evens out, eh? Karma."

The fog started to clear and the pilot gave a thumb's up. Wayne said, "Look Ted, I'd love to chat, but I gotta go. We're flying up there to survey the New Discovery site and do some costing for restoration. We've got the contract and it's going to be a big one."

"Who's got what contract?"

"The Indigenous people who never ceded the land. I'm working with them to restore that valley. They're reclaiming their traditional territory. Too bad you're out of commission Ted. You would have liked this job, but maybe not. After all, it's on the right side of justice."

"You really have landed on your feet. And what about those hippy squatters you were so protective of?"

"The Indigenous people have this crazy notion that both New Discovery Gold, and the squatters, have occupied and defiled their land for long enough. Those people you call squatters have gone too. I think they're somewhere down in the Slocan or something. I don't really give a shit Ted," said Wayne with even more sarcasm and smiling at Susan.

Wayne and Susan could hear Ted pleading as Wayne touched the button to end the call.

By the time they climbed into the Cessna 185, the fog had blown farther north into Tuck Inlet and it was clear to take off. Once in the air, it was a glorious, sunny fall day, so rare on this rain coast. They flew over the small mountain range and dropped down into Mirage Inlet. Flying up the inlet Wayne had brief panic flashbacks of all that had happened. But that was in the past. Susan had been there for him. Now he was staying with her in Rupert and with her parents over in Metlakatla, and getting past those events more every day.

They flew around the mine site to get a view from all angles. The path the tailings had torn through the wetland and creek was a vicious scar in the natural setting. A new watercourse was forming, running clear and toxic over the tailings, into the sea. From the air, the tailings fan running into the inlet was clearly visible under the water's surface. Wayne couldn't imagine how this mess would ever be cleaned up.

The place where the explosion had occurred stood out like an open wound above the partially blocked mine portal.

Looking out the plane's window Susan said into the intercom, "Do you think Dave and Jimi detonated that explosion?"

"I really don't know Susan. This whole place, and everything that happened here was weird. So many unexplained loose ends. Maybe the provincial mines department enquiry and the trials of Axel, Cody and Ted will explain some things." For a moment he said nothing as he stared out the window. "But Dave, Starshine and Cedar have disappeared from the face of the earth. And I heard Jimi and Chelsea went down to Mexico or farther south."

"Maybe. But maybe the land was just striking back. The ancestors."

Wayne looked over at Susan and shook his head, not in disagreement, but in wonder. He knew he had so much to learn about this other way of seeing the world, and he had now become an avid student.

The pilot dropped to the water surface and spray flew off the floats as the plane touched down. He reversed thrust and the aluminium floats settled into the salt water. They taxied over to the camp barge where Klaus met them.

"Klaus, what are you doing here?" asked Wayne as he stepped onto the float and climbed up to the barge deck.

"I'm closing up some things and keeping an eye on the site. A caretaker for a while I guess you could say."

"I'm surprised the police let anyone from the company stay out here."

"Oh Constable Stasiuk and I go way back. He trusts me."

"Do the Tsimshian trust you?" asked Wayne looking over at Susan with questioning surprise in his eyes. "What will you do when all of this winds down and people start going to jail?"

Klaus smiled at Wayne and said, "I'll be alright. Moving on though."

"Where to?"

"Ian Verster's started a new company. They're on the stock exchange now and have raised enough capital to go ahead with a project farther north. I'll be going up there to manage the site for him."

Wayne looked at Klaus, over at Susan and back at Klaus shrugging his shoulders in disbelief and thinking, 'How could this be?' After a moment he said, "Well best of luck to you, I guess."

"Thanks Wayne. You should come work for us. With Ted most likely going to prison for quite a while, Ian's going to need a good reliable environmental consultant. I think that could be you, once you get past all this bleeding heart stuff. And you could make lots of money on the stock. I'm sure Ian would welcome, even encourage, your investment."

Wayne smiled wryly and said, "You know Klaus, the idea is really tempting." Susan was becoming enraged until Wayne burst out laughing. "There's no way Klaus. Ian Verster's a crook and anyone who gets near him gets burned. You be careful."

They toured the site, taking notes and pictures. Later, taking off in the plane, Susan put on her headphones, turned to look at Wayne in the back and said into the intercom, "You really just about finished me there, finished us."

Wayne smiled and reached forward to take her hand. She let him. This was the rain coast where nothing is as it seems. End of the road. He'd be staying, maybe for a long time.

ABOUT THE AUTHOR

Glen A. Packman studied Marine Biology at the University of Guelph and completed a career in environmental science, regulation, policy and consulting on all three of Canada's coasts as well as in Ottawa. He has been involved in a wide range of major project types including, mines, oil and gas exploration and development, hydroelectric dams, and pulp mills from the assessment, regulatory, proponent and monitoring perspectives. His first publication was a review of environmental information for the Fraser River Estuary in 1974. He worked in Prince Rupert with the halibut fishery and conducted environmental studies at the Port Edward Pulpmill. He conducted contaminant surveys in Prince Rupert Harbour.

This is his second novel. His first novel, published on Amazon, was *Pipeline Underground* which the Nikkei Voice praised as "a deep dive behind the controversial pipeline project."

He has a wife, Sharon, and two children who are now on their own, forging their own paths.

ACKNOWLEDGEMENTS

First of all I would like to thank my wife Sharon and our two children Alex and Katherine for all of their love and support over a lifetime together and during the struggles writing this book. I would also like to thank David Hamilton for showing me the way and for editing the final version. Members of the Ottawa Writing Workshops group: Debbie Bhangoo; Nick Forster; Frank Kitching; and Mike Marshall all provided valuable ideas, perspectives and critiques. The input of Anne Ashley, Susan Noda, and Laura Ashley was very helpful in shaping and finalizing the story. Thank you all!

THANKS FOR READING!

PLEASE ADD A SHORT REVIEW ON AMAZON.

LET ME KNOW WHAT YOU THOUGHT!

Made in the USA
Middletown, DE
11 February 2025

71211124R00189